DRAGON AGE™

ASUNDER

DAVID GAIDER

DRAGON AGE™

ASUNDER

TITAN BOOKS

BioWare

This is a work of fiction. All of the characters, organizations, and events portrayed in this novel are either products of the author's imagination or are used fictitiously.

Dragon Age: Asunder
Print edition ISBN: 9780857686473
E-book edition ISBN: 9781781162293

Published By
Titan Books
A division of Titan Publishing Group Ltd.
144 Southwark Street
London
SE1 0UP

First edition December 2011
10 9 8 7 6 5 4 3 2

www.titanbooks.com

Did you enjoy this book? We love to hear from our readers. Please email us at readerfeedback@titanemail.com or write to us at Reader Feedback at the above address.

To receive advance information, news, competitions, and exclusive offers online, please sign up for the Titan newsletter on our website: www.titanbooks.com

A CIP catalogue record for this title is available from the British Library.

Printed and bound in India.

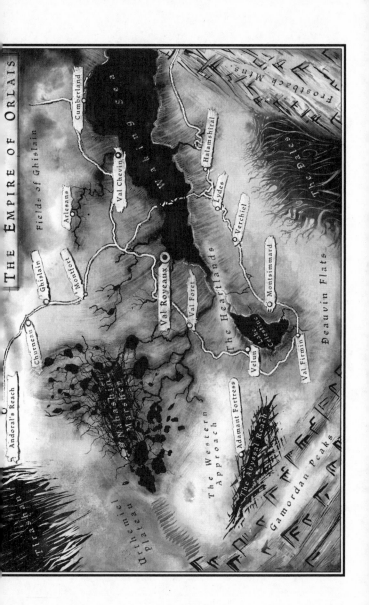

DRAGON AGE™

ASUNDER

1

I am the Ghost of the Spire.

It was an unpleasant thought, one Cole had turned over and over again in his mind. They said ghosts didn't exist, that the dead didn't really walk amongst the living, but some people believed in them even so. They believed a dead man could become lost on his way to the Maker's side, forever adrift in a land of shadow.

Cole wasn't dead. Yet at the same time, he didn't exist, and he walked amongst the living.

He'd overheard a pair of mages talking about him once, even if they'd no idea they were doing so. He'd discovered them late at night, huddled in one of the White Spire's dark hallways. There were many such hidden corners in the great tower, places where mages went to escape from the suspicious eyes of watching templars, and Cole knew them all.

Cole knew far less about the mages themselves. He knew, however, they'd taken a great risk sneaking out of their chambers. Few of the tower's templars were kind, and most believed that mages constantly conspired to commit unspeakable horrors . . . when the truth was usually much more mundane. Most of their conversation consisted of gossip. The mages whispered secrets to each other, sometimes idle speculation about romantic entanglements and other times much more serious things they knew to be true but could never talk about in the open. Occasionally he came upon mages meeting for a romantic liaison instead. They secretly pressed flesh upon flesh, a desperate act of intimacy between people for whom such fleeting moments could only be stolen.

He'd found the pair who spoke of him only by chance, over-hearing their muted whispers as he passed in the shadows. One was a homely woman with long hair the color of straw, the other a gangly elven boy. Both he recognized, but only by sight. They were older apprentices, the sort who had little talent for magic and who'd already spent too long preparing for the inevitable. Someday soon they would be called away by the templars for their final ordeal, and Cole would never see them again . . . or he'd see them roaming the halls as emotionless Tranquil, stripped of their abilities and doomed to spend their lives in passive service to their tormentors.

Cole remembered the dread in their eyes. The homely woman sported a bruise on her cheek, its mottled purple already begin-ning to fade. From their hiding place the pair watched furtively for any sign of wandering guards, starting at the slightest sound. Even the skittering of a passing rat caused them to jump, yet they did not budge from their hiding place.

For all their alertness, they'd been completely oblivious to Cole's approach. Not that he expected anything different. He'd walked right up beside them, leaning in close to listen.

"I tell you I saw it," the woman insisted, her voice tinged with awe. "I was walking through the lower passages to get a book for Enchanter Garlen, and there it was."

"The ghost." The elven boy didn't bother to hide his incredulity.

"Oh, there can be dragons but not ghosts?" Her voice grew in-dignant. "The Chantry doesn't know everything! There are things in the Fade they couldn't possibly begin to—"

"It could have been a demon."

She paused, her face blanching in sudden fear. "But . . . it didn't try to speak with me. I don't think it even saw me. I thought maybe it was a visitor, someone who'd gotten lost, but when I followed it around the corner it was just gone."

The elven boy frowned, his voice lowering to a whisper difficult even for Cole to overhear. "You know what they teach us. When a demon comes, it won't seem harmful at first. It'll be something to make you curious, until later when it begins to corrupt you. . . ."

She stared off, her mouth pressing thin with worry. She looked right through Cole, but only a single thought ran through his mind: *Did she really see me?*

The elven boy sighed and hugged her close, murmuring comforting words about how he didn't mean anything by his warning. Maybe she was right. The woman nodded numbly, fighting back tears. "What did it look like?" he eventually asked.

"You're humoring me."

"No, I want to know. Maybe it was a templar?"

"You think I don't know every templar in the tower by now? Some of them far better than I'd like." She touched the bruise on her cheek, and the elven boy scowled but said nothing. "No, he wasn't in armor or robes. He was just a man, not much older than you. Shaggy hair, maybe blond? Leathers that looked like they badly needed washing. There have been others who've seen him, and their descriptions match what I saw."

"Perhaps he was a laborer working in the tunnels."

"When was the last time anyone did work down here?"

He was at a loss, and shrugged. "I know, it's just . . ."

"I got close enough to see his eyes." The woman frowned, thinking back. "He looked so sad, like he was lost down here. Can you imagine?" She shuddered, and the elven boy grinned reassuringly.

"So that's the infamous Ghost of the Spire. The others will be so jealous."

Her answering smile was faint. "We probably shouldn't say anything."

"Probably not."

They stayed there for a while longer, and Cole lingered. He'd hoped they might talk some more about what the woman saw, but they didn't. They held hands in the dark and listened to the muted sounds of the chant that floated down from the tower's chapel far above. When the midnight service ended there was nothing left but silence, and the pair reluctantly returned to their chambers.

Cole hadn't followed them. Instead he'd sat where they sat, letting the silence fill him. He knew he wasn't a demon. He'd never seen one before or spoken to one, that he knew of, and unless someone could be a demon and have no inkling of it, that just wasn't possible. A ghost, however? That he wasn't so certain of.

He remembered when he first came to the tower. Like every other mage before him, he'd arrived in terror, dragged through the halls by a templar's rough hands. He'd no idea where this strange place was, or even how long they'd traveled to get there. Much of the journey had been spent blindfolded and unconscious, and his unsympathetic captors refused to tell him anything. As far as he'd known, they were going to kill him.

He remembered being pushed down a dark corridor, empty save for a few apprentices who scurried to get out of the way. Most of them averted their eyes, and that only served to heighten Cole's fear. He was being brought to a dungeon, a black pit from which he was never going to emerge, for his crime of being a mage. The templars called him that word in curt, ugly tones when they needed to call him anything. Mage. Before that day it wasn't a word Cole had associated with himself. It was something he'd only heard on the tongues of priests, a watchword for those who had been cursed by the Maker.

And now that's what he was. Cursed.

They'd tossed him into a cell. He'd lain there on the damp stone floor, whimpering. He expected a beating but none came. Instead, the cell door had slammed shut with a deafening crash;

while Cole was initially relieved, once the men were gone that relief evaporated. They'd left him alone in the dark with only the rats for company. The creatures scurried invisibly around him, nipping at him with razor-sharp teeth. He'd tried to crawl away from them but there was nowhere to go, nothing to do except curl up into a ball and pray.

There in the cold and the nothingness, he'd prayed for death. Anything would be better than waiting for the templars to return, anticipating whatever new torment they had planned for him. The priests said demons were drawn to mages, to transform them into terrible abominations—but Cole couldn't imagine anything more frightening than the templars themselves. He couldn't shut his eyes enough to block out the memory of their uncaring eyes.

He didn't want to be a mage. He didn't want to discover how one became a mage, and found nothing wondrous in the idea of magic. Fervently he prayed to the Maker, over and over again, for deliverance. He prayed until his voice was hoarse, prayed for the templars to forget he even existed.

And then he'd gotten his wish. That's exactly what they did.

Perhaps he'd died there in the darkness, and forgotten. Maybe that was how ghosts came to be: they were those who passed on and refused to accept it. Thus they remained, lingering in a life that didn't want them anymore.

He shut his eyes tight. *Maker above,* he thought, *if I'm dead then give me a sign. Don't you want me at your side, just like the priests all said you would? Don't leave me here.*

But there was no answer. There never was.

If he was dead, why did he still sleep? Why did he still hunger, and breathe, and sweat? These were not things that a dead person did. No matter what they called him, he was no ghost and no demon.

But that didn't mean he was real.

Up above, the White Spire swarmed with people. There were

many levels in the great tower, filled with sunlight and wide spaces. Cole rarely went up there. He was much more comfortable down below, among the things the templars had forgotten as well as the things they *wanted* forgotten. The bowels of the tower reached deep into the earth, and they were his home.

The first few floors of the tower's lower chambers were innocent enough. They contained the kitchen stores, as well as the armories, giant chambers filled with enough equipment and weapons to outfit an army of templars. Beneath that were the archives—rooms upon rooms filled with the books they didn't keep in the upper libraries.

There were books about magic there, as well as books of music and philosophy, books in forgotten languages, and even the forbidden books they put under lock and key. Normally the archives stood empty, but sometimes Cole would find a mage spending long hours reading by candlelight. He would never understand what they found so interesting about words and pictures. Books were all just old paper to him.

Far more interesting were the levels that lay beneath the archives. The oldest part of the tower was called "the Pit," and few but Cole ever explored its depths. There were flooded passages down there long ago sealed behind bricks, only to crumble from neglect. Rickety stairwells led to ancient storerooms, some filled with only dust, and others with strange-looking relics. A great mausoleum stood as silent testament to templars who had died centuries ago, faded statues of forgotten heroes towering over marble caskets. He'd found hiding places for treasures, the owners of which had long since perished. He'd followed dark tunnels that went in circles, or had collapsed, or even led into the city's sewers. Did anyone up above even know about those?

He knew every part of the Pit, all save for the area that lay at its heart. The dungeons were there, hundreds and hundreds of cells on multiple levels. More than the templars could ever want, and far more than they used. The oldest were filled with little more than the silent echoes of the tormented, left like indelible imprints in the stone. It made his skin crawl. Cole avoided the dungeons, only going there when he absolutely had to. When he needed to.

Like now.

Torches weren't used in the dungeons. Instead they put glow-stones inside glass lamps, things which flickered like flame but cast a cold and blue light. Magic, he knew, for he could feel the whisper of it caressing his skin as he passed. Even so, only a scant few were used. Just enough for the guards to see their feet.

There was one entrance, an intimidating stretch of hall with a vaulted ceiling and multiple iron gates, which could be closed in an instant. Anyone caught within when that happened would be skewered by spikes flying out of dark holes in the walls. Cole shuddered as he walked through. It wasn't the only death trap in the dungeon. The templars would rather have their prisoners die than make it out, and the old scorch marks on the walls told of those who had made the attempt.

On the other side of that hallway was a single guard station, a simple room with a small table and a couple of chairs. He saw an open bottle of wine and two half-filled goblets, and plates covered with the cold remnants of the evening meal. A cloak hung on the wall peg, with two dirt-smeared helmets sitting on the floor beneath it. No guards were present, and the inner doors stood wide open. They must be within.

Cole hesitantly stepped into the prison. The stench of fear, old and new, immediately assaulted his nostrils. The cells here were used often. How many prisoners might be present now he had no idea, though he knew there was at least one. He heard fearful whimpering farther down the hall.

There was laughter, too, along with the idle chatter of two men. Their voices echoed. Cole crept inside until he saw the first hints of blue light ahead. Two armored templars stood in front of an open cell, one holding up a glowlamp. Neither wore a helmet, and thus he recognized them—not enough to know their names, for he knew few, but enough to know that these two were merciless hunters, templars who had served their order for so many years that whatever pity they'd once been capable of had been ground into dust.

"Careful," Lamp Holder cautioned. "This one knows how to conjure fire."

The other, whom Cole thought of as Big Nose, snorted contemptuously. "I'd like to see her try it."

The whimpering came from within the cell. Lamp Holder rolled his eyes and turned away. "I wouldn't worry. There wasn't much fight left when we caught her. Even less now."

"Huh. Think she'll make it?"

"Probably better if she didn't." The pair exchanged knowing glances as the despairing cries became louder. Big Nose shrugged and slammed the cell door shut, fumbling with a large ring of iron keys until he found the one he wanted. The lock slid into place with an ominous sound.

The templars turned and walked toward Cole, whispering to each other. A joke, followed by cruel chuckling. He stayed where he was, nervously holding his breath as they drew close. When they reached him, however, they did what most everyone did: they walked around him, completely oblivious that they'd done so. It was never a sure thing, and Cole always half expected that someone might see him. Half hoped, even.

The key ring he lifted from Big Nose's belt as he passed.

Then they were gone. The glowlamp was gone with them, the only source of light in the prison, and now it was plunged into darkness. Cole slowly let out his breath, waiting for the sound of their footsteps to fade. He could still hear faint weeping behind the cell door. Nearby, water dripped onto stone with a rhythmic *tap-tap-tap.* Rats squeaked as they emerged from the walls. But he heard nothing in the other cells. If there were prisoners, they were asleep or as good as.

He should move. He tried to will his feet into motion, but they were frozen. He felt immaterial, as if he were made of the same substance as the shadows and the first step would cause him to be forever lost in them. The panic rose, and his heart pounded. Sweat poured down his face.

Not now, he quailed. *Not yet!*

Cole reached out for the wall. Part of him was fearful his hand would merely pass through, that he would stumble and fall . . . and keep on falling. Down and down he would go, one final scream swallowed by a black oblivion. But his hand touched stone. Blessedly cool stone. He gasped gratefully and pressed his face against it, letting its chill hardness scrape his skin.

His breathing slowed. He was shaking, but he was still real.

It's not too late.

Fumbling in a pocket, he produced a small bundle of cloth. Carefully he unfolded it and the azure radiance of a glowstone emerged. For what was coming next, he would need light.

It took several tries until he found the key the templar had used. It turned ever so quietly until the lock sprang with a jarring *clank.* Then he paused—the weeping inside had abruptly halted. Not waiting to see if the noise elicited a response from the guards, Cole pulled the door open and stepped into the cell.

The glowstone revealed a tiny cell, encrusted with filth. It was empty save for a single bucket and a girl cowering in the corner, dressed in filthy rags splattered dark with blood. Hers? Or someone else's? The girl's black hair hung in wet ropes down her shoulders, and she protectively shielded her face with her arms.

For a long moment Cole did nothing, shifting from foot to foot as he watched her. Then he hunched low, placing the stone on the floor beside him. Its flickering intensified, sending his shadow dancing madly across the walls. He could smell the girl even over the cell's foulness: heavy sweat, laced with sick. She trembled, no doubt certain he was here to hurt her. So he waited.

After a time, a pair of reddened eyes peeked out from behind her arms. She was pretty, or had been once. Now she was haggard, exhausted by whatever ordeal she'd gone through to get here. The girl blinked at the glowstone's light, incomprehension warring with terror. She stared at Cole and he stared back.

"You can see me," he said. His relief was palpable.

The girl yelped as if struck, scrambling to get as far away from him as she could. She backed herself into a corner of the cell like a caged animal, panting rabidly. Her filthy hands clawed at the walls, as if doing so might allow her to get through. Cole waited until her desperate efforts slowed and she locked eyes on him once again.

"You *can* see me," he repeated, more confidently this time.

"I didn't mean to burn it down," she whispered through ragged breaths. "The fire came out of my hands, but I don't even know why. It all happened so fast, I tried to warn them. . . ." The girl clamped her eyes shut, tears spilling down filthy cheeks. She wiped her face with a shaking hand, smearing the dirt across her face.

Cole waited. Eventually, her sobs quieted and she looked over at him again, more guardedly this time. Still crouched across from her, he hadn't moved, and he saw the first glimmer of curiosity.

"Are you a mage, then?" she asked. "They said one would come."

He hesitated. "No."

"Then . . . who are you?"

"My name is Cole."

That was hardly the answer she was looking for. She stared expectantly at him, but he said nothing. "But . . . if you're not a mage," she finally asked, "then what are you doing here? What do you want from me?"

"I came because you can see me." He reached under his leather vest and drew a dagger from its sheath. It was an ornate blade with an elaborate brass hilt carved in the shape of a dragon's head. The length of it gleamed in the blue light, and the girl's eyes fixed upon it in stark disbelief. "I felt it when they brought you here," he continued. "I knew you would, even before I met you."

The girl's mouth opened, and then clicked shut again. When she spoke her voice was very small. "Are you . . . going to kill me?"

"I think so. Yes."

A small gasp escaped her. "Because I'm a mage?"

"No, it's not that."

"Then . . . why? What have I done to you?"

"You haven't done anything to me." Emotion welled up, a desperation that he had pushed deep down inside him now fighting to escape. It left him breathless, and for a moment he cradled his head on his knees and rocked back and forth. Part of him wondered if the girl would use her magic on him while she had the chance. Would she conjure fire, like the templar warned? What would that be like? Could she kill him?

But she did nothing. Cole fought to regain his center and exhaled once, long and slow, before looking up again. The girl was frozen. She couldn't look away from his dagger, and perhaps hadn't even considered she could do something to stop him.

"I'm . . . fading away," he muttered. "I can feel myself slipping through the cracks. I have to do this, I'm sorry."

"I'll scream."

But she didn't scream. He saw the idea crumble inside with the realization that doing so would only call the templars back, if it brought anyone at all. Even faced with an armed man directly in front of her, that possibility was still worse. It was something he understood all too well. Slowly she slumped to the ground, defeated.

Cole inched forward, his heart thumping madly in his chest. He reached out and touched the girl's cheek, and she didn't flinch away. "I can make it go away." The words were gentle, and he held the dagger up to prove his promise. "The pain, the fear. I can make it quick. You don't have to stay here and see what they have in store for you."

She studied him, eerily calm. "Are you a demon?" she finally asked. "They say that's what happens to mages. The demons come and turn them into monsters." Then she smiled, a lifeless grimace that matched her dead eyes. "But you don't need to do that. I'm already a monster."

He didn't respond.

"I said I didn't mean to burn it down. That's what I told *them*, too. But I lied." The confession spilled out of her like cold venom. "I listened to my mother, my father, all of them screaming, and I did nothing. I wanted them to burn. I'm *glad* they're dead."

Her secret told, the girl took a deep breath and blinked back tears. She looked at Cole expectantly, but he only sighed. "I'm not a demon," he said.

"But . . . what are you, then?"

"Lost." He stood and offered his hand. She hesitated, but then numbly nodded. He brought her to her feet, where she stood only inches away. There in the glowstone's blue light, a strange intimacy enveloped them. He could see every mark on her skin, every stain the tears had left on her cheeks, every strand of hair.

"Look at me," he asked her.

She blinked in confusion, but complied.

"No, *look* at me."

And she did. The girl looked at Cole, looked *into* him. He was going to kill her, and she knew it. He went through life, unnoticed and quickly forgotten by all, but to her, at that moment, he was the most important thing in the world. She knew what he was, now. Cole was her deliverance, a way out of a world filled with terror. He saw weary relief in her eyes, mixed with the fear. In those eyes he was anchored, and he felt real.

"Thank you," he breathed, and plunged the dagger into her chest.

She gasped in shock, but did not look away. He thrust up, digging the blade deep into her heart. She convulsed, a spurt of bright blood erupting from her mouth. Then, with a final shudder, she collapsed into his arms.

Cole held her close, staring down into her eyes. He drank in every moment as the life ebbed out of her. It was an instant that seemed to stretch out into forever . . . and then she was gone.

Trembling, he allowed the body to slide off the dagger and slump lifelessly to the floor. He was only dimly aware of the warm blood covering the blade, his hands, the entire front of his leathers. He couldn't stop looking at those eyes, staring off into nothing. He knelt down and closed them, leaving a streak of scarlet across her lids. Then he stumbled back, leaning against the cell wall. It was difficult to breathe.

You need to stop.

It took every bit of will he had left, but he tore his eyes away from her. Like a drunken man, he stumbled toward the glowstone and snatched it off the floor, wrapping it back up in the cloth until the cell was plunged into blessed darkness once again. He took slow and deliberate breaths as he brought himself under control.

He'd almost forgotten what it was like to be connected, to feel like he belonged in the world. Part of him was certain the templars were about to come running, that the entire White Spire would realize all at once who he was—the escaped mage who walked in their midst. The Ghost of the Spire.

They would come with their spells and their swords. They would wrestle him to the ground, and then he would be locked away in a cell again. He would be lost in that blackness until they came to deal with him once and for all. This time they wouldn't forget him. This time the door would open and they would see him lying there, and by then he would be begging them to end it.

But no one came.

No one ever came.

2

Among the nobility in Orlais, custom dictated that masks were to be worn when in public. These delicately crafted works of art were painted to indicate the affluence of one's family. Some were anointed with tiny jewels laid out in tasteful patterns, while others were inlaid with silver and gold. Still others went over the top with their decorations of peacock feathers or glittering dragon scales. To have a more beautiful mask than one's rivals was seen as an advantage, and thus the Empire's maskmakers numbered among the most influential and sought-after of its artisans.

Servants wore a simpler version of the mask traditional to their master or mistress's household, a clear message to any who saw them: *I am owned, and you harm me at the risk of incurring the wrath of the one I serve.* To wear a mask to which you were not entitled was extremely dangerous. A wise nobleman guarded his masks like he guarded his reputation.

To be without a mask in Orlais, then, was a statement. It said you were either a peasant not even useful enough to be part of a noble house, or that you considered yourself above the Game. To the elite, however, nobody was above the Game. You were either a player or a pawn, nothing else.

Justinia V, Divine of the Chantry and the guest of honor at the evening's festivities, was not masked. Nor were the flock of priests attending her. The priesthood wasn't above the Game, precisely, but an exception to it, and any nobleman was expected to maintain an unimpeachable veneer of respect when speaking to a priest regardless of what they wore. Many priests engaged in the Game even so, and some even claimed the Divine was one of its best players. The priesthood simply played by different rules.

Evangeline also wasn't wearing a mask. As a templar, she technically fell under the same exemption as the priesthood. It was an exemption, however, that the nobility largely ignored.

She was also the only one in the palace ballroom wearing armor and carrying a weapon. Her templar plate had been polished to a shine, and she wore her finest red tunic, the one with the Chantry starburst sewn in gold thread. She'd even put her black hair up into the sort of elegant braid used by the ladies of the court. Even so, it paled in comparison next to all the glittering gowns, the bouffant wigs with their fancy combs and pearl strands, the resplendent jewelry twinkling in the firelight, and she knew it.

Evangeline knew very well what the ladies of the court who looked her way were thinking, and she knew the sorts of things they were whispering to each other behind their delicate fans. Someone as pretty as she could have found a husband. The fact that she had joined a warrior order meant she either came from a poor family or, far worse, was too *uncouth* to join the ranks of proper society.

Neither of those things were true, but it didn't matter. She wasn't there to play the Game. She was there to serve as the Divine's honor guard, a visible reminder to those who might use the celebration as an excuse to cause trouble.

Ostensibly the ball was being thrown by the Empress, but Her Imperial Majesty was nowhere in evidence. According to everything Evangeline had been told, she was instead at the Winter Palace in far-off Halamshiral—either enjoying her latest lover's attentions or dealing with a rebellion, depending on who you asked. Either way, it was clear the event had been arranged by palace bureaucrats, not that any of the guests seemed to mind. To show up was to prove you were worthy of an invitation, and that fact alone made it worthwhile. The ballroom was packed.

The Divine sat in an enormous, ornately carved wooden throne that had been brought in especially for the occasion. It was high up on a dais, providing a vantage point from which she could overlook the entire chamber. It also meant that anyone who approached her needed to do so from below. Orlesian nobles disliked being reminded of their subservience, even by someone who was unquestionably their superior, and so, once the long line of polite well-wishers earlier in the evening had ended, few chose to approach at all.

Thus the guest of honor sat there in rigid silence, with only attendant priests keeping vigil at her side. She watched the throng of dancers whirl around the ballroom, her expression kept neutral so none could accuse her of boredom. If she felt uncomfortable in the voluminous red robe and the glittering headdress, she made no indication of it. Evangeline thought the Divine was the very picture of icy grace, yet most of the comments she overheard were about the woman's age. Her predecessor had held the office for almost fifty years, so long that the Empire had become accustomed to the idea of a doddering and ancient Divine. Now things had changed, and some expressed a desire that Justinia V not live to get any older.

In typical Orlesian fashion they only did so quietly, of course, and with daggers hidden behind their backs. This was the Maker's chosen they were discussing, after all. Evangeline found their eagerness to justify such sacrilege with petty sneers and barbs almost sickening, but such was the way of the Empire.

The musicians, a large troupe assembled high up in the ballroom's upper gallery, suddenly started a faster tune. Those on the floor below applauded their choice and began assembling themselves for the *tourdion*. It was a lively dance that had become popular ever since a recent rumor claimed the Empress favored it.

The dancers lined up across from each other and assumed the *posture droit,* right foot slightly in front with the weight evenly distributed. Then they began: a small kick in the air with the left foot followed by a small hop with the right, alternating until on the fifth step they performed a small jump back into posture. Then it began again.

All the kicking and hopping made for quite the spectacle. There was much drunken merriment on the ballroom floor, though some of the dancers clearly devoted themselves to the endeavor with practiced grace. The crowd on the sidelines clapped loudly in admiration, and even the Divine and her priests joined in.

As the tempo of the music increased, the pace of the dancing became frenzied. Suddenly there was a cry of alarm—a young woman spilled to the ground, tearing her skirt and taking three others down with her. Worse, her mask flew off and landed on the floor with a great clatter. The music ground to a halt as a murmur of interest mixed with amusement erupted.

No one moved to help the young woman. She was left to scramble awkwardly to her feet, holding up the remains of her skirt as she chased after her mask. An imperious-looking woman in a towering wig of white curls, clearly her mother, ran out onto the floor to grab her arm and pull her off. The mother's face was hidden by her golden mask, but her every movement spoke of mortification rather than concern.

An adept observer might have noticed that another young woman in a brilliant yellow gown had been the culprit responsible for the fall. They might also have noticed that as the musicians began a new, slower song to recover from the interruption, she moved to intercept the gentleman across from whom the fallen girl had been dancing. Truth be told, Evangeline suspected everyone present knew exactly what she had done and why. They would also quietly approve of her maneuver. The Game was as merciless as it was contemptible.

Evangeline kept her place in front of the Divine's dais, scanning the crowd carefully. Her legs were sore from standing for so long, and the musky stench of sweat covered by sweet perfume was slowly becoming difficult to bear. Still, she had to be vigilant. The trouble with so many masks was that any of them could hide an assassin. Anyone here could be a stranger, and not a single other guest would be aware they didn't belong. She had to hope the army of guardsmen just outside the ballroom had been diligent in their duty. In the meantime, she could only wait. Another hour, perhaps, before the Divine politely retired, and then her duty would be ended.

"You cannot wait to get away, I see."

Evangeline turned to see that one of the Divine's attendants had approached her from the dais. This was one she'd seen before: a woman with short red hair and vividly blue eyes who carried herself in a manner so controlled and graceful that Evangeline wouldn't have been surprised to discover she wasn't a priest at all, despite the robes. A bodyguard, perhaps? It certainly made sense that the Divine wouldn't trust her fate to a lone sword. Evangeline was hardly offended.

"Her Eminence need not fear I'll abandon her," she replied.

The woman held up a hand, smiling disarmingly. "Oh, I did not mean to imply that you might. You do a better job of guarding your feelings than most templars I've encountered. Even so, this must be a very boring assignment for you."

Evangeline paused, not quite sure how to respond. "I think my Knight-Commander believed I might be more . . . comfortable in this setting, considering the family I was born to."

"But you're not."

"I left that life behind a long time ago." She looked out over the crowd of dancers, who were just finishing the latest song. They vigorously applauded the musicians in the gallery, and then dispersed into conversation. It was like watching a pack of wolves at work. They ferreted out the weakest of the pack, isolating them in anticipation of the kill. The only violence done, however, was with soft words and promises. The ballroom was a battleground, already littered with bodies, and yet no war was being won. At the next social gathering this scene would play out again, and again at the next, as regular as the tide. "All that wealth and influence, and what do they use it for? Their own advancement, while their world crumbles around them."

The red-haired woman seemed impressed. "I would agree with that. I know Her Eminence would, as well."

"That makes at least three of us, then."

She laughed heartily, and extended her hand. "Pardon my atrocious manners. My name is Leliana."

"Knight-Captain Evangeline."

"Oh yes, I know. There was a great deal of discussion as to who would be guarding the Divine tonight. Many of those in your order of similar rank, after all, have expressed certain . . . attitudes which cause us great concern."

There was a tone in the woman's voice which roused Evangeline's interest, as if there was far more to what she was saying than she was letting on. When Leliana strode a short distance away to a side table and poured a glass of wine, Evangeline followed.

"What do you mean?" she asked. "What sort of concern?"

"You're aware what happened in Kirkwall."

"Isn't everyone?"

Leliana gestured to the row of stately windows on the far side of the ballroom, through which the White Spire was clearly visible. It was one of the few structures besides the palace itself which could be seen from anywhere in the capital city, and at night it was lit by magic to make it appear a brilliant sliver of white cutting across the dark—the sword of the Maker, as the templars liked to call themselves. "The Circle of Magi in Kirkwall rebelled and plunged the city into war, and we've been feeling the effects across Thedas ever since. The templars now have two ways they can view it: either as a challenge to their authority . . . or as a lesson to be learned."

"And what does that have to do with me? I don't believe I've expressed an opinion one way or the other."

"Haven't you?" Leliana sipped from her glass, studying Evangeline over it with amusement twinkling in her eyes. "You say the nobility do nothing useful with their influence. Am I not to read from this that you feel the templars are different?"

Again with the hidden meaning. "Of course I do. We protect the world from the mages and the mages from themselves—not because they ask us to, or because the task is an easy one, but because it is the right thing to do."

"That sounds like an opinion to me."

"It is one I happen to share with the rest of my order."

"If only that were so." Leliana appeared somber for a moment, but then shrugged. "There are many who believe a war is inevitable, and that the Chantry has not done enough to support efforts the templars have made to prevent it. They say we must begin picking sides."

"And you're saying I was chosen to guard the Divine tonight because you believe I've picked a side?"

"I cannot say. That might be worth a discussion."

Evangeline paused, taken aback. The red-haired woman continued to drink her wine, her innocent air making it appear as if they discussed nothing of importance.

Across the ballroom another templar entered into view. This was a young man, one of the junior members of the order, and the sheen of sweat on his face said he'd come here quickly. He spotted Evangeline with a look of immense relief and raced through the crowd toward her. "Ser Evangeline! Thank the Maker I found you!" He stopped short as he drew near, belatedly realizing he'd interrupted their conversation.

Leliana laughed lightly, not seeming the least bit offended. "There is no need to worry, young ser, though I hope you have a good reason for bringing your sword. There is only supposed to be the one, after all." She tilted her head toward the blade that hung at Evangeline's belt.

The young templar glanced down at his weapon, still in its sheath, and blushed with embarrassment. "I'm sorry, I didn't think . . ."

"You have a purpose here?" Evangeline reminded him.

"I, uh . . . I do!" Relieved, he took a folded parchment from his tunic and handed it to her. "I was sent by the Knight-Commander. There's been another murder at the White Spire."

"There has?" A chill ran down Evangeline's spine as she opened the parchment. It was a note summoning her back to the tower as soon as the Divine retired for the evening. It also mentioned the Lord Seeker had taken a personal interest in this latest murder. Reading between the lines, it was clear the Knight-Commander considered this an unwelcome development. "Tell him I will return as soon as I'm able."

The templar nodded, but instead of leaving, he hesitated. He stared at Leliana, chewing his lip uncertainly, and she arched a curious eyebrow in response. "I'm sorry, madame, but I think I might have a message for you as well."

"Oh? From the templars?"

"No, there was a servant outside looking for you. A red-haired priest with the Divine, he said. I was told there is an old friend asking to see you."

"An old friend?" She appeared intrigued. "Did this servant say which one?"

"No, madame. He said this person came from Ferelden, if that helps."

"It does." She turned to Evangeline and curtsied. "It seems our conversation will have to continue another time, good ser. Maker watch over you until then."

"And you." Evangeline watched the woman leave with the young templar, and found her curiosity piqued even more than before. It was said that the Divine kept agents at her side, and that some of them were bards—master manipulators of the Game, sometimes spies and even assassins. If this woman was one, then their conversation had been a very dangerous one.

Evangeline casually glanced around the ballroom, wondering how many people had witnessed their discussion and remarked on it. Would word get back to the Knight-Commander? This was a difficult time for the templars. The rebellion in Kirkwall had sparked unrest in every Circle across Thedas, and the resulting crackdown had made things very tense. Everyone was jumping at shadows, with conspiracies seen in every corner. The White Spire was no exception.

Thankfully, no one appeared to be paying her any attention. The Divine was an ornament to these proceedings, as far as the Orlesian nobility was concerned, and Evangeline was a bodyguard to be paid no heed. She let out a slow breath and returned to her post in front of the dais. What she should be concerned about were the murders. Her investigation had gotten nowhere, and in the current climate that was an unforgivable failure. With any luck, there would be more evidence this time.

The ball was slowly winding down, the musicians already making their final bows and putting away their instruments. Some of the men were retiring to the palace's "evening room," which was a polite way of saying they were going to drink heavily and smoke kohl pipes and otherwise engage in activities their wives wouldn't approve of. Conveniently, this left the women free to complain about their absent husbands and indulge in some matchmaking. Others were already making apologies—those would be the ones cutting their losses, getting out before they did further damage to their reputations—even if leaving before the guest of honor would be seen as an admission of weakness.

As if sensing the opportunity, the Divine stood from her chair. The priests beside her stepped forward on the dais and began clapping loudly to get the crowd's attention. It was effective, and there was a general din of excited conversation as everyone assembled in anticipation of a speech. Evangeline moved aside so as not to block anyone's view.

Nodding thanks to her attendants, the Divine raised her hands. She was an impressive figure in her ceremonial robes and headdress, and by rights the nobility should have been bowing low and thanking the Maker Himself for having been granted the opportunity to meet His chosen, rather than treating her like just another guest with a fancy title. Naturally those present were far too jaded, or too proud, to show such obeisance—but they were willing to feign respect, and after a long moment the room was completely silent.

"Honored citizens, brothers and sisters," she began, her voice ringing out. "We gather here tonight to give our thanks to the Maker, for it is by His will that we enjoy so many privileges: prosperity, freedom, an empire that stretches across half of Thedas. It is in this city that the Chant of Light first began its journey to the four corners of the world, and so it is fitting we stop to consider our role as the Maker's favored children."

The Divine paused, and with an enigmatic smile she descended from the dais. Evangeline almost choked in surprise, and the barely concealed alarm on the faces of the priests still on the dais told her this was very much unexpected. In fact, it was unheard of.

Marveling whispers spread through the ballroom as Her Eminence approached those closest. Some backed away uncertainly, while others had the good grace to curtsy or kneel. The leaders of the Chantry had always been aloof figures, rarely coming out of the Grand Cathedral except for state occasions. That this one agreed to come to a ball, even at the Empress's request, had been something of a surprise. There was thus no real precedent for the nobles to draw from for anything but a formal audience.

She took the hand of a curtsying elderly woman in an elegant bronze dress, and the woman practically shook as she lifted her mask and kissed the Divine's rings. Smiling gently, the Divine walked forward into the crowd; they parted readily before her. They practically recoiled, in fact, and Evangeline pictured them as a sea of hissing serpents despite all the wigs and fancy dresses.

Belatedly, she remembered her purpose and edged closer to fall in behind the Divine. Her eyes scanned over the crowd, which kept its distance even as it pressed in. Despite the horror behind those masks, it was easy to tell their curiosity had been piqued. An advantage, perhaps, of having a younger woman wearing the holy mantle?

"We should not allow fear to cloud our reason," the Divine continued. "We must remember all of those who have defended us in the evil times of ages past, who allowed us our prosperity through their sacrifice. We owe them a debt, and yet we have been shamefully forgetful of that fact."

The Divine paused dramatically, her eyes scanning over the hushed audience. "I speak of mages. The Chant of Light says, 'Magic exists to serve mankind, and not to rule over him.' And so it has been. The mages have served us well, in many wars over many centuries, yet in times of peace how well have we served them? We mean them no harm, yet have we not harmed them even so?"

"You lie!" The cry rang out from the crowd. For a moment, it seemed as if nobody was sure who had spoken. There was a murmur of shock, and quickly the nobles parted once again as a new man stepped forward. He looked no different than many of the other noble guests, a balding yet distinguished-looking gentleman in a black velvet surcoat. When he tore off his mask, however, it revealed a face twisted by grief and rage.

"You mean us every harm! It's the Chantry that teaches them to fear us!" he continued. "You keep us under your thumb, reminding us again and again how you let us live only because we're *useful*!"

The people on the floor continued to back away, giving the man a wide berth until he stood practically alone with the Divine, Evangeline only a few steps behind. She placed a hand on the hilt of her sword. If this man was a mage as he claimed, that meant he was dangerous. If she drew her blade, or if the guards outside clued in to the disturbance, then the Divine's life could be placed in jeopardy.

To her credit, the Divine remained calm, raising her hands in supplication to the crowd. "Please, everyone," she called out. "There is no need to be frightened. There are better ways to get an audience, I'll grant you, but I'll happily hear this man speak."

The audience twittered nervously, not entirely convinced. Neither was the mage. "You'll hear me speak? You've disbanded the College of Enchanters, silenced our leaders! You've done anything *but* listen to us!"

"I am listening," she replied, "but order must be kept; surely you realize that. If there is to be peace, it cannot be accomplished through threats and demands. The lives of many more than just the mages are at stake."

Evangeline watched the mage carefully. The man shouldn't be here. From his words, he belonged to a Circle—perhaps even the White Spire, though she didn't recognize him—but he had clearly escaped his templar watchers to come. She doubted it was merely for a chat.

He was trembling, seemingly only moments away from breaking down into tears—yet his fists remained tightly clenched at his sides. "We see no peace being accomplished," he spat. "If Kirkwall was any example, it showed us that nothing will be accomplished unless we fight for it."

With that he raised his hands, and bright red power began to coalesce around them. The chamber filled with an electric charge that tickled the skin, a thrumming that reverberated deep in one's skull. Magic. The dam that had kept the crowd's panic at bay suddenly broke. People screamed in alarm, and some began to rush to the ballroom doors. They pushed down whoever was in their way, trampling them if need be, and the panic gave way to cries of terror.

Evangeline leapt in front of the Divine. In a flash she drew her sword and brandished it at the man. Their eyes locked: templar and mage, the oldest of enemies. "Stand down," she warned him. "You know what I can do. There is no need for this to end in blood."

He let out a sound that was half laugh, half desperate sob. "And where else should it end? I'm dead already."

The mage extended his hands, a wide arc of flame bursting forth, but Evangeline was already moving. "Get back, Your Eminence!" she cried, hoping the Divine would hear. She charged into the path of the fire, feeling the heat of it lick against her cheeks, and brought her sword down onto his chest.

She had power of her own, the same power that all templars shared. It was a power the mages feared. As the blade struck him she channeled it forth, feeling it surge through her and into her weapon. There was a bright flash as the mage's flow of mana was disrupted, his flames guttering to a halt.

"Bitch!" he cried, staggering back. There was blood where his surcoat was rent. He ran his fingers in it, staring at the blood as if shocked to see it there. Then he looked at Evangeline, his face twisting into blind hate.

She rushed at the mage, realizing what he was about to do, but it was too late. The blood on his hands sizzled and evaporated as he drew mana directly from it. The blood on his chest smoked, and his eyes burned with a dark and evil power.

Evangeline felt the wave of force hitting her before she reached him. She attempted to raise her aura of protection, but the magic shattered it as if it were thin glass. It knocked the breath out of her, and she felt herself flying back through the air. She crashed to the marble floor, tumbling end over end as she slid. Her head hit something hard.

She lie there, the world spinning dizzily around her as she tried to push herself up. Her arms didn't seem to want to cooperate. The screams in the ballroom were deafening, seeming to come from everywhere at once. She could also hear the shouts of the guards trying to get inside, but there were too many nobles trying to push past them. Somewhere behind her the priests were shouting, begging the Divine to run.

Evangeline felt the blast of heat before the flames struck her. She only barely managed to summon her aura once again, and this time it held. Even so, it buckled under the assault, and the pain as the flames seared her skin was agonizing. She screamed. Her vision dimmed, and she felt the last vestiges of power inside her ebbing away.

It might have been a moment or an hour later when Evangeline reopened her eyes, she wasn't sure. She was crouched low on the floor, her blistered hands covering her head. Her sword was gone. She must have dropped it in the fall. The air was filled with the acrid smell of smoke—something in the ballroom had caught fire, and it was quickly spreading. The panic had redoubled, reaching a fever pitch as the guests tried to get out in whatever manner they could. Someone threw a chair through one of the vaulted windows, and it shattered with a resounding crash.

Then she looked up. She saw a pair of black boots. They belonged to the mage, and he was walking toward the Divine. Her headdress had fallen off, but her red robes were unmistakable even through the haze. She had retreated to the far side of the ball-room, backed against the wall like a cornered animal. She watched the mage approach her warily, refusing to give in to terror as every-one else had.

Evangeline saw the mage hold up his fist, power forming around it. "They already fear us," he snarled. "Now let them have a reason."

With a great cry, Evangeline pushed herself up. Gritting her teeth against the pain, she lunged toward the mage and just barely caught his surcoat. As she yanked him back, he attempted to twist around. Flailing hands sent a gout of flame hurtling upward. For a single moment it seemed as if the entire ceiling was awash in ribbons of red and black, a sea of fire that roiled and bubbled as it spread.

She threw the mage down to the floor, hard. He snarled at her, attempting to push her away. One of his hands caught her face and she felt his fingers digging into an eye, but she refused to be dislodged.

Her gauntleted fist came down on his face—once, twice, three times . . . and then something made a cracking sound. She stopped. The ballroom was still aflame, but none of it was the mage's any longer. He was still, his features twisted in a mess of blood, vacant eyes staring up at her in silent accusation.

And then everything went black.

When Evangeline came to, she found herself seated on the floor of the terrace just outside the ballroom. Normally it was where the palace's guests might have come to take in the evening air, a place of tranquility, but at the moment it was pure chaos. Swarms of people milled about, some weeping on the ground, some shout-ing. A noblewoman in a tattered dress wandered nearby, close to hysterics as she called out a man's name. A fat nobleman sat on the ground nearby, his expensive surcoat blackened with blood as a guardsman tried to tend his wounds. In the distance she could spot the city guard running into and out of the palace, desperate to restore order.

How long had she been out here? Was the Divine safe? It was all too much to take in, the confusion flowing around her in a sea of random voices. She tried to get to her feet, but the pain slammed into her like a fist. Gritting her teeth, she eased back down and tried to maintain consciousness.

Smoke billowed out from the palace windows, and only now the fire brigade arrived with buckets in hand. With any luck they would get the flames under control before half the palace burned down. If that happened, the Empress might be less than impressed when she returned from Halamshiral.

That was, Evangeline reminded herself, if the Empress wasn't somehow involved in the attack. Her absence the very night a mage slips into the palace to attack the Divine seemed more than coincidental. If that were the case, there was little the templars could do about it. If it wasn't, someone would pay.

She was wracked by a spasm of coughing, and her vision blurred. "Are you all right, Knight-Captain?" someone asked her.

It took several blinks before she recognized Leliana, the red-haired woman she'd spoken to earlier. She knelt down next to Evangeline, a look of sincere concern on her face. "What?" Evangeline responded dumbly, feeling as if a fog seeped through her mind. She rubbed her forehead, and only belatedly noticed the blisters on her hands were gone. Her skin was whole.

Leliana smiled, reassured. "There are mages here now. I had one of them heal you, but there will still be pain. You inhaled a great deal of smoke, I think. I was worried . . ."

"I'm fine. Thank you." Evangeline shook her head. The shouts around her were much clearer now, like the world was coming into focus. "The Divine . . . she wasn't hurt, was she? Did she get out?"

"She did. She's been taken to safety." Evangeline breathed a sigh of relief. One less thing to worry about, then. "I want to thank you," Leliana said. "I should have been here. If something had happened to Justinia while I was away, I would never have forgiven myself."

"I understand."

"Her Eminence is extremely grateful as well, I want you to know that. If there is ever anything you need . . ."

Evangeline nodded, but couldn't bring herself to do more. Satisfied, Leliana squeezed her shoulder and then left. Already more templars were arriving. Order was being restored. Taking a deep breath, she got to her feet and straightened her armor. Despite the healing magic, it still felt as if her bones were covered in bruises and her lungs filled with soot.

Magic can't do everything, she reminded herself.

3

Rhys sat in the Knight-Commander's antechamber, waiting for the inevitable summons into his private office. It was a bare room of grey stone, furnished only with a pair of wooden chairs, little to recommend it beyond the enormous bay window that dominated the far wall. From there one could look down at the entirety of Val Royeaux, even as far as the port district at the sea's edge. It was a spectacular view of the capital, one that few mages got to see; they were rarely invited into the upper levels of the White Spire—unless something had gone wrong, of course.

Which it had. None of the templars would actually say what had happened, but their grim faces spoke volumes. There had been another murder.

He glanced over at Adrian, grinning as she stormed from one end of the small room to the other. Back and forth, back and forth, like she was just getting going when a wall balked her and forced her to turn around. Then she would spit angrily and glare at the Knight-Commander's great oaken door, as if willpower alone could command it to open. In all the years they'd served together in the Circle of Magi, he'd never known her to back down from a confrontation, imagined or real. Some people said it wasn't very mage-like of her, a comment that could get her frothing at the mouth.

Rhys tended to chuckle at those remarks. What was a mage *supposed* to be like, anyhow? He knew what the common folk outside the tower thought. If they were kind, they'd say a mage was a thin old man with a white beard who spent all his time surrounded by scrolls and books. If they were unkind, then a mage was a sinister-looking fellow with black hair and a pointed beard, someone who lurked in shadows summoning demons whenever the templars weren't actively preventing him from doing so.

Adrian was about as far from their idea of a mage as it was possible to be. She was tiny, for one, with a shock of red curls and freckles that still made her look like a child even though she was only a few years younger than Rhys, and he was rapidly approaching his fortieth. She despised such comparisons, and only Rhys could get away with the occasional teasing. If she was in a good mood. Plus, she swore like a fishwife.

Come to think of it, Rhys wasn't all that mage-like himself. Adrian said he was too handsome, a comment that always made him laugh. He *did* think the grey that was starting to show in his beard was terribly distinguished, but it didn't cause women to swoon as he passed. That he noticed. Beyond that, Rhys was terrible at lurking in shadows, and not what most people would consider "scholarly." He'd done a great deal of field research in his time, but locking himself into a library and staring at books until his eyes became tiny was far from his idea of a good time. Not unlike being summoned to the Knight-Commander's office.

It made him angry. Both he and Adrian were senior enchanters; having served the Circle of Magi faithfully in the decades since their Harrowing made them mages in full . . . but here they might as well have still been apprentices for all the consideration that got them today.

"This is bullshit," Adrian swore. As always, she was far more willing to show her rage than Rhys. She stopped pacing for a moment and shot him a scathing look that said *Why aren't you doing something?*

"You're cute when you get like this."

"You want to see cute? How about I set this room on fire? I wonder just how cute you'd think I was then."

He chuckled lightly. "Well, *I'd* still think it was cute. The templars, on the other hand, might not agree."

"It would bring them running," she fumed. "I'm tired of being ignored."

"Well, why don't you tell them? They're right in there, after all."

"You think I won't?" She spun around to face the office door. "We've been waiting over an hour! They can't treat us like this!"

Rhys didn't know whether to laugh or be horrified, and settled for a little of both. "Maker's breath, woman! Calm down, will you? You know why they've brought us up here. Don't plant more ideas in their heads."

"You think those ideas aren't already there? They've decided that one of us is guilty. Now they're just trying to prove it." She marched over to the empty chair beside him and sat down. Then immediately leapt back up, as if sitting was a concession she wasn't willing to make just yet. "For all they know, it could be a templar doing these murders! Have they considered that? Who else has keys to the dungeons?"

Rhys sighed, rubbing his temples. It was, of course, only the fifth time in the last hour that Adrian had mentioned her favorite theory, as if he were the one who needed convincing. "You're giving me a headache with all the yelling, you know that?" he complained.

"You're as mad as I am, admit it."

"If you mean mad as in crazy, then certainly. We're both of us completely insane." He gave her a sly wink, and though she rolled her eyes, she also chuckled ruefully. It worked to calm her down a little, as it always did. "I heard not all the victims were in the dungeons, actually. One of them was an apprentice."

"You don't mean Jolen, do you? I thought he failed his Harrowing."

"That's what everyone thought, but I overheard some templars talking about it in the courtyard a few days ago. They mentioned Jolen by name."

"They talk where you can hear them?"

He winked at her. "You'd be amazed at this spell I know that involves looking really busy while actually listening. It's amazing, and works even on templars."

She ignored his jest, tapping her chin thoughtfully. "Jolen was doing so poorly with his lessons. Enchanter Adria said all he wanted to do that last week was hide in his cell, he was that terrified of his Harrowing. When he didn't appear as a Tranquil, I just assumed . . ."

"So did I." He nodded. It wasn't unusual for apprentices to simply vanish. The templars gathered you for your Harrowing in the middle of the night, without warning. Succeed at the test and you were a mage in full. Fail and you were dead. If you refused the test, you were put through the Rite of Tranquility and rendered an emotionless neuter. It was a preferable fate for some, but Rhys found that hard to believe—he couldn't get near a Tranquil without shuddering. He would rather be dead than spend the rest of his life looking at the world through those dead eyes.

When someone failed their Harrowing, however, the rest of the mages weren't told. The apprentice was just gone. It happened frequently, and considering a mage's life was never his own—you could be transferred to another Circle or whisked off to some duty assigned by the Chantry without so much as a by-your-leave— one became accustomed to people coming and going. You didn't question it. There could have been many more murders than any of the mages suspected, and only the templars would know for sure.

"They should tell us." She seethed, her thoughts obviously mirroring his own. "They should at least tell the First Enchanter. They can't keep us in the dark forever."

"I suspect they would argue otherwise."

He fully expected Adrian to explode once again, but instead she looked pensive. She turned and walked toward the bay window, staring out at the city below. He knew what she was thinking. He'd taken his Harrowing almost twenty years ago, and since then he'd let himself believe he was someone of importance to the Circle, that they valued his abilities and his contributions. It wasn't easy to be reminded how untrue that was.

Ever since the Chantry ordered the closure of the College of Enchanters, things had been steadily growing more tense. Permission for travel had been suspended. Gatherings were forbidden, and even on those rare occasions when assembly was allowed in the White Spire's great hall, the First Enchanter had little to tell them. He was supposed to be their leader and their advocate, but now it seemed he was reduced to a figurehead.

There was talk of rebellion, of course. There was always talk. Mages in the far-off city of Kirkwall had rebelled a year ago, and considering what happened to them Rhys wasn't surprised the talk never went further than that. It did make him wonder if that might ever change. If Adrian had her way, it would, and sometimes he even agreed with her.

He jumped as the door to the Knight-Commander's office suddenly opened. Adrian spun around, her vexed expression indicating she planned to give the man a piece of her mind, but both of them were startled to see a woman standing in the doorway instead. It was Knight-Captain Evangeline, wearing full templar regalia and clearly in no mood to be trifled with.

The First Enchanter was at her side. Edmonde was an elder statesman among the White Spire's mages, a man so grizzled and bent by age it seemed like he could barely wear his black robes without collapsing. Now he looked defeated, his limbs trembling with such weariness it was only by leaning on his staff that he was even able to remain upright. He glanced at Rhys, his bleary eyes full of apology—for what he had told them or what was about to come, it couldn't be said—and slowly tapped his way out of the room without a word.

Ser Evangeline watched the First Enchanter leave, and for a moment her rigid demeanor faded. She closed her eyes and sighed, the small and tired sound of someone forced to do the unpleasant. When she opened them again, it was as if the moment had never occurred. "Enchanter Rhys," she said, indicating for him to enter.

Adrian stepped forward. "And what about me?" she demanded.

"In good time."

"So I'm to be left out here until you're bloody ready? Why are we being treated like criminals? If you want our help with an investigation, this is hardly the—"

"In. Good. Time," the templar repeated in a steely tone. Her warning look said that her patience was wearing dangerously thin, and it was enough to give even Adrian second thoughts. Rhys shook his head at Adrian in a manner he hoped she would find discouraging. She clenched her teeth and glared at him, but kept her silence.

Rhys followed the Knight-Captain inside.

The office was unchanged from the last time he had been there. The same war trophies from the Knight-Commander's younger days as a soldier. The same dull painting by some relative preoccupied with the pastoral Orlesian countryside. The same bookshelf filled with long-winded treatises on history and Chantry dogma. The fireplace had settled into a dull smolder, but put out enough heat to give the room a warm, smoky feel. About the only thing that was different about the office was that the Knight-Commander wasn't there.

Instead, there was a stranger seated behind the massive oaken desk. Salt-and-pepper hair showed the man had some age, but his face was hewn from solid stone. The armor he wore was like a templar's, but was charcoal black and emblazoned with a strange image that looked like the Chantry's sunburst but with an eye in the center. Most noticeable were the man's grey eyes: sharp and cold. This man was a warrior, and one who would kill without a second thought. For the first time Rhys wondered if he was in real danger.

"Sit," the man snapped, nodding to the small chair across from the desk. Rhys found himself complying before he realized it. He sat there quietly as the man perused several sheets of parchment. The air was tense, and Rhys couldn't decide what made him more nervous: the idea that whatever was written on those sheets was about him, or that Ser Evangeline stood at crisp attention next to the desk, her face completely blank.

He cleared his throat. No need for this to be unpleasant, after all. "Is the Knight-Commander going to be joining us?" he ventured.

The man glanced up from his reading, raising his eyebrows curiously at this impertinence. For a moment it seemed like he might say nothing. Then he put the sheets down, straightening them into a neat pile with slow deliberation. "Knight-Commander Eron is no longer the head of this order. I am Lord Seeker Lambert, and I will be in command of the White Spire until further notice."

Rhys felt a chill run down his spine. He may not have recognized the symbol on the man's armor, but the name he'd heard of. The Seekers of Truth, an order that stood above the templars as personal servants to the Divine. Nobody spoke of them except in whispers, and even then only to say that when a Seeker showed up you knew there was trouble. "Does this have something to do with the murders?" Rhys asked.

The Lord Seeker paused, his eyes boring a hole into Rhys's skull. "You know about them?"

"Everyone knows. Just because you don't tell us what's going on doesn't mean we won't figure it out. We're not idiots."

The Lord Seeker glared over at Ser Evangeline, but she steadfastly refused to meet his gaze. The slight twitch in the corner of her mouth said *I told you so*. Then he looked back at Rhys, folding his arms. "Odd that every other mage in this tower professes ignorance on the matter. I'd be curious as to what you think you know."

Rhys could lie, but what would be the point? It was entirely possible the Lord Seeker already knew what he was going to say. Still, it galled him to give in. He didn't possess Adrian's talent for invective, but he believed in standing up for himself. These templars didn't control the tower because the mages asked them to, after all. They did it because they could, and because the Chantry said it was their holy duty. Mages were required only to be obedient, and Rhys wasn't the sort of mage who could accept such an imbalance of power without chafing.

"I think there've been five," he said lightly, "but I've heard as many as twelve. Nobody knows how many for sure."

"Go on."

"The first one was an initiate. A farm boy who was brought in from the southern Heartlands. We never even got to find out his name because he was killed in his cell two days after the templars brought him in."

"Strange you would hear anything."

"Not so strange. Initiates aren't the only ones you stick in those dungeons, and they're not soundproof. Someone heard screaming from one of the other cells, and not the normal kind. The day after, the templars were buzzing around the tower like hornets."

The Lord Seeker shrugged. "Initiates die."

Rhys felt his temper rising. The way the man said it, you'd think young mages dying was of no consequence. He tried to maintain his casual demeanor, keep the smile on his face, and not let this man get the better of him. It wasn't easy. "Not screaming like that they don't," he managed through gritted teeth.

The Lord Seeker ignored him. "How did you hear about the others?"

"We . . . knew initiates were being brought in, but then we wouldn't see them later as apprentices. The templars told us they'd been transferred to another Circle, but you can always tell when a templar's lying like that. There were too many questions and surprise searches. And then Jolen died."

The man glanced over at the Knight-Captain. "The fourth one," she said with a nod.

"Ah," he said. "Yes, I suppose it's unsurprising that the order here wouldn't be able to keep that quiet."

"And why should you?" Rhys demanded, feeling his anger bubbling up despite his efforts to keep it under control. "If someone's going around killing mages, don't we have a right to know? The templars are supposed to be protecting us! Isn't that part of why we're locked up in here?"

The Lord Seeker leveled an icy glare at him, and he regretted his outburst instantly. He didn't want to regret it—he wanted to keep on yelling, make these people see just how wrong it was to treat grown mages, mages with *power*, like they were recalcitrant children. In the face of that look, he knew it didn't matter. He was a good judge of character. Given an excuse, this man would slit Rhys's throat before he even got off a single spell. And he would do it with the same cool, unblinking demeanor that he had now.

The Lord Seeker frowned, drumming his fingers on the desk as if deciding just what sort of response was required. "Protecting you is part of the reason you're in the tower, yes." His tone was suddenly pleasant, which somehow made it all the more frightening. "The other part, of course, is that magic is dangerous. It can be dangerous through no intention of the mage, should a demon take hold of them, but not all mages have good intentions, do they?"

The question was ominous, and not entirely without merit.

"Do you know a man by the name of Enchanter Jeannot?" the man asked.

"Yes, of course. He's a senior enchanter here, as am I."

"Was, I'm afraid. Last night he attempted to assassinate the Divine, in front of many witnesses, and was slain." The man watched carefully as he allowed that news to sink in.

Rhys felt cold, as if discovering he was walking on far thinner ice than he'd realized. There was more going on here than just the murders, much more. Jeannot tried to murder the head of the Chantry? How would he even get out of the tower? To do so without help seemed . . . unlikely. Suddenly it made sense why the Knight-Commander was gone, why the First Enchanter acted as he had. "I . . . I see" was all he could manage.

"He used blood magic during the attempt," the Lord Seeker continued. "Were you aware that Jeannot knew such forbidden arts?"

"No, not at all."

"Interesting." The drumming fingers continued, the only sound in the room. Rhys felt a bead of sweat slowly crawling its way down his forehead. It was impossible to keep an entire tower of mages under complete control, not without locking all of them in cells like prisoners. The templars knew that mages snuck around behind their backs and gossiped, and it wasn't unreasonable to think they shared other types of knowledge as well. Where there was one blood mage, there could be more. There could be dozens.

They think I know. Or that I am one.

"There have been six murders in the White Spire to date," the Lord Seeker announced. "Four initiates and two apprentices. Whatever other numbers you've heard are speculation. Those six, however . . . they were interesting." He indicated that Evangeline should explain. She seemed unconvinced this was a good idea, but acquiesced.

"All of them were stabbed in the heart and allowed to bleed out," she began, her tone clinical. "No weapon was discovered. No evidence was found on the victims. As near as we can tell, whoever did this was able to get past the guards, unlock the cells, and leave without being noticed. By anyone."

A sneaking suspicion wormed its way into Rhys's head. He tried to refuse it, banish it from his mind completely, but it wouldn't go away. *Without being noticed . . . by anyone.* It was all he could do to keep his thoughts from giving him away, and from the way both templars stared at him it seemed he wasn't particularly successful.

The Lord Seeker leaned forward on the desk, steepling his fingers as he stared intently. "Now, it is *possible* that a templar could do this, and have his fellows cover up the deed. Perhaps a group of them, dedicated to acts of maliciousness against the very people over whom they are supposed to watch. It is deplorable, but has been known to happen."

"I questioned the templars first," Evangeline explained to Rhys, perhaps a little defensively. "We began alternating guard duties, transferred—"

"It is also *possible*," the Lord Seeker interrupted, "that a blood mage could cause a guard to fall asleep or make him forget whatever he witnessed. Such spells of mind control are one of the reasons blood magic is forbidden. Blood spilled from a sacrifice, meanwhile, could be used to power something much, much worse. Something we can't even guess at yet."

"It could also be a demon," Evangeline offered.

"If so, then it is a demon powerful enough to influence the mages of this tower." The man shuffled through the pile of parchments until he found one in particular. He tapped it. "It says here that you are a medium, Enchanter."

Rhys kept his face calm. "Yes."

"You have a rare talent to detect and communicate with spirits and demons."

"Yes."

"Have you ever detected or communicated with any here in the White Spire?"

Another bead of sweat found its way into Rhys's eye. He wiped it away, hoping his hands weren't visibly shaking. "Yes, but . . . the Veil is thin here. That's part of my research. It should all be accounted for in the First Enchanter's—"

"I'm aware of your research," the Lord Seeker snapped, his tone carrying heavy disapproval. "I'm also aware it was discontinued almost a year ago, after the rebellion in Kirkwall. Well before the murders began. What about recently?"

"No, there's been nothing." That much was true, at least.

"It seems to me that someone with such talent wouldn't allow templars to keep him from doing as he wished. We cannot follow you across the Veil. You could be speaking to demons on a nightly basis, and no one would be the wiser."

"It's not that simple," Rhys insisted. "Consciously entering the Fade requires preparation, a group of mages working together. My research required painstaking work to protect me from the spirits I was contacting, in case—"

"In case you were corrupted," the man finished for him.

"Learning more about spirits is important if we're ever going to protect ourselves from them more effectively. Knight-Commander Eron scrutinized me after every ritual. He trusted me. If he didn't . . ."

The man neatly replaced the sheet of parchment in the pile. "Knight-Commander Eron's judgment did not assist him in safeguarding his charges, nor in finding a blood mage in his midst."

Ser Evangeline scowled at that, but Lord Seeker Lambert didn't notice. Rhys frowned, not liking where this was going. Not one bit. "Am I being accused of something?" he asked.

"Not yet."

The Knight-Captain cleared her throat, ignoring the warning look she received from the Lord Seeker. She leaned toward Rhys. "I've seen you with Jeannot," she said gently. "Both you and Enchanter Adrian. All three of you are part of the Libertarian fraternity. I think you can see why we're concerned."

And there it was. Rhys had been wondering when that was going to come up. The fact rankled enough to make him put aside any efforts to contain his anger. "So you think the Libertarians have all become blood mages? We'll do anything to attain freedom for the Circle, even become the very thing that brought about the Circle in the first place?" He sat forward, glaring at both of them in turn. "Let me tell you this: I didn't know Jeannot was a blood mage, nor why he did what he did. We weren't close. If I'd known, I would have told the First Enchanter. It's mages like that who give the fraternity, and us all, a bad name."

"Then tell us who he was close with."

Rhys folded his arms. "No."

The Lord Seeker's eyes widened. "You're refusing to answer?"

"I am. I won't be a party to persecuting my fraternity. We're the first to blame for everything."

"Then give us another answer."

"You're not looking for answers." Rhys stood up, defiant. "This isn't an investigation. Someone tried to kill the Divine, and you're not going to be happy until you can string together a conspiracy that makes sense to you. So whatever you're going to do, I suggest you do it. Lock me in the dungeon. Perhaps I can be the murderer's next victim? That should clear me of suspicion quickly enough."

There was a long and tense silence, punctuated only by Ser Evangeline's sigh of disappointment. The Lord Seeker was coldly outraged. He rose from his chair and stiffly straightened his breast-plate. "That was foolish."

If the man expected a response, he didn't get one. Rhys re-mained where he was, and the two of them locked glares. He knew this would probably get him imprisoned. They could leave him in there to rot, or even make him Tranquil—just to be safe. But Rhys no longer cared. A vanished apprentice was one thing, but he was a senior enchanter and a member of the Libertarians. Let them explain that to the rest of the Circle, to Adrian, and see how that worked out for them. Given the mood in the tower that had been building this past year, it wouldn't be pretty.

"Get out," the Lord Seeker finally growled.

Ser Evangeline stepped forward and took Rhys by the arm. He fought against being led away, still matching the Lord Seeker's gaze. The man wanted a fight, and Rhys was tempted to give him one. But then he relented and allowed himself to be pulled out of the office, reminding himself that he was getting off easy.

He did, after all, know more than he'd let on. And they knew that now, too. Walking out of that room, he felt as if a noose had been slipped around his neck, just waiting for the right moment to tighten.

Adrian's interrogation went no better than his. Far worse, if the extent of her later rage was anything to judge it by. Hours later she was angrily stalking from one end of the commons to the other, ranting to any mage who would listen about the conspiracy they were dealing with.

The commons weren't really intended as a gathering area. It

was a glorified landing outside of the mages' chambers on the middle floors of the tower, allowing access to the central stairwell. There were no furnishings to speak of, just cold stone floors and a few small windows that let the chill in every winter. Statues lined the area at each supporting pillar, grave-looking depictions of warriors from an age long past. Rhys had always hated them. He felt their proud eyes staring down at him, judging him for having the temerity to possess magic.

But there was nowhere else for the mages to go. Rumors of the Lord Seeker's presence had spread like wildfire, as had word of the attempt on the Divine's life. By the time Adrian and Rhys had walked into the commons it was already packed. Everyone spoke in hushed voices—as if anything above a whisper would invite the wrath of the templars. The smell of raw fear permeated the chamber, but along with it came an undercurrent of anger.

What if the Lord Seeker invoked the Rite of Annulment? Rhys heard that question asked more than once. The thought of every last mage in the tower being put to the sword was difficult to contemplate. It was a right the templars possessed, meant to be used only as a last act of desperation when a Circle of Magi was completely lost to corruption. That was supposedly what had happened in Kirkwall. If the Rite of Annulment hadn't been invoked since then, it was no doubt because the templars feared further rebellion—but how far could they be pushed?

According to Adrian, the same question should be asked about the mages. She didn't believe what the Lord Seeker said about Jeannot. How could one man have gotten so close to the Divine? Adrian thought the entire thing suspicious, and suggested it was a templar ploy to turn popular opinion more firmly in their favor.

Rhys wasn't as certain. There were rumors among the Libertarians of those who were no longer satisfied with peacefully seeking freedom, even more so now that the closure of the College of Enchanters had removed that option entirely. They wanted action, even if it involved dragging the rest of the mages kicking and screaming along with them. Rhys wouldn't put it past such people to perform forbidden rites to give themselves an advantage, not to mention keeping their activities secret even from the rest of their fraternity. The templars had every reason to be nervous.

But they didn't have all the facts, did they? As Rhys stood there in the commons, watching the crowd roil in its discontent like a sea before the storm, he felt only guilt. He was keeping a secret, from the templars as well as his fellow mages. He couldn't tell anyone the truth, and the chances he would be able to do anything about it were looking slim.

Adrian marched over to him, already working up another head of steam. What was this, now? Her third wind? The talk in the commons had gone around in circles, and it was no closer to going somewhere productive now—though that certainly wasn't for lack of Adrian's effort. "Aren't you going to *do* something?" she snapped.

He grinned at her. "I am doing something. I'm watching."

"Do something else!"

"Dearest Adrian," he chuckled. "What would you have me do, exactly? You seem to have the outrage covered. It's taxing just to watch you."

He tried to take her by the shoulders, calm her before she did something rash, but she pulled away with a resentful look. "Don't give me that. You know as well as I do they'll listen to you before they'll listen to me. They always have."

"That's not true," he demurred. But it wasn't entirely false, either. Some of the younger enchanters had approached him already, probing with hopeful questions. Others were watching their exchange even now. They were waiting for him. He could see it in their eyes. It was an uncomfortable feeling.

"The First Enchanter is doing nothing," she said, just loudly enough for the man to overhear. Edmonde stood not far away, gazing listlessly out a window. He'd spoken to no one, and his only reaction to Adrian's statement was to close his eyes with a pained expression. Rhys felt badly for the man and the position this entire affair had placed him in. Couldn't she see that? Rhys raised a hand to urge her to keep her voice down, but she knocked it out of the way. "The other senior enchanters are no better. *You* can do something, Rhys. Take charge!"

It was always the same demand. Adrian was headstrong and thus made enemies. Rhys was more charming, she said, and thus better liked. He could get her point across to those who wouldn't listen, despite his protests that this would put him in the same position as she was in. "That's not going to help," he told her.

She sighed bitterly, her shoulders sagging. It was just one more time he'd disappointed her, after all. Adrian had been his friend for a long time—in fact, for a while they'd been more than friends, as much more as their life within the confines of the Circle would allow. But he would never be the leader she expected him to be, and so friendship was all they were left with.

"At least tell everyone about the murders," she muttered. "You know they're dying of curiosity, and I didn't even get *that* far with the Seeker. Pompous, arrogant bastard that he is."

Rhys hesitated. The murders were the very last thing he wanted to talk about. It turned out that he didn't need to make a decision regarding that anyhow, as a moment later several guards entered the commons and ordered everyone to retire to their chambers. He wasn't surprised. In normal circumstances Rhys and Adrian would be in the dungeons by now, along with anyone else who'd so much as greeted Jeannot in passing. Thankfully, the templars weren't interested in provoking the mages further.

Adrian, of course, felt no compulsion to return the favor. Rhys saw outrage flash in her eyes, and waited for the inevitable scene to follow. Thankfully, the First Enchanter chose that moment to intervene. Edmonde turned from his window and quietly sug-

gested everyone do as the guards asked. Tomorrow would be another day. That took the wind out of Adrian's sails, and slowly
everyone in the commons dispersed.

Rhys was relieved. This might give him the chance he was waiting for.

He spent the next several hours in his chambers, staring up at
the ceiling from his cot. Occasionally he heard the footsteps of
guards passing his door. It was fortunate that senior enchanters
got their own rooms. As spartan as they were, they allowed privacy the dormitories didn't. One could sneak out of a dormitory
easily enough—apprentices did it all the time—but not without
being seen by others sharing the room. Where Rhys needed to
go, he had to be absolutely certain nobody else knew about it.

By the middle of the night, an utter stillness had crept over the
tower. There had been no footsteps for well over an hour. *It's now
or never,* he told himself. Slowly, he sat up in the darkness, listening intently for the slightest shuffle outside that might indicate a
sentry. Nothing.

Feeling around blindly, Rhys found his staff leaning against
the wall. The wood felt warm to his touch, awakening from its
slumber. The crystalline orb greeted him with a soft glow that filled
the room, but Rhys darkened it again with a wave of his hand.
Light was the last thing he needed.

Then he jumped. Something in the room had moved, just as
the light went out. Steeling himself, he willed the staff to glow
once more—and sighed when he realized it was only his reflec-
tion coming from the ornate standing mirror in the corner. A gift
from Adrian, something she'd bought for him years ago when
outings into the city had still been permitted. "You can admire
yourself in it," she'd laughed, and she so rarely laughed that he
couldn't refuse. It was the one extravagant thing he owned, however, and he still wasn't used to its presence. Peevishly, he wanted
to kick it over.

Calm down, you idiot, or you'll do the templars' work for them. He allowed himself to chuckle, and the fear drained out of him a little. The emptiness that remained left him shaky and feeling more than a little foolish.

Rhys darkened the staff again and crept toward the door. He worked the latch, trying to press it slowly, and was rewarded when the door cracked open with only the softest click. He peered out into the hall. A glowlamp was hung by the central staircase, but that was quite far away. Everything nearer was swallowed up in shadow. There was no one in sight, but that was difficult to trust.

Gathering his magic, he reached his mind across the Veil and summoned a spirit through. It was tiny, a wisp of a creature with barely any consciousness to call its own. The shimmering orb hovered over the palm of his hand, its magical hum tickling the hairs on the back of his neck.

"I need you to be quiet," he whispered. "You can do that, can't you?"

The wisp bobbed excitedly and dimmed. He barely even saw it now. Tossing it up into the air, he sensed its excitement as it floated out into the commons. Even such a small spirit took great joy in coming into the real world. They found the oddest things of endless fascination: a wooden chair, a piece of steak, a feather. Left to its own devices, a wisp would bob around random objects for hours, making strange trilling noises as it explored its environment.

The templars frowned on the use of even such benign spirits, although it was not strictly forbidden. The best healers, after all, summoned spirits of compassion to assist them. Such spirits did not linger and immediately returned whence they came, but the Chantry looked upon any who had the talent to contact them with suspicion—such as himself. Still, it had its uses.

Rhys waited. Just as he was beginning to fear the wisp had become distracted, he sensed its return. It came to rest on his open palm, emitting an odd set of excited sounds. He closed his eyes and tried to gather what impressions he could from its memory. The first images he saw were confused, and made it seem like the commons was filled with a dozen or more templars. Then he realized it had been looking at the statues, and couldn't tell the difference. Typical.

But one of the figures had moved. He focused on that one sighting and received enough impressions from the wisp to figure it out. A sentry on the far side of the staircase. The hall was being watched after all.

"I need you to do one more favor for me," he quietly asked it. The wisp floated off his hand, already quivering with anticipation. "I need you to lead the man away. It doesn't matter where. Just a few minutes and you're free to return to the Fade."

It was a fairly complex command. The wisp twirled in place, shimmering slightly as it considered, and then floated off once again. Within minutes, Rhys heard a muted swear from the unseen guard. Footsteps followed, heading down the stairs at a rapid pace. Good. That would give Rhys the time he needed.

Slipping out into the hall, he turned not toward the staircase but toward the darker part of the commons. A tiny storage room lay hidden next to the dormitories. He crept there as quietly as he could, letting himself inside.

It was pitch black within, the air thick with the stench of stale smoke. He stifled a cough and willed his staff to glow. The light revealed a room barely deeper than his arm could reach, lined on both sides by rickety shelves filled near to bursting with the things the Tranquil used to service the mages' chambers. There was also evidence that the apprentices frequented this storage room: the floor was a mess of breadcrumbs, ashes left by illicit kohl pipes, and depleted glowstones.

Funny, then, that the apprentices hadn't discovered the loose stone on the back wall. If they had, they would have realized they didn't need to hole up in a closet. Pressing the stone opened a hatch, and that led to a crawlspace beyond. From there, one could climb unseen past the kitchens and into the tower's underground levels. There were many such passages in the White Spire; the few mages who knew about them guarded their secret jealously, lest the templars seal them up.

The next hour was spent crawling through interminable darkness and dust to find his way. Near the kitchens he had to shuffle between the walls, trying not to choke on the fetid air. Then the crawlspace finally turned into an exceedingly steep staircase. He could stand, but the walls were so narrow he could barely squeeze through. Everything felt closed in. Stifling. Suffocating.

His relief was palpable when he finally felt the air change. He knew the stairs led to an open chamber below, a room that belonged to one of many unused portions of the lower floors, and he was getting close. Rhys eagerly made his way down—too eagerly, in fact. One of the last steps crumbled under his weight, and with a cry of alarm he pitched forward.

The staff flew out of his hands, its light winking out as it landed below with a clatter, and he was not far behind. Trying to slow his descent by clutching at the walls, he only managed to make his fall more awkward. He twisted and bumped, smacked his head against the wall, and then finally met the ground at full force.

Ow.

Rhys lay there in the darkness, getting used to the pain. There was a lot of it, sharp and throbbing. Slowly he tested the extent of his injuries. Hand flexed fine. His feet moved. Nothing was broken, though his body begged to differ. A relief, to be sure.

There were no sounds of footsteps, nothing to indicate someone had heard his fall and come to investigate. That wasn't surprising. This place wasn't far from the dungeons, but the way sound traveled in the Pit, it was unlikely someone could find the source even if they overheard it. The guards didn't generally roam this far anyhow, but there was always a first time.

Groaning, Rhys pulled himself to his knees. He felt around for his staff. His hands encountered dust, dust, and more dust. There were loose stones, as well, and rotten pieces of wood. Once this might have been a storage room, although how long ago was anyone's guess. There were a few ancient crates and barrels, long empty and now just purchase for spider webs. Was there still a stool? Some intrepid mage had brought one down ages ago, but it wasn't safe to sit on any longer.

Finally he found his staff. Closing his hand around it, he willed the orb to shine . . .

. . . and gasped in shock. Someone was in the room with him.

A young man sat on his haunches not five feet away, staring with haunted eyes from under a mop of unkempt blond hair. He was clearly neither a mage nor a templar, dressed in worn leathers near covered in dust and grime, and hadn't seen a bath in ages. There was a furtive tension to the way he crouched, like a cellar rat caught out in the open—paralyzed by fear and yet desperate to run.

"Cole," Rhys breathed, taking deep breaths to slow his racing heart. "You scared the life near out of me!"

The young man bit his lower lip, squirming uncomfortably. "I haven't seen you in a long time," he said. His voice had a raspy quality, no doubt from lack of use. "I thought you'd forgotten."

"I haven't forgotten. I told you it was becoming more difficult to get away, didn't I?" Rhys stood up carefully. He brushed off some of the filth, frowning at the tears and bruises that would be more difficult to explain later. Then he stopped, remembering the reason he had gone through all this effort in the first place. He turned to look at Cole, wary of just how he should broach the subject. The young man was nervous enough as it was.

"There are some things I need to ask you about," he began. "Important things."

"Oh." The way Cole twisted in place, like a guilty child eager to find any excuse to leave but unable to tear himself away, told Rhys everything he needed to know. Cole knew exactly what he was going to ask. He knew and had come to find Rhys anyhow, because he couldn't help himself.

"It's you, isn't it? You're the murderer."

4

It had been nearly a year since Rhys had first seen Cole.

He remembered the time well, because the White Spire had just received news of the rebellion at Kirkwall. The mages buzzed with fear, templars present in the halls in force. Amidst all that, Rhys caught rare glimpses of a stranger lurking, a young man who wasn't running about like everyone else but instead simply . . . watched. Although this stranger was oddly dressed, Rhys didn't give it much thought. A new apprentice, or a visitor sanctioned by the templars. No one else seemed to pay this stranger much mind, after all, so why should he? Back then strangers weren't a common sight in the tower, but they weren't unheard of.

Later, during a lecture in the great hall, Rhys saw him again. Sitting in the back of the chamber and watching the proceedings with a perplexed expression. The young man seemed entirely out of place, so Rhys turned to Adrian and asked who she thought he might be.

Adrian looked to where he indicated, and frowned. "Who are you talking about? There's nobody back there."

"Are you sure?"

"Is this a joke? What are *you* seeing?"

That shut Rhys up. If he was seeing something Adrian didn't, then it was either his imagination . . . or worse. It might be a spirit, or even a demon, and that meant trouble. Still, he was a medium. If this young man was a demon, why didn't he sense him as such?

So Rhys passed it off to Adrian as merely a misunderstanding, half convinced that was the case. Afterward he did some asking around—carefully. Had anyone seen something strange in the tower? Someone who didn't belong? That's when he heard about the Ghost of the Spire.

It was ridiculous, of course. Everything his research had told him said ghosts didn't exist. At best they were spirits masquerading as the dead, or confused. When people died their souls went . . . somewhere. If the Chantry was to be believed, they went to reside with the Maker in some realm beyond the Fade. Even the spirits themselves claimed not to know, if the word of such beings could be relied upon.

Yet these rumors caused him even more concern. So he watched carefully for the young man to reappear, determined to confront him and find out for certain. Like the old saying about watched pots, waiting for a sighting of the young man meant there was suddenly no sign of him anywhere.

So Rhys went down into the Pit to look for him. That's where anyone who mentioned this mysterious ghost agreed it could be found. If it was a spirit, Rhys owed it to his research to find why he couldn't sense it—and owed it to himself to prove that he wasn't being influenced by a rather clever demon.

He looked in the archives. He poked around some of the forgotten areas of the tower, even places that were technically forbidden. Just when he started to suspect the entire thing was his imagination, he had stumbled upon Cole. Or, rather, Cole had stumbled upon him.

Rhys remembered turning a corner and nearly running into the young man standing there, watching him. When Rhys spoke to him, the young man jumped as if struck. The shock of finding someone who could see him had been considerable, evidently, and it took more than a little convincing to calm him down. He'd been drawn by Rhys's search, but never once considered that it might be because Rhys had seen him previously. He'd long ago stopped watching for other people noticing him, because it never happened.

That first conversation was . . . illuminating. According to Cole, he'd been brought in by the templars and thrown in a cell. He didn't remember when, and he didn't remember clearly how he got out—but now he found himself lost in a world that couldn't see him. Rhys had never heard of such a thing. In fact, he had to touch the man to be certain that this was, in fact, a real person.

"How can you be invisible?" he'd asked.

"I don't know."

"But . . . people *have* seen you. Fleeting glimpses, anyhow. I've heard the stories."

"Sometimes. I don't know why."

Cole's answers were evasive. He was uncomfortable being questioned, and frightened of what Rhys was going to do with the knowledge of his presence. He begged not to be turned over to the templars, to the point of becoming frantic. Rhys had reluctantly agreed—who would believe him, after all, if he said an invisible man was stalking the tower halls? Especially if that man did not want to be seen.

So he left Cole there, promising to return in the future, and didn't understand why the young man's response was silent incredulity until he found him again several days later. At that point, Cole was startled once again. He said he'd managed to get people to notice him before, he could do it if he really tried. But they always forgot about him again soon after. He just slipped their mind completely, and he assumed the same would happen with Rhys.

But it didn't. Rhys kept coming back, at first because he was intrigued by this strange puzzle. If he could figure out what was making Cole invisible, perhaps it could be undone. Perhaps there was something to be learned by this power. Rhys was no scholar, but interesting research had always attracted him—especially if it could help someone.

And Cole needed help. The young man never spoke of it, but it was obvious he was desperately lonely. As much as companionship was strange and frightening to him, the fear was never enough to keep him away. Eventually it stopped being about helping him; Rhys still wanted to find out the truth, of course, but now it was because he liked Cole. The young man was slow to talk, but had a sharp mind and a curious nature. He was also a perfect example of why the Circle didn't work. What if mages had been there to greet his arrival at the tower, with understanding rather than fear and scorn? What if he had been made to realize his talent wasn't terrifying, but unique and fascinating?

So they met as often as Rhys dared. They played card games by the light of a glowlamp, and Cole showed him some of the mysteries he had uncovered in the Pit—things Rhys hadn't even suspected might be down there. They talked about anything, as long as it was inconsequential. Questions about how Cole became like he was, or even the possibility of helping him often led to him withdrawing back into the shadows.

They were discovered exactly once, by a templar guard patrolling the archives. The man came into the room unnoticed, startling them both as they mulled over a chess board. The guard stood there, staring, and then asked if Rhys always played games by himself. Rhys stuttered through an excuse that he was working out strategies, and the guard moved on with a bewildered shake of his head. Until that moment, Rhys had privately wondered if Cole wasn't simply hard to notice, if someone presented with direct evidence would see him normally. But that wasn't so.

And then the College of Enchanters was shut down.

With that came increased scrutiny on every mage in the tower, and thus less opportunity for Rhys to go anywhere without his absence being noted. His visits became infrequent, and when he did come he found Cole withdrawn and listless. The young man was convinced each time that Rhys had forgotten him, despite assurances to the contrary. Afterward he would be sullen, expressing a doubt that if Rhys hadn't forgotten him now, then he no doubt soon would.

So Rhys redoubled his efforts to find an answer. His search in the archives turned up little. He considered broaching the subject with Adrian—but what would she say? What could anyone say? Ignoring the possibility of the templars discovering his secret, what advice could anyone offer regarding someone Rhys couldn't even prove existed? Being unable to help made him feel guilty, as did the notion his visits were making Cole feel worse rather than better.

The last time Rhys came down to the Pit, he had to search for hours to locate Cole. It was unusual, because normally the young man found him first. Rhys dared not call out, instead combing the forgotten corners where Cole lived, half dreading that he might come across a lifeless body.

Eventually he found Cole in the templar crypts, perched atop a massive sarcophagus like a sad raven. The young man seemed unhealthy and pale, like he hadn't slept for weeks. He didn't say hello as Rhys approached, just watched warily, and then asked out of the blue if Rhys thought he was dead.

"You're not dead," Rhys insisted. "You're as real as I am."

"Maybe *you're* not real. You could be a demon sent to torment me."

"Is that what I do? Torment you?"

Haunted eyes. "Yes. No."

Rhys reached up to touch Cole, to reassure him, but the young man only scrambled farther up the sarcophagus. "Leave me alone," he muttered, although it didn't sound convincing.

"Is that what you really want me to do?"

"No."

"Cole, come with me. I need to bring you to the First Enchanter, *make* him see you. We can write things down, so nobody forgets. Then we can get you help. I'm sorry, but I just can't do it on my own."

Silence.

"Don't you *want* help?" he asked.

"I don't want anyone to hurt me." Cole was a grown man, but this was the frightened plea of a child. Rhys stood there for a long time, staring helplessly up at him.

"You could leave, you know. You don't have to stay in the tower like I do."

"Where would I go?"

Rhys didn't have a good answer for that. *Nowhere. Anywhere but here. If I were you I would walk past those templars, leave the tower, and go somewhere they could never find me.* But he wasn't Cole. The young man avoided the upper floors of the tower because people frightened him. The city outside the tower was an impossibility, so terrifying in its chaos that he probably couldn't even imagine it. And what sort of life would that be, watching a world bursting full of excitement in which you could only be a spectator?

So Rhys reluctantly left him there, walking out of the crypt with a pair of eyes boring into his back. That was a month ago, and until he'd sat in the Knight-Commander's office today he'd never once made a connection between this sad young man and the murders. The idea that he might be anything more than a victim never even entered his mind.

Now Cole crouched there before him, staring with that same sullen expression as the last time they'd met. Was Rhys in danger? He thought he'd known what this young man was capable of, but he was wrong. More than wrong; he was an idiot. Part of him clung to the notion that there *must* be an explanation for this.

"Tell me this isn't true," he demanded. "Tell me you didn't actually kill those people, that there's some other explanation."

"I can't."

"Was it blood magic? Were you trying to . . . cure yourself with some ritual you found? Something in the archives?"

Cole looked perplexed. "I don't know any magic."

"Then *why*? Tell me that much."

"I needed to."

"You needed to kill them? How can—" Rhys stopped short, a terrible idea coming to him. "Was it Jeannot? Did he find you, speak to you? Did he tell you to do this?"

"I don't know who that is."

"A mage like me, but older. Less hair. I know he comes down here . . ."

"Does he eat peaches? There's a man who looks like that who goes to the archives. Sometimes I see him in the crypt, but only when he's talking to the others."

"Others? What others?"

Cole shrugged. "They talk in the dark, about boring things. He leaves peach pits on the floor. That's how I know he goes there."

Rhys thought about it for a moment. Secret meetings in the crypt? If Jeannot was part of that . . . then the Lord Seeker's assumption about there being a conspiracy in the tower might not be far off. A chilling thought. "Why didn't you tell me about this sooner?" he asked.

"I didn't know you didn't know. Or that you wanted to."

"Could they have seen you? Maybe they cast a spell to force you to do these things. For all we know, they might be the ones who made you like this in the first place."

Cole considered the idea. For over a minute he idly drew lines in the dusty floor, frowning. "They didn't see me," he finally said. "Nobody can see me, except for you. And the ones I . . ."

"The ones you killed."

Cole nodded.

"Was that why you killed them? You thought they would tell the templars?"

"No. They didn't see me until I went to them. But I knew they would." Cole chewed his lip, an expression that Rhys had seen before whenever the man was trying to put a difficult thought into words. "Have you ever been underwater?" he finally asked.

"Of course."

"There's a pool in one of the lower halls. I go there sometimes." He seemed lost in thought. "You can float when you're underwater. If you close your eyes, it's like you're floating in nothing. You're surrounded by darkness, and all you can hear is yourself. Everything else is far away."

"I don't understand."

Cole sighed in frustration. "Sometimes I feel like I'm underwater, and I won't ever get out again. I just keep sinking and sinking, and there's no bottom. The darkness is going to swallow me up." He stared at the floor, embarrassed. "I'm falling into the cracks between what's real and what's not real, and if I don't stop myself I'll be lost there forever. The only way I can stay is to . . ."

Rhys backed away. Just a step. He didn't mean to do it, but Cole noticed nonetheless. The grief that twisted on his face at that realization was difficult to watch. Rhys found himself torn between fear and concern. He liked Cole, and always had, but it was too difficult to reconcile the harmless young man he knew and a murderer who had stabbed six helpless mages in the heart. "The only way you can stay," he said, his voice small and strained, "is to kill someone?"

"I know they'll see me," Cole whispered. "I don't know why, but I do. So I go to them. The moment they die, they look at me. They know I'm the one that's killed them, and that makes me the most important thing in the world." His face became wracked with grief again. "I've never been that important to anyone." The words came out as a hoarse croak.

"And . . . being important makes you real?"

Cole looked up at him with wide, uncomprehending eyes. "Doesn't it do that for you?"

Rhys didn't know how to respond. There was a more important question that lingered in the back of his mind: Would Cole kill him, too? He could see the man, after all, just like his victims. If Cole became convinced that killing Rhys would somehow make him real, wouldn't he do it? As much as Rhys wanted to help this young man, it was becoming clear he was delusional. He was beyond help.

"Cole," Rhys said firmly. "You have to listen to me. You're not going to disappear. Murdering innocent people isn't going to change anything."

"You don't know that. You once said you had no idea what was wrong with me."

Rhys stepped forward and grabbed Cole by the shoulders, lifting him to his feet. The young man's eyes went wide in shock, but he didn't struggle. "Cole, you have no idea what kind of trouble this has caused. Not just for me, but for all of us. They think a blood mage has been killing everyone. You *have* to come with me."

"No!" Cole struggled to break free, but Rhys held him.

"We have to *make* them see you! Tell them whatever happened to you is affecting your mind, that it's not your fault. I don't know, something! This is the only way you're ever going to get help, Cole!"

"They can't help me!" He twisted out of Rhys's grasp, quickly retreating to the far wall. "They won't!" His look was one of abject terror and betrayal.

Rhys hesitated. Of course Cole was right. Even if the templars could be made to see him and not forget, they wouldn't help. Chances are they'd consider him someone who'd fallen under the sway of a demon. The mages, meanwhile, would see someone who had murdered six of their fellows . . . and Rhys wasn't sure he should try to convince them otherwise. Cole was sick. He killed people in order to help himself. Didn't that deserve punishment?

He put up his hands to forestall Cole from running. "You can't keep doing this," he warned. "One way or another, this has to stop."

"Please," Cole sobbed. He looked so agonized it was difficult not to feel sorry for him. "I never meant to make you angry. I don't want you to stop talking to me, too."

"Then come with me."

"I can't!" Cole darted toward the door. Rhys lunged, but with one hand holding his staff he could only grab on to the edge of Cole's leather jerkin with the other. It wasn't enough, and he almost toppled over as Cole escaped into the dark hallway outside.

"Blast!" He didn't want it to be like this. He ran after Cole and stopped just outside. His staff illuminated a passage that went straight ahead, as well as winding stairs to the right. If he remembered correctly, ahead eventually led to the dungeons, but the stairs went deeper into the Pit. Down below, there was a labyrinth of old corridors that included the templar crypts. He couldn't see which way Cole had run, and the echoes of the man's footsteps came from everywhere.

Rhys raced down the stairs. There would be templars at the dungeons, and while they wouldn't see Cole, he doubted that would make a difference. He took the steps two and three at a time, careening off the stone walls each time the stairs turned. Part of him feared taking another tumble, a more serious one this time, but he didn't care.

Finally he got to the bottom. Within moments he caught a glimpse of the young man in the distance, running as fast as he could. "Stop!" He channeled mana through his staff, unleashing a bolt of white energy that lanced down the corridor. It struck the wall near Cole, causing the stone to explode with a crack of thunder. Rocks flew everywhere.

He heard Cole cry out in fear. Rhys covered his mouth, coughing at the deluge of fresh dust, but kept running. He found the young man cowering near a pile of loose stones, with smaller ones still crumbling from the ceiling. He was filthy but otherwise unhurt. Good. Rhys hadn't intended to kill him.

"Cole, don't make me do this," he shouted as he drew close, trying to catch his breath. "You have to come with me. There's no other choice!"

Then he slowed to a halt. Cole wasn't cowering. He was crouched low to the ground, eyes glinting dangerously. In his hands was a dagger with a jagged blade, a killing weapon. And it was clear he knew how to use it.

"I don't want to hurt you," Cole warned, his voice low and threatening.

They locked eyes, neither willing to give. It made Rhys angry, to think of all the time he had spent worrying about this young man, only to discover he was a wolf in sheep's clothing. Even if Cole had never claimed to be anything else, Rhys still felt betrayed.

"Why not?" he snapped. "I can see you. Won't killing me make you more real?" He may as well have slapped Cole across the face, considering how the man flinched at his accusing tone. Rhys didn't regret it. He was done with coddling. "This is your last chance." The orb on his staff crackled with white energy.

Cole's eyes narrowed, and for just a moment Rhys thought he might attack. Then he suddenly leapt in the opposite direction. Startled, Rhys unleashed a blast from his staff, but Cole nimbly dodged to the side and it missed its mark. More rocks flew, spreading an even thicker cloud of dust, and Rhys staggered back, coughing.

When he recovered, wiping his eyes, Cole was gone. Grit trailed down from large cracks in the ceiling. He would have to be more careful—the last thing he wanted to do was cause a collapse down here. He wasn't going to stop, however. While Rhys loathed the idea of bringing anyone to the templars, this had to be done. The only way to prove that the murders weren't done by mages was to have Cole in hand and pray to the Maker the young man's strange ability wouldn't mean they'd forget he'd done so five minutes later.

Steeling his nerves, Rhys rushed through the cloud and chased after Cole. He held his staff in front of him, already channeling mana into it. He wasn't going to miss again.

Evangeline felt exhausted. Had she stayed asleep in her chambers like she'd planned, then she wouldn't have discovered Enchanter Rhys missing from his quarters. Not knowing would have absolved her of any responsibility to act, and chances were the mage would have been back in the morning with nobody the wiser. She knew very well how the mages snuck around this tower. Like rats they managed to sniff out every dark corner and secret passage where they could find some privacy. Under normal circumstances, she wouldn't consider this an issue.

But these weren't normal circumstances, and she did know. One last check on the sentry she'd posted in the mages' commons and then she'd rest—that's what she'd told herself. The man at first had stammered and insisted he hadn't left his post, which of course meant he had. He tried to sound dismissive when he mentioned the light he'd seen on the stairs, someone carrying a torch, or so he thought. She knew right away what had happened.

After so many years of watching over their charges, one would think templars would be used to the idea that mages could use their spells to do more than fling lightning bolts. Evidently imagination wasn't something the order could train. Considering Enchanter Rhys possessed a facility with spirits, it wasn't difficult to piece together who was responsible.

So now she followed First Enchanter Edmonde up the long flight of stairs that led to the phylactery chamber. He lit the way with his staff, although the shadows still pressed in from all sides. The old mage stumbled on every second step, stopping to wipe the bleary fatigue from his eyes. She sympathized, but they had little alternative.

It wasn't long before the stairs finally opened onto a foyer. A single stone room, holding only a massive vault. The door was an elaborate mechanism of dwarven construction, a series of interlocking circles made of brass and steel and other alloys Evangeline couldn't begin to name—strong enough to withstand even the most concerted magical attack. The entire tower could be brought crashing to the ground and it would remain intact. Everything inside would be destroyed, of course, which made her wonder why they hadn't put it underground instead. She imagined the order liked to keep the phylacteries high out of reach from the mages, like a shiny bauble dangled over a desperate child's head.

On each side of the vault door a glass plate shimmered with a faint reddish glow. Two keys for entry: one for a templar and one for a mage. That was the only way inside, as dictated since the Circle's inception.

A guard in templar armor stood in front of the vault, his posture so erect there was little doubt he'd been asleep only moments before. "Knight-Captain!" he saluted smartly. It deserved a reprimand, but this *was* the most boring post in the entire tower. It hadn't even required a guard until after the Kirkwall rebellion; Knight-Commander Eron decided prudence demanded it. One wouldn't normally expect the chamber to be needed in the middle of the night, even so. The guard's lucky day, she supposed.

"Hard at work, I see?" she said as she approached.

"Yes, ser!" The guard blinked hard, a sheen of sweat on his forehead. He had the soft face of one noble-born, some second or third son from a forgotten corner of the Empire who no doubt despised the fact that rising within the order wasn't as easy as he'd hoped.

"Stand aside." She waved her hand at him irritably; he almost yelped as he scrambled out of her way. She turned to the First Enchanter beside her. "Shall we?"

The mage looked almost as if he'd topple over from exhaustion. "Is this really necessary, Ser Evangeline?"

"One of your people is missing, the night after an attempt on the Divine's life. It was also not long after we questioned him regarding the murders. I think that warrants suspicion, don't you?"

"Questioned, but not accused."

"If you prefer, we can wake Lord Seeker Lambert and ask for his opinion."

The First Enchanter's shoulders sank. Letting out a laborious sigh, he shuffled over to the plate on one side of the vault and placed his hand on it. The red light reacted to his touch, shifting and swirling until it became blue. Nodding, she strode to the other, removing her gauntlet and touching her bare hand to it. She channeled power through her skin; it tingled as the plate slowly changed to blue as well.

The vault began to shudder, letting out a resounding groan that echoed throughout the chamber. Gears turned, and the metallic circles that were part of the door began to slide in different directions. She watched, fascinated, as each layer slowly lined up one by one . . . until the lock emitted one final clank and was done. A small panel in the center of the door slid open, revealing a handle.

She marched over to it, waving at the gawking templar to stand back, and pulled. The entire door opened far more easily than its weight suggested, making so little sound its great hinges might have been oiled yesterday rather than centuries ago. Those dwarves certainly knew their business.

The windowless chamber inside was enormous. It contained six great pillars that reached to the very top of the ceiling, five around the edges of the room with the largest in the center. Each pillar was lined with delicate glass vials and encircled by a metal staircase. Each of those vials held but a few drops of blood, taken from every mage as they were inducted into the Circle, and imbued with magic that made the blood glow. They made it seem as if the pillars were covered in glittering, dark jewels, and collectively the vials suffused the entire chamber in a ghastly crimson pallor. The color of forbidden things.

Evangeline had always disliked this room. The vials emitted a vibration you felt more than heard. The sensation built and built the longer you remained, until it almost drove you mad. In her mind, the phylacteries were too similar to blood magic—but since the templars found it useful, it was permitted. A bit of hypocrisy in the name of the greater good.

First Enchanter Edmonde stood next to her, staring up at the pillars with obvious distaste. He rubbed his forehead with a withered hand, and then noticed her watching. "Rhys is a good lad," he said, as if replying to a question.

"Would you have said the same of Jeannot?"

"No, although I doubt you'd believe me now."

"You're right." She walked to the large central pillar, touching the metal stairs that twisted around it to make sure they were solid. It seemed impossible they would hold the weight of a person all the way to the very top, but they had never once so much as wobbled beneath her. Still, for her own peace of mind she tested it every time.

Evangeline climbed carefully. She noticed a number of the vials had stopped glowing. Usually that meant the mage it belonged to was dead. She would have to remember to suggest the Tranquil clear out the defunct vials, an undertaking that was long overdue. Although who would she tell? The Lord Seeker? She had her doubts the man was interested in simple matters like the tower's day-to-day administration.

Enchanter Rhys's vial was about halfway up. She checked the runic marking over it against the record to make sure. It occurred to her to wonder if the Tranquil record-keepers were ever wrong. They were inhumanly methodical, and their passive nature made them reliable—but did the templars trust them too much? All of them had once been mages, and while they harbored no emotions, she wondered if it was possible for a Tranquil ever to turn against them.

The Chantry had always claimed it could never happen. But once upon a time the Chantry had considered the idea of a mage rebellion unthinkable as well.

"So are we mages now confined to our chambers?" the First Enchanter called up to her. "Traditionally we have always been given the run of the tower. You cannot squeeze people into a smaller and smaller box and hope they will disappear."

"Or there will be a rebellion? As in Kirkwall?" She allowed more annoyance into her voice than she intended. As she descended the stairs, blood vial in hand, she tried to keep her temper under control. "Conditions were harsh there, I'll grant you that. Considering all that's happened, I'd hope even you might agree it's not the same thing."

He shrugged. "An attack on the Divine was foolish, without a doubt. All I ask is that we not all pay for one man's crime."

Evangeline reached the bottom of the stairs and turned to him. "Perhaps Enchanter Rhys is not involved after all. What if he is being stabbed right now, to cover up someone else's guilt? The templars are here to protect mages, whether you like it or not."

"Even if it kills us?" The man absently waved away her immediate retort. "I apologize for that. It is late. You have what you need?"

"I do."

"Then let us be off."

They walked out of the chamber, and Evangeline allowed the First Enchanter to go on his way. He ambled down the main stairwell without further comment while the guard meekly shut the vault behind her. He was clearly torn between wanting to pretend nothing had happened and sucking up to a superior officer. She planned on letting him sweat.

She held up the phylactery vial and studied it. *Now let's see where you got off to,* she thought. Concentrating, she channeled a bit of power into it. The crimson glow of the blood pulsated and then slowly intensified.

Still in the tower, then. That was a start.

Evangeline walked down the stairs, keeping an eye on the vial. The lower she went, the brighter the glow became. It wouldn't tell her in which direction Enchanter Rhys lie, but it would tell her if she got close—and as she descended past the levels where the mages kept their chambers, she realized he was lower still. Definitely a secret passage, then, unless the sentry had wandered farther from his post than he claimed.

She continued to move through the dark halls of the tower, the phylactery's eerie glow lighting her way. The inner courtyard was empty, devoid of the templars who spent their time training. The chapel was silent, with only the Eternal Flame in the holy brazier to indicate it was ever used at all. She was utterly alone, with only her echoing footsteps to keep her company.

Eventually the vial led her down to the Pit. Not unexpected, really. If the man was as close as the glow indicated, and wasn't on the mage levels, then this is where he'd be.

The first thing she did was head to the dungeons. Not because she expected to find Rhys there—unsurprisingly, the phylactery agreed with her assumption—but because she wasn't about to start wandering around in the dark looking for a potentially dangerous mage without telling someone. Her encounter at the ball had reminded her that even one mage could make a formidable opponent.

The dungeons were a morbid place. A relic from a time when this tower did not belong to the Chantry at all, but instead served as the ruling fortress of Emperor Kordillus Drakon. It was he who had founded the Chantry, during a time of great upheaval when cultists were everywhere and magic ravaged the lands. Once, she supposed, these dungeons had been full, and the ancient torture chambers had seen regular use. She shuddered at the thought that those devices might ever be dusted off once again.

It could come to that, if the mages pushed it. Evangeline wasn't foolish enough to imagine otherwise, and hopefully neither were they.

The two templars at the dungeon's guard station were playing cards, and she shook her head as they started to rise. "Up late, Knight-Captain?" one of them asked.

"I'm looking for a missing mage." She indicated the vial.

"We haven't seen anything."

"No, I don't suppose the dungeons would be his first destination," she chuckled wryly. "But I wanted to let you know before I headed farther into the Pit. Just in case."

The men exchanged significant glances. "Expecting trouble? Want one of us to come along?"

"No. Check the cells. Make sure everyone is still in one piece." Evangeline turned to go, but then paused as she noticed the other templar looking anxious. "Something on your mind, ser?" she asked.

The man guiltily ducked the glare from his companion. "Err . . . there's been noises. From below, I mean."

"What sorts of noises?"

"Just the usual," the other insisted.

Now she was interested. She crossed her arms and arched a questioning brow at them both. "What constitutes 'the usual,' exactly? It's been some time since I pulled guard duty in the dungeons. It could, however, be the first of many for some."

"Now, listen here." The templar put his hands up defensively. "There's all sorts of noises in an old place like this. You hear them down below. Things break apart, or something gets in from the sewers. If you go chasing after every single thing you hear, you'll spend all night running around in the dark."

"Could be the Ghost of the Spire," the other suggested, a bit sheepishly.

Evangeline rolled her eyes. She'd heard that rumor, the sort of nonsense spouted by mages. She wouldn't expect that from a templar. The possibility that such a "ghost" could be a demon, particularly if there were blood mages in the tower, made it somewhat less of a joke. In fact, it might be something she had to take quite seriously.

She left the dungeons, moving urgently now.

She was still finding her way to the lower passages, unfamiliar with the area, when she heard the first strange sound. A distant blast, like thunder . . . or an explosion. She ran faster, racing down a flight of stairs, drawing her blade at the same time. Then she heard something different: a sharp, electric crack. Spells were being cast.

What in the Maker's name was going on down there? A battle?

Evangeline raced through the corridors, holding the phylactery in front of her to judge its brightness. Twice she had to double back when she encountered a dead end, and then a third time when she realized the passage wasn't going in the direction she needed it to. She swore under her breath, half directed at herself for not waking the entire tower when this business began and the other half at whichever idiots thought the bowels of a tower were an excellent place to build a labyrinth. The order should have sealed off these parts of the Pit centuries ago.

Then she entered the templar crypts and saw him. Enchanter Rhys stood next to one of the larger sarcophagi, the statue over it having tumbled to the ground and shattered in a hundred pieces. Dust hung in the air, along with the acrid stench of smoke. The mage himself was filthy, smeared with dirt and grime, and was that blood on his face? His staff crackled with brilliant energy, ready for the attack.

"Stand down, mage!" she cried, brandishing her sword. "This is your one and only warning!"

Rhys jumped at her voice and spun around. She half expected a fight, but as soon as he recognized her the brilliant light around his staff faded. He offered a wry grin. "Why, hello, Ser Evangeline. What brings you to this part of the Pit?"

"The noise. And a missing mage."

He nodded, more seriously this time. "I suppose that was inevitable."

Somehow he managed to be handsome even under the grime. It was the eyes, she thought. They were a warm brown, kind like her father's. With any other eyes, a man with such chiseled features and dark beard might look cold, or even sinister. It made him difficult to judge. Certainly, the way he had stood up to the Lord Seeker said something of his courage . . . or his foolhardiness.

She advanced on him. "Mind telling me what you're doing?"

For a moment she thought he might actually tell her. It was clear he was considering it, frowning thoughtfully. But then he shook his head. "You wouldn't believe me."

"Wouldn't I?" She got as close as she dared, her extended sword just short of touching him. He glanced down at it, but his posture remained relaxed. It wouldn't be a battle, then. That was good. "What am I expected to think? The Lord Seeker questioned you and then you sneak down here to . . . what? Demolish the crypt? Work out some anger?"

"Not exactly, no."

"You were fighting someone. Who?"

Evangeline was watching him carefully, and caught him glancing toward a dark corner on the far side of the crypt. She followed his gaze but saw nothing there except stone slabs, scorch marks, and smoke. He'd definitely been casting spells at . . . something.

"Do you see anyone for me to fight?" he asked, his tone evasive.

She paused. It was possible that whoever he'd been fighting had run off. She'd come through the only entrance, but for all she knew there were a dozen secret passages leading out of here. Still . . . something didn't seem right. "No. I don't." She lowered her blade slightly. "But that's hardly an answer."

The mage said nothing, and absently wiped his cheek. There was definitely a gash there amid the dirt, and when he pulled his hand away he seemed startled to see the blood. "Well," he said lightly, as if this were a casual conversation they might be having in the tower halls. "What are you going to do now?"

"You leave me no choice. It's a cell for you, until I figure this out."

"A cell? I don't know that—"

Evangeline didn't give him time to finish. She lunged forward, twisting her sword around so she could strike him in the back of the head with the pommel. He was taken completely by surprise, and went down like a sack of potatoes. His staff winked out, leaving only the crimson light of her vial.

She stood over him, keeping her sword ready as she scanned the rest of the crypt. There had to be something here, but she saw only the smoke rising from the fallen statue and a cloud of dust wafting through the air. Everything else was still, literally as silent as the grave.

Maker's breath, man! What were you doing?

Was that movement she caught out of the corner of her eye? Tightening her grip on the sword, she crept over to the corner of the crypt. She looked carefully at the spaces between each sarcophagus, searched the shadows for someone hiding.

Nothing.

She shuddered. There were too many statues in here, of men dead so long their names had faded even from their epitaphs. And there was too much talk of ghosts. It left her stomach in knots, and she hated that. Fear was not something she could fight.

Evangeline walked back to the unconscious Enchanter Rhys. Sheathing her sword, she heaved him with difficulty over her shoulder and walked out. As she left, the hairs on the back of her neck stood on end.

She couldn't escape the feeling she was being watched.

5

Rhys awoke in the dark, with no idea where he was.

First there was agony, a throbbing pain that threatened to split his head apart. Then panic followed, until he remembered Ser Evangeline's threat. His hands were manacled. His nostrils filled with the sour stench of sweat. He was in the tower's dungeon, without even a blanket to keep him warm.

He lay there for what must have been hours, shivering and almost sick from nausea. Fitful sleep came and went. When Ser Evangeline finally appeared, he was almost delirious. It could have been weeks he was down there, for all he knew, and he was startled when she tersely informed him it had been little more than a day.

Questions followed. What had Rhys been doing in the lower levels? How did he get there? Who were his accomplices? All of them elaborations on what she'd asked in the crypt, only now was his last chance to answer. He remained silent; the time to answer those questions had passed. Even if he thought the templars had any chance of believing the truth, which he didn't, such a strange story would now only seem like a deception to save his skin.

And it was obvious what she was looking for: a confession that he'd gone to the crypt to meet with Libertarian conspirators. He almost asked her what conspirators those might be—were there any other mages missing from their rooms that night? Perhaps she thought he was in league with templars. There was a chilling thought. If only there were a lie he could spin that she might accept.

In the end, she shook her head in disgust and walked out. He almost begged her for water first—but what was the point? Dying of thirst would probably be a mercy compared to what they had in store for him.

So there was nothing left to do but wait for the inevitable. Time passed slowly in the dark. The ache in his head eventually faded, replaced by a new one in his stomach. He chafed at the manacles and struggled to find a comfortable position on the stone floor. Sometimes he slept but didn't dream. Other times he just lie there, alone with his bitter thoughts.

Would Cole come for him? There he was, someone who could see him, now bound and helpless. The templars would assume his death the act of mages trying to keep from being named. Would Cole even know the manacles prevented Rhys from casting proper spells? He might be able to summon a spirit, perhaps he might even be able to open the door. But what then? The only way out was past a guarded hall filled with ancient traps that could skewer him instantly.

Each time Rhys opened his eyes he expected to see Cole crouched across the cell, staring with his sad and haunted eyes. There were moments Rhys was sure he would react in terror. Others he felt nothing but rage, and longed to yell at the young man for getting him into this mess. *I wish I'd never seen you,* he wanted to say. Then, in the darkest moments when he lie there starving and thirsty, he wondered if he wouldn't be glad. A friendly face, come to save him from a fate worse than death.

After those moments he wept, and tried to banish such thoughts from his head.

The smart thing to do would have been to walk away when Cole refused to go with him to the templars. Just go back up the stairs and hope for the best. But what if Cole killed again? The templars would see their fears confirmed, and everyone in the tower would suffer.

In fact, that could still happen. It was only a matter of time. Whatever they did to him, eventually Adrian would be next . . . and any other mage in the tower to whom their suspicion turned. Perhaps he *should* tell them the truth. If they were going to kill him anyhow, what did he have to lose?

But perhaps they wouldn't kill him. They might make him Tranquil. What would it be like to walk through life, never caring about anything? To be safe and content, knowing what had been done to you but never caring? Would he tell them about Cole? Confess everything he knew without concern for what they might do with that information?

How dare they. No evidence. No trial. Just suspicion and finding him in the wrong place at the wrong time, and that was enough to erase him from all existence? All because they feared what he might be capable of?

Defiance warmed his heart a little; in that cold cell, it was a sort of comfort. Let them come. Let Cole come. He would summon what magic he could and fight, consequences be damned.

By the time the door opened again, he felt ready. He lay in wait, a kernel of magic he had painstakingly gathered nestled deep in his heart and waiting to explode.

"Enchanter Rhys," the templar at the door stated. The man's voice sounded bored, and he tossed down a small pile of folded cloth. "Get dressed. I'm to take you to the bath."

Rhys wasn't certain what to make of that. "The . . . bath?"

"You're being released."

"How long has it been?"

"Since you got put in here? Four days. Now hurry up." The man spun on his heel and left, the door staying open. Rhys blinked several times, not quite believing it. Four days? It felt like a week, if not longer, though without food or water he probably would have died by then. He tried to hold on to his anger, but it drained away like sand through his fingers. For whatever reason, they were letting him out.

He exchanged his dirt-encrusted robe for the new one, and edged out into the hall. He heard men talking and even laughing down at the guard station, so he walked toward them. It was, without a doubt, the most surreal stroll of his life. There were three templars in the room, drinking cups of wine, and they looked over at him as if nothing were amiss.

"Water on the table," the guard who released him said. "Food, too."

Rhys looked to where the man nodded, and saw a pewter mug along with a bowl of stew. The smell of the meat lured him closer, and before he knew it he was digging into the meal with a vengeance. It was cold, practically congealed, but he didn't care. He shoved it into his mouth so fast he almost gagged, but it was still the best meal he could remember. The water poured down his throat like ambrosia.

And then he keeled over, his stomach protesting violently. Kneeling on the ground he clutched at his guts while the men laughed. Eventually the pain went away and the guard hauled him up by the shoulder. "Come on," the man chuckled, not without sympathy.

It wasn't long before Rhys found himself in a small room elsewhere in the tower, sunlight streaming in through a window. It hurt his eyes, and it was all he could do to blink at the pain and wonder what he was doing there. Through the door he could hear water being poured into a tub, and smelled the bath salts. A sense of foreboding came over him. He felt like a lamb being prepared for the slaughter.

Moments later, a young elven woman entered. She wore a simple grey robe, and he immediately noticed the pale sunburst mark on her forehead. A Tranquil, then. "If you are prepared," she said in a monotone voice, "the water is ready."

She held out a slender hand, but he didn't take it. "Does . . . it hurt?" he asked.

"The water will not harm you."

"No, the . . ." Rhys gestured at the mark. It seemed like it might be a personal question to ask, but then he reminded himself that a Tranquil couldn't take offense. Still, that seemed like a poor excuse. Considering he had been around the Tranquil his entire life in the tower, as they performed every menial and administrative function, he should be more comfortable in their presence. He never was, nor were most mages he knew. Most often they tried to pretend the Tranquil were a part of the background, and hadn't once been just like themselves.

The elven woman blinked, and tilted her head in what might have been confusion. He couldn't really tell. "The Rite of Tranquility," she stated. "I am not permitted to speak of it. You know this."

"If I'm going to be made like you, I want to know."

"I am not preparing you for the Rite. You are to be brought to a gathering of mages in the great hall." She turned and glided into the other room, and he numbly followed after her. "The Lord Seeker requested that you be cleaned, so that is what I am here to assist you with."

Sure enough, the other room contained several brass tubs, one of which was now filled with steaming water. He'd never seen the place before, so he imagined it must be in the templar quarters. How bizarre. He turned to the elf, stunned. "I'm free? Just like that?" he asked.

"I have no knowledge to offer regarding this."

He only hesitated a moment before removing his robe and stepping into the water. Modesty was another thing the Tranquil would have no use for. She watched him with blank eyes and handed him a towel once he was immersed. He mumbled thanks, trying not to stare at her forehead, and she walked toward the door.

She stopped and turned to look at him. "If I felt pain," she said softly, "it is meaningless to me now. Once I knew only fear, but now I know only service. Whatever pain there was, I believe it an acceptable trade."

The Tranquil left. Though Rhys sat in near-scalding water, he felt a chill race through his heart.

An hour later he was in the great hall. The massive chamber stood in a structure not within the White Spire but instead attached to its lowest floor. It served as the tower's main entrance; through here kings and queens had been brought before the man who later became the first Emperor of Orlais. The throne had long since been removed, of course, but the palatial arches and stained glass windows served as a reminder of that glorious past. Now it was a testament to the power of the templar order, and on the rare occasion when the mages were allowed to gather here they could not avoid being reminded of it by their surroundings.

The hall itself was incredibly long, the floor made of glistening marble in a black and grey checkered pattern. On either side stood rows of chairs, but all were currently empty. Instead, everyone milled about in the middle of the room, clumping in groups and talking excitedly. As near as Rhys could tell there were more than several hundred mages here, even the youngest apprentices. The entire complement of the tower's Circle of Magi.

He stood at the entrance, staring in amazement. They weren't due for another assembly for at least a month, and with the attack on the Divine he would have assumed the templars would forbid even that.

Then he saw a familiar shock of red curls as Adrian made a

beeline toward him from the crowd. "They let you out of the dungeon?" she asked as she drew near. "That's a bit of a surprise."

He grinned at her. "My sparkling personality won them over."

"Oh, I'll just bet."

Rhys gestured at the other mages, some of whom were surreptitiously glancing his way. "So, this is interesting. Mind telling me why the entire Circle's here?"

"I thought *you* might know. It's a mystery."

"Oh, I like mysteries! An announcement, maybe?"

"That was my thought. The Lord Seeker wishes to address us, perhaps?" She smirked. "Or gather us all into one spot. Less work for the templars to slaughter us that way."

"You have to admire their sense of efficiency."

Adrian chuckled mirthlessly, then took his arm in hers and led him into the hall. Their footsteps echoed loudly on the marble, drawing curious looks from those present. She seemed oblivious to it, but Rhys was a little uncomfortable. Did the others think he was responsible for what was happening? How much had they been told? Evidently reading his thoughts, Adrian leaned in close as they walked. "You've been the talk of the tower. The First Enchanter said you'd gone missing, but that was it. The templars refused to tell us anything."

"Then how did you know I was in the dungeon?"

"We raised a ruckus, of course, and I led the charge. There was a whole group of us staring down the templars. They had their swords out and everything. You missed the excitement."

"All that for me? How touching."

"I wasn't going to let you vanish, only to turn up Tranquil in a few weeks. Not without proof you'd even done anything." Adrian scowled, a look she normally reserved for whenever she paid someone a grudging compliment. "First Enchanter Edmonde backed us up. He was there with all the senior enchanters, demanding to speak to the Lord Seeker."

Rhys merely nodded, a bit speechless. He could joke all he wanted, but the idea that the other mages would defend him even at the risk of their own safety was daunting. Would he have done the same in their shoes? He liked to think so. "So what happened?" he finally asked.

"Ser Evangeline showed up." Adrian rolled her eyes at the name. She could never keep her feelings about anyone secret, templars least of all. "She ordered her men to stand down, and told us you'd snuck out of your room in the middle of the night. Went down to the Pit, maybe even got into some kind of battle." She paused as they reached the center of the hall, looking at Rhys with guarded curiosity. "It's . . . not true, is it?"

Ah, so here it was. He noticed there were a few others nearby who halted in the middle of their conversations, pretending not to listen even though they clearly were. Adrian was dying to know the truth. They all were. "It's true," he admitted.

"Which part?"

"I went down to the Pit," he said carefully. "I needed to find someone. I got caught, and that was the end of it."

"You needed to find *someone*."

"Yes."

Her eyes flashed with annoyance. "Fine, then. Don't tell me." Adrian pulled him forward again, sternly silent. Rhys couldn't blame her for being angry. If anyone would believe him about Cole, she would, but what then? She would be determined to do something—even if she had no idea what that might be. As much as he longed to be able to talk about it, getting Adrian mixed up in his mess would just make things worse for her and everyone else.

He looked around, hoping to spot the First Enchanter in the crowd. He felt as if he should go and thank the man, or at least apologize for putting him to so much trouble. The idea behind finding Cole, after all, was to spare the Circle from suffering—not to instigate more of it. But he couldn't see the man anywhere.

Finally Adrian got to her destination: a small group of senior enchanters, all of whom Rhys recognized. Members of the tower's Libertarian fraternity—except for Jeannot, of course. One of them, an elven man with long black hair and the strange alien eyes typical of his kind, nodded grimly as they approached. Garys had been the unofficial leader of the fraternity before Adrian effectively supplanted him—not through any scheming, of course, but by virtue of the fact she couldn't *not* be the leader and still have things done her way.

Consequently, Garys cared little for either of them. Rhys felt the same in return; Garys was one of the reasons he'd never much associated with the White Spire's Libertarians except through Adrian. "Good to have you back," the elf said. It didn't sound sincere.

"Oh, I was going to stay in the cells a little longer, but who could miss this? An assembly, already? Exciting!" He chuckled inwardly as the elf's jaw clenched in irritation.

Adrian folded her arms, frowning severely. "It seems Ser Evangeline was telling the truth. He snuck out of his chambers that night, just like she said."

Garys raised his eyebrows in surprise. "More the fools us for defending you, then. What would possess you to do such a thing? And why would they let you out at all afterward?" His eyes narrowed suspiciously. "Just what did you tell them?"

"He didn't tell them *anything*," Adrian insisted. Then she glanced at Rhys, suddenly uncertain. "You didn't tell them anything, did you?"

"I don't know anything."

"That wouldn't stop you from making something up," Garys growled.

Rhys shrugged. "I didn't give the templars a reason to blame the Libertarians, if that's what you're asking."

The elf appeared unconvinced, but Adrian waved the idea away.

"It doesn't matter. We're together now, and we need to talk about what our next step is. If we sit back and do nothing, they'll end up pinning the attack on the Divine on us. You know they will."

"That depends," Garys said. He turned to Rhys. "The Libertarians stood behind you, and perhaps that's what got you released. What I want to know is whether you'll return the favor? You've never truly been part of the fraternity, I know that. . . . But will you stand with us now?"

There was a tone to the elf's voice that gave Rhys pause. He glanced around and noticed only other Libertarians close by. The fraternity was planning something, perhaps something serious. They wanted his help, or they wanted to test him. Either way it made for a dangerous conversation, particularly in the middle of the great hall.

It also made Rhys wonder. *Had* they been involved in the attempt on the Divine, and not told him? Was Adrian part of it? It seemed unlikely, as she was terrible at keeping secrets, and yet . . .

Adrian looked at him expectantly, as did the others. "Well?" she asked.

Thankfully, fate intervened before he could say anything. The din of conversation in the hall suddenly increased. The mages moved to the seats on either side of the chamber, their steps a clatter of loud echoes that made it difficult to talk. Rhys saw one of the Tranquil circulating among the groups, quietly urging everyone to clear the floor.

"It seems our time is up," Garys muttered.

"We can speak later," Adrian said. "Provided this isn't the Lord Seeker's way of telling us what new privileges we're having revoked, and we're all to be locked in our rooms." She strode quickly toward a pair of open chairs—in the front row, of course—and waved for Rhys to follow. He did so, leaving Garys to scowl with the other Libertarians.

It wasn't long before a sudden hush descended. First Enchanter

Edmonde had appeared. He wore ceremonial robes: thick black brocade with a golden border, as well as a mantle of white fur that looked heavy enough to bear him to the ground. The man favored his staff, each tap ringing loudly on the marble. As everyone quieted, the tapping became the only sound in the chamber. By the time the First Enchanter reached the center of the hall, he had everyone's rapt attention.

He looked about, and initially didn't say anything. The weariness in his posture was just as pronounced as in the Knight-Commander's office. "I am pleased," he began, his voice barely audible, "that you have all attended this assembly, and that you are well. These are dangerous times, my friends, and I would not wish to see us adding to the strife. Our gifts can do so much good, if we only allow it . . ."

He trailed off into silence, closing his eyes. Nobody dared to speak, and the only sounds in the entire hall were a few uncomfortable coughs. When the man opened his eyes again, he raised a hand and nodded. "I know, I know. I am old, and here I find myself your leader with so very little to say. Would that I could do better." He turned toward the doors. "There is, however, someone who may have the words I do not."

All eyes turned to the doors. An elderly woman walked in, but whereas the First Enchanter had been worn down by his years, she carried hers with pride. She wore a robe of blue silk and a regal white cloak that swept along the floor behind her. Her grey hair was tied up into a matronly bun, but it was easy to see she had once been a beautiful woman. Now she might be called handsome, her face carrying the careworn maturity of one accustomed to power.

This woman needed no introduction, for every mage in the hall knew of her: Wynne, archmage and hero of the Blight in Ferelden nine years before. Despite this, she received no hero's welcome here. There was a smattering of polite applause, but most of the crowd was shocked into silence. It was she, after all, who had led the College of Enchanters to vote against independence from the Chantry prior to its closure. There were many here who believed that made her a traitor.

Rhys groaned inwardly. Of all the people he might have expected to see walk through that door, she was the very last. He would rather it have been the Lord Seeker. Anyone but her.

"Can you believe it?" Adrian hissed in his ear.

"Not really, no."

Wynne ignored the tension in the hall, instead nodding politely to the First Enchanter as he withdrew. Her cool gaze swept across the audience, perhaps sizing it up or silently daring those who resented her presence to speak up. None did. Rhys thought her eyes lingered on him, and he did his best to avoid meeting them. Then she raised her white staff high over her head. With a blinding flash, an arc of lightning raced out of it toward the vaulted ceiling. It was followed by a thunderclap that reverberated throughout the chamber, rattling the stained glass windows.

The audience gasped, and many threw their hands over their heads in anticipation of the roof caving down upon them. Nothing happened. Wynne lowered her staff, regarding those seated with a stern expression. "That is our power," she intoned. "We may unleash great destructive force, or we may control it. It is a choice we must make wisely, for this power can bring great suffering to others."

She paused, raising her free hand. Her fingers moved in an elaborate pattern as she cast a spell, and slowly a spirit began to manifest. It had a vaguely humanoid shape, as if knitted together from gossamer strands of light. The spirit hovered in the air beside her, bewildered, and Wynne held her hand out toward it. Her fingers passed through its form, leaving ripples in their wake. Her expression was tender, almost motherly.

"And then there are times when that choice is taken away from us." She waved her hand and the spirit blinked out of existence. "There are spirits far less benign than that one, and should they force their way into your mind, you will become a creature of chaos." She took a few steps toward the apprentices' side of the hall, looking straight at a boy who couldn't have been more than twelve. The lad shied away uneasily. "Even the most innocent among us could become a terror, and there is no way to know who will fall."

Sadness crossed her face, and she turned away. Facing the rest of the audience again, her tone softened. "If I tell you things you already know, it is because we forget how very remarkable we are. We forget the reasons others have to fear us, and that they are good ones. We see only the harsh restrictions placed upon us, and they seem very unfair indeed."

Rhys heard the susurrus of angry whispers around him. Beside him, Adrian was livid. He could all but feel the grinding of her teeth as she kept herself from exploding. He felt his own temper stirring as well, try as he might to suppress it.

"What is our alternative?" Wynne continued. She waited for an answer, but none was forthcoming. "Shall we ask to watch over ourselves, without the Chantry's help? Ask the people of Thedas to trust that we would not repeat the mistakes of the Tevinter magisters, mistakes that have brought the world to the very end of destruction on more than one occasion?"

She held her white staff in front of her now, and a fiery aura blazed into life around it. "Or shall we fight?" The aura intensified until it shone so brilliantly Rhys was forced to look away. Others did the same. "We stand up against our oppressors and show them their error in underestimating us!" The light suddenly died, and at that the hall became deathly quiet. "To what end?" she whispered. "Even if we could kill them all, it would change nothing.

"I counsel patience, now just as I did a year ago at the College of Enchanters. Yes, things must change . . . but if we do not show ourselves willing to bend, how can we expect those who fear us to do so?"

"Patience!" a new voice cried out, the echoes ringing throughout the hall. Rhys was startled to discover it was his own. He was standing, fists clenched at his sides, and now a hundred robes rustled as all eyes turned toward him. So, too, did Wynne regard him with a curious lift to her brow.

"Have you something to add, Enchanter?" she asked.

He was sick of the theatrics. This woman lecturing them like they should be grateful for their treatment . . . it filled him with rage. Even so, he hadn't planned on speaking. This was the second time he'd let his temper get the better of him: once with the Lord Seeker and now this. If he were smart, he'd mumble an excuse and sit back down.

Still. That would mean giving in.

"I do," he finally said. Adrian stared at him in shock, but also amusement. It was she, after all, who had a reputation as a troublemaker. Gritting his teeth, he pushed on. "Who are you to counsel patience? You have more freedoms than any of us. You're not locked into a tower, herded into your chambers at night like a child. Nobody's threatening you with the Rite of Tranquility for stepping out of line. It's easy to be *patient* when you haven't been through what we have this last year!"

There was a smattering of applause, most prominently from Adrian and the other Libertarians, but he heard opposition as well. Several voices rose in complaint, while others argued; the general level of noise began to escalate. Wynne raised a hand, and slowly the talk quieted.

"I do have freedoms," she admitted. "They were earned through years of service, and as a reward for my part in defeating the darkspawn. I worked to gain the trust of the Chantry; I did not expect it to fall into my lap."

"And what have we done to be denied that trust, those who

have spent our entire lives doing everything asked of us? Why are we all held accountable for the mistakes of a few?"

The applause was louder this time. The First Enchanter appeared, approaching Wynne with a look of concern, but she shook her head. "What would you have them do?" she asked Rhys, speaking over the general babble. "Argue over procedure while the tower falls around them? We are all in the same boat, young man, and it behooves everyone to paddle, lest the current carry us away."

Rhys was going to respond, but a warning look from the First Enchanter made him change his mind. It didn't matter anyhow. Mages on both sides of the hall had leapt from their chairs, booing or shouting angrily. Others were determinedly clapping in support of Wynne, or arguing with her detractors. The entire chamber was erupting in a cacophony of noise.

Wynne regarded the reaction with an air of resignation. First Enchanter Edmonde whispered something into her ear. Whatever he asked of her, she reluctantly agreed and turned to leave. Everyone was so caught up in their arguments they barely noticed her departure.

Beside Rhys, Adrian stood up. She wasn't taking part in the arguments, and instead marveled at it all with a bemused expression. "Not bad," she commented. "I couldn't have done better myself."

"Yes, well, apparently my mouth has a mind of its own."

"I like your mouth. It should do more of your talking for you."

Rhys watched in disgust as two mages started shoving each other nearby. One was a Libertarian, while the other was part of the Loyalist fraternity—"Chantry apologists," as some liked to call them, for they advocated obedience to the Chantry and bitterly opposed all attempts at independence. He winced when the men started knocking over chairs, drawing others into the fray.

"Well, don't look now, but the fun's about to end." Adrian indicated the main doors, and he looked just in time to see templars storm in. There were at least a dozen, swords in hand, already shouting at the top of their lungs for everyone to return to their quarters.

The younger apprentices, most of whom had watched the goings-on with wide eyes, immediately scrambled to obey. The others were slower to react, so the templars began wading into the stands to force their point. They grabbed whoever was nearest, roughly hauling them down to the floor area. This prompted general chaos; the mages began abandoning the seating area all at once, some fleeing while others angrily accosted the templars in defense of their fellows.

The tension seemed at the point of turning into something ugly. Rhys held his breath, half expecting someone to cast a spell—a single spark of flame, even a staff pointed in the wrong direction, and that would be the end of it. The templars would be forced to act, and there would be bloodshed.

But it didn't happen. With excruciating slowness, order was restored. Rhys remained where he was with a handful of the senior enchanters, all of them watching the proceedings with dismay. Adrian shook her head. "Shall we go, before the templars drag us out as well?"

He nodded. More of them were arriving, and the mages were allowing themselves to be herded out. The shouting had given way to a sullen hush, marked only by the clatter of footsteps on the marble. As Rhys and Adrian made their way through the thick crowd at the doors, they were intercepted by an aged Tranquil in grey robes.

"Enchanter Rhys?" the man asked.

"That's me."

"The Lord Seeker has asked for your attendance in his office. I'm to take you there immediately."

Rhys exchanged a wary glance with Adrian. That was quick. Considering that he hadn't expected to be let out of the cell, being thrown back in—or worse—wasn't exactly a shocking prospect.

"I'm going with you," Adrian vowed. He could tell from her tone there wouldn't be any arguing with her.

"Your funeral."

The long walk back to the Knight-Commander's office, now the Lord Seeker's office, felt more like a death march. As they ascended into the upper levels things became quiet, like a shroud had descended over the entire tower. The tension was palpable. None of the templars they passed said a word, and the Tranquil was content to silently lead the way.

Rhys leaned in close to whisper to Adrian as they walked. "If they decide to punish me, I want you to promise you won't try to stop them."

"Are you mad? Of course I will."

"And give them an excuse to punish you, too? You can't help me, Adrian, and you can't help the rest of the mages from inside the dungeons."

She frowned but said nothing, and avoided his persistent looks afterward.

It wasn't long before they were in the office foyer once again. Twice in a single week—that had to be a record. The large window was wide open this time, letting in a breeze laced with sour smells from the city below. It also admitted the late autumn chill, making Rhys shiver.

Two templars stood at attention outside the office door, so stiff in their alertness one could almost smell the fear coming off them. Fear of the Lord Seeker, Rhys assumed. They barely acknowledged the Tranquil, who bowed and glided back out without a word.

"You're expected, Enchanter—alone," one of them said, and frowned at Adrian. His breath was visible in a fine mist.

"I'm not going anywhere," she growled.

The man hesitated, and then shrugged. Evidently he would

rather the mages suffer the Lord Seeker's displeasure than risk it
for himself, so he opened the door and stood aside.

They entered. As before, Lord Seeker Lambert sat behind the
desk with Ser Evangeline standing at his side. In the chair across
from him, however, sat Wynne. The old woman stood immediately. Her gaze was cool and appraising.

"Hello, Rhys," she said quietly.

Of course she would be here. He shouldn't be surprised.

"Hello, Mother," he said.

If Adrian's eyebrows could have shot up any higher, they would
probably have climbed into her hairline.

The Lord Seeker cleared his throat, leveling a disapproving
glare at Rhys. "I'm informed you caused quite the disturbance in
the hall."

"Isn't that why I'm here?"

"It's not. Enchanter Wynne requested your presence after the
assembly was finished. Why did you think you were allowed out
of your cell?" Rhys was taken aback by that. Now it all made sense.
The man looked at Adrian and frowned. "She did not, however,
request the attendance of anyone else."

"I invited myself," she said defiantly.

"It is no bother," Wynne interrupted before the Lord Seeker
could retort.

He eased back in his chair, clenching his jaw in silent fury.
"Do what you came to do," he said through gritted teeth.

Wynne nodded, satisfied, and turned to Rhys once again. "I'm
afraid there's nowhere for either of you to sit," she began, searching about the room as if expecting chairs to suddenly materialize.

"I can stand," he said. "What's this about?"

"I need your help."

"My help?" Rhys glanced at the Lord Seeker, and then Ser
Evangeline, but their stony expressions offered no enlightenment.
"What could you need my help for? And why would I offer it?"

"Would you rather go back to the dungeons?" the Lord Seeker interjected.

Rhys didn't answer. Inwardly he rankled at the threat.

Wynne merely nodded, as if his reply was nothing more than she expected. "An old friend of mine has been turned into an abomination," she began. "I intend a rescue, and that means going into the Fade to wrest control from the demon that has possessed him. It's a difficult task, and not one I can do alone. I'll need you to come with me to help perform the ritual."

The Lord Seeker let out an angry growl and slammed his fist down on the desk. "You said *nothing* about taking Enchanter Rhys from the tower!"

"Nor did I need to, until now."

"Have you forgotten about the attack upon the Divine? This man is involved, and I cannot allow him to leave. I will not."

"I thought you might say that." She reached into a pocket in her white cloak and produced a vellum scroll, the wax seal bearing the symbol of the Chantry. The Lord Seeker snatched it away with a scowl. Breaking the seal, he unrolled the scroll and read. "As you can see for yourself, the Divine has given me full authority to perform my mission as I see fit." She smiled slightly. "And I see fit to take Enchanter Rhys with me. He is a spirit medium, after all, and thus his abilities will prove useful."

The Lord Seeker ignored her and continued to scan the document. Carefully. Finally his scowl deepened. "Where did you get this?"

"From the Divine, obviously. An old friend introduced us."

He rolled the scroll back up and tossed it onto the desk as if it were refuse. "You seem to have a great many old friends," he sneered. "And I'm supposed to let you endanger one mage just to save another? What is so special about this man?"

Wynne considered. "He is Tranquil," she admitted.

Rhys almost spat in surprise. "What? That's impossible!"

The Lord Seeker also seemed surprised, and his eyes narrowed at Wynne suspiciously. "The Rite of Tranquility severs a mage's connection to the Fade forever. They cannot be possessed by demons; that is the entire *point*."

"Even so, it has happened." She looked at Rhys. "You have performed research into demons, according to your First Enchanter. My friend has done the same. If he contacted a demon with extraordinary powers, we need to know what it is and whether this can happen again. If, however, this is a failing of the Rite of Tranquility . . ."

"The Rite has never failed," the Lord Seeker insisted.

"If it has," Rhys said, "then we all need to know it."

Lord Seeker Lambert chewed over the idea, making a face as if tasting something unpleasant. Eventually he made up his mind. "Absolutely not," he said curtly. "I can't allow such an ill-considered venture."

Wynne smiled sweetly. "That's not for you to decide."

"I am responsible for the safety of all mages within the Circle."

"If you prefer to have the Divine order you personally, that can be arranged."

The Lord Seeker glared at her. It was the dangerous look of a man who wouldn't soon forget the insult being handed to him. Wynne refused to give in, and a silent battle of wills ensued as the others looked on in tense silence. Rhys wondered if it was about to come to violence.

Instead, the man gave in. "Ser Evangeline will accompany you," he said curtly, "and ensure that Enchanter Rhys is returned to the tower once your task is done."

The templar's eyes went wide, and her mouth opened as if she were about to protest, but then thought better of it. Wynne had no such hesitation. "I don't remember asking for an escort," she said.

"Nevertheless, you will receive one." He glanced at Evangeline, and she nodded acknowledgment of the order. "I'm certain the Divine would not object to my providing extra protection for this mission of yours, not to mention some assurances a dangerous mage won't mysteriously elude our grasp while he's absent."

"Now I'm dangerous?" Rhys snorted.

"Yes." Lambert fixed him with a dangerous glare. "You think us fools? Ser Evangeline finds you in the crypts, with no explanation for your presence or your behavior? You know far more than you admit to. That in itself is an indictment I will not ignore." The last was delivered in a tone so forceful it made Rhys retreat a step.

"Take him," the man barked at Wynne. "But if your intention is to spare your son from justice, you will not be successful. Even the Divine will not protect you if our investigation is interfered with."

"So I see." She replaced the scroll in her cloak. Then she sat back in her chair, raising a curious brow at Rhys. "Are you willing to help me now? I won't force you to come, if you do not wish it."

He considered. Refusing would no doubt mean a return to the dungeon, but he didn't trust Wynne's motives. At least here he knew what to expect. Then again, this friend of hers researched demons, just as Rhys himself once had. What if the man possessed knowledge that could help with Cole's curse? That could also prove Rhys's innocence in the murders. It was a long shot, but it might be the only chance he'd get.

"Very well," he agreed reluctantly, already regretting it. "But from what I know of this ritual, you'll need more than just the two of us. There need to be three mages . . . at a minimum."

"That's right," Adrian suddenly piped up. "You should take me."

She exchanged a significant look with Rhys. She wanted to come, that was clear. He didn't care for the idea of taking her into danger any more than going himself—but then again, he couldn't think of anyone else he'd rather face it with. Getting her away from the tower would also prevent her from becoming his replacement in the dungeon.

"Yes," he agreed. "Adrian should come with us."

Wynne allowed herself a pleased smile. "You should both go and prepare, then. We leave in the morning, and it's a long journey to the Western Approach." She looked at Ser Evangeline. "You too, my dear, although you'll have to provide your own horse. I only brought the one extra."

"That shouldn't be a problem."

Nobody moved. After an awkward minute of tense silence, Rhys unceremoniously turned and walked out. There wasn't really anything more to say. Adrian followed on his heels.

"You owe me an explanation," she hissed in his ear as soon as they were out the door.

"I'll bet."

They passed through the chilly foyer, both guards studiously ignoring them, and back into the corridor outside. If there was one good thing about all this, he thought, it was that he was finally getting out of this templar-infested tower. Even if the respite was nothing more than a delayed sentence, hovering over his head like an executioner's axe, it would still be a chance for fresh air. The problems of the Circle of Magi could be left behind, for a time.

As would Cole. That thought darkened his mood considerably. *What in the blazes are you doing now, Cole?*

6

Rhys was leaving.

Cole had never spent so much time on the upper floors of the tower. The presence of so many templars made his heart race. As each one passed, it was all he could do to keep himself from pressing against the nearest wall and holding his breath, despite the unlikelihood they might see him. He still expected them to. Rhys could see him, after all, and there had been others . . . why not a templar? One day a hand would grab his shoulder, and he would turn around and see one staring back at him, full of questions.

What would he do then? Kill the man? Cole had drawn his blade on Rhys. He hadn't meant to, but Rhys had meant his threat. Cole had betrayed his only friend in the world, and even if he'd only been trying to protect himself, that still left him feeling more alone than ever.

He found Rhys easily enough, but even though he was desperate to talk to the man, he lingered at a distance. What could he say, after all? Words had never been his strong point. Even if Rhys bothered to listen, Cole couldn't imagine an argument that might sway the man. So instead he was forced to watch from afar, vacillating between fear and indecision.

He saw Rhys carrying a pack, accompanied by the freckled mage with the cloud of red hair. Where they were going, Cole had no idea, but everyone he overheard said they were leaving the tower. Going somewhere secret.

There was someone else going with them, too. A tall templar woman with black hair, the same one who had found Rhys in the crypts. He remembered her well. She'd stood not five feet away, her eyes falling right on him even though she never knew, before she finally turned away. He'd breathed a sigh of relief when she left.

Cole had seen her before. He thought of her only as Knight-Captain, for that's what everyone else called her. They treated her with respect, which meant she was someone important.

So he followed Knight-Captain now, instead. Maybe she might say where Rhys was going, and if he was even coming back. That meant Cole would be spending more time in the templar levels of the tower than he ever had before. It left him feeling exposed, but what choice did he have?

Knight-Captain was busy. First she spent over an hour in the courtyard talking to one of her men, presumably about what he should be doing while she was gone. Cole barely listened, except to hear that she didn't know how long she'd be gone. A week, perhaps.

Then she met with another woman, this one a templar as well, to discuss what "happened" in the great hall. Cole didn't know what that was. He'd heard the commotion even from the lower levels, but curiosity alone hadn't been enough to draw him up there. At the time he'd known only that Rhys was let out of his cell.

Before they'd taken Rhys away, Cole had sat in front of that cell for hours. He stared at the door, knowing Rhys was inside. He kept wondering if he should open it, if it would be better to talk to the man when there was nowhere he could go. But Rhys would have assumed Cole was going to kill him, wouldn't he?

Cole couldn't have taken that, seeing the same look in his friend's eyes he'd seen in the others. He would rather die.

He followed Knight-Captain to various other places, and then finally to the upper floors, above where the mages lived. Cole shuddered as he walked up those stairs—this part of the tower he rarely came to at all. Everything had a stark, cold feel to it. Even the templars looked nervous when they came here.

He kept close to the woman, almost stepping on her heels when she stopped to open a door. Were these her bedchambers? Was this where important templars lived? Why would someone so important be going anywhere with Rhys? Was he in trouble? Was Cole the cause?

He longed to ask her. That's what normal people did, and he vaguely remembered a life before he came to the tower, when even he could ask someone a question and expect to receive an answer. Now he was left to wonder, awash in a sea of silence broken only by Rhys's infrequent visits. He always felt worse when Rhys left again; it made the silence that much harder to bear.

The templar walked into the room and Cole followed, slipping in just as she shut the door. It was indeed a bedchamber, if a small one. There wasn't much inside save for a cot and an armoire that took up almost half the space. A small window peeked out onto the city below, and on its ledge sat a number of tiny figurines carved out of stone. Curious, he walked over and picked one up. It was a mottled grey, looking a little like a sitting wolf with baleful red gems in its eyes. Strange.

He put it back on the ledge, and the small tap from the contact was enough to make Knight-Captain spin around. Cole froze, cursing his stupidity. If he drew attention to himself, she might notice—just because she would forget later didn't change the fact that she would see him *now*.

She had been undoing the leather straps on either side of her breastplate, and now paused midway. She looked around the room, brows knit in confusion. Cole felt a trickle of sweat rolling lazily down the side of his face. He wanted to run, but dared not. Then she would see him for sure. But if she took one step forward . . .

She didn't. Frowning, the templar returned to the task of removing her armor. Cole let out a slow breath. That was close.

He quietly watched her undress. He'd seen naked flesh before: the mages when they coupled in the dark corners, for instance. He'd seen people bathe in the big metal tubs they filled with hot water, and wondered why they went to all that trouble when there were perfectly good pools in the Pit below. He used to watch the mages as well, fascinated with their daily routines, and that included when they changed their clothes and prepared for sleep. Eventually it lost its appeal. It made him feel like a child pressing his face up against a window, peering into a warm and cozy room he could never enter.

Knight-Captain removed her armor in pieces. The bulky breastplate first, then the shoulder guards, then the braces on her forearms. As soon as she kicked off her metal boots she was down to her sweat-stained tunic. Why would the templars walk around in so much metal, day in and day out? Did they really expect they'd be called into battle at a moment's notice? Against people who didn't even wear armor? Yet another question he could never ask anyone.

She sighed in relief as she pulled the tunic over her head. There was a small nightstand by her bed, on top of which was a bowl of water. She punctured the thin layer of ice that floated on its surface, and wet a cloth to wipe herself down. Cole noticed numerous scars on her muscular body, and wondered how she came to get them.

The woman finished washing and opened the armoire, slipping on a new tunic. Cole noticed her eyes lingering on something else within. She slowly took out a book, a dusty tome with the sunburst symbol embossed on its leather cover. What it might be, Cole couldn't imagine. The leather looked so worn and cracked, it seemed like it might crumble at her touch.

Knight-Captain handled it carefully. She ran a finger along the cover, her face softening with a look that was both gentle and sad. The binding protested loudly, and she inhaled the smell of the book's yellowed parchment.

Cole didn't understand. What was so special about a book? The archives in the lower levels were full of so many, some far older than this one. They did little more than collect dust, and held no interest for him or anyone.

There was a firm knock on the door, and both of them jumped. Knight-Captain snapped the book shut, and quickly replaced it in the armoire. "Yes?" she called out. Her voice sounded a little odd—like there was a lump in her throat.

There was no response, but the door opened and a man entered.

Not just any man. This one wore dark armor with a strange insignia on his breastplate, and carried himself with a force of presence that left no doubt he was in command. There was an angular cruelty to his face that put Cole immediately on edge. But it was more than that. There was something about him that spoke to Cole like a dark whisper. This man had power, something completely different from the other templars.

Cole had never seen him before, and was immediately terrified.

"Lord Seeker Lambert," Knight-Captain spluttered. "I could have come to your office. There was no need for you to—"

The man held up a hand. His eyes did not look at her, but instead searched the room. They narrowed in suspicion, as if he had suddenly sensed something amiss.

Then Cole realized it. *He's looking for me.* He backed as far into the corner as he could, hiding behind the open armoire. Even that movement drew the Lord Seeker's attention. He stared in Cole's direction, not quite fixing on him . . . but the man knew *something* was there. He seemed like a grizzled mouser sensing its prey nearby, waiting for the moment to pounce and deliver the killing blow.

"There is something wrong," the Lord Seeker announced.

That seemed to alarm Knight-Captain. She sped across the room to where she'd lain her armor, grabbing up her sword from its sheath. She held it ready, and scanned the room for an enemy. Her gaze passed right over Cole.

The man barely noticed her. "What were you doing before I arrived?" he asked.

"Changing out of my armor."

"Nothing else?"

"Nothing important, my lord."

Cole held his breath. Just when he was certain the man was going to walk over to the corner and grab him by the neck, the man lowered his hand. Scowling in displeasure, he looked toward Knight-Captain. "This tower has set me on edge. I thought I felt . . . well, never mind that."

She lowered her blade, looking unconvinced. "Is there something you wished, Lord Seeker?"

"Yes." He closed the door behind him. Then he took something out of a belt pouch—it was a small bundle, wrapped in purple cloth. The woman took it, and when she opened the bundle it revealed a trio of tiny glass vials. Each held a small amount of liquid, glowing vividly blue. Cole felt the familiar tickle of magic.

Knight-Captain seemed to know what they were. She frowned, though, as if this was not a particularly welcomed gift, and quickly wrapped the vials back up. "Thank you, Lord Seeker," she said, "but you didn't have to bring me these personally."

"No." He stroked his chin, considering his words carefully as the silence grew tense. "What I have to say to you cannot leave this room."

"I see."

"I sent word to the Grand Cathedral. I don't know how Enchanter Wynne was able to procure such outlandish privileges from the Divine, but she told the truth."

Her brow furrowed. "And . . . that is a good thing, yes?"

"It means we proceed as before." The Lord Seeker clasped his hands behind his back and paced. Cole thought he looked troubled. "I have a suspicion, however, that the Divine is unaware of the full implications of this mage's mission."

"Implications?"

"It could be nothing. Enchanter Wynne's suspicions about this Tranquil could be incorrect, or the circumstances so bizarre they could never be repeated." He stopped pacing. "But if it's not, if he has been restored somehow and the Rite of Tranquility is proven to have any weakness . . ."

Knight-Captain paled. "Is such a thing possible?"

"I said no and I believe that." The Lord Seeker glanced out the window, shaking his head in disgust. "But I am also old enough to know that the impossible can and will occur when magic is involved. If this mage discovers *any* possibility that Tranquility can be reversed, I want you to ensure it never reaches any other ears."

She opened her mouth to speak, then reconsidered. After a moment she tried again. "And how do you propose I accomplish that, Lord Seeker? I will be traveling with three mages, none of them weak in power."

The man walked over to her, putting his hands on her shoulders and looking her straight in the eyes. His gaze was grim and intense. "You know what the Rite of Tranquility entails. It could hardly be called a kindness, but it spares mages too weak to resist the lure of demons from a more permanent alternative. If the mages of the Circle *believed* it was possible to escape Tranquility, whether it was safe or even wise to do so, we would have chaos." He squeezed her shoulders. "I am relying on you to do what you must, Ser Evangeline, in the name of peace and order. Of all the decisions Knight-Commander Eron made when he led the White Spire, it is clear that your promotion was his wisest."

Evangeline—for that was surely her name, Cole realized—straightened and set her jaw firmly. "Thank you, my lord." She nodded. "I will see it done, if it comes to that."

"Pray that it doesn't."

With that, the Lord Seeker walked out of the room. When the door closed behind him, Evangeline relaxed. She leaned against the cot, her legs looking like they might give out from under her. She tossed the purple bundle to the side and exhaled a long breath.

Cole shivered in the corner. He was relieved the frightening man was gone, but now he was torn. If he understood what had transpired, was Rhys in danger? His first impulse was to immediately find Rhys and tell him. But what if Cole was wrong? What if Rhys didn't believe him?

What was he going to do?

Rhys inhaled the fresh air, and found it far sweeter than he remembered.

They were finally out of Val Royeaux with its teeming crowds, its buckets of slop being thrown out of windows, and its everpresent stench of horse manure and fish. The guards at the city gate had given their group a sidelong stare: three mages, noticeable due to their staves even if they were in traveling clothes, and a templar in full armor. It clearly wasn't something these men saw every day, despite garrisoning a city that held the White Spire. They were so eager to let the group pass, they barely issued any challenge.

He'd forgotten what it was like to be not only out of the tower, but out of the city. Occasionally, the mages would be escorted somewhere by the templars, if their magic was required, but this was different. Rhys felt liberated. He admired the mighty oak trees lining the road, their leaves shades of yellow and burnt orange in the late autumn. He smiled at passing merchant wagons even if the drivers avoided looking at him. He laughed when a group of children assembled by the road, shouting out for *petit alms*. It was an Orlesian tradition, after all, and Rhys wished he had coins to throw them.

Adrian was far less enthusiastic. She sat behind him on the horse, her arms clutched tightly around his chest, speaking only to complain about the chill and her sore backside. She would never admit it, but Rhys knew she was afraid of horses. The leery look she'd given the beast outside the tower had been vastly amusing. She would cope, he was certain, but only out of sheer determination.

Evangeline remained quiet as well. She did not even look when they passed a village just off the road where lively music could be heard playing. People were dancing in the village square, a trio of elves playing harpsichords on a wooden stage. When Rhys wondered out loud if they might see what was going on, the templar dourly reminded him they were not traveling for pleasure. For the most part, she kept her eyes on the road ahead, her scarlet cloak fluttering in the crisp breeze, and attempted no conversation.

Then there was Wynne.

The old mage lagged behind the others; even when Evangeline pointedly mentioned they needed to make better time, she merely smiled and kept her steed at its easy pace. Wynne had wrapped a heavy shawl around her blue robes, and seemed content to pick through her packs and read while there was still daylight. When Evangeline attempted to ask her more questions about their mission, Wynne's responses were vague. Eventually, the templar gave up.

If there was any presence that could dampen Rhys's spirits, it was Wynne's. He imagined he should be grateful she had gotten him out of the tower, but that almost made it more galling. It nipped at the edges of his consciousness, reducing his initial joy until he was almost as quiet as the others.

Finally, Evangeline called for a halt at the first highway inn they reached. Such buildings were fairly common on the major roads, especially in the Heartlands. They were fortified stone structures with blue slate roofs easily recognizable from a distance, designed to offer safe shelter to merchants and travelers. This one seemed in good shape, the Imperial crest hanging outside its gate kept polished and the courtyard inside teeming with horses and wagons.

Evangeline didn't seem eager to go inside, but they needed traveling supplies they couldn't acquire at the tower. Adrian declared that she would join the templar, although Rhys knew it wasn't out of any desire of Adrian's to keep her company. She wanted off the horse.

So he was left alone outside with Wynne. The two of them sat on their horses just outside the gate, the only sound a gust of wind that rushed through the nearby trees. A pair of shutters on one of the inn's upper windows repeatedly flew open and slammed shut again.

Wynne closed her book and sighed. She was pretending not to notice Rhys staring at her, and looked speculatively up at the clouds. "It might snow," she commented. "That would be rather early, wouldn't it?"

"It would."

Her enigmatic smile faded into a frown. "Very well, Rhys," she sighed. "If you have something to ask, now would certainly be the time."

"You got it." He turned in his saddle to face her directly. "Why am I here?"

"I told you my mission."

"But not why you need me on it," he snapped. "And don't feed me that line about being a spirit medium. You're as skilled with spirits as I am, if not more."

"Very possibly."

"You need a mage or two to help you with the ritual to enter the Fade. It could have been *any* mage. So the only reason to ask for me is because . . ."

"Because you are my son," she finished for him.

Rhys felt himself about to say something rude and barely bit it back. He had to look away. His eyes fell upon a little girl hiding in the bushes not ten feet away. She couldn't have been more than eight years old, staring at the two of them with eyes as big as saucers. Staring at their staves, rather. Wasn't it odd how children could be so fascinated by magic? It took them time and the lessons of the Chantry to learn real fear.

"Is that the reason, then?" he asked. "I didn't even know about you until nearly ten years ago. You came after the Blight in Ferelden, and introduced yourself . . . and then I never saw you again."

"I wanted to meet my son," she said. "To see the man he had become without any guidance from me. I did that."

"Then what is your interest now? You didn't need me to come on this mission of yours. You didn't even need to come to the White Spire. Yet you did."

"I didn't come to the White Spire seeking you out, Rhys. It was the closest tower at hand after I met with the Divine." She pulled her shawl more tightly around her shoulders, staring in the direction of the inn's gate as if hoping Evangeline and Adrian would appear. "When I arrived, I was told you'd been thrown in the dungeons—the prime suspect in a murder investigation conducted by the Seekers of Truth." Then she looked at him, her eyes hard. "Ten years ago I found a man who needed nothing from me. That is no longer true."

"I don't need your help," he growled. "I didn't kill anyone."

"According to the templars you've done everything to convince them otherwise." She snorted derisively. "And you've mixed yourself up with the Libertarians, as well. I assumed you had more sense."

"Not every mage is interested in rolling over and playing dead like a well-trained mabari hound. We're not children, yet the templars treat us like we are."

"Because many of you act like you are."

"Is that what you think?" He felt the anger rising inside him again, and this time didn't try to fight it. "The mighty archmage lectures us on responsibility? Do you even remember what it was like to live in a tower, or ever consider what it must be like for those of us who still do? After the rebellion in Kirkwall—"

"Must we repeat this argument?" she interrupted.

"I suppose not. What's the point?" They remained there in their saddles, saying nothing as the wind howled overhead. The Imperial sign squeaked as it slowly swung back and forth on its post. It felt cold. Wynne felt cold. There was a wall between them built of all the things left unsaid, things he had been storing up in the years since he'd met her. He felt it growing larger, now.

The little girl let out a squeak of terror and burst from her hiding place in the bushes. She sped off into the distance, as if she was being chased. Neither of them watched her go, frozen as they were in their tense silence.

"Why did you help me at all, then?" he finally asked.

"Is that important?"

"It is to me."

"If I had known this was how you would react," she sighed, "then perhaps I would have left you in your cell. Perhaps that is where you belong."

That stung. He didn't know how to respond, so he just shook his head. "You've changed," he muttered.

"You don't know me well enough to say that."

"I remember the woman I met ten years ago," he said. "I assumed I'd come from a family in Ferelden, and had just been taken too young to remember them. All my life I'd wondered who my mother was, and then she appeared out of nowhere. She was this warm, kind woman—and she was a hero. That she was my mother made me proud."

Wynne said nothing, her eyes remaining fixed on some faraway place.

"That woman told me she was relieved we'd finally met. She told me she would return . . . and I never saw her again. I still wonder what happened to her."

"I am right here," she said stiffly.

"The woman I met wouldn't have stood in the great hall and told us that it's better to endure than to hope for better. She wouldn't have been the one who convinced the College of Enchanters that surrendering is our only option."

"Then I'm sorry to disappoint you."

He shrugged. What else could he ask her for? First Enchanter Edmonde told him once that this sometimes happened to mages. They lived their entire lives separated from humanity until finally they forgot they were ever part of it to begin with. The Wynne he remembered had been gentle and caring, not aloof and imperious; it didn't seem possible the same woman was across from him now.

But perhaps he should be grateful. Even if this was only a respite from his fate, it was better than nothing. For what it was worth, he was out of the tower—for now.

7

Evangeline was beginning to find the tension wearying.

As uncomfortable as these mages might be with the idea of a templar chaperone, it seemed to her they disliked each other far more. Adrian and Rhys whispered to each other on their horse from time to time, brief exchanges that the others were clearly not intended to overhear, but to the archmage they said nothing. The old woman might as well have been alone.

Until the moment Wynne and Rhys had greeted each other in the Lord Seeker's office, Evangeline hadn't realized they were related. None of the templars in the White Spire had. They'd known the man had been born to a mage, and raised in a Chantry orphanage until he was old enough to come to the tower. It was a common enough practice, seeing as the Circle was no place for a newborn. How Rhys had come to know of his mother, however, was a mystery. If they'd met, they did so in secret, although evidently not one kept hidden from the Seekers.

Their relationship did not seem to endear them to each other, however. It made her think of her own mother, who had passed away before she'd joined the order. They'd bickered, particularly because Evangeline had embraced none of the things expected from a young Orlesian woman of breeding. She had enjoyed neither dancing, nor music, nor outings to the city to seek a suitable husband. Instead she'd favored her father's teachings, the sword-play and martial skills he'd learned from his years spent as a chevalier in the Empire's service.

Yet when her mother died Evangeline had felt nothing but regret that they'd not been closer. All those years spent resenting a woman who'd wished the best for her, and only feared her unwomanly pursuits would lead to unhappiness. It hadn't, but she didn't imagine her life as a templar was what her mother pictured.

Without a husband or children, it also meant her father's estate had fallen outside of the family upon his death. She still remembered the day a messenger had arrived with the news. Knight-Commander Eron had asked whether she wished to retire from the order and take up her inheritance. It would have meant marriage, with scores of noble families arriving at her doorstep with younger sons they couldn't pawn off elsewhere but would assume a spinster like herself would be desperate to accept. Even so, it hadn't been an easy decision. Last she'd heard, her uncle had gambled away his fortune and sold the estate to a Nevarran merchant. This made her sad.

So the life she was left with was the one she had chosen, a life of protecting the world from all the harm magic could do. While many of the mages resented templars for it, she knew there were also many frightened of their abilities. What would they do without the Circle of Magi there to bring them into the fold, to teach them what they needed to know?

Order had to be kept, just as the Lord Seeker said.

It had been four days since they'd left the safety of the White Spire. Evangeline had led the group off the main roads, preferring instead to keep to the side paths that passed through the countryside, away from cities. Still, this was the Heartlands. Even those roads were busy with traffic. They passed merchants, pilgrims on their way to the Grand Cathedral in the capital, farmers bringing their wagons to market, taxmen, elven laborers looking for late-season harvest work . . . the list was almost endless.

What she didn't see were Imperial enforcers. Normally, soldiers flying the purple banner were a common sight, even on the side roads. Anyone traveling could expect to be stopped by a patrol at least once, but there had been no sign of any.

There were other things, too. On the third day they spotted a pillar of black smoke in the distance, and a pair of dwarven merchants they stopped told them of riots in the city of Val Foret. They said things were worse outside the Heartlands as well, telling a tale of roving bandits and press gangs hired by the country lords to force commoners into army service. Later they saw a disorganized group of refugees, ragged-looking folk carrying everything they owned on their backs, who said they were fleeing a battle in the east. They didn't even know who was fighting, only that the soldiers were killing everything in their path.

It was troubling to hear. News in Orlais traveled slowly even in the best of times, but it seemed to her that even insulated in the White Spire, she should have heard such things. The capital was a hotbed of gossip, and although there'd been rumblings of displeasure against the Empress and the usual talk of elven rebellion in Halamshiral, there'd been not a single whisper of a brewing civil war.

Just to be careful, Evangeline elected not to seek lodgings in any of the villages they passed. She'd purchased camping gear at the highway inn—indeed, her horse was laden down with it—and despite the protests of the mages, she insisted they sleep outside. Rather, it was Rhys and Adrian who protested. Wynne smiled when they did, and reminded them that she'd all but lived out of a camp during the Blight. If she could endure it, so could they.

It rained the first night, a bitterly cold downpour that kept the group huddling in their tents. The next morning there was a thin layer of ice covering everything, though it didn't last long into the day. Regardless, a chill permeated the air, and, combined with a sky of hazy grey clouds, told them the weather would be decidedly foul. By the time they returned from the Western Approach, there could very well be snow on the ground.

Adrian complained constantly. Not loudly enough for Evangeline to argue with her explicitly, but quietly muttering to herself and to Rhys. It was like an angry fly buzzing in her ear, one that wouldn't desist no matter how much she swatted at it. The redheaded woman's self-righteous indignation set Evangeline's teeth on edge, and had her wishing it would rain even more than it did.

"Why are we going this way?" Adrian demanded as they rode, the third time she'd asked in as many minutes.

"I intend to avoid Val Foret," Evangeline answered.

"Why? Because of what that vagrant said? He was drunk."

"Indeed he was. That doesn't make him stupid."

"I once knew a dwarf," Wynne suddenly announced, "who was drunk more often than he was sober. Yet he could still cleave a darkspawn in two without so much as blinking an eye."

Adrian rolled her eyes. "That's nice."

"My point," the old woman responded coolly, "is that some things don't require sobriety. Like knowing that your home village isn't a safe place to be."

"That's odd, isn't it?" Rhys asked. He looked questioningly at the others. "With all the trouble we've been hearing about, you'd think the Imperial army would be here in force. I can't even remember the last time I heard of there being so much chaos."

"It probably isn't—" Adrian began.

Wynne interrupted her. "It's the war," she said. "If I'm not mistaken, I believe Gaspard is making his move."

"The Grand Duke?" Evangeline blurted out, surprised.

"Of course."

"The only news in Val Royeaux was of a rebellion in Halamshiral. If the Grand Duke was moving against the Empress, everyone in the palace would have been buzzing about it."

The old woman chuckled lightly. "Oh, don't be silly, dear. Gaspard isn't going to send word into the capital, where Celene has all of her allies. No, the whole point was to lure her out east with that story of an elven rebellion."

Rhys nodded slowly. "So he could ambush her."

"I imagine Celene did not take as many soldiers with her to fight elves as she might have to confront Gaspard." Wynne shrugged. "Possibly he even has friends among the chevaliers. Either way, the more quickly and decisively he acts, the stronger he looks. The more chaos is sown in the Empire, the weaker Celene looks and the more desperate the Imperial Court becomes."

It made troubling sense. Evangeline had to wonder just how much worse this would be if the assassin had managed to slay the Divine that night in the palace. Half the Empire would be up in arms. Which . . . did make her wonder if the mages might be innocent after all.

She glanced at Rhys and Adrian on their horse. The redheaded mage was scowling and difficult to read, but Rhys seemed genuinely bewildered. Evangeline had to admit that were she going to assassinate someone, it would be clever to make it look as if the perpetrator were someone others would not question. Why would templars doubt that rebellious factions within the Circle were trying to lash out at the Chantry?

That did not explain the murders, however. Perhaps the two events were not connected? Lord Seeker Lambert insisted on a larger picture, and saw schemes within schemes. She had to look with clearer eyes. It was worthy of some thought.

"How do you even know this?" she asked Wynne.

"Because Gaspard tried to recruit me."

"Recruit you?"

"I came here from Ferelden, which meant I passed through the Dales and the eastern lands. Evidently Gaspard got wind of my presence, for he sent men to collect me at Jader." The mage grimaced at the memory. "They were rather insistent. I don't know why Gaspard thought such treatment would make me inclined to assist him. The man has enough arrogance to believe night is day just because he pronounces it so."

"But you refused him?"

"Naturally. He tried to force the issue, but I'm not without my own resources." She said it with the barest shrug of her shoulders, as if it were nothing of consequence, although Evangeline imagined there was far more involved. Grand Duke Gaspard de Chalons was renowned for his temper; what would he think of an old woman who refused his offer? She could only imagine.

"Then why didn't you tell anyone?" Adrian asked, shocked.

Wynne chuckled bitterly at that. "Who would I tell? Celene was already gone from the capital. Even were that not the case, I doubt I would tell anyone."

"What? Why not?"

The old mage smiled coldly at her. "Because I am Fereldan, for one. I have no love for the Orlesian Empire, so the thought of it falling to pieces causes me no distress. Plus, there are other benefits if there is war here."

"Benefits?" Adrian scoffed.

"She means the Circle," Rhys said, frowning sourly as he considered. "If there's civil war in the Empire, they'll come to the mages to ask for our help."

Wynne seemed pleased at his insight. "That is so. I know you believe I desire no improvement to the conditions we live under, but that's not the case. A position of strength will only increase our bargaining power as we move forward."

"With many innocent lives lost," Evangeline muttered.

Wynne gave her a level stare. "Innocent lives are already being lost."

She couldn't offer much argument. It was true, after all, that the Circle probably would be called if the Empire fell into chaos. The mages had been invaluable in the Blights, fighting against the darkspawn, and in the great Exalted Marches of ages past . . . and the amount of prestige the Circle gained after each of those wars was lost on no one. Could she honestly tell these mages they should be patriots? That they should care for people who feared and even reviled them? She couldn't, although that didn't mean she had to like such a mercenary attitude.

It was clear Rhys didn't like it, either. He said nothing, but gave Wynne a dark look that spoke volumes.

They rode on. The skies continued to darken, distant peals of thunder threatening a cold downpour. Adrian dug a blanket out of their pack and miserably huddled inside it. Rhys tried to sympathize with her, but got little more than grunts. As pleased as Evangeline was to have the woman finally quiet, she had to admit she wasn't looking forward to the weather taking a turn for the worse. It was only going to get colder as they headed south into the badlands.

Wynne pulled up beside her, the first time she'd moved from the rear of their party the entire trip. "Perhaps," the woman suggested, "we might consider a night out of the rain?"

"I thought you enjoyed camping."

"*Enjoy* is a strong word. I can tolerate it, even if I am not as young as I once was." She glanced back at the pair behind them. Rhys was regaling Adrian with a tale about an elven apprentice who'd become incredibly ill after staying out in the rain, and when the Knight-Commander decided she was feigning her sickness she'd proceeded to vomit all over the front of his armor. Adrian appeared unamused, and Rhys chuckled at her expense. "I think,"

Wynne continued, "it might behoove us to take shelter for the sake of the others. It will not be long before we're in the part of the country where that won't be possible, after all."

Evangeline considered it. "I know of a town up ahead, not far from where I grew up. Perhaps, if there's no trouble there . . ."

"That would be wise." The tone she used was just forceful enough to remind Evangeline that she was accompanying them on this journey, not commanding them. Then Wynne allowed her horse to lag behind once again, giving Evangeline no chance to argue.

They continued down the road for several more hours. It was all prime farmland, orchards here and vineyards up in the hills farther to the west. The men and women who worked the land had done so for generations, most under the auspices of a seigneur, but there were freeholders as well. They were the "poor man's land-owner," and her father had been one of them. He'd held just enough of a title to acquire his land from a baroness desperate for coin, and it had always been a source of pride that he worked it well.

Back when she was younger she used to roam her father's orchards. She loved the rich smell of the soil, and she'd climb the apple trees until her mother came running out of the estate, skirts in hand, to yell at her. Not an hour's travel to the east was Lake Celestine, its glittering surface enough to take one's breath away at the height of summer. Of course, now it was late fall and the lake would be choppy and grey, only fishermen braving its waters.

Part of her wondered if she shouldn't go to her family's old estate. Evangeline could probably come up with a pretext the others would believe. Perhaps the new owners might even invite her in, provided they didn't notice she was accompanied by mages. She burned with a morbid curiosity to see what changes they'd made—even if everything she saw would likely make her sad. No, perhaps it was best she stayed away.

The town of Velun came into view in the early evening, just

as it started to rain. The skies practically opened up, pouring down on them with such ferocity that even Evangeline started to feel uncomfortable. The village looked normal enough, really no different from those days she'd sat on her father's wagon when he went to market. The only thing that seemed out of place was the gibbet just off the road. Three iron cages, each with a man inside . . . or, rather, one had a man and the other two had rotting corpses. The man was well on his way to joining his fellows, and was too weak and dispirited to do more than look up as they passed.

"Grim," Rhys commented.

"That man is a rapist. The other two were thieves."

"How can you tell?"

She pointed. "The runes on the post above their cages."

"Are those dwarven?" He squinted, trying to make out the symbols through the rain. "Why don't they just put up a sign?"

"Because not everyone reads."

The mage nodded, although it was clear he didn't really understand. To someone who grew up in the Circle of Magi, surrounded by books, it was perhaps understandable to think everyone in the world must be the same way. The truth of the matter was that mages were afforded an education few others outside the wealthy received.

Velun was little more than a haphazard collection of buildings surrounding the central square—on market day it would be a bustling place, as the town swelled to several times its normal population, but tonight it was all but abandoned. Many of the windows were warmly glowing, however, indicating everyone was inside. Regardless of the quiet, Evangeline found herself heartened by the familiar sights. This almost felt like home.

A lone guardsman huddled under the eaves of a storefront, shivering from the chill. He nodded when Evangeline and the others rode toward him, their horses making loud clopping sounds on the cobblestones. "Good evening, ser," she greeted him.

"Late for travelers," he remarked without much interest, blowing on his hands.

"Indeed. Is the Spriggan still about? I didn't see it on the way in."

The guard squinted at her. "You're a local?"

"My family once owned Brassard-manot."

That seemed to brighten him a little. People from the provinces could be wary of outsiders. It would be even worse when they left the Heartlands. "The Spriggan burned down some years back," the guard said. "Old Man Lusseau built a new inn just past the Chantry. Just look for the blue lantern out front, you can't miss it."

That wasn't far. Evangeline smiled her thanks at the man and led the others through the square in the direction he indicated. She found herself looking at some of the buildings and trying to remember if they had changed in the years since she'd last been here. It was surprising how many had not. Such was the way of small towns.

"Did you really come from here?" Rhys asked her as they rode.

"Not Velun itself, but my family's estate was nearby."

He cracked a mischievous grin. "So . . . a member of the nobility, after all?"

"If you're picturing me in a fancy gown, it never happened. I preferred a sword to a dress from the time I could hold one in my hand."

"You must have been quite the sight at the country ball, then."

She chuckled at that, despite herself.

The storm was picking up strength, the wind howling to the point where it was becoming difficult to talk. So they rode in silence until the inn came into view. As advertised, a large lantern hung beside the door, the patina having turned its metal bright blue. The sound of laughter came from within, as did the aroma of smoke and cooked meat. Evangeline found her stomach responding with a hungry growl. After four days of dried bread and fruit, it would be good to eat something hearty.

The inn was the sort that one often found in country towns throughout Orlais, little more than a glorified tavern that rented rooms to weary travelers. The fire pit in the center of the main room filled it with a warm glow and the sharp scent of burnt tree sap. Small tables were scattered about, many of them filled either with local laborers or traveling merchants. They gathered in clumps, clinking their wooden mugs and laughing merrily. The place had a cramped, cozy feel to it. Friendly and inviting.

Or it did until they noticed who had stepped through the door.

All conversation stopped, and a dozen eyes looked their way in startled silence. Evangeline grimaced. She knew what they were staring at: her armor, for one, and the staves carried by the mages. The four of them crowded together in the doorway, water dripping onto the wooden floor as the tense scrutiny continued.

"Maker have mercy!" a jovial voice declared.

It was loud enough to make Evangeline's hand edge toward her sword, but then she hesitated as an enormously fat man strode out from the kitchen. He wore an apron stained yellow with old grease, and busily wiped his hands with a cloth almost as dirty.

"I had to come out and see if everyone had died!" The man chortled and then paused as he noticed his patrons continuing to stare. "What? Have none of you arses ever seen Chantry folk before? Back to your beers lest I tell Amelda to water down the next round more than usual!"

There was a murmur of discontent. Several of the men exchanged dark glances, but returned to drinking—albeit unenthusiastically. Evangeline caught a pair of the laborers glaring at her still. These were rough-looking men, the kind with small lives and smaller minds. It was exactly their sort that had led her to avoid populated areas until tonight.

The fat man rushed toward them, arms wide and an obsequious smile plastered upon his face. "Come in, my good friends! I trust the Chantry supplies its people with an abundance of royals, as usual?"

Evangeline jiggled the purse at her belt, letting the coins inside provide her answer. "Give us room and board for the evening and you'll be fairly compensated."

"What more can one ask?" He swept across the small room to a table beside the fire pit, unceremoniously yanking the chair out from underneath the weasely-looking fellow who occupied it. The man shot the innkeeper a hurt look as he rushed to a smaller table elsewhere. "Come! Have a seat!"

Normally Evangeline wouldn't have chosen something in the middle of the room, but it *did* look invitingly warm. She smiled at the innkeeper as she took her seat, and he bounded back to the kitchen with purpose. The mages filed in behind her, staring around dubiously at the tavern.

"Are we truly going to sleep here?" Adrian asked.

"If you prefer," Wynne smiled sweetly, "we can go back outside and find someplace more to your liking."

"Err . . . no."

"Then this will have to do, won't it?"

Evangeline noticed Rhys hiding a smile as he turned and warmed his hands over the fire pit. She took off her gauntlets and laid them on the table, and then unfastened her cloak. It was so heavy with water it felt like it weighed a thousand pounds. She would have to wring it out later, and peel herself out of her armor. The mages were no better off. They would all be lucky if they didn't catch their deaths.

A girl came out from the kitchen, wearing an apron in no better shape than the innkeeper's. Her father, Evangeline assumed.

They shared a bulbous nose, if not a taste for food; this girl was mousy and reed-thin. She dropped off a pair of mugs at one of the tables and then reluctantly walked over to theirs.

"Something I can get you?" she asked.

"Wine," Rhys said immediately.

Evangeline frowned at him. "Don't you get enough of that back at the Circle? Our stores are practically filled with wine caskets and little else."

"Filled because nobody wants to drink that piss."

She chuckled. "We drink the same piss, I'll have you know."

He flashed a charming grin at the serving girl. "Why don't you bring us a bottle of something that's been collecting dust in your cellar? A fine local vintage, something the templars wouldn't dream of serving to us lowly mages?"

"Charming," Wynne said dryly. She held up a hand to catch the attention of the serving girl, who seemed at a complete loss how to respond. "Bring the wine for them if you must. I'll have something a bit stronger. Do you have dwarven ale?"

"You must be joking!" Adrian guffawed.

"Why must I?"

"An old woman like you drinking dwarven ale? We'd be lucky to find you alive in your bed come morning."

Wynne seemed nettled by that. "I acquired a taste for it in Orzammar."

Adrian looked skeptically at Rhys. "She's trying to impress us."

"Not at all," Wynne said. She arched a brow at the serving girl. "Do you have it or not? I'll take Fereldan whiskey if I must, preferably something from the coastlands."

The girl nodded dumbly. "Father keeps a keg for the guild merchants."

"Excellent."

"Bring some for me, as well," Adrian said. She gave the old

mage a wicked smile. "I'm willing to bet I can finish my cup and most of yours, and you'll still be under the table."

"I doubt that."

"The . . . ale is very expensive, madame," the serving girl said cautiously.

Wynne reached into her robes and pulled out a small purse and tossed it on the table. Sodden though it was, it was easy to see it was filled with coin. More than Evangeline had, by far. "I think that should suffice. If that's stew I smell in the kitchen, bring that out as well." She glanced archly at Adrian. "*Some* people here are going to need something in their stomachs."

"Yes, madame." The girl ran off, relieved to get away.

"Well!" Rhys declared, smiling at Evangeline as he rubbed his hands together. "More wine for you and me, then!"

She kept her drinking to a minimum, sipping on her cup and letting Rhys have the rest of the bottle to himself. She only picked at the stew, as well, despite it being as delicious as it smelled. The rest of the tavern was too quiet for her liking. Some of the men had already slunk off, and those who remained stared at the mages more often than they talked. When they did talk, it was in whispers. The merriment they'd heard prior to their entry was gone.

Evangeline didn't trust it. The mages, of course, were oblivious. They drank quietly at first, Rhys cradling his dusty wine bottle like it was some lost treasure while the two women engaged in a battle of wills. Each of them drank as much of the murky black liquid as they could stand in order to show the other how little it affected them. Wynne was clearly far better at it, her cool façade undiminished, and that only seemed to aggravate Adrian all the more.

Evangeline didn't know how they could stand the stuff. Dwarven ale wasn't really ale—it was some concoction made from fungus, or so she heard. Normally only dwarves could drink it without making themselves sick. It remained to be seen whether that would be the case here.

"It *was* a dragon," Wynne insisted. Her composure was beginning to slip ever so slightly, words blurring at the edges. "We met it on the roof of Fort Drakon, where it had been forced down. The last battle to end the Blight, and a single swipe from that creature could have sent any of us hurtling to our death." She tossed back the last sip of ale in her cup for good measure, waving absently to the serving girl for more.

"A dragon!" Adrian exclaimed excitedly. She cradled her chin in her hands, staring at the older mage with bleary, awestruck eyes. Her red curls had dried into a frizzy mess of comical proportions. Unlike Wynne, she was a complete wreck. "A real, honest-to-goodness dragon?"

"Adrian is fond of dragons," Rhys explained with a smirk.

"It was an Archdemon," Wynne said, "a dragon tainted by corruption, transformed into a thing of evil with no match in all of Thedas." She couldn't contain the smallest of proud smiles. "Save for the Warden, of course."

"The Warden! The Hero of Ferelden?"

"The one and the same."

Adrian gesticulated inarticulately for a few moments before she realized she couldn't put her excitement into words. Then she stared at Wynne as if an incredible thought had just occurred to her. "They *let* you out of the tower to do all that?"

"Not quite. The Circle of Magi in Ferelden had been . . . disabled."

"I heard about this," Evangeline commented.

"Most of the mages had been overcome by demons," Wynne continued. "There were only a few of us left, really, when the Warden arrived."

"The Warden saved you?"

"Indeed."

"And took you away from the tower!"

"My help was needed."

"Lucky for you." Adrian picked up her cup, disappointing herself all over again to find it empty. She searched around for the serving girl and, not seeing her, tried to stand up. That only succeeded in nearly knocking over her chair, of course, and she stumbled back into it in the most ungraceful manner possible.

"Be careful, Adri," Rhys warned, grabbing her shoulder out of concern. She looked at him with a mixture of surprise and bleary affection.

"Oh! You haven't called me that since . . ."

He attempted to look blasé but failed. "You're drunk," he muttered. Adrian reached up and cupped his cheek, her expression suddenly so tender and sad that Evangeline felt embarrassed to watch. Rhys reddened and gently removed her hand, his grin apologetic.

"I didn't realize you two were . . ." Wynne left the thought unfinished, clearly uncertain how to end it. Rhys glanced at her, his eyes flashing with annoyance.

"We're not."

"All evidence to the contrary."

"I said we're not." He straightened in his chair, busily pouring himself another cup of wine—the last in the bottle, Evangeline noticed. "And even if we were, I don't really see how that's any of your business."

"Did I say it was?" She chuckled gaily. "I'm no stranger to the idea of a mage seeking the company of others in the Circle, Rhys. How do you think you were born?"

He looked disquieted. "I . . . don't want to think about that."

Wynne waved a hand dismissively. "You're a grown man, and then some. I'll assume that you can handle the notion of someone you barely know having lain with a templar forty years ago—even if she does happen to be your mother."

The old mage downed the rest of her ale even as Rhys's eyes widened in shock. He tilted his head awkwardly, as if not quite capable of processing this news. Adrian appeared to have no such problem. She slammed a fist down on the table, squealing with delight so loudly it drew the attention of the entire tavern.

"You laid with a *templar*?"

Wynne paused, apparently realizing what she'd revealed. "Well," she hemmed, "it *was* a long time ago." The old woman looked helplessly at Evangeline, and sighed when Evangeline just looked the other way. She wasn't getting involved in this conversation, no how and no way.

"That's marvelous!" Adrian cackled.

Rhys appeared mortified. "*I* don't think it's marvelous."

Wynne smiled patiently at him. "Demonize them all you like, a templar is a man like any other." The corner of her mouth twitched as it tried to form into a mischievous smirk. It succeeded. "Trust me," she chuckled.

The man groaned, and Adrian laughed so uproariously she had to pound the table several times in order to punctuate just how much she loved the entire notion.

"You robes seem pretty satisfied with yourselves."

The new voice was gruff, and cut through the merriment instantly. Adrian stopped laughing and stared. Evangeline turned in her seat to see a huge, burly man looming beside their table. His beard grew out of his chin like some wild, black bush, and his arms were thick as tree trunks. This was a man hewn from wood, probably one of the local freeholders or one of their workers. Indignant rage smoldered in his eyes like fire.

Adrian looked like she was about to retort, but Rhys spoke first. "We're just travelers who came in out of the rain," he said amiably. "How about we buy you a drink, in thanks for your town's fine hospitality?"

"And what are we going to toast?" the man growled. "You mages trying to kill Her Holiness?"

"We had nothing to do with that."

The burly man slammed his fist down on the table so hard it sent the wine bottle and cups clattering to the ground. The entire tavern went dead silent. "But it was you and your stinking magic that done it! If Her Holiness had a right mind, she'd tell everyone to string you up! Burn your curse out of this world once and for all!"

Wynne looked calm, but Evangeline saw her hand creeping toward her staff. Rhys remained still, his smile fading. Adrian, however, lurched drunkenly to her feet, her temper clearly aroused. "Our curse?" she spat. "Our only curse is to be faced with ignorant louts like you, as if you mundanes never did anything terrible in all of history!"

"History." The man repeated the word with disgust, his upper lip curling. "I don't care about history. I care about Jean-Petit. His farmhouse got burned down two weeks ago, with him in it. You know who done it? His daughter, a spiteful little thing the templars had to drag off before she killed anyone else." He loomed closer. "You think your magic impresses me? Impresses anyone?"

Several voices chimed in with the man now, as others got up from their chairs. The mood of outrage was thick. These men had been simmering, waiting for someone to express what they'd been thinking all along. The fat innkeeper came out of the back, his look of concern turning into fear. When his daughter started to pass him, he stopped her. They both retreated to the kitchen.

Adrian's eyes narrowed in hate. She held out a hand in front of her, an aura of blue flame crackling into life around it. The hum of her power reverberated around the room. "I don't know," she said, her tone low and dark. "We can be very impressive."

Evangeline jumped up. She reached out with one hand and grabbed Adrian around the neck, channeling her own power into the woman so quickly it disrupted her magic. The flames disappeared with a flash. Before Adrian could do more than widen her eyes in shock, Evangeline shoved her hard. She stumbled back over her chair, falling to the ground and slamming her head against the side of the fire pit.

Evangeline felt, rather than saw, the burly man move. She grabbed his thick arm before he could touch her, spinning around and shoving him back. Enraged and clenching his fists, he made as if to charge her—

—and halted. Her sword was out, and pointed at his throat.

"Don't be a fool," she warned him.

Other men were drawing closer now, fists clenched at their sides. Wynne rose, staff held protectively; thankfully she had enough sense not to invoke more magic. Rhys knelt down by Adrian's side, helping her up as much as restraining her.

"You're going to kill us? For these mages?" the man snarled. "You of all people should know what they are."

"I'm here to protect them, and to protect you from them. Nothing more."

"They don't deserve protection!"

"What they don't deserve," she stated firmly, "is to be strung up by an angry mob. I know you're angry. What happened to Her Holiness was unforgivable. But you'll not condemn the innocent for it, not while I stand."

"How are they innocent?" he shouted. He turned to face the growing crowd, holding his hands out to them in supplication. "It wasn't just Jean-Petit. Last year there was the man in Val Bresins who turned into a demon in the middle of the marketplace! The hedge witch who blighted the Arlans crop! The Wickens boy who talked to ghosts—you *know* it was him that was killing our poor dogs!" The gathered crowd murmured in agreement. "How long are we going to stand by and let this evil fester? The Maker would not have it!"

"The Maker does have it!" Evangeline roared. She glared challengingly at the crowd, and many of them shrank back. "These mages serve the Chantry, as do I! Do not forget that in wars past it was *we* who have stood between the good folk of Orlais and oblivion!"

Adrian wrested herself free from Rhys and lurched forward. "Yes!" she shouted belligerently. "You should all be grateful!"

Evangeline wheeled on her. "Silence, you foolish woman! It is *you* who should be grateful, grateful that you have the luxury to worry just how free you are. Do you honestly think mages are the only people in this world who *suffer*?"

Adrian took a step back, startled, and bumped into the table. For once, she seemed at a loss for words. Rhys stepped between her and Evangeline, an angry look on his face. "No," he stated. "We don't think that."

"Yes, you do," Evangeline snapped. "You live in an ivory tower, without the slightest clue just how much worse it could be."

"I know how much worse it could be," Wynne said. The old woman frowned as she turned to address the crowd. "Please, good folk of Velun. We meant no harm to any of you. Leave us in peace, and we shall do the same, I beg you."

There was a mutter of discontent among the men, but none of them seemed willing to press the issue any further. Even the burly giant who began the fight did little more than glare. What was one man, even one as large as himself, to do against an armed warrior and three mages? That one of the mages appeared to be no more than an old woman took the wind out of his sails.

"You're not welcome here," he said gruffly. "We would have you gone."

"We'll go," Evangeline assured him. "In good time. And we won't be back."

The man looked around at the others with disgust. Finally, he let out a frustrated growl and stormed toward the door. Evangeline watched him go, keeping her sword at the ready until the others in the tavern began to follow. They complained quietly, reassuring each other that things could have gone very differently. Within minutes the room was almost empty, save for a few scattered merchants who stared purposefully at their beers and pretended they were elsewhere.

Wynne approached Evangeline. "That was well done."

"I did it to keep you drunken fools from using magic to hurt these poor people. They wouldn't have stood a chance."

"It was well done, nevertheless."

"Is that how you protect us?" Adrian snapped. She lurched toward Evangeline, standing close enough that the stench of ale on her breath was all too apparent. "I wasn't the one looking for a fight! Yet you would have let them drag me out into the street!"

"That didn't happen."

"Thanks to the generous protection of the templars!" she said mockingly. "We mages in our ivory tower and our heads in the clouds, we don't know anything about abuse or what it means to stand up for ourselves!"

"Adrian," Rhys warned her. He gently guided her away by the shoulder, and she resisted him for only a second. Her glare lingered, even as Rhys nodded to Evangeline. "Thank you," he said. "I know we don't seem appreciative, but if that mob had pushed it . . . we would have had no choice but to use magic. Nobody wants that."

He didn't give her time to respond, instead leading Adrian out the front door. The innkeeper poked his head out not a moment later, looking vastly relieved to find his tavern empty of bloodshed. He simpered over to Wynne and Evangeline, clutching his hands nervously.

"My, that was . . . unexpected!" he declared.

"Sadly, it wasn't." Evangeline took out her purse and handed him some coins. "This should cover the drinks, and any damages. We won't stay in your rooms, just in case those men decide to come back. If you have a hayloft, we'll sleep there and be gone by morning."

"There's one in the stables out back." He hesitated, obviously torn between wanting the templar and her mage friends gone and hoping for more coin. "I . . . just want you to know that Velun is not always like this. Had I known the men would be so uncivil . . ."

"These are strange times," Wynne assured him.

He had to be satisfied with that, and could only watch anxiously as they left.

The rain had slowed to a fine drizzle, coating Rhys's skin like ice. He shivered uncontrollably. It would have been nice to have a warm room in which to dry off completely. As it was, he felt as if he would never be warm again. If he'd been wise, he would have stayed in the hayloft with everyone else. It wasn't the warmest place to sleep, but at least it was out of the rain.

As it was, he was creeping through the town streets in the middle of the night. The windows were all dark now and, short of the occasional hungry dog that wandered up to him with its tail wagging hopefully, everything was still. The guardsman they'd met on the way in was nowhere in evidence, but Rhys still kept to the shadows as much as he could. He didn't need to answer awkward questions, not from the guard and most certainly not from his companions.

They were asleep, thank the Maker. Adrian had collapsed into a blanket, still wound up from the incident in the tavern and furious at Evangeline, but too drunk to stay awake even so. She would be impossible to live with come morning. Wynne had retired without so much as a word. Evangeline stayed up for almost an hour longer, however, watching for any sign of the townsfolk returning to make trouble.

Rhys had pretended to sleep, watching out of the corner of his eye until finally she nodded off. He'd been certain the creaking of the old ladder would give him away, but she hadn't stirred. He could thank his lucky stars, for once.

Now he was beginning to wonder why he'd bothered. The hush of the town was impenetrable, and for all his searching, he was finding only empty alleyways and more shadows. Perhaps he should give up and go back. If someone woke, he could always explain that he'd needed to use the privy.

Then he caught a glimpse of movement. A silhouette darted into the alley between two dark shops, and Rhys raced toward it. He turned the corner, half expecting to discover it was just his imagination, but instead was greeted by the sight of a man crouching by the wall. He looked like a drowned rat, blond hair plastered against his face and his leathers drenched black. He shivered miserably, staring up at Rhys with a mixture of fear and wariness.

"Cole," Rhys sighed. He kept his distance, a firm grip on his staff just in case the young man decided to attack . . . or run, as he had last time. Rhys had first noticed someone was following them only yesterday, keeping far enough back on the road so they were just out of sight. As soon as Rhys realized that Evangeline, alert as she was, didn't spot their shadow, he knew exactly who it must be.

"I'm sorry," Cole moaned.

"Did you follow us all the way from the tower? What, in Andraste's name, are you even doing here?"

The young man rubbed his shoulders, his teeth chattering. "I had to come. I had to warn you, but I was afraid . . ."

"Warn me?"

"I saw Knight-Captain speaking with a man, a frightening man in black armor. He told her that if you found something, nobody else could know about it." Cole looked up at him, his expression full of concern. "I couldn't let anything happen to you; you're my only friend! I just . . . I was so afraid that you'd never . . ." He buried his head between his knees, misery overtaking him.

Rhys stared, unsure what to think. Could Cole be lying? Perhaps making up some story to earn his way back into his good graces? That seemed unlikely. Cole might omit the truth, but there was little guile to him. That much Rhys was still certain of, if little else.

"You came all this way to tell me that?" he said, shaking his head in disbelief.

"Yes," Cole said. "I was so scared I might lose sight of you, and I wouldn't be able to find my way back. I'd be lost forever. I didn't realize it would be so *far!*"

Despite himself, Rhys felt bad for the young man. He knelt down beside him, sighing. Cole flinched, and then realized that Rhys wasn't going to attack him. He clutched desperately at Rhys and hugged him tight.

Rhys hugged him back. What else could he do? Yes, Cole had killed people . . . but he wasn't doing it out of malevolence. Nobody had taught him how to control his magic, or given him an answer he could understand. He was frightened and lost, and a part of Rhys understood that.

But what now? He couldn't take Cole along, and the idea of leaving him to his own devices had no more appeal. It would be like abandoning a child in the wilderness. Maker only knew how Cole had been feeding himself so far. Stealing his food, probably, with no one the wiser . . . but there would be nowhere to steal from once they were in the badlands.

"Cole, you have to go back," he said.

The young man disengaged long enough to give Rhys a hurt look. "I can't."

"Yes, you can. If you find one of the main roads, it should lead you straight back to Val Royeaux. It's a hard city to miss."

"I need to protect you!"

Rhys patted the man's shoulder sympathetically. "It's enough that you've warned me. I can take care of myself, Cole."

"No, you can't. They took you away to the dungeons, and I should never have let them. I should have listened to you! I should have gone with you; I'm so sorry!"

"We can deal with that when I get back to the tower."

"No." Cole backed away and stood up. "I'm not going to let anything happen to you. I won't let them hurt you again." Without another word, he turned and ran off into the darkness.

Rhys watched him go. Giving chase would be as pointless as it had been the last time, although he couldn't help but have misgivings. What was Cole going to do? Would he try to hurt Evangeline? He might not realize how much more trouble that would mean for them all.

Even so, it was a relief to once again see a glimpse of the young man he'd known. It was troubling to think of Cole as a murderer, and the shock of the discovery still lingered. How much more was there about Cole that he didn't know? If he didn't find a way to help the young man or stop him from killing again, the blood of his victims would be on Rhys's hands. He had to remind himself that while Cole wasn't a monster, that didn't mean he wasn't dangerous.

There wasn't anything more he could do now, however. He stood up, sighing, and slowly made his way back to the inn. Several times he looked over his shoulder to see if Cole was following, but there was nothing. Rhys just hoped the young man wouldn't do anything foolish. With luck he would turn around and go back to the tower on his own.

Rhys walked around the side of the inn, feeling his way in the near-darkness, until he was in sight of the stables. The moon was almost completely obscured by clouds, but there was just enough light to see someone standing in front of the stable doors. A woman in templar armor, crossing her arms and waiting impatiently.

So much for returning unseen.

Evangeline arched an eyebrow when she spotted him. "Already returned from your little jaunt?" she asked.

"Call of nature?"

"Funny, then, that you were nowhere near the privy . . . or anywhere else nearby. You must have searched far and wide for privacy."

He spread his hands and grinned at her. "You caught me. I went to consort with a demon, of course. He gave me the loveliest recipe for blood magic pie. You should try it."

The joke fell flat. The silence dragged on as Evangeline stared at him, baffled. "You're not very good at staying alive, are you?"

He coughed uncomfortably. "Evidently not."

"It's a good thing you're charming."

Oh? "You think I'm charming?"

She suppressed a wry smile. "Like a stupid dog is charming, perhaps." Then her expression hardened. "I'm no fool, Rhys. What were you thinking? Those men from the tavern could have spotted you, alone and away from the rest of us."

"They didn't."

"This is the second time I've caught you wandering off. If I didn't think you were smarter than that, I'd suspect you were trying to make a run for it. What were you really doing?"

He paused, remembering what Cole had told him. Could it be true? "I've a question for you, actually. If we find something with Wynne's friend that the Chantry wouldn't care for, what are you supposed to do? What orders did the Lord Seeker give you?"

Evangeline's eyes narrowed. "What do you mean?"

"It's true, isn't it? You're here to protect the Chantry's interests."

She stepped away from the door, walking up to him with a look that said she meant business. "There is more than our self-interest at stake here. I will do whatever I must to protect the greater good."

"Does Wynne know that?"

"She would be a fool not to." She sighed unhappily, and for a moment Rhys saw the woman behind the templar mask. There was doubt in her eyes. It was good to see he wasn't dealing with some unquestioning creature of the Lord Seeker's. "I'll admit," she said, "I hope what we find is inconsequential, an aberration we can deal with together. I have nothing against you or the others, but I will do my duty."

"Even if that means trying to kill us."

That he'd said "trying" wasn't lost on her. A single templar against three senior mages would not be much of a battle . . . assuming that they were all on the same side. "Stop trying to evade the question," she growled. "Where have you been?"

"You wouldn't believe me if I told you."

"Try me."

He considered carefully. What would change if he told her about Cole now? The templars already thought Rhys was the murderer, and it seemed pointless to provide her with yet another lie she would see through instantly. If Cole truly intended to listen to him now, then he would need to go before the templars eventually. And if he didn't . . . it's not like Rhys's fate could get any worse.

"Very well," he finally said. "There's been someone following us since we left the tower. I went to find him."

"I've kept a close eye on the road."

"No, you wouldn't have seen him. He's invisible."

Evangeline gave him a skeptical look, evidently trying to decide if he was making a fool of her. "Invisible," she repeated. "Are you joking?"

"This would be an incredibly poor time to joke, wouldn't it?"

"Disastrously poor."

He gave up and sighed. "Yes, he's invisible. It's . . . a special ability, I guess you would call it. Most people don't see him, and even those who do forget about him. I can see him, and I know some of the mages in the tower have caught a glimpse. They've been calling him the Ghost of the Spire, although I don't know if a templar would have heard about that."

Her look of recognition said she had. Even so, she seemed suspicious. "You're saying he lives in the tower."

"He was brought there by the templars, yes, and he's never left . . . until now."

"He *could* be a demon."

"I can sense spirits. I would know the difference."

"Demons are masters of deception."

"I know that, too." Rhys shrugged. "I've been visiting him in the tower's lower levels for almost a year now, trying to figure out how to help him. I couldn't tell anyone because they wouldn't believe me."

She thought about it. "And this is who you were fighting with when I found you?"

"Yes."

"Why?"

"That's . . . a long story."

She didn't believe him, just as he assumed she wouldn't. He could see it in her eyes, in the way she folded her arms again and began circling him, as if looking for a weakness. "Do you have any proof of what you're saying?" she demanded. "Can you produce him?"

"Not yet. He's frightened of the templars, and with good reason."

Evangeline stared at him a moment longer. Then she nodded. "You may be telling the truth, or you may be under the influence of a demon . . . in either case I'll have to watch you closely. Regardless, this isn't the time for this conversation. We will discuss this further when we return to the tower."

He let out a slow breath. "I thought you might try to drag me back there now."

"I would," she said, "but I doubt Wynne would come with me. My duty is to help her mission. What comes afterward is another matter." Her glare became hard. "And for your sake, I pray you're telling the truth, and this 'invisible man' is what you believe he is. Maker help you if he's not."

That seemed to be the end of it. Evangeline turned to leave, but paused when she noticed his incredulous expression. "I half expected you to run me through, regardless of what I said," he admitted. "You're all right. For a templar."

She snickered, rolling her eyes. "Such high praise from a man filled with wine." With that, she walked back inside the stables.

Rhys remained outside, watching her go. There was definitely a woman underneath all that armor, and a fine-looking one. But then he chided himself for the thought. *You must be drunk,* he thought. *She would eat you alive.*

He sighed, and his thoughts darkened as he looked around one last time in search of Cole. Still nothing.

Go back, he wanted to tell the man. *Go back to the tower and wait for me.*

It was no use. If Cole intended to keep following them, there was nothing he could do. This would play out however it was going to.

Maker help them all.

8

The next morning was the finest since they'd left Val Royeaux. The group walked out of the stables to discover a clear sky bursting with pink and gold as the sun peeked over the horizon. The ground was still wet, covered in a faint layer of frost that lent a bite to the air. Rhys would have called it beautiful had the memory of the previous night's ugliness not lingered, leaving a bad taste in his mouth. The townsfolk were already stirring, and the way they stared so suspiciously told him word had clearly gotten around.

It reminded him of the time he spent at the Imperial consulate in Teraevyn. As a young man, he'd been apprenticed to an elderly elven mage by the name of Arvin. He remembered the man as resembling an old leather glove, all disapproving scowls and squinting eyes. Arvin had been a taskmaster, only grudgingly moved to praise when Rhys shed sweat and blood to please him. It had been a miserable time, one that Rhys had been sure would never end. He'd been overjoyed when Arvin informed him of a transfer to the consulate—and astounded when the man invited him along.

It was unprecedented. The opportunity to not only leave the tower for more than the shortest jaunt, but to voyage into another land completely? Into the Tevinter Imperium, an exotic and forbidden land where mages were said to rule? Even though he'd been certain Enchanter Arvin only wished a lackey to fetch his meals and polish his boots, Rhys had still been overjoyed. He stayed up long nights in the dormitory, staring at the ceiling and almost quivering in anticipation of the voyage.

The mere fact that the enchanter had gone out of his way to take Rhys seemed unthinkable at the time. The man wouldn't even say why, he would just harrumph at the question and demand more chewing salts be fetched from a shop in the capital's alienage. They made his breath stink of raw fish, enough to make Rhys's eyes water whenever the man leaned over his shoulder to explain something, but by then Rhys would have endured far worse to avoid his displeasure.

He still remembered arriving at Teraevyn. Even the grandeur of Val Royeaux, with all its palaces and gleaming buildings, didn't compare to this Tevinter city. Signs of age were everywhere: crumbling statues of dragons, the remnants of ancient temples, decrepit buildings covered in moss. It was as if the entire city was built on the bones of older places, and those older places built on top of ones older still, with the past poking through like weeds and refusing to stay buried. Enchanter Arvin was unimpressed, but Rhys was transfixed.

Even the consulate itself had seemed special. Marble pillars and the acrid smell of incense that the Tevinters burned to mask the smell of sewage in the streets. Tiled murals so decayed he could never figure out what those faceless warriors were actually battling. There was even a fountain in the Summer Garden, crafted long ago by magic and not dwarven pumps. The marble dragon was missing its wings and both its front legs, but its head looked so malevolent Rhys was certain it depicted an Old God.

There were slaves, as well. Rhys had been too young to understand what that meant, or why Arvin got so angry whenever he saw one. An elven slave once offered the man a tray of figs, and he knocked it out of her hands and shouted until the Consul came running. Rhys had read about how the Tevinter Imperium conquered the elven lands long ago, but those were only words on a page. The slaves were just another exotic feature to be admired and gawked at.

It wasn't until weeks later that Rhys had realized he wasn't welcome. Orlesians were constantly at odds with the Tevinter Imperium, and had been in all the years since the Imperial Chantry had split off from the Grand Cathedral in Val Royeaux. That was the history, but the truth of it felt much different. The locals were suspicious, and they became hostile whenever Rhys revealed his accent. He found himself avoided, cheated by merchants . . . not a single local would so much as talk to him.

It was difficult living in such an air of hostility. The novelty of the exotic city quickly wore off, and he started to find it drab and ugly instead. He felt lonely.

Eventually there was an incident: on his way to comb the Teraevyn bazaar for salt chews, Rhys found himself surrounded by three older boys. They were apprentices to a magister, as well as nobility, and clearly feeling superior enough to pick on an Orlesian. They pushed him down and kicked him, until finally Rhys's temper surfaced and he used his magic. He scorched one of the boy's faces, and they responded in kind. He'd been badly hurt, and would have died had the fracas not drawn the attention of nearby city guardsmen.

If only that had been the end of it. The incident reached the ears of the magister, who made an official protest to the consulate. Arvin sat him down and said he'd been left with no choice. Rhys would have to be sent back to the White Spire. He told Rhys that a talented young man like himself shouldn't take what happened to heart; there would be other opportunities, other chances to find a life worth living, even under the restrictions of the Circle.

It was the only compliment the man had ever paid him. He'd been dumbstruck; hours later when he found himself on a carriage with a templar chaperone and heading back to Orlais, he regretted not trying to respond in kind.

He wrote Arvin a few times, and even saw the old man once when he returned to the White Spire for a brief visit. Eventually, it was Arvin who sponsored him to gain the rank of senior enchanter. Not long afterward, he was told Arvin had died. The templars wouldn't say exactly how, but Rhys heard rumors of poison. It seemed Arvin's position in the consulate had been that of a spy and not really an "advisor" at all. Strange how it had all seemed so innocent to him back then.

Thus he didn't object when Evangeline insisted they avoid any more towns and camp near the road instead. Neither did Wynne or Adrian. They didn't need a repeat of the previous night's performance; short of disguising themselves and somehow hiding their staves, it would surely only get worse the farther they traveled from the Heartlands.

Their time on the road moved quickly. Adrian remained quiet, sore from the previous night's drinking, just as he suspected she would be. At least she hadn't complained when he'd woken her; she was as eager to be away as everyone else. Wynne remained contemplative, commenting only that there seemed little traffic. It was true; for all intents and purposes they had the road to themselves. With the sun shining and the rain finally passed, it should have been a pleasant day of travel.

Except that it wasn't. Evangeline tersely refused to speak to him. Even Adrian, wrapped up in misery as she was, noticed and gave Rhys a questioning look. He sighed and said he would explain later.

And he did. After they set up camp the first night, Rhys told Wynne and Adrian he needed to talk. Evangeline raised an eyebrow but made no comment, and elected to busy herself elsewhere. He explained everything to them: how he met Cole, the man's strange curse, and how he'd followed them from the tower. The only thing he didn't mention was that Cole had killed the mages.

Evidently, he didn't have to. Adrian's expression grew more

and more annoyed as he spoke. Eventually she interrupted. "If he's invisible," she said, "how do you know he's not the killer? You said yourself the templars didn't see anyone."

Rhys hesitated to answer, and that was enough.

"It's him!" she spat. "And you know it's him! Why didn't you say something?"

"I didn't find out until it was too late."

"You could still have denied it! They think you're the killer!"

"And what would I say? The templars wouldn't be able to find him, and Cole wasn't willing to approach the templars. He's terrified of them. I couldn't even force him to go." He threw his hands up, frustrated. "Look, I don't condone what he's done. Far from it. But telling the templars about him would just make them think I was under the influence of a demon."

"How do you know you aren't?" Wynne asked.

He glared at her. "I would know."

"In my travels, I've encountered a great number of things that defied explanation. There are more spirits than we understand, Rhys, and some of them are capable of things we can't imagine. Considering your research, you should understand that better than anyone."

"I do, but I've spent time with Cole. He hasn't tried to tempt me. There's nothing about him that says he's a spirit of any kind."

"Other than the fact that he cannot be seen." She held up her hands to forestall his retort. "If it were easy to know that one was being influenced, far fewer mages would succumb to it."

"Well, if he's a demon, he could hardly be the one killing the mages, could he?"

"Are you certain he is?"

"He told me—" Rhys cut himself off, sighing. "I didn't see him killing anyone, no. But Cole is no immaterial spirit. I've touched him, unless I imagined that, too." The last he added with a note of bitterness.

"You said his memory was confused. He may be a spirit who's forgotten he is a spirit. Or this may indeed be a young man, some-one a spirit has possessed."

"He would turn into an abomination."

"Not all possessed mages become abominations." This she said with a bit of heat, enough to surprise even Adrian, who looked at the old woman curiously.

"What do you know about it?" he asked.

"I know enough." With that, Wynne tossed the remains of her provisions into the fire and stood up. Her crisp demeanor had re-turned. "I suggest you avoid dealing with this young man and save yourself a great deal more trouble in the future." She walked off before Rhys could respond.

"What I want to know," Adrian demanded, "is why you didn't tell *me*."

"Because you would have tried to do something about it."

Fury flashed in her eyes. "Damned right I would! You see him again, you point him out. I'll gladly kill him."

"Considering what happened to him, I'm surprised you don't have more sympathy."

"I have every sympathy." She stood up, fists clenched at her sides. "If I saw a mage turn into an abomination, I would still kill them, no matter how much I sympathized."

"Yet we're traveling to save an abomination."

"That's not my choice," she said. "Some things you can't come back from. Remember that your friend is a murderer." With that, she, too, stormed off. Rhys was left staring at the fire. Adrian had a point, of course. They all did. If he had connected Cole to the murders sooner, or reported him immediately . . . but he hadn't. It was done, and there was nothing he could change about it now.

Not far away, Evangeline looked up from cleaning her sword and gave him a dubious look. He wondered how much she had overheard. It probably didn't matter anymore.

They spent the next several days making good time on the southern roads, moving out of the Heartlands and into the Provinces. Gone were the verdant hills and farmlands. Instead, the vegetation clung to the rocks with a sort of desperation. Everything was muddy and brown, some parts of the road so flooded they needed to navigate carefully lest their mounts trip and fall. There were fewer travelers by far, and what few villages they passed were filled with mean-looking folk who appeared glad to see them go.

The tone of the group had changed considerably, as well. Adrian ignored Rhys, her cold indifference to him magnified by her amiable chatter with Wynne. She pressed the old woman for details about her past, details she wasn't about to receive now that Wynne was sober. That only made Adrian more determined, of course; by the second day, she was riding behind Wynne instead, the two of them arguing over the Circle. Rather, Adrian was arguing—Wynne was content mostly to listen, and responded only when the red-headed mage became too aggravated.

Evangeline, meanwhile, kept her eyes on the road. Every time she spotted more than a lone traveler she would hold up her hand to warn the others. They would then give whomever they spotted wide berth, or stop and wait until they passed. Considering everyone they saw seemed equally wary, Evangeline's caution wasn't without reason.

Once, when they were just to the west of the city of Montsimmard, the templar saw a group of men standing on a sharp bluff overlooking the road. Rough-looking men in leathers, perhaps even bandits. There was no way around, and too many hiding places amidst the rocks, so Evangeline hesitated to bring them through. The men, meanwhile, seemed satisfied to wait.

Fortune smiled on them when Imperial soldiers appeared. Adrian was the first one to spot the purple banners, and even Rhys felt cheered when well over a hundred men in armor marched toward them. They were led by a handful of mounted chevaliers, warriors in ornate silver armor with feathery plumes of gold and green fluttering from atop their helms. Even their mounts were adorned with fancy barding, some of which looked to be more for show than for actual protection. Regardless, the force appeared daunting. Whether they were present to safeguard the roads or not, the bandits atop the bluff quickly vanished.

Which was fortunate, as the Imperial soldiers neither slowed nor even looked their way. Rhys thought they looked grim-faced, as if they were marching off to war . . . but what war, he wondered? No answers were forthcoming. Evangeline guided the group off the road lest they get trampled, and as soon as the soldiers passed she led them swiftly past the bluff before the bandits got any clever ideas about returning.

For his part, Rhys was the odd man out now. No one wished to talk to him, and he wondered if he should regret telling them about Cole. Every now and again his eyes would wander to the road behind them, looking to see if there was any evidence of the young man. There was nothing. Why Cole would bother hiding himself when only Rhys could see him, he didn't really know.

Eventually, Evangeline noticed where he was looking.

"Your invisible friend is behind us, I assume?" It was the first time she'd said a word in two days, her tone laced with thinly veiled incredulity.

"I don't know. I don't see him."

"You don't find that odd?"

"He might not be following us anymore."

She stared at him a moment longer, her look speculative. Then she shook her head and turned away.

"You're trying to decide if I'm insane?" he asked.

"No," she said. "I'm trying to decide if I should do something. My duty compels me to act should I see a mage succumbing to corruption."

"And?"

She didn't respond. He wasn't certain if he should take that as a good sign or not. Considering he still had his head, he chose to take an optimistic view—but he still worried about Cole. Not knowing if the young man was still following was unnerving, as was the thought that he might come upon them when they least expected it. Such as at night. The thought made him shiver.

The land slowly grew drier as they moved into the Western Approach. How the area got its name, Rhys really couldn't imagine. There wasn't anything farther west to approach other than steppes crawling with monsters and forests so deep and dark that explorers never returned from them. The badlands wasn't a place that someone went *to*. At best, it was someplace you came *from*. Fled, more likely.

According to the texts Rhys had read, this area was the site of one of the great battles of the Second Blight. Hundreds and hundreds of years ago, the darkspawn had swarmed out of a great chasm and corrupted the land so severely it never quite recovered. The blood of too many men fell upon the sands here, trying to force those creatures back before they spilled across the entire world. For those men and women it must have felt like the skies had opened up and rained black death down upon them all.

The Approach had a strange sort of beauty to it even so. It was a desert, but not a warm desert with glowing yellow sand. It was a cold desert, mottled purple like an unhealed bruise. Rocky pillars jutted out of the sand like brittle, twisted bones; there was a sense that the howling winds had long covered everything else. Even so, it didn't seem forbidding and horrible . . . just stark, and perhaps even a little sad. It was as if the world mourned a mortal injury inflicted long ago.

"There," Wynne said. She pointed to a shape off in the distance, a tall tower of iron barely visible through the blowing sand.

"That's what passes for a path in these lands. As we reach each one, we should be able to see the next."

"And if we don't?" Evangeline asked dubiously.

"Then we wait until the wind dies down. You don't want to wander too far out into the sands. Not all of it is stable, and precious little is safe."

"Of that I have no doubt."

Adrian guarded her eyes against the wind, scowling. "Why would anyone even live in this Maker-forsaken place?"

"The fortress Adamant lies at the lip of the chasm," Wynne explained. "Once it belonged to the Grey Wardens, for they wished to ensure the darkspawn did not rise from its depths as they had during the Second Blight. Eventually the Wardens abandoned it, but some residents have lingered. Life can exist, even in lands such as this."

"And your friend?" Rhys asked her.

She frowned, refusing to look directly at him. "My friend's name is Pharamond. He lived . . . lives . . . at Adamant because the Veil is so very thin. It has helped with his experiments."

Now it was Evangeline's turn to be curious. "Experiments?"

"Pharamond is a Tranquil. He is engaged in research at the behest of the Chantry, I believe. Without their permission, I doubt a Tranquil would possess the curiosity to engage in such a thing."

"At the behest of the Chantry?"

"So I understand."

"Was he researching the Rite of Tranquility?" Rhys asked.

Wynne put up her hands. "I was never privy to the details. I only found out what happened to Pharamond when I visited the fortress a month ago. I was seeking aid for a friend, and instead I found another in even greater distress."

"You saw him? As an abomination, I mean?"

"I saw the fortress filled with demons, and sensed what had

become of Pharamond. I did not encounter him while I was there. If I had, there would have been little choice but to kill him."

"So instead you risk us all."

Wynne glared at him. "I would like to think, my dear, that I might do the same for you one day . . . or you for any other mage you found in a similar condition."

They proceeded into the badlands. According to Wynne, it wasn't a long trip to reach Adamant, though it could be lengthened if the winds became poor. To Rhys, trudging through the sand felt like it would take forever. He kept his head down, shielding his eyes, and tried not to let the slow pace of the horses get to him. If it weren't for the vague shape of the tower slowly becoming clearer before them, he'd swear they were riding around in circles.

At one point, Evangeline drew her sword. She pointed with it to a tall ridge that cut sharply across their path not far away, its rocky surface black as pitch and polished almost to a shine by the blowing sand. Rhys peered closely, but he couldn't see more than blurry figures moving about on top. They were too far away, and moments later they vanished out of sight entirely.

"Darkspawn," Wynne said.

Evangeline visibly shuddered. "Will they attack?"

"Not until it grows dark."

That sped them up, and they reached the first tower while there was still light in the sky. It was at least a hundred feet high, a monstrosity of rusted iron that had clearly been patched numerous times and yet still looked ready to fall over. Someone could clamber up the side fairly easily to reach the tiny bird's nest, although Rhys could only imagine what the winds would be like up there. The Orlesian flag fluttered up top—or at least he assumed that's what it was, as it was too tattered and faded to be identifiable.

Evangeline pushed them forward, claiming she wanted to reach the second tower before nightfall. No doubt she had the darkspawn in mind, and none of the others complained. The way the horses occasionally fidgeted and nickered, as if they sensed things out in the sands, made them all nervous.

Then the wind stopped all at once. It was almost as if someone had turned it off. Rhys had been huddled on his saddle, leaning into the wind with his head down, and just about fell off his horse. He looked up in surprise. "What happened?"

"The air grows still at night," Wynne said.

That was an understatement. There was still a faint breeze, and occasionally a gust would blow between the rocks, whipping up a dust devil that died as quickly as it began . . . but otherwise it was silent. The sun was going down now, setting the grey skies aflame with hues of amber and bronze.

Then he saw it. Off in the distance, beyond the rocky pillars, it looked as if the land was cracked in two. A jagged chasm, easily a mile across, extended in either direction as far as the eye could see. They had probably been near it for hours, but couldn't see it through all the blowing sand.

"What *is* that?" Adrian breathed behind him, her eyes as wide as his own.

"The Abyssal Rift," Wynne said. "It gets much larger as we head west."

"How deep is it?"

"Nobody knows. Some say it extends down into the Deep Roads, perhaps even farther than that. Fortunately Adamant is on this side of it."

"Come," Evangeline snapped, although she too stared toward the chasm in wonder. "We don't want to wait for those creatures to come out of hiding."

The next tower was now easily visible, a thin sliver several miles away. With the light quickly fading, it wouldn't be for long. They raced toward it, leaving a dust cloud in their wake. Rhys almost

worried someone's mount would trip, but by the time all light in
the sky faded to black they reached the tower.

Evangeline pulled up her horse, and paced around trying to
control the steed as she scanned behind them for signs of pursuit. Rhys watched, as well. Nothing. A curtain of shadow had
descended, and along with it a chill that crept through his robes.
It was going to be a cold night.

"We camp here," the templar said, although she seemed unconvinced.

Adrian slid off the horse, wincing and rubbing her backside as
she hit the ground. There was a fire pit next to the tower's base,
surrounded by a wall of piled rocks almost two feet high. Even
then, it was half-buried in sand. When she started picking at the
blackened pieces of wood within the pit to see if any were still
serviceable, Wynne waved her staff.

"We'll want to avoid a fire."

"But it's freezing!"

"Then prepare your spells for combat. We can do battle by firelight."

Adrian seemed less than thrilled by the notion, and tossed one
of the charcoal logs back into the fire pit. She rolled her eyes at
Rhys, and all he could do was smile and shrug. It seemed odd
anyone would create a fire pit where it was dangerous, but perhaps
most of the travelers who passed through the badlands did so in
armed groups. While a group of skilled mages and a templar might
be able to fight off darkspawn, he didn't relish the idea of finding
out just how many of them were out there.

The night grew colder by the hour. Rhys shivered at the bite on
his skin, his breath plumes of white quickly sucked away by the
dry air.

I should be back at the camp.

But he wasn't. He stood on the lip of the Abyssal Rift, as Wynne called it. The chasm was much closer than it had seemed, only a brisk ten-minute walk through the sand until suddenly he was standing on bare rock and staring into blackness.

He might have fallen in, had the sky not been alight with strange, shimmering ribbons of light. He'd never seen its like before—each one flowed like liquid into the next, then separated and multiplied or disappeared into nothing. It was a slow, majestic dance across the blank grey sky that transfixed him and offered the faintest illumination to the desert. Just enough to anoint the rocky pillars and the edges of the chasm with a silvery sheen.

He heard not a single sound. Rhys held out his hands over the chasm that yawned beneath him and drank in the stillness. What lay down there? He couldn't see a thing within but he could *feel* its depth. He imagined taking a single step off the lip and plunging down into that sea of shadow. It seemed like he could fall forever, swallowed by the peaceful silence until he was lost to eternity.

The thought was somehow both strangely attractive and terrifying *because* it was attractive. He was reminded all too clearly of Cole's words when the man spoke of drowning. Maybe it wasn't so hard to understand Cole's fear after all.

"Ser Evangeline is completely beside herself," a new voice said behind him.

He scowled as Wynne approached, but tried to control his annoyance at her intrusion on his solace. It was easy to pretend he was alone out here in this vast emptiness, that all his problems were a bad dream best forgotten, but it just wasn't so.

"Do none of you people sleep?" he mused.

"You snuck away when her back was turned. She would have come hunting for you herself if that didn't mean leaving Adrian and myself unguarded. I said I would look." Wynne had a blanket wrapped around her shoulders, but even so she still shivered in the cold and leaned heavily on her staff. Then her eyes widened in alarm as she realized just where he stood. "Rhys . . . what are you doing?"

"Freezing."

"No, what are you doing *there*?"

Rhys sighed, turning to stare down into the chasm again. There was a faint smell that wafted up from below, acrid and sharp like brimstone but not entirely unpleasant. Faintly, he wondered if the edge could crumble under his weight. The jet-black rock looked worn from the blowing sands, maybe weak from the passing ages, but it felt solid under his feet.

"Just admiring the view. I . . . couldn't sleep." He stepped away, though Wynne hardly seemed relieved. She clutched her blanket close, staring at him in concern, and for a long moment he stood there and accepted her scrutiny in silence. "Are you angry at me?" he finally asked.

She let out a slow and weary sigh. Looking around, she spotted a large rock nearby and ambled over to sit on it. "Angry," she repeated uncertainly.

"When I told you about Cole . . ."

"I'm not angry about that."

"Then what?"

She thought about it. "You need to be more careful, Rhys. I barely know you, and yet I see you careering toward a terrible end. What do you think will happen?"

"I don't really know."

"Yes, you do," she snapped, growing irate. "If I had not intervened, you would be Tranquil. This Cole . . . whatever he is, the fact that you've continued to associate with him is what has drawn you into this mess. You know what he's done."

"Yes, but I don't think he's in his right mind. He needs help."

"*You* need help. You need to protect yourself, now more than ever."

"I can't stand by and do nothing."

"That's exactly what you should do." She paused, shaking her head. "But here I am, arguing with you again. I suppose I should have more sympathy for anyone with a penchant for lost causes."

Rhys couldn't help but grin. Perhaps he was partly to blame for her anger that night. He'd questioned her willingness to help a friend, despite the risks, and this after earlier accusing her of being heartless. Both those things couldn't be true. In fact, despite all her protests to the contrary, she did seem to care about his welfare. She may not be the kind old woman he met so many years ago, but that person wasn't gone entirely.

He was about to say so when he heard a faint whistling sound. Then something thudded into his chest. He looked down to see it was an arrow, a black and wicked-looking thing impossibly protruding out of him.

That can't be right, can it?

"Rhys!" Wynne cried, leaping up from the rock.

The darkspawn came out of nowhere. The pale creatures bared their fangs and hissed, raising crude swords over their heads as they charged. Rhys stared at them in stunned disbelief—he'd known they were out in the desert, but to see them up close seemed strangely surreal. He stared at the strange blackness that bled out of their eyes and mouths, the glassy hatred in their eyes. Time moved at a snail's pace.

Wynne raised her white staff; it pulsed with power, sending out a brilliant flash that pulled Rhys out of his stupor and made the darkspawn reel back in pain. The arrow still stuck in his chest, and only now was he beginning to feel it—like a strange tightness that grew more intense by the second. It made him gasp as it overcame his shock, and when he tried to move he succeeded only in stumbling to his knees. His every movement seemed too slow, like he was stuck in quicksand.

Wynne spun the staff around her, and suddenly a great storm of electricity erupted around them. Arcs of it raced through the air, leaping from stone to stone and from darkspawn to darkspawn. The thunder threatened to make his ears explode.

He watched as one of the creatures was hit dead-on by a bolt, and it screamed in agony as the power cooked it from within. A darkspawn roared in fury and raced at Wynne, and the old mage spun around again. She held a hand out in front of her and the creature suddenly froze solid, encased in a block of solid ice, before it finally shattered into a thousand pieces.

Another ran at her from behind. Rhys began to call out a warning, but there was no time for her to react. He summoned mana from within, ignoring the throbbing pain it caused where the arrow still lodged in his chest, and *pushed*. A wave of force surged out of his hands and slammed into the darkspawn. It was lifted off its feet and thrown back into the chasm, the earsplitting screech of terror as it fell drowned out by the thunder.

Something hard slammed into the back of his head. He scrambled forward, trying to get away from whatever was attacking him. The flashes of lightning were too bright, too disorienting for him to see properly.

His attacker grabbed his shoulder from behind. Sharp talons dug into his flesh, and he screamed. Reacting instantly, Wynne held out her staff; a white-hot beam of energy lanced forth. Rhys felt rather than saw it strike the darkspawn behind him, and heard its grunt of pain.

He wrested free, falling to the ground. The arrow shaft cracked under his weight, and a new jolt of pain shot through him. Nausea filled him, and his vision swam.

How many were there? The sound of thunder suddenly seemed so distant, like he was hearing it through a tube. . . . He caught a glimpse of Wynne's blue robes, her boots in front of his eyes. He saw the lightning performing its blinding dance. He heard another of the creatures scream as it was struck by a magical blast. A pool of black darkspawn blood soaked the sands by his hands, the sickly sweet smell assaulting his senses.

Rhys tried to summon more of his magic. He closed his eyes and trembled from the concentration; he wasn't going to let Wynne fight alone. But the mana wouldn't come, the pain was too severe.

"Rhys, get up!" He heard Wynne shouting in his ear, but he couldn't quite place where she was. "There are more coming!"

Oblivion reached up and dragged him down into its blissful embrace.

9

Evangeline smiled as she watched Rhys stir on his horse. The way he blinked in confusion, not quite comprehending where he was or why he was moving, was a little amusing. Considering all he'd put them through the previous night, she couldn't help but think he was due a little discomfort.

Adrian sat behind him, and grabbed him before he slid off. He had a heavy cloak wrapped around him to keep him warm, and the red-haired mage had been more or less supporting him since they left camp. Evangeline didn't want to risk waiting until he woke to get underway. If it took too long, after all, they might end up spending another night under that tower—and draw another attack.

"Where am I?" Rhys rasped.

"On a horse."

He stared at her, not realizing she was joking, and then finally offered a weak grin. "All right, yes, that explains the smell—but what about the darkspawn? I remember . . ."

Wynne pulled up beside them. The old mage looked pale and drawn, and for good reason. Evangeline couldn't begin to imagine the kind of power she had tapped. She'd lit up the badlands with her magic, and when Evangeline had gone running she half expected to find the entire side of the chasm crumbled into its depths.

"I healed you, of course," Wynne said.

"But how did we even survive?"

"You almost didn't. If Ser Evangeline and Adrian hadn't ar-rived in time . . ."

He sighed dejectedly. "I shouldn't have wandered off."

"I was going to say that," Evangeline said. When he shot her a guilty look, she chuckled. "I would be angrier, but it seems you lived. We could easily have been attacked at the camp. Perhaps the lure of easy prey drew them off?"

He looked back at Adrian, grinning crookedly. "You hear that? I'm a hero!"

"You woke me up," she grumped.

"Rhys," Evangeline said, her tone now serious.

"Yes?"

"Don't do that again." When his eyebrows shot up, she added a little more sternly: "Remember that you're still a mage of the Circle. You wander off once more and I'll treat you as an apostate."

He made no comment.

The winds had resumed shortly before the sun rose, or what passed for sun in these blasted lands. The grey haze in the sky was light enough to navigate by, and that would have to do. Just as Wynne claimed, the chasm became wider as they traveled west, and the other side could no longer be seen. Now it seemed less like a massive crack and more like the very edge of the world.

Evangeline found these lands cold and uninviting, and not for the first time since they arrived she wondered what she was doing here. Following orders, of course, but how she was expected to do that when she couldn't even keep track of one mage's whereabouts unsettled her. She had a bad feeling regarding what was to come, but kept her thoughts to herself.

Adamant fortress was slowly coming into view, its vague outline discernible through the blowing sand. It wasn't large but, through sturdiness and defensibility, had clearly earned its name.

Tall walls of dark jetstone, and a massive gate with archer towers on either side. It perched almost precariously on the edge of the chasm, like a bird of prey waiting to swoop down upon its victim. Any attack against the place could only come from one direction—unless it came out of the chasm itself, of course, and considering its history, that wasn't implausible.

As they drew closer, the fortress took on a decidedly sinister air. It was completely silent, for one. The towers were unmanned, and the gate stood half-open. A black haze wafted up from the court-yard, as if from a fire that had only recently been extinguished. Evangeline could smell something as well—even with the wind and the sand, the stench of carrion was unmistakable.

Her horse shied away and fought against direction; she strug-gled to maintain control until she realized what it was avoiding: bodies, half-buried in the sand. There were dozens of them, fan-ning out in all directions from the open gate, now little more than suspicious mounds that only hinted at what lay beneath: an arm, a hand, the edge of a sword . . . all that remained to tell they were riding through a graveyard.

Wynne's lips thinned into a grim frown. "These were the in-habitants of the fortress," she explained. "When we arrived, they rushed out to attack us. Mindless corpses, possessed by demons."

Evangeline shuddered. She steered well clear, trying not to notice the wisps of blond hair on one of the exposed heads, now fluttering in the wind. A young woman in her prime, desiccated and taken by the badlands. If she was dead when she'd attacked, she was even more so now.

"We?" Rhys asked.

"I didn't come here alone."

Adrian pointed down at the ground. "Are they still here? There's a lot of tracks, and they can't be that old." She was right. The sand was disturbed in many places near the gate, and with the wind blowing as it was, it wouldn't take long for such tracks to be covered. Numerous horses had arrived here, a day ago or perhaps less.

Wynne appeared suspicious. "This is too many. Someone else is here."

"There." Rhys pointed off into the distance with his staff.

A group of twenty men on horseback emerged from the swirling winds, slowly riding around the far edge of the fortress walls. They were in heavy armor, and it took a moment of squinting before Evangeline realized what they were: templars.

"Friends of yours?" Rhys asked.

"I have no idea why they're here." She cautioned the others to remain behind and urged her mount forward. Why would there be templars here, of all places? Had one of the other towers heard about the abomination? Were they too late? It didn't seem likely—if the templars had already dealt with the threat, they should be long gone.

As Evangeline drew within range, the templar at the head of the group waved at her. She scowled as she realized she knew him: Arnaud, one of the lieutenants the Lord Seeker had brought with him when he assumed command of the tower. The man was far too handsome and arrogant, and clearly assumed he would be taking her position in the tower before long. Perhaps he was right. Either way, she didn't care for his superior air, and had made certain to speak to him as little as possible.

"Ser Evangeline!" he called out. "You finally arrive!"

She pulled her horse to a halt and appraised Arnaud's group. They were templars from the White Spire, every last one. "Indeed," she said to him, with a little more frost in her tone than she'd intended. "I'm curious, however, as to why you're here to greet us."

"We were sent by the Lord Seeker, of course."

"Oh?"

He glanced to the mages waiting at the gate behind her. "As I understand it, you may need some . . . assistance. If things don't go as well as you hope."

"I hope for nothing. I'm here to keep Enchanter Wynne safe for the duration of her mission, one agreed to by the Divine. Should she discover something that will prove harmful, I will deal with it then."

"And that is why we're here. To help you deal with it."

She bristled at the idea. It sounded almost as if the Lord Seeker *expected* Wynne to find something harmful. Did he know more than he let on, or was he merely being cautious? Either way, she wasn't about to push things in a direction they didn't need to go. "Then let's hope your help is not required," she told him. She pulled her horse around and began riding back to the gate. "Stay here until we return."

"And if you don't?" he shouted after her.

She didn't respond. If she didn't return, after all, then the matter would be out of her hands . . . and Arnaud would have to figure out a way to impress the Lord Seeker on his own. When she got back to the mages, they looked at her expectantly. "They come from the White Spire," she told them. "To help."

Adrian looked dubious. "Are they coming in with us?"

"No. They're staying out here."

She hoped.

The gate was open just enough for their horses to ride through. Evangeline noticed the amount of sand that had accumulated just within—the gate would take an incredible effort to close again, if anyone cared to reoccupy the fortress once their task was done.

From what they saw in the courtyard, that idea seemed unlikely. The keep itself looked intact, the doors at the top of the stairs still closed, but everything else was a ruin. A battle had been fought here. The buildings that stood inside the walls had been burned to the ground, their charred remains no longer providing any clue as to what they had once been. Scorch marks were everywhere, evidence of magical combat, and the cobblestones around the shattered cistern in the middle of the courtyard were black and covered in ash.

Evangeline noticed a pile of corpses, all of which had been recently burned. They were the source of the smoke they'd seen from afar. Everything else was long cold.

The only thing that seemed out of place was the statue that stood at the base of the stairs. It seemed crudely built, about seven feet tall and made of bulky stone and crystals—an odd choice for a statue, truly, and not at all like the fine sculptures she would expect to see in an Orlesian castle.

Then the statue moved. Its head swiveled around to face them, eye sockets glowing malevolently. "Watch out!" she cried, instantly drawing her sword.

"Hold!" Wynne warned.

Evangeline watched, stunned, as the old mage slid off her horse and walked toward the statue. Rhys jumped down and made to grab her, but Wynne merely shrugged him off and continued on.

"The elderly mage took its time returning," the statue complained. Its voice was booming and gravelly, sounding like rocks grating together.

"I told you to come with me, didn't I?"

"And allow the creature within to flee? Perish the thought." It gestured to the pile of burned corpses. "I spent my time cleaning. Like a servant. What a pleasure it is to once again perform dull errands at the behest of a mage."

Wynne chuckled lightly, and then looked back as she noticed the others gaping at her. "This is Shale," she said, indicating the statue. "She was with me when I arrived. I was, in fact, hoping Pharamond might be able to help her . . . condition."

"Little chance of that now," it griped.

"I'm truly sorry, Shale."

"Is that . . . a golem?" Adrian asked.

"Did you say *she*?" Rhys said. "It doesn't look female."

The statue seemed almost indignant. "I most certainly am not!"

Wynne sighed. "She is a golem, yes. Shale was with us when we fought against the darkspawn in Ferelden. We discovered she has the soul of a dwarven warrior placed into this stone body long ago, and she's been trying to regain her living form ever since." She patted the statue on its big arm sympathetically. "We've had little success."

It appeared unmoved. "The advantages of a flesh body seem dubious at best."

Evangeline dismounted, keeping an eye on the golem. She'd heard of such creatures—constructs made by the ancient dwarves, an art they'd since lost. Since golems didn't age, there were still many to be found, although she understood most were quite mad. She'd certainly never heard of one *talking* before. It made her suspicious, not least because Wynne had failed to mention it earlier.

"Is it tame?" she asked.

The golem turned to look at her directly, its eyes flashing with annoyance. "Perhaps the insolent templar would enjoy being crushed into pulp and discovering the answer for itself?"

"That's not necessary, Shale," Wynne said. She turned to study the doors to the keep, squinting her eyes in concentration. They looked solid to Evangeline. If they were locked, they'd have a difficult time gaining entry. "Do you sense anything, Rhys?"

Rhys closed his eyes. "There's definitely a demon within. Maybe more than one. The Veil is even thinner here than at the White Spire."

She nodded. "Would you prefer to wait out here, Ser Evangeline?"

"I prefer to stay by your side."

"As you wish." She looked expectantly at the golem. It sighed, and stormed up the stairs to the doors, each one of its heavy footfalls *thooming* loudly in the courtyard. Rather than trying the handles, it sank its thick fingers directly into the wood. The doors let out an excruciating groan as iron reinforcements twisted. Finally, with a great heave, the golem ripped the doors off their hinges, large chunks of wood and metal hurtling out into the courtyard.

Evangeline dove out of the way, just barely avoiding getting struck by one of the larger pieces. "Are you mad?" she cried.

The golem looked back, and shrugged. "It is agile enough."

Nobody was hurt, at least. The others seemed less perturbed than Evangeline, and more interested in the now-vacant doorway into the keep. Wynne walked boldly inside, and everyone else quickly followed. Evangeline had no choice but to do likewise.

The keep was dark, and cold—colder than it had any right to be, even with the building being made of stone. Even worse, what little light came through the doorway offered a nightmare: an entry chamber splattered with dried blood and gore. It covered the floors, it was smeared across the walls . . . the smell of it was musty, thick. There were no bodies, but in the distant shadows she could hear things moving. Large things, dragging themselves across the ground. Her imagination conjured too many images.

Wynne stamped her white staff on the ground; a ringing sound echoed as it began to glow. The shadows seemed to recoil from the light, revealing a grand staircase and passages leading off, but it didn't make Evangeline feel less uneasy. She felt like an intruder. Foreboding slithered across her skin like a cold eel.

"There's writing on the wall," Adrian said in a hushed voice.

Words were smeared in blood right beside the doorway. Most of them were unintelligible gibberish, but one sentence was clear: "WE WANT OUT."

Evangeline frowned. "The doors were barred from the inside, weren't they? If they wanted out, couldn't they have . . . left?" She immediately regretted the volume of her voice as it echoed throughout the hall, and tried not to imagine who "they" might be. More possessed corpses, or something worse?

"They weren't barred," Shale grunted, "they were sealed."

"How?"

"Its guess is as good as mine."

Rhys stepped away from the writing, looking distinctly queasy. Evangeline felt much the same. "Where do we go?" she asked. "Up the stairs?"

Wynne shook her head. "Down. Adamant is built into the side of the chasm. This part of the keep is merely the living quarters. Pharamond's laboratory lies below."

"Down," Rhys repeated. He gave himself a shake, as if throwing off something unpleasant. "Of course it would be down, wouldn't it? One day I'd like to find a demon that enjoys pleasant, well-lit surroundings."

"Not today."

"The old mage is still eager to find its friend?" Shale asked.

"Yes." Wynne's answer was not confident.

They stood there in the darkness, the winds whistling outside the doorway with a vengeance. There was nothing further to say. They had best get started.

Rhys had told Cole to go back to the tower, and there had been a moment when Cole considered it. He'd watched from the shadows as their horses rode out of the village, and he thought about what Rhys had said. He could retrace his steps, find the proper road, and go all the way back to that huge and terrifying city on his own. It could be an adventure.

But then he felt lonely. He never knew that being out in the world, surrounded by a multitude of strangers, would make him feel more invisible than ever. In a way, going back to the tower would be a comfort. A place he knew, and safe. But Rhys wouldn't be there. Rhys would be in danger, and he might never come back. Cole would be alone forever. That thought drove him forward.

So he followed them. For days he kept as far behind them as he dared, worried that Rhys would notice and force him to leave. The man kept looking back from his horse, searching, and each time he did, Cole flinched. He kept off the road and in the brush as much as he dared, but then a thought began to hit him: What if Rhys *couldn't* see him?

What if he was invisible to Rhys now, as well?

That fear began to gnaw on him, worming its way into the pit of his stomach and sitting there like cold lead. He woke up each morning, covered in dew and shivering, gripped by the immediate fear that Rhys and the others had already left their camp. He raced to find them, his heart pounding, until finally he saw them sleeping. Only then did he breathe a sigh of relief, even if part of him desperately wanted to wake Rhys up. Just to talk to him. Just to hear another voice.

Sometimes when he followed the group, he walked in the middle of the road, hoping that Rhys would look back and do *something*. But it didn't happen. They were often so far ahead they were little more than a speck in the distance, and each time they disappeared around a hillside he started to worry. What if they turned off the road and he didn't notice? What if he became lost out here for good?

And then the land changed. It became dry, and then nothing more than wind and purple sand. It was a strange desolation, as if the entire world had died and just shriveled away. The wind was a lonely howl that cried of pain and neglect; the sadness of it tugged at Cole's heart. He never imagined such a place could exist, or why anyone would want to go there.

The one benefit was that Rhys and the others became easier to follow. The horses moved more slowly, and even though he couldn't see them through all the swirling sand, they left a trail for him. It didn't last long in the wind, but it lasted long enough.

There were creatures in that land. Dark things that lurked in the corners. Cole couldn't see them, and didn't want to. He worried that they could see him, however. That first night was a horror, spent hiding in a rocky crevasse and shivering from the cold. The darkness was so total it threatened to sweep him away.

And worse, there was the music. He didn't know what it was, but it seemed to come from far, far off. It called to him, but not in a pleasant way—it had an urgency that sped his heart and made his blood burn. The dark creatures, the lurkers, they listened to it. He didn't know how he knew that, but he could *feel* them out there, craning their necks, raising taloned hands toward that call.

He put his head between his knees and covered his ears. When the other sounds started, the sounds of magic and fighting, he trembled. Somewhere in the distance he heard Rhys shout in pain, but Cole remained where he was. He felt like a coward. The darkness outside of his hiding place was too daunting. The creatures were everywhere. If he could have run back to the tower right then, he would have.

Sometime during that night, exhaustion overcame him. It wasn't sleep. It was a torment of strange dreams. Memories stirred in him, like old wounds ripping open and spewing forth rot. He saw faces, but didn't know why they terrified him. He was hiding, but it wasn't between two rocks . . . it was somewhere else, somewhere dark and small that lay in the distant past. He wanted nothing more than to get out. And run.

And then he woke. The music reached a tendril down into the dark waters he floundered in and dragged him up into the light. The winds had begun again, and rather than being immediately worried about what had become of Rhys, his only thought was *I am alive*. He felt relieved . . . and utterly alone.

Cole rose from the rocks, stiff and caked in grit . . . and froze.

One of those creatures was standing not ten feet away. It looked like a man, but wasn't. It was a man who had been eaten away by something evil inside, eaten until the darkness oozed out and spat upon the world. And it reacted. It spun around, staring at Cole with terrifying glassy eyes, a window into its tormented existence.

Of all the things he would want to see him, this wasn't one.

And then, ever so slowly, the creature's gaze shifted. It wasn't looking at Cole after all . . . or, rather, it didn't see him. It *smelled* him.

It sniffed, and then let out a ragged hiss. It took a step toward the rocks where Cole stood. He inched his hands toward the dagger on his belt. He didn't want to draw it. Yet. One more step and he would have no choice. And then . . . then the other creatures would come. They would know.

But the music saved him again. It swelled suddenly, just as the wind did, and the creature's gaze moved upward. Sunlight managed to worm its way through the grey clouds, just for a moment, and the creature recoiled as if in pain. It scrambled up the rocks and away . . . and within moments it was gone.

It hadn't been easy to discover which way Rhys and the others went. Cole found the little camp at the base of the metal tower, a spike jutting out of the sand like a skeletal finger that beckoned to him from afar, but the wind had already erased their trail. What little he could find showed there had been all sorts of movement around there, perhaps the previous night. Cole felt utterly helpless.

And then he did the only thing he could: he followed the chasm. It was a wound in the side of the world. Long ago, something had split the ground apart and let out something dark, something that lingered like the smoke after a fire. The sight of the chasm left him awestruck, dwarfed by its immensity, and he felt nervous being so close to it. But he had no other choice—Rhys had been heading in this direction so far; Cole had to assume he would continue on.

And that's when he found the castle that perched on the very edge of the chasm. There were templars outside on horses, waiting around and laughing at jokes as they drank from canteens. He recognized some of them. Big Nose was there. Why, he had no idea. They hadn't come with Rhys, after all.

He ignored them, and picked his way gingerly through the rubble in the courtyard. He didn't like this place. There was a . . . presence here. The music had withered away to nothing during the day, but now a whisper had replaced it. It spoke words in his ear, too faint to be discerned but enough to set his nerves on edge. Death filled this place up, and it was more than just the pile of burnt corpses he didn't want to see. Terror was imprinted on the stones, as clear as if written there yesterday.

Why would Rhys come here?

There were horses in the courtyard, which meant Rhys had gone into the keep—but how long ago? Cole entered, shuddering as he passed through the doorway. The whispers were worse inside. They told him to be afraid, and he was.

Worse, there was no trail to follow in here, either. No voices, no sounds of footsteps, nothing. Cole waited, rubbing his arms briskly to warm them up.

"Rhys!" he called out.

The echoes answered back: *Rhys! . . . Rhys!*

"Are you here? It's Cole!"

Cole! . . . Cole!

Nothing.

He kept hoping someone would walk into the entry chamber, anyone he could then follow farther within. What he didn't want to do was go exploring on his own. But he was left with no choice, wasn't he? Up? Down? One of the side passages?

He chose up. Down seemed too . . . he would only go down those dark stairs if he truly had to.

The stairs were littered with strange things, like some animal had been busy strewing them about: bloody pieces of clothing, broken furniture, a child's doll. People had lived here. This castle was someone's home, or had been.

For over an hour he roamed the halls of the upper floors. There were bedrooms, or at least they might have once been such. The beds were demolished, the furniture ripped apart. Blood was everywhere, but not a single body. Everything was still. What few windows existed were all barred, and the faint light they admitted did little more than show thick clouds of dust hanging in the air. Everything smelled stale, and strangely meaty.

Cole's heart began to pound. What if Rhys wasn't here after all? He called out several more times, but still there was no response. What if Rhys couldn't hear him? Cole could be fading away, even now, just as he'd always feared.

He stopped in a dark hallway and leaned against a wall, sweat slowly pouring down his face. He felt like he was burning up, despite the chill. What was he going to do? He'd been around and around these abandoned rooms, but whoever had been here was long dead or long gone.

And then he paused.

There was someone nearby. He knew, in the same way he knew when the templars brought someone to the tower—someone who would see him.

Slowly he stepped away from the wall and crouched down low, drawing the dagger from his belt. His senses felt alive, and he reached out through the darkness to find where this person was hiding. *Almost. Almost. . . .*

There.

Cole moved through the darkness. He could hear their heart beating, like an insistent lure drawing him close. He could *feel* their despair. In the silence it was like a clarion call. How could he not have heard it sooner?

Up the stairs again to the top level of the keep. Down a dark hall almost devoid of litter and blood. Whatever had happened barely touched this place. There was dried blood on the wall, a few smears on the floor . . . but some of the rooms were almost intact. One bedroom he passed looked like it might have been a nursery, a carved wooden crib just waiting patiently for its babe to return.

And then he was there. Some kind of sitting room, maybe. He'd never seen a room like this in the White Spire, so he had nothing against which to compare it. Someone wealthy might have lived here, once. There was a fancy-looking chair with a red leather cushion, a cold fireplace, a massive bookshelf that covered all of one wall . . . all of it untouched. Even the books were still where they were supposed to be.

But someone had died here. A rumpled rug covered in patterns of red and gold lay in the center of the room, and in the middle of it was a large and ugly pool of blood. Black and dry. They had fought hard, he thought—there were long splatters of blood along the wall nearby, and a large splash on the bookshelf. The smear leading from the rug said they'd been dragged out.

Another door led beyond, but that didn't matter. The person he sensed was in here. He crept around the room, trying to listen. The faint buzzing of flies, nothing more. But they were *here*. He knew it.

Suddenly Cole leapt at the rug and threw it back. He was rewarded with the sight of a wooden trapdoor hidden beneath. It, too, was stained with blood . . . but someone was beyond. He knelt down and pulled it open, its hinges creaking loudly.

A dark cubbyhole was revealed, and a figure cried out in fear and cowered. It was a young woman, and she tried to squirm out from under the trapdoor's opening—unsuccessfully. He stared at her: skin stretched thin over her bones and black hair wild from fear. Homely, dressed in only a dirty smock. Covered in filth from head to toe. Surrounding her was evidence she'd been in there for some time: bits of dried food, a stained blanket, and the overpowering stench of urine.

He'd seen people who never slept, kept in the tower's dungeon until their minds reached the breaking point. She was like that. She trembled as much from exhaustion as she did from fear.

And she could see him. The sense of relief he felt was palpable.

It was some time before she peeked out from under her hands. Her eyes rapidly darted to his dagger and then back to his face. "Are you . . . going to kill me?" she asked, her voice barely a whisper.

"Do you want me to kill you?"

She didn't answer.

"I can take this all away, if you like. I can make it quick."

She stared into his eyes; inch by inch, her trembling eased. There was nothing but silence between them, and he realized she understood. She knew what he offered her: a way out of the pain and the fear. But she couldn't bring herself to say the words.

Cole ran his thumb along the edge of his blade. She couldn't move. He was the guardian on the precipice between life and death, no one else. Already he felt that familiar stirring inside him, that old fear demanding he fight to stay in this world. *Never give up,* it said. *Don't fade away into the night.*

But what would Rhys say?

He would say that Cole was mad, that he shouldn't listen to that stirring. That killing someone didn't help him, or make him more real. But was that true? Looking down at this girl, knowing what she had been through—would it be any better to leave her as she was? Every one of those people he found in the tower had agreed to release, in their way. He struggled with the idea, turning it over and over in his head.

"I'm not going to kill you," he finally said.

The young woman began to weep. At first he thought it must

have been the wrong choice, but then he realized her tears were of relief and nothing more. She covered her face and cried so hard she trembled. Cole felt sad for her, and decided it was best if he left her alone. He turned away.

"No!" she cried. Then, more hesitantly: "Please . . . don't go."

He stopped. She continued to stare at him, but still didn't move from the hole.

"Have you seen Rhys?" he asked.

She looked confused. "I don't know who that is."

"How long have you been in there?"

"I . . . go out sometimes, to get food. But I have to hide at night."

"Why?"

Her eyes became dark. "Because they come for you at night."

So there were others. Somewhere. Cole knew where, of course: down. The place he didn't want to go, but would have to now. He got up to leave.

"Please!" she shouted, then covered her mouth in horror at her volume. Slowly she sat up in the cubbyhole, poking her head over the edge and staring around at the room with wide eyes. Her breathing was rapid and loud.

He waited, and eventually she crept out onto the floor, alert for the slightest sound. When he began to move toward the doorway, she ran after him and clung to his shoulder. Her nails bit into his arm. "Where are you going?" she begged.

"I have to find Rhys."

"They'll kill you!"

Cole couldn't think of a good response for that. If whomever she spoke of was going to kill him . . . then they were going to kill Rhys, too. That worried him. What if Rhys was already dead? His only friend gone, and he'd come all this way and not even been able to protect him. Knight-Captain might have killed him, too. Maybe that's why all the templars were here.

Her face was inches away from his own. It seemed like she would crawl under his skin if she could, but he tried not to mind. It had . . . been so long since anyone had touched him. He couldn't even remember the last time. It felt good. Like he was real. It was even worth the smell.

"Do you have a name?" she asked him quietly.

"Cole."

"I am Dabrissa."

He tried to remember what people did when they met each other. Shake hands? But she was already touching him. So he shrugged awkwardly. "Do you want to leave, Dabrissa?"

"I can't. The keep is sealed."

"But the door is open."

The girl stepped away from him, staring at him suspiciously. Then she bolted past him out into the hall. Cole remained there for a moment, unsure if he should follow—but where else did he have to go? He found her at the top of the stairs, looking down at the main floor where the wide-open entryway was plain to see.

"See?" he said.

Dabrissa shook her head in disbelief. "There . . . was so much noise. I thought, *Something is happening! I must hide!* But I could have left. I could have . . ." More tears welled up in her eyes; she buried her face in her hands.

Cole reached out and awkwardly patted her on the shoulder. It seemed like a useless, impotent gesture. He had no idea how to comfort someone, nor was he certain why he felt the need to. "There are men outside, on horses." He thought about it for a moment. "They might help you. I don't know." He had his doubts. When had the templars ever helped anyone? She wasn't a mage, but he wasn't sure that even mattered.

Still, the news seemed to cheer her up. "Will you come with me?"

"No. I have to find Rhys."

She nodded, accepting his mission even if she didn't understand it. She began to move toward the doorway, but before she went more than a couple of steps she stopped and turned toward him. "You saved me." She smiled. It was a shy smile, but full of gratitude. "I will remember you forever."

"No. You won't."

He didn't look at her, and eventually he heard her walk down the stairs. Two tentative steps at first, and then she fled out the door as fast as her legs would carry her. And she didn't come back.

He touched his shoulder where she had clung to him, feeling the first whispers of his emptiness return. If he was going to find Rhys, he had best get underway. The dark depths of the keep beckoned.

10

"At least we're off those stupid horses."

The cramped passages swallowed Adrian's voice. Gone were the echoes, replaced by a suffocating sense of claustrophobia the farther they descended. Rhys glanced at Adrian, and saw she was nervous and pale. She jumped at nearly every shadow cast by Wynne's glowing staff.

"It's all right," he whispered to her. "Calm down."

"No, it's not all right. What are we *doing* here?"

"You volunteered, remember?" He gave her his best grin.

It didn't help. "Don't remind me."

Shale turned to stare at them, the light in the pits of its eyes glowing red. "Perhaps the two mages wish to cease their nattering, lest they draw unwanted attention? I care not, but soft and fleshy creatures should take greater care for their innards."

Rhys was tempted to point out that the golem's heavy footfalls more or less announced their presence already. Even attempting to move quietly, it was a constant litany of *thoom thoom thoom*. The golem seemed in no mood for such a reminder, however . . . if a walking statue could be said to have a "mood." Rhys was reminded of the solemn templar statues in the mage commons, and wondered what they might be like if they suddenly got up and started walking around.

Somehow he doubted they would be nearly as sassy.

Evangeline took point, warily keeping her sword at the ready.

It was for good reason: the sounds they'd heard earlier were louder now. Things were moving, but the way the passages worked he could never tell how far away they were. Sometimes it seemed as if they'd be around the next turn, or just behind him. It was unnerving.

After coming down the long stairs, they first passed through what might have been an antechamber. It was empty save for the blood that covered the floor and walls. Scraps of bloody cloth, bits of jewelry. It smelled like a charnel house. Still no bodies, however.

"I'll give them this," he muttered. "These people really know how to redecorate."

"It's very welcoming," Evangeline agreed humorlessly.

"Perhaps the White Spire should consider a similar theme?"

"Where would we get all the blood?"

"With a tower full of mages? That's not a serious question."

"True."

Adrian glared at him incredulously. He couldn't tell whether it was because he was joking, or because he was joking with Evangeline. Knowing her, it was probably both. Rhys clammed up, but it only made him more nervous. The silence, punctuated by those distant slithering sounds, was almost unbearable. He would have screamed until something showed its face, just to get it over with, if he thought that might help. Somehow he doubted it.

Suddenly there were more stairs, and branching hallways leading out from the bottom landing. Wynne confidently steered the group in the right direction: right, then left. Down a flight of stairs, then around a corner. It was dizzying . . . if Rhys had to find his way back, he wasn't sure he could manage. The place was so much larger than he'd imagined.

"How many people lived here, anyhow?"

"Several hundred, as I recall," Wynne answered.

"But there's room for a thousand."

"As I said, this was once home to the Grey Wardens. At the height of the Second Blight they very likely had more than a thousand men . . . and griffons."

That perked Evangeline's interest. "Griffons?"

"Of course. The old weyrs opened onto the chasm. They're sealed up now, but I understand they're still down there. Either way, this place has stood mostly empty for centuries."

"But if there were hundreds of people here . . ."

The thought was left unanswered. There had been, at best, two dozen bodies in the courtyard. That left a lot of people unaccounted for. All the blood left little to the imagination as to what had become of them, but how had they died? And where were their bodies?

They proceeded through several more rooms, once used for storage. The crates looked as if they'd been torn apart by animals, leaving a mix of grain and foodstuffs strewn about. It was everywhere, some of it mixed with blood, much of it rotting. Flies filled the room like a cloud.

And there was noise coming from the room beyond. It was pitch black there, only the threshold lit by Wynne's staff . . . but they could see the hint of movement. He heard a low droning, and the sound of many things shifting about. Hundreds of things.

Evangeline tensed, staring into the darkness. "Arm yourselves," she whispered.

Rhys hoped it wasn't as bad as it sounded, but that seemed unlikely. He willed his staff to come to life, slowly channeling magic until it crackled with white energy. Adrian did the same. He saw the sweat pouring down her brow.

Wynne quietly cast a spell, moving her hands in arcane patterns until gossamer streams of energy appeared and settled onto each of them. His skin tingled, and he could feel the protection her magic was offering. "Shale." She motioned to the golem. "You go first. Ser Evangeline will be right behind you."

"Flesh creatures are so easily pulverized," it agreed. Clenching its huge stone fists, Shale charged into the room. The others followed right on its heels, Wynne causing her staff to flare so brightly that Rhys at first recoiled. He covered his eyes, and had to blink to get his vision back.

As soon as he did, he wished it would go away again.

The room might once have been a barracks of some kind, but now it had been turned into a gruesome lair. In the glaring light, he could see a huge crowd of people . . . or what had once been people. Now they were twisted creatures, hunched down and feasting on human remains. They crawled over piles of bones and even each other like primitive beasts, fighting over scraps. Wallowing in the gore. Their skin was covered in blood and filth, little more than rags remaining of whatever clothes they'd once worn.

And their eyes. As they spun around to stare at the intruders, their eyes shone like malevolent beacons. It was as if some dark force spilled out from inside them. As they bared sharp and bloody teeth in angry hisses, they took on a decidedly demonic appearance.

Rhys had never been so terrified in his life.

"Beware!" Evangeline cried. She raced forward as the nearest creatures rushed at her. The first she cleaved nearly in half with her sword, but the others leapt on her and almost bore her down. She threw them off with a great heave. One immediately sprang back up, hissing loudly, and she took off his head.

Shale was already ahead of her. The golem charged forward, each step making an earth-shattering boom. It scooped up several of the possessed men and women in its arms and threw them across the room. They screeched as they sailed through the air, plowing into others and knocking them all down.

Already others were climbing over Shale. As it tore each one off, another replaced it. Shale resorted to ignoring them, swinging about with its fists as the creatures tried to get to the mages. Each one it struck was sent flying from the impact.

But more were coming. A surge of them rushed into the room, howling and screaming in bloodlust. Wynne gave Rhys and Adrian a dire look. "Are you ready?"

They both nodded.

Rhys was first. He fought down his fear and concentrated, focusing instead on the power welling up inside. It grew stronger and stronger until he shook, until he felt ready to explode. Then he extended a hand, directing the energy outward.

The thrill as magic coursed through his body was unbelievable. A ball of black energy burst from his fingertips and hurtled across the room. It flew past Shale and Evangeline, and when it struck the far wall it expanded. It became a sucking void, drawing the nearest creatures into it. They disappeared into its depths, screaming. And then it grew, its power becoming more immense. A corona of blue energy surrounded it, sucking air and debris and everything else into its core. Creatures not close enough to be drawn inside were slowed. As if fighting against a powerful wind, they bent down and struggled to take even the slightest step.

Adrian was next. She closed her eyes and took a deep breath, and Rhys felt the heat radiating from her. When she opened her eyes they glowed red with flame. She held up a palm and a swirling ball of fire coalesced over it. Then she threw it, and as it flew it grew larger and hotter. It struck a group of creatures and exploded into an inferno. They emitted earsplitting screeches as the flames engulfed them.

Wynne fired lightning from the tip of her staff. As each bolt struck a creature, killing it instantly, the energy arced to another nearby. Still more of the creatures managed to get by Evangeline and Shale, and as they rushed at Wynne she unleashed a wave of cold. The entire group froze solid where they stood.

Still others ran around their frozen comrades, ignoring them completely. Wynne blasted several, but one leapt high up into the air. It descended with fangs bared, knocking her to the ground.

"Wynne!" Rhys cried.

Panic gripped him. He launched a magical bolt from his staff, hitting the creature just as it was about to sink its fangs into her neck. It was blown off, and as it scrambled back to its feet Wynne blasted it with an ice spell. The creature froze, and then shattered into a thousand icy shards.

Wynne gave Rhys a grateful look, but just then something slammed into him from the side. He fell hard, and twisted around to see the creature's face inches from his own. It was a woman— her skin mottled and diseased, blond hair hanging in stringy clumps from her scalp. She hissed, baring fangs coated with black saliva and blood.

He desperately tried to push her off, but she was stronger than he ever would have believed. Just as she was about to overpower him, something struck her on the side of the head. A staff. Adrian loomed over them, face twisted by terror, and hit the creature again. It leapt off of him, and spun about to hiss at Adrian, and she fired a jet of flame at the creature. It was hurtled back into the shadows, screaming.

"There's too many!" Adrian shouted, although he could barely hear. Each lightning bolt Wynne fired filled the chamber with thunder. That, combined with the screaming of the creatures as they swarmed Evangeline and the golem, made it deafening.

"I know!"

Adrian looked out at the mass of creatures. Rhys did the same. Already, more pushed past Shale, who all but crawled with them. Even though the golem was made of stone, they were still strong enough to slowly tear it to pieces. Evangeline was wounded as well, blood coursing from a gash on her forehead down her face and over her armor. Wynne was hard pressed—they were all sweating, and wouldn't be able to keep this up for long.

"I'm going to summon the storm!" Adrian concentrated, pressing her palms together and forming a kernel of red flame, which slowly began to grow in intensity.

"No! You'll kill Evangeline!"

"It's either that or we're all dead!"

He leapt up, throwing caution to the wind. Several creatures charged at him. He summoned what power he could and unleashed it as a wave of pure force, and they were sent flying. He raced toward Evangeline, who swung her sword in wild arcs. The creatures had her surrounded, and her grim expression told Rhys she knew she was about to fall.

"Evangeline!" he called, as loudly as he could. She didn't hear him. He rushed toward her, blasting several of the nearest creatures. She spun as he drew close, only prevented from chopping him in half at the last second, as she realized who he was.

She stared at him in shock, her face covered in blood. "What are you doing?!"

"Down!" Rhys tackled her, bearing both of them to the ground. She struggled, as much in anger as in fear of the creatures now racing toward them.

And then the firestorm began.

The flames swept across the ceiling, dancing like eddies of a hurricane wind. Gouts of fire swooped down with a great roar, rushing across groups of the creatures and turning them almost instantly into cinders. Rhys could see Adrian, her hands outstretched and surrounded by a corona of fire even though she remained unharmed. She floated off the ground, red curls flying, a terrible and vengeful goddess.

Rhys buried his face against Evangeline, and she covered her head. The heat was blistering. The roar reached a force that was almost physical. It pounded at Rhys and pressed him down, threatening to tear him apart. He tried to scream, but nothing came out. He could barely breathe.

And then, almost as soon as it began, it was over. The firestorm vanished, followed by an eerie silence. No screeching, no thunder or roar of flames, just a faint sizzling sound accompanied by the smell of charcoal and burnt flesh.

He lifted his head. Evangeline did the same, and stared at him with a stunned expression. There were no words to speak—he felt dizzy, strangely empty. Rhys willed power into his staff, and as the blue glow expanded, he saw the battle was over. Charred corpses lined the room from one end to the other, black smoke still rising from their bodies. Shale stood not far away, irritably brushing hot ash off its stony skin.

"Mages are occasionally useful," it grudgingly admitted.

Both Wynne and Adrian lay on the floor not far away. Neither moved. Quickly Rhys jumped up and ran over, coughing at both the stench and the smoke. Wynne looked singed and disheveled, but otherwise unhurt, and waved him away with a scowl. Adrian was deathly pale, barely breathing.

He touched her cheeks: cold. "Adri?" he whispered, fear gripping him.

Slowly she opened her eyes, just a little. "Am I dead?" she moaned.

He laughed in exhausted relief. "Not yet, no."

"That's a shame . . ."

Evangeline walked over, sheathing her sword. Coated in blood and soot, she looked every inch the battle-hardened warrior. "There doesn't seem to be any more. We're safe, at least for the moment."

Wynne lit up her staff again, nodding with approval when she saw Shale was unharmed, and looked about. "The passage on the far side leads into Pharamond's laboratory. He is inside."

Evangeline looked incredulous. "You can't think he's still alive!"

Wynne gave her a serious look. "I do."

It felt strange to consider simply proceeding with their mission, as if the battle had been nothing more than an obstacle. These

creatures had been innocents, possessed by demons; if Pharamond's experiments had caused this, Rhys questioned if they
should be trying to save him at all. But he remained quiet. What
else could they do but move on? And Wynne was correct. Now
that the fight was over, he could feel that dark presence again.
Whatever had happened here, the heart of it was in the next room.

He didn't feel particularly eager to discover what it was.

The first thing that struck Rhys as they entered was the laboratory's size. It had multiple levels, and seemed to be something
between a library and a workshop—and that was only the parts
of it he could see by the light of Wynne's staff. Most of it was
shrouded in darkness. More strangely, it was utterly untouched by
the chaos present everywhere else in the keep. The books remained on their shelves, the workshop tables were cluttered with
papers and strange instruments. It looked not dissimilar to the
workshops one might find in the White Spire.

The exception was the elven man sitting in a luxurious chair in
the middle of the room.

Or what had once been a man. Now he looked misshapen, his
flesh hideously twisted across his frame. His arms were too long
and thin, his fingers ending in talons, his lips pulled back from
his teeth in a disturbing grimace. The only reason Rhys could tell
he was even an elf was his pointed ears, although now they re-
sembled horns. His eyes, however, appeared completely clear . . .
and he watched them from his chair with an air of calm fascination without rising.

The presence Rhys sensed was inside of him. A demon burned
in every fiber of his being, pulsating with a malevolence that infected the room.

Wynne stood not far from the man, Shale beside her. At first
he wondered why she wasn't doing anything, but as they entered
she held up a hand in warning and then gestured to the floor. That's
when Rhys saw them: runes, inscribed in a circle around the chair.

There was powerful magic in them; the familiar tingle of it on his skin told him that much.

"Greetings to you all." The demon leaned back redolently in its chair, tapping its talons on the arm. Rhys found its voice was oddly cultured, though the unearthly timbre of it made him shiver. *"I have waited so long for guests. You will have to excuse my lesser brethren. They become so . . . excitable . . . after passing through the Veil."*

"Are you Pharamond?" Wynne asked carefully.

"Can you not tell?"

"I believe you were once Pharamond. Now you are something else."

"Poor Wynne." Its lips pulled even farther back from its teeth, in the semblance of a smile. *"You have lived through events that would make a lesser human beg for mercy . . . and what have you to show for your efforts? It must be distressing for one so favored by fate to discover it has nothing more to offer her."*

She scowled but did not respond. Evangeline stepped forward, keeping a wary eye on the demon and her sword at the ready. "I don't understand," she whispered to Wynne. "How does it know your name? Why is it just sitting there?"

"Those runes form a circle of binding. The demon cannot cross them, and I suggest we stay on this side. As for how it knows my name, it's reading my thoughts . . . or using Pharamond's memories."

The demon's grin grew wider. *"Clever mage."*

Evangeline knelt down, studying the runes more closely. "These are enchanting runes. The sort the Tranquil use."

Wynne nodded, but now Rhys spoke up. "So Pharamond created the binding circle? That means he . . ."

"He did this on purpose." Evangeline completed his thought. "Created the binding circle and placed himself within it. This demon is no accident."

The idea took a moment to sink in. Everything they had seen

in the keep was the doing of demons, dark spirits that had bled into this world from the Fade . . . and here was evidence that Pharamond had brought them here. Perhaps it hadn't been his intention, but he'd known enough of the risk to create the binding circle. It might even have been him that sealed the keep's doors. If they were precautions, they clearly hadn't been enough.

The only questions that remained were how . . . and why?

Evangeline stood back up and faced Wynne. "I trust you've seen enough. Whatever your friend was researching, he did so through the use of demons. No good can come of this."

"I haven't determined that, yet."

"What is there left to determine? This is folly!"

Wynne set her jaw stubbornly. "I came here to save Pharamond, a goal which has the full support of the Chantry."

"The Chantry would change its mind if it knew what he was doing."

"And it will." Wynne glared at Evangeline. "We do not have all the answers yet, and I will not jump to conclusions. You are free to help me or not, as you choose."

The demon chuckled with amusement, drawing their attention. It slowly rose from the chair, its skin stretching with a leathery creaking sound. Shale took an aggressive step toward the circle, only to be stopped by Wynne. The demon smiled again, holding its arms wide. *"By all means, creature. Come into the circle and destroy me, if you dare."*

"Let me squish it," Shale grunted.

Wynne shook her head. "No. That's not why we're here."

"I know why you are here, Wynne." The demon extended a long arm toward Evangeline, who raised her eyebrows but did not move. *"But do you know why the templar is here? Why she urges you to desist your efforts?"*

"What do you mean?"

"Ah! Then Rhys did not tell you?"

Wynne glanced back at Rhys, and he felt guilty. He'd told Wynne and Adrian about Cole, yes, but not what he'd learned about Evangeline's true purpose. Now he wished he had. "She is here to find out what Pharamond was researching," he said hesitantly. "And whether that knowledge would damage the Chantry."

Adrian pushed away from Rhys. She wavered from weakness, but still had enough presence of mind to stare at him suspiciously. "What does that mean?" she demanded. "What if she doesn't like what we find?"

"Then it remains here," Evangeline said grimly. "No matter what."

"Meaning you'll kill us." Adrian's eyes went wide in realization. "That's why the other templars are here, isn't it? Admit it."

Wynne backed away from Evangeline, her eyes glaring dangerously. "Is this true?" Shale took half a step in front of her, looming protectively as if the templar were about to attack.

Evangeline remained still, one hand on the hilt of her sword, but she made no move. She looked guardedly at the others, and then nodded. "I did not ask them to come. But yes, that is why they are here."

"I knew it!" Adrian spat. "For all your talk of protecting us, you're doing what the templars *always* do—protecting yourselves!"

"It was feared the Divine might not have been fully aware of the implications of your mission," Evangeline said firmly, "and I see that was correct. I am here to watch, and decide. I take no pleasure in this, but I will do my duty."

"And what about your duty to do as the Divine asks?" Wynne asked.

"I am operating on the orders of the Lord Seeker, he who is the hand of the Divine. It is not my place to question his judgment."

"So you're just following orders?" Adrian hissed. She held out her hands and a wreath of flame began to form, curling around them. Rhys tried to restrain her, concerned she was overtaxing herself, but she jumped away. "And you! You kept this to yourself! Why would you do that, Rhys?"

"Oh, I don't know," he sighed. "Maybe it's because you're so predictable?"

That was the wrong answer. She drew herself up, eyes flashing with rage. "Should I be *grateful* a templar's been sent along to kill us? Is there *another* reaction I'm supposed to have?" She turned back to Evangeline, the fire around her hands glowing brighter. "Do you really think we'll let you get away with this?"

The templar seemed undaunted. "Do you really believe there is knowledge worth finding here? Save the man or don't save him, his research was dangerous enough to condemn every innocent soul in this keep to death. It is forbidden magic I have sworn to guard the world against, to my dying breath."

"Forbidden magic!" Adrian laughed contemptuously. "What you templars call anything you don't understand!"

"What more is there to understand?"

"Don't you want to know how a Tranquil could be possessed?" Adrian shook her head, as if disgusted Evangeline could have forgotten. "Isn't that the entire reason why we're here? Who cares how he managed to do it—it's been done!"

"Oh, I can help with that," the demon interjected.

Wynne looked at it suspiciously. "Is that so?"

"There are only two possibilities." It smiled, tapping its chin as if trying to think the matter through. *"Either I am so powerful that even the mind of a Tranquil is not denied me . . . or the man you see before you managed to reverse his condition. He is no longer Tranquil."*

"That cannot be done," Evangeline objected.

"Yet here I am. Ask yourself which possibility is more likely." It chuckled at her grim expression. *"Ah, yes. If the Rite of Tranquility can be undone, templars would have to watch over the Tranquil as well as the mages. Suddenly no one is safe."*

She looked disturbed, but before she could respond Adrian

rushed toward Wynne. "Stop her," she demanded. "It's not going to matter what we find out, and you know it. They don't want your friend saved, and if what the demon says is true they'd rather die than let anyone know their precious rite is worthless."

Evangeline spun to face them, angry. "And you think that knowledge would be of benefit? To anyone?"

"Yes, I do." Adrian was defiant. "All those mages the templars have mutilated, turned into servants and worse! Why wouldn't I jump at the chance to undo the damage you've caused?"

Evangeline's face grew hard. "You speak of those who do not have the strength to command their gifts. There is little other choice, save to watch them become prey to demons they could not hope to fight."

"And how do you judge them? You throw a demon at them in a test to the death, where their only alternative is to submit to your ritual? It's barbaric!"

"What would you rather we do? Execute them?"

"It would be more honest! Instead you get to pretend like you're not all murderers, like you're doing us a favor!"

"You *are* a stupid girl." Evangeline shook her head.

Adrian screamed in outrage, flying at Evangeline with her hands extended to claw out the templar's eyes. Evangeline raised her sword, but before they could collide Rhys interposed himself. Adrian tried to get around him, but he grabbed her. She struggled, snarling furiously, and when she realized it was useless she slapped him.

"Stop!" he shouted. "Don't you realize this is exactly what the demon wants?"

That gave her pause. He looked at Evangeline. "Even when demons aren't lying," he said, "they'll manipulate the truth to get the results they want. Don't listen to it."

Wynne, who up until this point had watched the confrontation with a dangerous glare, slowly nodded. Even Adrian reluctantly nodded, though her scowl indicated she didn't like it. In all the years he'd known her, she could always be talked down from a true fury—but this had been a close thing.

"Thank you," Evangeline said.

"Yes, heroically done," the demon applauded him, smirking. *"Perhaps you should tell your companions why you didn't inform them of the templar's mission, Rhys. They might not think you such a hero then."*

"I didn't tell them because I knew this would happen!"

"Oh? Not because you sought the templar's favor? Protection from the fate that awaits your return to the tower?"

"No!"

"I see." It nodded. *"Then perhaps it is merely the templar you wished to protect. She is a pretty thing, is she not?"* It laughed with delight.

Adrian detached herself from his hands, but avoided his gaze and was silent. "Adrian," he said quietly. "Remember what I said. The demon is just trying to goad us with lies."

"I do not need to lie, not when the truth is so much more delicious."

He wheeled on it, enraged, and summoned mana to his command. He wanted nothing more than to wipe that twisted grin off its face, blast it into ashes.

Wynne stamped her staff down on the ground, hard, interrupting him. All eyes turned toward her. "Heed your own advice," she commanded, "and ignore the demon." Then she turned to Evangeline. "We are going to continue with the ritual, and I will go into the Fade and face the demon there. Do you intend to stop me?"

Evangeline considered. "No," she finally said.

"Excellent," the demon agreed smugly. It sat back down in the chair, arranging itself like a king greeting his subjects. *"By all means, come into the Fade and meet me on my own terms. I do not, after all, have anywhere else to go."*

Tense silence followed. It was the golem that finally interrupted it. "Does this mean the argument is finally over?" it sighed. "It really is quite dreary to listen to."

"Yes, it's done," Wynne snapped.

"Until you bring back Pharamond," Adrian added. She glared meaningfully at Evangeline, who kept her expression deliberately neutral. Her eyes met Rhys's only for a second, and he looked away. He felt embarrassed. What must she think of him now? She was attractive, it was true. More than that, if he was any judge of character he believed her to be honest and even noble—rare traits in a templar.

She was still a templar, however, and he was still a mage. Anything more was impossible, and even if it wasn't the entire idea seemed sullied now. He tried to ignore the flush that crawled up his face.

Wynne waved her staff toward him. "Take a position on the other side of the binding circle. You as well, Adrian."

"What about the Veil?" Rhys asked. "It's thin here, worse than at the White Spire. I didn't want to summon any spirits earlier because I was afraid what else might come through. If we make a mistake . . ."

"We will do what we must." She looked at Shale. "It will be up to you to guard us, old friend. Do you remember when we did this at Redcliffe?"

The golem rolled its eyes. "*I* have not become senile, unlike the elderly mage."

"Good. Then I trust you won't fall asleep."

"If I slept, I might be tempted."

Adrian scowled as she stood next to the circle, alternating between glaring at the demon and glaring at Evangeline. Rhys took his position on the other side, and was simply glad to be getting this underway. The quiet was excruciating. He almost wished for the thunder and roar of the combat they'd been engaged in only minutes before.

"Are you sure you're strong enough for this, Adrian?" he asked. She didn't look at him. "I'll be fine."

The demon swiveled its head around, looking appraisingly at Rhys with its too-human eyes. He tried not to meet its gaze. During the course of his experiments, he'd interacted with a number of spirits, some of them demons—none of them as powerful as this one. To stand in the same room with it, to have it sitting there so calmly, was more than a little surreal.

"Of course, she will be fine," it chuckled. *"There is nothing at all to fear."*

"Shut up."

"I am but offering you one more opportunity to engage in discourse with a demon, Rhys. I am surprised your templar companion permits this at all."

He could see Evangeline frowning. She looked down, fingering the hilt of her sword. Perhaps she was considering killing them as they attempted the ritual? If so, she had only the golem to stop her. Still, he doubted she would try.

A new thought occurred to him. He stared suspiciously at the demon. "What do you mean 'one more opportunity'? Do you know something about Cole?"

Wynne rummaged through her pack, pulling out a large bottle filled with a glowing blue liquid. Pure, unrefined lyrium. Even from here, Rhys could hear its faint song, a melody that played in his head and danced upon his skin. "Don't speak to it, Rhys," she warned. "Anything it tells you will be a lie."

Adrian snorted derisively. "It hasn't lied to us yet."

"But what if it knows what Cole is?" Rhys felt helpless, caught between his wariness and the faint chance the demon might be able to tell him something useful. He didn't truly believe Cole was a demon. He could sense this one, right here in front of him— why would Cole be any different? But what if he was?

"It preys on your doubt," Evangeline suddenly said. "Put your mind at ease. If answers come, they will not be at the hand of this creature." She looked at Rhys with unexpected concern, and he found himself relaxing a little. She was right. He nodded back to her gratefully.

Wynne stood. "We may begin."

She unstoppered the bottle, careful not to let any of the blue liquid spill on her. Raw lyrium was dangerous to a mage. Even to an ordinary person it could cause madness. Lyrium smugglers from the dwarven lands sometimes grew sick and died, screaming at invisible torments. The shock of absorbing so much mana, however, could instantly kill a mage.

He watched anxiously as she poured the lyrium into a small brass bowl. As soon as it touched the metal it began to bubble, sending out a small burst of energy that sent a shiver through his skin. The demon watched with clinical fascination, almost trilling with delight as a cloud of blue vapor rose from the bowl.

Wynne closed her eyes, concentrating. She began to move her hands around the vapor, coaxing and teasing without ever touching it. It branched out like a growing vine, sending out tendrils toward Adrian. She held out her hands to welcome it, and the vapor slowly swirled around her.

Rhys held his hands out as well, focusing his mind on the music. It was getting louder now, a chorus of power that thrilled his soul. The vapor reacted as if alive, undulating toward him, curling around his body. Wherever it drew close to his skin, he felt a strange charge, like electricity. It set his hairs on edge.

Everything was drowned out by the music, that insistent sound that seemed to pull him out of his body. The blue vapor slowly wandered back toward Adrian, and when it connected with the tendrils of vapor in front of her, the circuit was complete. A ring of power now surrounded the demon and began to grow in intensity, to grow in urgency until it was all Rhys could bear.

It was too much. Too much. He shut his eyes, the music so

overwhelming it felt as if he were about to vibrate out of existence. He violently shook his head, but it only grew worse.

I . . . can't . . . this is . . .

And then the Veil ripped open.

11

Cole's mind rebelled.

That music, at first so strange and different from what he felt when he saw the tainted creature in the badlands, had become a nightmare. It invaded him, filled him up and then tore him apart . . . and didn't stop there. He remembered falling to the ground, covering his ears and trying to scream. But there was no other sound at all, just a wrenching that lifted him up and bore him into the darkness.

And now . . . now there was silence. But he was somewhere else.

He was outdoors, in the middle of an unfamiliar city and in the middle of a war. Buildings burned, people were running and screaming. Chaos was everywhere. A sinister darkness filled the sky, like some evil rot had spread and infected the world. Worse, it was all *wrong*. It felt as if he were looking through tinted glass, everything real and yet completely unreal at the same time. The world was too vivid, too in focus, yet it all seemed to blur at the edges of his vision.

Cole wanted to grab someone, make them see him and demand to know where he was. What was that mountain that dominated the skyline? He'd never even seen a mountain before. What were they running from? Why was everything burning? But he was too terrified, and everything was happening too quickly.

He dashed to the side of the road, getting out of the way of a group of fleeing elves—families dragging their crying children and carrying their worldly possessions—and took refuge in the doorway of some burned-out shop.

There were charred corpses inside. He didn't want to look at them. The entire city stank of death and smoke. His heart wouldn't stop thumping in his chest, and he wanted to scream. *What is happening?*

And then he saw them. The same sort of monster he'd seen in the badlands, things with pale flesh and tainted hearts. They ran into view, carrying crude swords and shouting their bloodlust. But there was something wrong with them, too. He didn't hear the music, that insistent melody with its tendrils reaching out for him. They were shells and nothing more.

But they saw Cole. It took a moment for that to register as the monsters pointed at him. They roared and pounded the ground with their swords, and then charged.

The first he slashed across the throat with his dagger. He hadn't even realized he'd drawn it; he'd reacted instinctively, and there it was. Black ichor spurted from its neck, and it gurgled as it stumbled past him into the shop. The second swung its sword and missed, the blade chopping into the burnt doorframe and sticking there. Cole slashed its arm, forcing it to let go of its weapon, and then spun around with enough force to plunge the dagger into its sternum.

It collapsed with a bestial cry, but already others were coming. Too many. Cole turned and ran. He darted through the shop, leaping over the dead bodies and escaping out of a collapsed section of the back wall.

He had no idea where he was going. He heard the wailing cry of the creatures behind him as they gave pursuit, and that only made him run faster. He charged through winding alleyways, through choking black smoke, and past frightened people who cowered from him as he passed.

Eventually Cole spilled out onto some kind of square, drenched in blood and gore. A battle had occurred there—bodies of dead soldiers lay scattered about, most of them human and all of them wearing colors he didn't recognize. Their throats were cut, their limbs hacked apart. One man no older than he lay nearby, his tongue swollen and purple, horrified eyes staring up at nothing. The smell made Cole want to vomit.

A scream of terror in the alley behind him forced him to move. Across the square was the opening to a larger street, one that wasn't completely choked with flames. That could be a way out. Cole picked his way across the square, stepping between the bodies as quickly as he could.

He was only halfway across when he heard the savage cry of discovery. He turned back and saw the creatures spilling out of the alley now, dozens of them charging into the square with wild abandon.

There was no way he would make it in time. Cole gripped his dagger tightly, sour sweat pouring down his face. He looked at the dead soldiers, wondering if he should take one of their shields . . . or perhaps a sword? He'd never used either, and those things didn't seem to have helped the soldiers.

Die like a man. The command wormed its way through his head. Where did it come from? He'd heard it somewhere, and now it made him clench his teeth. He tensed and waited. The creatures ran toward him almost slowly, as if running through murky water, but it wasn't true. He was the one who slowed.

And then there was an explosion.

Cole stared in stunned disbelief as a great burst of fire sent the creatures flying. They sailed through the air, arms flailing, and hit the ground hard. All of them were burning, screaming horribly.

"Cole!"

He turned toward the sound of the voice . . . and saw Rhys running into the square. The other mages were with him, the old woman and the red-haired one, and Knight-Captain, too. A great statue made of stone and crystals lumbered behind them, something Cole would normally have been startled to see. Today it was just one more piece of strangeness to heap upon the others.

"Rhys?" he asked quietly.

Rhys stared at him, mouth agape in shock. Knight-Captain stared as well, although her expression was far more wary. She held her sword at the ready, as if concerned Cole might run at them and attack. It was the furthest thing from his mind.

The other two mages walked toward the creatures still standing. They held out their staffs and unleashed bolts of power. The blasts scattered the pale monsters, and that's when the stone behemoth rushed past the mages. It pounded the ground with both fists, hard enough to send out a shockwave that toppled the rest of the monsters to the ground.

A few more bolts of fire and lightning and the monsters finally fled. They picked up their weapons and abandoned their dead comrades, disappearing back into the alleyway. Cole watched them go, having never moved from the middle of the square. In the quiet that followed, punctuated only by the distant sounds of fire and screaming, he realized everyone was staring. At him. They could all see him.

Rhys took a step closer, but Knight-Captain reached out and stopped him. "Cole, what are you doing here?" Rhys asked, perplexed.

"I know you didn't want me to follow you . . ."

"No, how did you get *here*?"

Cole felt nervous. He wasn't used to having so many people looking at him, and they weren't *doing* anything. He desperately wanted to hug Rhys, beg the man's forgiveness. . . . He'd pictured this reunion so many different ways, but never like this. "There was music," he said quietly. "It was so loud, it filled me up and took me here. But I don't know where here is."

"This is the Fade," the old woman said. He'd never gotten a close look at her before. She might have seemed like a kindly grandmother had it not been for those sharp eyes. They looked right through him and sized him up, and there was something else . . . something behind them that made Cole shiver. He didn't like it. He almost wished he were invisible again. "The realm of spirits," she continued. "And this is a dream, of sorts. I believe it might be mine."

The red-headed mage frowned. "Your dream?"

"Denerim. This is the capital of Ferelden, and we are in the middle of the Blight. This is the battle when the Archdemon was slain and the darkspawn at last routed."

"But that's a good thing."

The old woman's face sagged, and for a moment she looked tired. "Look around you, Adrian. This was a nightmare. The victory came at a terrible cost, and has haunted me ever since."

They did look around, at the burning buildings and the terrible blackness roiling in the sky. The screams made Cole shiver. He didn't want to stay in this square, standing among so many dead bodies. If this was a dream, why couldn't they just wake up?

The walking statue lumbered over, its stony face twisted into a scowl. "The old mage has brought me into the Fade again. I didn't like it the first time."

Old Woman nodded, sighing. "It wasn't intentional, Shale. It seems everyone was drawn through the Veil, rather than just me."

The statue turned its glowing eyes toward Cole. "And this one, as well? Shall I squish it now? It looks unpleasant."

Rhys suddenly snapped out of his stupor. "No!" he cried. "Leave him alone!"

"We don't know what he is," Knight-Captain said. "Think about it, Rhys. Nobody can see him, but suddenly he's in the Fade? Right where you are? Don't be a fool."

"He's *not* a demon."

"I don't know," Old Woman said uncertainly. She stepped toward Cole, and he backed away. He still held his dagger, and now he began to wonder if he would need to use it. "I don't sense he's a spirit, but what does that mean here in the Fade? I didn't sense those creatures chasing him as spirits either, but they certainly weren't darkspawn."

A moment of tense silence passed, and Cole looked at Rhys. "Are . . . you still angry at me? I only wanted to protect you."

"You can't protect me, Cole. That's why I told you to go back."

"I couldn't."

Red Hair glared at Cole angrily, though as near as he could tell she always looked angry. Her voice penetrated like knives. "Why couldn't you?" she demanded. "Do you have *any idea* what you've done to Rhys?"

He backed up another step, but she pursued him. "I didn't mean to do anything to Rhys," he said quietly.

"And what about the mages you murdered? Did you not mean that?"

Cole felt as if a hole were opening underneath him. How could he explain it to her, when he was barely able to explain it to Rhys? She didn't know those people he'd killed, the tormented ones in their cages, and she didn't know him.

"*This* is the murderer." It was Knight-Captain who said that. She did not look surprised, but instead disappointed. She glared at Rhys. "You didn't mention that."

"I . . . thought you overheard."

"You should have told me yourself."

"So you could do what?" he demanded harshly. "You barely believed me as it was. You would have thought I was lying to you, in order to look innocent."

She stared at him, and then slowly nodded. "You're right." Then she turned toward Cole and drew her sword. "Demon or murderer, there is only one solution."

Cole jumped back, crouching low. He didn't want to run off into the city again, where those pale creatures were surely lurking, but he also didn't want to leave Rhys after spending so long searching for him. Knight-Captain was pretty, and seemed nice for a templar, but he knew why she was here. He wouldn't let her do that, any more than he'd let her kill him.

"Stop!" Rhys ran up and grabbed Knight-Captain by the shoulder.

Red Hair shook her head at him. "Don't, Rhys. How else do you think this is going to end? Why would you defend a murderer?"

Rhys seemed unable to answer. From his look of uncertainty, the way he glanced at Cole with that lingering question in his eyes, it was clear what his answer would be. Cole desperately wanted to defend himself, to prove to Rhys that he was still the man's friend, but he didn't know how. Nothing had ever felt so painful as watching Rhys slowly release Knight-Captain's shoulder now.

"I believe the matter is settled," she said, turning with a grim expression toward Cole. He prepared himself, tightening the grip on his dagger.

And then the world shook.

A deafening roar sounded from the sky, so loud it beat down upon Cole like a physical force. It drowned out everything. He covered his ears and doubled over, his head threatening to explode from the pain. The sound seemed to go on forever, and only when it finally stopped did he dare to look up.

Cole had seen pictures of dragons before—there was a faded mural in the White Spire's archive, and it showed a dragon surrounded by a group of knights with great spears and nets. It seemed to struggle against its attackers, but was heavily wounded and losing the battle. Cole had always thought it looked noble, a beast wrongly hounded by men that refused to see its savage beauty.

That dragon was nothing like this one. The dragon that filled the dark sky was a behemoth, and it didn't have a body covered in smooth scales. It was all muscle and sinew, eaten away by worms that writhed just under the surface. Like someone had taken rotting flesh and constructed a dragon out of it.

"The Archdemon!" Old Woman cried in horror.

There was no time to react. The dragon descended onto the square with the force of an earthquake. Cole tried to dive out of the way, but the massive wings of the beast beat once and sent a hurricanelike wind sweeping through the square. He was lifted up, along with many of the dead soldiers, and flung through the air. He slammed against a stone wall, hard.

The world spun around him. Cole found himself on the ground, gasping for breath and wincing at the pain running through his body. He felt disoriented. There were people yelling, but he couldn't tell where they were. Somebody shouted, "Get out of the square! Quickly!" but he had no idea who.

The dragon roared again, louder this time. It was little more than a giant black mass to Cole, the smoke being sucked into the square by its beating wings almost too thick to see through. He scrambled to his feet in a panic, glad not to have lost his dagger, and looked around for Rhys.

There. Three barely discernable figures in robes sprinted across the far side of the square. The dragon reared up, its serpentine neck curling. It then lunged forward, belching a blast of black flame from its mouth. Cole watched in horror as the mages were engulfed, and for a moment he thought they were surely dead. Then as the smoke cleared he saw Rhys down on one knee—the man had erected a shimmering shield of magic, and that had protected them. Even so, the shield was buckling under the strain. Rhys crumpled to the ground.

Old Woman and Red Hair darted in front of him. They extended their staves, one firing a bolt of lightning and the other a blast of pure power. Thunder shook the square as both struck the dragon on its chest. Even though it seemed unhurt, the beast spread its wings in fury.

Then the walking statue appeared, as if out of nowhere. Cole watched as it charged the dragon, smashing both its fists into its flank. "I killed it once," the statue bellowed, "and I'll kill it again!" The blow was strong enough to stagger the beast, and it seemed like it might topple. But then it twisted around, swatting at the statue as if it were an annoying fly.

The statue hurtled like a cannonball toward one of the stone buildings near Cole. It smashed through the wall with a resounding crash, bringing the entire building down on top of it. A cloud of dust billowed out, choking Cole and forcing him to scramble for safety.

The next moments were a blur. The dragon spun around, and Cole barely saw the tail swinging toward him as he leapt aside. Out of the corner of his eye, he spotted Knight-Captain swinging her greatsword at one of the beast's legs. The blade cut deep into the rotted flesh, black blood spurting out. It reacted violently, spinning about once again. Knight-Captain dove out of the way just as Cole had.

Then the air erupted into lightning. He felt his flesh stirring in response to the magic, heard the sizzle of the bolts randomly striking things around him. Several came close, and Cole danced out of the way . . . only to be confronted with the dragon looming over him. Two baleful black eyes stared down, full of malevolence and deep as forever. Its lips curled around fangs as large as his arm, and with a contemptuous snort the gaping jaws lunged down toward him.

It seemed to happen so slowly. He saw its forked tongue, the dripping saliva, the ridges of black flesh lining the inside of its mouth. Tendrils of corruption spread across each tooth. The dragon's breath stank of decay.

Someone far off shouted his name. Almost instinctively he rolled to the side, over rubble and dead bodies, and heard the jaws snapping shut with a terrible gnashing sound right behind him. The bite would have torn him in two, he was sure of it. The dragon swung its body around, but Cole was already moving. He sprinted as fast as he could, the world around him alive with lightning flashes, but to him it felt like he was running through water.

The air shifted, and he ducked. One of the creature's hands passed right over his head, each talon curled and shiny black. He saw Knight-Captain not far in front of him, getting back to her feet. There was blood on her face, and for a single moment their eyes met. In her horrified expression he saw what was about to happen next.

Cole turned and saw the dragon inhaling.

A ball of fire struck it from behind, exploding into an inferno. Again it was unharmed, but the force of the blast was enough to distract it. Cole took the opportunity and dove underneath the beast itself.

What are you doing? A small voice in his head kept asking him that. *Why don't you run?* He tried to tell it to be quiet, but it wouldn't go away.

The belly of the dragon slithered just over his head. He was certain the creature would crush him, or that one of those feet moving about would rip him to shreds. He had to keep crawling, the rocks scraping against his stomach. Without thinking he stabbed upwards with his dagger, the metal ripping into the leathery flesh, and sliced as he moved. Blood spurted down on him, hot and rank.

It got a reaction. The dragon tensed and leapt up with such force that Cole was almost sucked up with it. He looked up and saw the creature rising past the cloud of lightning, black wings spread wide over the entire square. It bellowed a challenge into the sky.

Each downward thrust of its wings sent winds screaming in every direction. Rocks flew, bodies flung about, a couple of the buildings collapsed. Utter chaos. Cole gasped for breath and held on to a larger piece of crumbled masonry for dear life. He saw the grey-haired old woman tumbling past him, white staff ripped from her hands, but there was nothing he could do.

And then the dragon landed again on the far side of the square, with such devastating force the ground caved in underneath it. Cole screamed in terror as he felt himself lifting up. Before he could start tumbling toward the beast, he scrambled back. A huge crack lay between him and safe ground, rapidly getting larger and farther away.

Cole jumped. He flew through the air, arms flailing, beneath him a gap that led down into darkness. It was like the chasm that split the cold desert, filled with nothing but a cold emptiness. And then he was falling into it. Desperately he grabbed on to the far edge. His fingers found purchase, but the crumbling rock began to give way. With a burst of strength he pulled himself up and onto solid ground.

The dragon roared again. Smoke was everywhere, and his eyes stung. He heard Knight-Captain shouting, and the blast of spells. Then someone grabbed his arm.

He looked up. Rhys stood over him, his robe bloodied and badly burned.

"Cole! Get out of here! Run!"

"I'm not leaving you!"

Just then, Cole saw the dragon leap across the square toward them. It descended fast with talons extended. "Look out!" he cried. He grabbed Rhys and pulled him away, the creature landing just where he had been a moment before. The impact sent both of them tumbling.

Rhys got back to his feet, furiously turning to face the dragon. Magical energy suddenly swirled around him, so bright Cole was almost blinded. The power built until Rhys screamed with the effort, and unleashed it in a torrent.

The dragon reeled, the magic crackling along its hide and burning wherever it touched. It screeched in rage, but before it could act a giant boulder flew through the air and crashed against its head. Cole spotted the walking statue emerging from a pile of rubble. It was scowling, and began picking up more rocks and hurling them.

Then a jet of white flame struck it from behind. The red-headed mage was on top of a large rock, battered but grimly determined. The fire streamed from her staff and grew stronger and stronger.

The dragon writhed from side to side under the combined assault, unable to get its bearings as it was pummeled by rocks and blasted by spells. It let out one last defiant screech that resounded across the heavens, and leapt high up into the sky.

The draft of wind beneath it sent both Cole and Rhys stumbling and sliding toward the edge of the square. Rhys grabbed on to an outcropping of rubble, but Cole couldn't find purchase anywhere. He slammed against the ground, agony spiking through him as he rolled into one of the alleyways.

There he slid to a halt. Cole lay still, breathing raggedly as he stared up at the walls on either side of him. One of them began to fall apart. He stared in confusion, watching large cracks race up its side, not realizing the danger until a giant piece of mortar began descending toward his head. With a cry of alarm, he rolled out of the way and the rubble smashed against the ground.

The entire building was collapsing.

Cole jumped up. He turned to run back into the square, but a giant piece of the wall landed right in front of him. Then something struck his head; he didn't even see what it was. Dazed, he backed up. A chain reaction began as the building across from him also began to fall. More mortar rained down, filling the alleyway as he quickly retreated.

He reached an intersection, and stared at the ruins before him. His heart pounded in reaction. The worst appeared to be over.

Then he heard a low growl. Spinning around, he spotted one of the pale creatures at the far end of the alley. It raised its sword, glaring at Cole with an eager hunger in its dead eyes. More of the same appeared behind it.

He didn't have his dagger. Had he dropped it? "Rhys!" he called out. The terrible thunder of the earlier combat had been replaced by an uneasy silence, but there was no shout of response. For all he knew, Rhys could be dead.

He ran.

Rhys slowly picked himself off the ground. His head was spinning, and he felt completely drained. *I could sleep for a week . . . except I'm technically already asleep, I suppose.* It had been a long time since he'd used magic in the Fade. He forgot the sheer power it offered, and how it left him dried up and aching afterward.

The square was a ruin. A great crack split it in two, the other side almost completely caved in. Most of the buildings were gone, and now a shroud of dust hung over everything. It was eerily quiet. Even the distant screams and sounds of war seemed to have vanished. With the black clouds still roiling overhead it seemed odd, like he was trapped in stasis. A single, horrible moment belonging to a place he'd never been.

"Are you hurt?"

He looked up and saw Evangeline offering her hand. Blood splattered across her face, and she was caked in mortar dust, but somehow still managed to carry herself like a proud warrior. Also a very unhappy warrior. Her glare of displeasure was scathing. He hoped it wasn't directed at him.

"I'll live." He took her hand and stood up. Then the thought struck him: Where was everyone else? Looking around in panic, he was relieved to see a battered-looking Wynne being helped to her feet by Shale, and Adrian dusting herself off on the far side of the square . . . but Cole was nowhere to be found. The alleyway he'd slid into was now filled with rubble.

He ran toward it, panicked. "Cole!" he called. Desperately he began pulling at the rocks, realizing even as he did so that it was pointless. If Cole was under there, he was dead. If he wasn't, there was no way he was going to be able to clear a path.

Adrian walked up behind him. She looked battered and bloody, as did Wynne. The old woman's grey hair was askew, her blue robe torn and covered in dirt. She was limping, helped along by the golem. "He is not dead," she said firmly.

"How do you know that?"

"Because I saw him run when the buildings collapsed."

"Then I have to find him."

"There isn't time. We have a mission to complete."

Evangeline strode forward, her face set into pure rage. "Your mission," she grated through her teeth, "is what has put us in this predicament. This is your doing, Enchanter, and I will not allow you to drag us heedlessly into further danger."

Wynne's eyes widened. "You will not *allow* me?"

"That is correct." Evangeline paused as Shale took a step toward her, looming overhead in a threatening manner. She was undeterred. "I am ending your mission. Now."

Rhys exchanged a nervous glance with Adrian, but found little sympathy there. She was no doubt as thrilled as he was to find herself in the Fade, but after the scene in the laboratory she lacked sympathy for Rhys and Evangeline both. She looked away, scowling.

Wynne drew herself straight. Despite her disheveled appearance, the imperious woman Rhys saw in the great hall made a sudden return, now bristling with anger. "You have no right to do that, Knight-Captain."

"I have every right. How many lives do you wish to put at risk, all for the sake of a man who apparently sought his fate?" She drew her sword, an act which made Shale's eyes flashed dangerously. Evangeline ignored it. "I am not prepared to share in it, nor am I prepared to allow you or anyone else here to do the same."

Wynne touched the golem's elbow, and it backed off—although it remained no less wary. "Do you believe you actually hold that sword in your hands?" she asked. "The blade may cut, but only because you believe it will. Templars are masters in many places, but not here in the Fade." Her smile was grim. "Demons are drawn to us because we shape reality to our will. That is our curse, but here . . . here it is our power."

Evangeline frowned, and slowly she lowered her sword. She did not step away. "I cannot force you, it's true. Is it your intention, then, to put us in further danger?"

"We know nothing of the circumstances which led to his act. I would prefer to wait until he's free of the demon before I judge him. So, yes, I intend to finish what I started. I never claimed this task to be risk-free, and I didn't ask for your company. You're here now, however, so it would be better if we remained together." Wynne looked back at Rhys and Adrian with a questioning brow.

"I'm not going," Rhys said firmly.

Adrian snapped her head toward him, her expression shocked. "What do you mean, you're not going? Where else will you go?" Then she paused, realizing. "You still want to look for him? That murderer?"

"He saved my life. That dragon would have killed me."

"That doesn't change what he did," Adrian said.

Evangeline shook her head. "It doesn't matter. You're not running off on your own, Rhys—not again. I don't approve of this mission any more than you do, but my duty is still clear."

"And what about your duty to Cole?" She looked at him, confused, and he had to control the rage in his voice. "I know perfectly well what he's done. I also know that he's been lost and frightened in the tower ever since the templars brought him there. They had a duty to protect him, to protect everyone from what his magic could do, and he slipped through their fingers." He stabbed at Evangeline's breastplate with an angry finger. "And now you can see him. You didn't believe me before, but here he is. Instead of trying to help him as you ought to do, you'd rather judge him. And me."

Evangeline frowned, but did not respond. Adrian, however, stepped right up to him. She barely came to his chin, but glared up at him with a ferocity that was daunting. "You're being an idiot, Rhys," she snapped. "I know you mean well, but you need to start thinking of yourself. You're staying with us, and we're going to find Pharamond and then get out of the Fade."

He hesitated. What hope could he have finding Cole on his own? Even if the dragon didn't reappear, who knew what other creatures could manifest themselves? "I could use your help, Adri."

But he needn't even have asked. What hope he had died when she coldly shook her head. "No," she said. "I'm not going to do that."

"I'll go with him."

Rhys was startled, and had to look twice to realize that it was Evangeline who said it. The templar scowled grimly but seemed determined. He didn't even have a chance to express his shock, as Adrian beat him to it.

"You must be joking," she scoffed.

"But he's right," Evangeline said grudgingly. "If this Cole was indeed a mage brought to the White Spire . . . then we are responsible for him, and his actions, at least in part." She glanced at Rhys, her expression softening to embarrassment. "Whatever he is, a man who risks himself for another cannot be beyond redemption. Like Pharamond, we can worry about his guilt once we are safe."

Rhys felt relieved. He smiled gratefully at her, but didn't know what to say.

Wynne frowned. For a long moment she looked at him—was she disappointed? Angry? He couldn't tell. "Is this truly what you wish to do?" she asked.

"You could come with me. We could find Cole first, and then look for Pharamond together."

Her smile was thin. "You have your friend to seek, and I have mine." With that, she looked up at Shale—who stared disinterestedly off into the distance. "I hope *you'll* be coming with me, at least?"

"Oh? Is it done chattering? I thought we were waiting for the dragon to return."

Wynne smirked. "Isn't this the point where you tell me you aren't afraid of the Archdemon, because it could swallow you whole and you'd still pass through its bowels unharmed?"

The golem almost blanched. "That would not be my first choice."

"Well, good. Then we can be off!"

As Wynne and the golem marched off, Adrian began to follow—and then stopped. She glanced at Rhys dubiously. "Just watch her," she warned. It took him a moment to realize she was referring to Evangeline. "You find this mage, or whatever he is—remember she's still a templar. She's not here to protect us." She left without waiting for a response.

Rhys and Evangeline were left alone. He looked sideways at her and cleared his throat uncomfortably. "Thank you."

She didn't smile. "Don't thank me yet."

12

Evangeline stared at the world around them, her skin crawling with unease. Not moments before, she and Rhys had been making their way through the ruins of the city—and then it abruptly changed. Now they were standing in what appeared to be a desolate farmer's field. The land had recently been burned, as far as the eye could see, and now smoldered. The acrid smoke hung in the air, stinging the eyes.

Off in the distance a hovel stood. Not the proud home of a freeholder, but the sort of mean shack one expected to see in the provinces. Desperate people lived there, barely subsisting off the overworked soil, and the house reflected it: greying planks, peeling paint, and a sense of loneliness that carried in the wind.

"Are you sure this is it?" she asked Rhys.

He nodded, his expression grim. A small orb of light floated next to his head; a spirit he'd conjured, which he said would lead them to Cole. She was leery of any spirit, even ones so small, and worried it might lead them astray. According to Rhys, such spirits barely had a will of their own, and knew the Fade far better than any mortal being could ever hope to. She hoped he was right.

Now that they were out of the city, or the nightmare—whatever it had been—the tainted sky had been replaced with an emptiness that yawned overhead. Instead of stars and clouds there were floating islands and strange, shimmering bands of light. They fluctuated from green to gold, sometimes sharpening and at other times spreading like a sick miasma to fill the void.

Off in the far distance, barely visible through the haze, there was an island that gave the impression of being much larger, and on it spread a city shrouded in darkness. The Black City, once the seat of the Maker and now a testament to mankind's folly. She had read about it in books, and been told it was the only constant feature in the Fade, visible from any point . . . but she'd never thought to see it personally.

She shuddered. How oddly out of focus everything seemed. The mages claimed that men came to the Fade on a nightly basis, to dream, and merely did not remember their journey. To her, it felt as if the living did not belong in this place.

They walked slowly through the field, clouds of ash rising with each step. There was no indication anyone was in the hovel. The front door stood open, banging rhythmically in the wind. A line of laundry was hung, the sheets stained black from the smoke and half of them having fallen to the ground. The entire place stank of neglect.

"What is this place?" she said.

"I don't know. Cole's home, perhaps."

"What do you know about him?"

"Nothing. He said he didn't remember where he came from." He looked around. "I guess there's a part of him that does. This is a memory he's fled to."

Evangeline didn't need to ask if it was a good memory or not. There didn't seem to be anything good about this place. They stopped just outside the door, looking for any evidence of movement within. There was nothing but darkness. A mangy kitten crawled out from under the steps, one of its ears badly singed, and it mewed pitifully at them.

She knelt down and held out a hand to the creature. It sniffed hesitantly and then, realizing there was no food to be had, redoubled its desperate cries. Even though part of her knew it was only part of the dream's landscape, she couldn't help but feel sorry for it. There was nothing to offer, however.

"It's easy," Rhys said. He knelt beside her, and in his hands was a small slice of raw meat. The kitten leapt on it ecstatically, pulling the meat off his hand with gusto and gnawing away at it. "Remember, you only have your sword because you think you do."

"So you can change anything here?"

"Not anything, no."

She shook her head, confused. "Is the Fade always like this?"

"The spirits see the world in our minds, and they try to emulate it. They don't understand that what they're seeing isn't how it truly is. It's mixed up with memory and emotion—but they think it's real, and they find it fascinating. They're drawn to it. But not all dreams are created by spirits."

Evangeline nodded as if she understood, although she didn't really. All of this was the province of mages, and she would have to trust him. And she did, in a way. As foolish as Rhys was, she truly believed he had good intentions.

He cleared his throat awkwardly. "Look, about what the demon said . . ."

"This isn't the place to discuss it."

"I just don't want you to think . . ."

"Let's find your friend." She stood up, watching the kitten drag its prize back under the stairs. Rhys only nodded glumly. What else was there to tell him? The demon's words were obviously meant to drive a wedge between him and Adrian . . . and had done so, as near as she could tell. The girl was far too willing to believe the worst of everyone.

As for whether or not there was any truth behind what it said . . . well, that didn't matter, did it? Rhys was a mage, and she a templar. Despite the man's charms, she doubted he looked at her in such a fashion, and nor should he.

They walked up the creaking steps and through the open door. It was far darker inside than was natural. None of the light from outside seemed to penetrate more than inches past the doorway. There was also a shocking chill to the air, their breath appearing in fine plumes of mist.

Evangeline drew her sword, exchanging a wary glance with Rhys. He held out his staff, and the crystal at its top began to glow. It showed a room almost barren of furniture. A few chairs, one of them broken. Several filthy blankets. Wine bottles lay scattered about, and some of them had been smashed against the wall. All of it was covered in a fine layer of frost.

"What happened here?" she whispered, not daring to speak too loudly.

Rhys clearly knew no better than she. Whatever it was, the memory of it clung to the room. It felt like terror. She had seen it before in mages brought to the tower, people so terrified of their magical gift they prostrated themselves and begged to be put to the sword. The raw edge of their fear touched her then as it did now.

A small kitchen lay off to one side, filled with small cupboards and shattered dishes. A large pool of frozen blood lay on the floor, smeared in such a way as to suggest a body had been there until only recently.

The small spirit floating around Rhys agitated, and he made soothing noises at it.

"What's wrong?" she asked him.

"I'm not sure. It's . . . sensing something unusual."

"There's not much about this I would call usual."

But he seemed distracted. Perhaps he was communicating with the tiny spirit; she couldn't tell. It whirled about, dimming and then pulsating in distressed sequences. She gripped her sword nervously. Unless it was her imagination, the shack had become much colder.

Then she heard something, a sound coming from one of the cupboards. A whimper. She turned around, trying to detect where it was coming from . . . but just then, a shout echoed throughout the house.

"COLE!"

Rhys jumped, and the spirit quivered in terror and whisked off out of sight. Evangeline raised her sword, aware that the cold had intensified even further. Rhys was shivering, and frost was forming on her armor. "Where is that coming from?" she asked.

"The cellar, I think."

"Cole, you little bastard! You think you can hide from me forever?"

Heavy footsteps came up the stairs. Evangeline stepped out of the kitchen, watching a small door in the back of the shack rattle in its frame. "What do we do?" she demanded nervously.

"Fight it. It's a demon, keeping Cole trapped here."

The door flung open. Beyond it stood a barrel of a man, grizzled and bald and wearing a smallshirt stained red with fresh blood. The imprint of a hand could clearly be seen upon it. The man's face was gaunt and pale, flesh sagging from his skull like that of a corpse just beginning to rot. *"Come out and die like a man!"* he screamed, spittle flinging from his lips. *"You know what the punishment is!"*

She carefully advanced on the man. Some demons had magic, and if she could disrupt it she could keep the creature from gaining an advantage. "Leave," she warned. "We've come for Cole, and nothing else."

The man looked her up and down. *"You're worthless,"* he sneered. *"A mistake I should have drowned long ago. You've evil in you, boy, passed down by your mother. You'll pay the price just as she did."*

Evangeline lunged at him with her sword, channeling as much of her power through the blade as she dared . . . and then froze in mid-swing. The sword stopped not inches from the demon's face. She couldn't move a single muscle.

He leaned close, the stench of carrion rank on his breath. *"What did I tell you?"*

"Leave her alone!" Rhys roared. He rushed past her, striking at the demon with his staff. When the orb touched it, a powerful light flashed and the demon screamed in agony. It fell back, flailing wildly, and just barely caught the sides of the doorway before tumbling down the cellar stairs.

"Maker take you and your foul magic!"

Its mouth gaped wide, stretching all the way down to its chest, and an icy blizzard belched forth. The blast whipped painfully across Evangeline's face, and she would have screamed if she were able. Rhys reeled back, but at the same time summoned a magical barrier that spared both of them from the worst of it.

He quickly grabbed her around the waist, dragging her like a statue back into the kitchen. There he dropped her onto the floor. Breathing hard, he touched a hand to her forehead. She felt the spell rushing into her, pushing out the paralysis all at once.

She gasped for breath. "Watch out!" she cried.

The demon screeched as it leapt on Rhys from behind. He was knocked to the floor, and it sank its teeth into his shoulder as they landed. Blood spurted, and Rhys shouted in agony. He struggled, trying to wrestle the demon off his back, but it was too strong.

Evangeline jumped to her feet. She lifted her sword high with both hands and brought it down on the demon. The blade struck home, digging deep into its back, and her power disrupted its magic.

It released Rhys's shoulder, rising as bluish blood seeped from its wounds. Baleful eyes glared at Evangeline. *"You have learned nothing, you wicked fool!"*

"Maker take your evil!" she snarled. With a great swing of her sword, she took off the demon's head.

The head disintegrated before it hit the ground. As the body stumbled back, hands grasping blindly in the air, black energy roared up from the bleeding stump. And then its body began to fall apart, dissolving into a brackish morass until finally there was nothing.

She breathed heavily, her heart racing in reaction. Rhys stared up at her from the floor, cradling his wounded shoulder. "I . . . think that should do the trick," he said.

"Let's hope so."

"Nice swing, by the way."

Already the room was changing. The biting chill had lifted, and the pool of blood on the floor was gone, but the darkness remained. They were left in a dark and empty farmhouse, like a place long abandoned . . . any signs that something terrible had happened there were gone, but she could still feel the evil soaked into every floorboard.

Evangeline looked around, keeping her sword ready just in case. "Why isn't it all gone? I thought you said the demon created this."

"The demon kept Cole trapped here, but the nightmare is his." Rhys began casting a spell, its soothing blue light sinking into his shoulder and knitting flesh back together. "Now we just need to find him, before another demon swoops in. They're very territorial."

She didn't like the sound of that. Part of her had hoped the demon was the one from the laboratory, but apparently not. That demon would undoubtedly be wherever Pharamond himself was. The idea that it could be in two places at once baffled her . . . but then again, wasn't she? Her body was in the real world, and the rest of her was here in the Fade.

While Rhys healed himself, she searched for Cole. Initially she considered the cellar. That was where the demon had ascended from, and it struck her as the sort of place a demon—and, indeed, a father—might try to trap someone.

When Evangeline opened the door, however, she found it led

down into pitch blackness. A raw fear pulsated down there, something that spoke of childhood terrors and long hours submerged in hopelessness. She closed the door quickly, her heart racing, and berated herself for such foolishness. She was a warrior. Her father had raised a hand against her only when she deserved it, nothing more. These fears were not her own.

And yet they seemed so real.

And then another thought occurred to her: Why would the demon have come looking for Cole if he was already in the cellar? The suspicion nettled her . . . until she remembered the whimper she'd heard in the kitchen.

"Is something wrong?" Rhys asked as she walked back inside.

She didn't answer, and instead listened carefully. Nothing. Slowly she began to open the kitchen cabinets one by one. Each was empty, containing only dust and evidence of long neglect.

"What are you looking for?" Rhys asked again, annoyed.

And then she opened the last cabinet. Inside crouched a filthy young boy, perhaps twelve years in age and with shaggy blond hair hanging in front of his eyes. His face was filled with stark terror, wide eyes having long drained of tears that now stained his cheeks . . . and worst of all, a little girl was squeezed in there with him. She was half his age, held in a crushing grip, with one hand clamped over her mouth as if to keep her quiet.

Only she was dead.

The young boy began shaking, fighting against sobs that threatened to overwhelm him. "Please don't tell," he begged Evangeline in a quivering whisper. "Mama told us to hide. We have to hide."

"Cole?" Rhys approached behind her, horrified.

Evangeline didn't know what to do. The little boy shook even more profusely, new tears welling in his eyes—but he made not a single sound. She wasn't sure he even knew who they were . . . or who he was.

She reached out and removed Cole's hand from the little girl's mouth. "Bunny was crying," he explained in a tiny voice. "Mama told us to be quiet. I only wanted her to be quiet."

Gently Evangeline took the girl from his arms, and he only reluctantly gave her up. She weighed almost nothing, just skin and bones and the slightest wisp of a yellow dress. The sort a child would have been proud to own, something she might have thought was pretty. The dead girl dissolved into nothingness the moment she left the cabinet.

She looked helplessly at Rhys. He gently moved her aside and crouched down next to the cabinet. "Cole? Do you know who I am?"

The little boy stared at him, terror visibly fighting with alarm. His breaths became rapid and anxious. Rhys reached out to touch him, but then stopped . . . a dagger had appeared in the boy's hands. Cole's dagger. The boy held it up in an obvious threat, a desperate rage slowly overtaking his face.

"I won't let you hurt Mama anymore," he seethed. "I'll *stop* you."

Evangeline almost pulled Rhys back. She had no idea if they could be killed in the Fade, but she wasn't eager to find out. But Rhys simply held up his hands to the boy in surrender. "Shhh," he whispered. "I'm not here to hurt you, or anyone."

The shaking dagger slowly raised, the point of it touching Rhys's neck. The little boy held it there, alternating between sharp sobs and frightened whimpers. His eyes were incredibly intense.

And then the boy's shaking stopped. "Rhys?" he asked with sudden recognition, his voice so pitiful and hopeful it was heart-wrenching.

Rhys nodded.

The dagger clattered to the floor, and all at once the little boy spilled out of the cabinet. Only he was a little boy no longer. He was the young man Evangeline had seen earlier in the city square, older and dressed in blood-splattered leathers.

He buried his head in Rhys's chest, agonized sobs ripped from somewhere deep in his soul, and Rhys simply held him. He said soothing things, and that made the young man cry all the harder.

And then the shack was gone. Evangeline looked around, and saw they were back in the burned field. It was completely empty, as if the farmhouse never existed. But it had existed, once. Deep in her heart, she knew that for Cole it had gone from being a nightmare to a memory . . . an awful memory the Fade had dredged up from some dark and dreadful place where it should have remained buried.

She stood there, watching awkwardly as Rhys cradled the young man, and her heart broke.

As Adrian walked through the city with Wynne and the golem at her side, she noticed everything had become strangely empty. The city no longer burned, and the streets seemed abandoned. There were no fleeing people, no rampaging darkspawn . . . just dark windows and a lonely wind that fluttered Wynne's white cloak.

In fact, it seemed as if the buildings themselves had changed as well. The architecture was different, more like the peaked roofs and whitewashed stone she would expect to see in Orlais. It wasn't until she saw the white tower rising in the distance that she realized this was Val Royeaux.

"We're in the capital?" she asked incredulously.

Wynne nodded. "Someone's version of it. Perhaps Pharamond's."

Adrian had been out of the tower often enough that she knew Val Royeaux's main streets fairly well . . . yet she didn't recognize where they were. It was like an impression of the city, or a painting created by someone who had never been there but had had it described to them, and forgot to add in a single sign that it was inhabited by anyone.

It was oddly unsettling.

A summoned wisp led the way, although truth be told it was

already obvious they were heading toward the White Spire. The trick, as it turned out, was navigating through the city. Val Royeaux's streets were winding and even sometimes confusing in real life; here in this Fade version they were a literal maze. Several times already they'd encountered dead ends and been forced to double back, Wynne scowling irritably at the delay.

"What if you had come here on your own?" Adrian abruptly asked her. "What would you have done if we hadn't been here to help you?"

"Died," Shale said.

Wynne shot the golem an annoyed glance. "The demon is hiding. It has created all of this for our benefit, forcing us to hunt it down. Had we not all been drawn through the Veil, it might have been bold enough to confront me directly."

"And then what would you have done?" Adrian persisted.

"Died," Shale snickered.

"I would *not* have died," Wynne archly corrected them. "I would have defeated it, as I shall when we finally reach it."

"Just as it defeated the Archdemon?"

"Technically speaking, I created the Archdemon."

"Technically speaking, I watched the elderly mage be blown across the square."

"You know very well, Shale, that demons do not create everything in the Fade. They set the stage, as it were, and we fill it with our own dreams and nightmares."

"Perhaps it should try having less potent nightmares."

"We could always have ended up in *your* nightmare, Shale, and encountered a giant pigeon instead of the Archdemon. Would that have pleased you more?"

"I would have enjoyed fighting it more."

"I'll keep it in mind for our next visit. Maker knows we all exist to please you."

Adrian watched as the two of them carried on. They were

clearly old friends, accustomed to each other's foibles and unafraid to point them out. It was also clear that Adrian was an outsider. The way they walked just a bit faster than her, subtly excluding her from their company and conversation, was enough for her to notice even if she didn't comment on it. It made her miss Rhys all the more.

Thoughts of Rhys made her heart clench a little. She should have gone with him, she knew that now. At the time she wanted to punish him, not for what the demon claimed but because it was obvious he didn't trust her. It hadn't seemed that long ago they were confidantes. But now? Now he kept secrets. How many opportunities did he have to tell her about Cole, and yet remained silent? He'd learned the truth about Ser Evangeline's mission and didn't say a thing. That told her he thought she either couldn't keep a secret or didn't possess the judgment to not make things worse.

Yes, she had her faults, but so did Rhys. His temper was almost as bad as hers, and he trusted far too easily. She was constantly watching out for his interests because he refused to. Sometimes she wondered if he intended to die. He certainly couldn't go about it any more efficiently if he did.

Adrian had few friends within the Libertarians even though she led them—actually, if she were honest about it, she had none. The other mages viewed her as useful, the kind of person who spoke her mind even when they were too timid. Rhys had always supported her, however. He stood by her side and believed in the same things she did, believed that the Circle was a place of oppression and that mages needed to be free. With him, achieving change seemed possible. Without him, she simply felt alone.

And now she'd abandoned him, possibly when he needed her the most. All Adrian really wanted to know was why he considered this Cole more important than anything else . . . and why he protected a templar. The thought that she might truly lose him, forever, filled her with dread.

Adrian sped up to walk beside Wynne. The old woman did a poor job of hiding her scowl. A fine thanks, Adrian thought, for continuing to help even after they'd all been dragged unwillingly into the Fade. Why Rhys thought anything of the woman at all, she couldn't imagine. She was one of the most prominent mages in the Circle, true, but she was nothing like him . . . and she couldn't think of someone less motherly.

"Why are you doing this?" Adrian asked, annoyed.

Wynne seemed surprised by the question. "Rescuing Pharamond?"

"You could have gone with Rhys. Instead you're choosing to rescue . . . what? A friend? Over helping your own son? What if something happens to him?"

"If you were concerned about Rhys's safety, then you should have accompanied him."

"But I'm here with you, and I think I'm owed an explanation. Do you do this sort of thing for all your friends? Are they more important to you than your family?"

Wynne clenched her jaw, stifling outrage. "You know nothing of me."

"But I know Rhys," Adrian insisted, "and I know he deserves your help."

"I've already helped him."

"And now he's gone running after that invisible mage, or whatever he is . . . because he wants to help the man, not because it could prove his innocence. But I think it'll just make things worse for him, especially with that templar there."

Wynne smiled with amusement. "The way you say 'that templar' . . . you truly don't care for her, do you? Personally, I mean."

"Is there any reason I should? You heard what Ser Evangeline said. She'll do her duty, no matter what. I don't think Rhys understands what that means."

"And you do?" The old woman shrugged in a condescending

manner that irritated Adrian. "I made a commitment to the Chantry. That is important to me. It just so happens that Pharamond is also my friend, and I refuse to see him abandoned to his fate."

"Even after what he's done?"

Wynne stopped. She turned and leveled a cool glare at Adrian. "For a Libertarian who claims to have the interests of all mages at heart, you seem remarkably willing to cast aside those who fail to meet your standards. It seems the templars are not the only ones quick to judge."

Adrian was taken aback, unsure how to respond to that without getting into another argument. Wynne seemed to take that as acceptance, however, and knowingly nodded. "As I thought," she said. "If it's me you wish to judge, you may certainly do so. I would suggest you consider the fact that I, at least, have a mission as well as a friend to help. You have neither of those things. If there is anyone you should be asking these questions to, it's yourself."

With that the woman sped up her pace and marched off. Adrian was left standing in the middle of the street, nonplussed, with the golem staring down at her. The glowing points of light where its eyes should be made it difficult to tell what it thought, but Adrian imagined it was amused by the spectacle.

"It should be more careful," the golem announced.

"Oh? Why is that?"

"The elderly mage will squish it like a bug if it angers her."

Adrian snorted. "She may have more experience, but I am a senior enchanter for a very good reason. Nobody will be squishing me."

"There are things it does not know about the elderly mage," it insisted.

"Such as?"

The golem refused to elaborate, however, and instead stomped off to catch up with Wynne. Adrian stood there, frustrated. The old woman was a powerful mage, but she certainly hadn't defeated the Archdemon single handedly, had she? How could she be so confident that she expected to walk right up to the demon that ruled this portion of the Fade and defeat it? What was Adrian missing?

They proceeded through the empty city streets for a time, the wisp unerringly guiding them. Open doorways dotted the buildings they passed, and Adrian asked why they didn't use one of them to reach the tower. A doorway in the Fade, after all, was simply a transition—it could be used to reach almost anywhere one desired. Wynne was suspicious, however, and claimed they could be a trap laid by the demon. So they remained on foot.

Not everything was unfamiliar. Adrian noticed the Imperial Palace far off on its hill, looking as resplendent as she remembered. They passed the streets of the Belle Marché, but whereas they would normally have been bustling with merchants and entertainers of every variety, here it was simply empty. The marketplace was *never* empty, as she recalled. Even at night it was filled with people, the taverns overflowing with revelry.

The White Spire loomed ever larger the closer they got to it, the pale tower shooting straight up into the sky like a lance, almost as if it would reach the far-off floating islands or even beyond. It was not nearly this large in real life, Adrian realized. This was the product of someone for whom the White Spire—perhaps the entire Circle of Magi—dominated their mental landscape. She could sympathize.

Finally, as if the city had given up trying to confuse them with its twists and turns, the entry to the tower appeared. The ivy-covered wrought iron gate stood open, as did the massive doors leading into the great hall. Whereas normally there would have been templars guarding the compound, or at least visible as they traveled in and out of the tower, the area seemed utterly abandoned.

"It seems we are made welcome," Wynne commented.

The golem peered at the gate and scowled. "It's going to shut behind us, isn't it? Does the elderly mage wish me to rip this off its hinges?"

"What would be the point? What we seek lies within." She waved her hand at the hovering wisp and it bobbed gratefully before winking out of existence. They were left alone, the only sound the faint whistling of the wind between the buildings behind them.

"I don't like it," Adrian complained.

Wynne sighed. "There's very little to like about any of this."

They walked inside. The great hall looked just as it should: the checkered marble floor, the vast arches, the foreboding windows of colored glass. Unlike every other part of the city, this seemed exactly right. She almost expected the interior doors to fly open, and a horde of mages to file in for their assembly. None came. The golem kept looking at every corner of the chamber, clenching its fists so tightly Adrian could hear the crunching of the stone. It made her more nervous than she already was.

They saw their first living person as they moved into the main floor of the tower. Templars should be training in the interior courtyard or at least present in the halls. These first floors were their main barracks, after all; they should be everywhere. But it was a single mage that greeted them. Then Adrian saw the grey robes and corrected herself: this was no mage, but a Tranquil.

The man walked up and bowed. His placid smile was the same as most Tranquil assumed, not because they were pleased about anything but because they knew it put others at ease. Adrian found it off-putting. In fact, she found everything about them off-putting. The idea that this could just as easily be done to her was at once both unsettling and outrageous.

"I greet you all," the Tranquil said. "Is there something you seek here?"

Wynne studied him carefully. She raised a hand to stop Shale from attacking, without looking in the golem's direction. Shale pouted, but remained still. "I'm looking for Pharamond," Wynne said. "Where would I find him?"

The man nodded, as if expecting this, and pointed up. The meaning was clear: the top of the tower. Somehow Adrian wasn't surprised.

"And who might you be?" Wynne asked him.

"I am no one of significance, merely one who is now content."

The way he said it, so evenly and with conviction, made Adrian shiver. "How do we know this isn't the demon?" she whispered to Wynne.

"He's not. I would sense it." Wynne didn't seem certain, however.

The man only smiled patiently. "I understand if you do not trust me. I have lived my entire life as a danger to others, and though that time has passed it would not surprise me to learn there are those who still harbor suspicion."

"What do you mean 'that time has passed'?" Adrian asked him.

He gestured to the tower around them. "Do you not see? This place stands as a memorial to an era best forgotten. The Circle of Magi is no longer needed. The templars are long gone, and those of us who remain do so only because we wish to."

"I don't understand."

"Come, I will show you." He beckoned to them, and headed up the stairs. Shale made as if to grab at him, but Wynne shook her head no. She tapped her staff on the ground, lighting up the tip with an aura of power. Exchanging a glance with the others that they should be wary, she followed him.

They saw more people as they ascended, men and women roaming sedately through the halls. None of them spoke, and the only sound Adrian could hear was the faint rustling of their grey robes.

Some stopped and nodded pleasantly as they passed, but there was no sense of concern or danger.

It wasn't until they reached the level occupied by the mages that she began to understand her rising apprehension. The commons was crowded, just as Adrian had often seen it before. People stood in clumps, speaking of things in calm whispers. None of them were mages, however. They were all Tranquil. All of them.

"Do you see?" the man asked them. He appeared almost pleased as he waved to the crowd. Some of them looked their way, though none of them smiled. "As I said: the templars are no longer needed. Order has been restored to the world."

A shiver of horror ran through Adrian. This was Pharamond's nightmare, then—and in many ways it mirrored her own.

Wynne walked into the commons, her eyes searching the crowd. Her lips pressed together in grim disapproval, but she seemed nowhere near as affected by the scene as Adrian was. Everyone was so *calm*. The aura of peace that pervaded the tower was like a shroud, and Adrian wanted nothing more than to run from it screaming.

"Where is Pharamond?" Wynne demanded.

All conversation ceased. Every eye in the room turned toward them, and Adrian felt her hackles rise. In the utter silence that followed, she became very aware these were *not* truly Tranquil. They were part of the dream, perhaps even demons themselves, and they could turn hostile in an instant. Considering how many there were, that would be very bad indeed.

Shale stepped beside Wynne, fists clenched. "Shall I crush them?"

"Not yet."

"Whatever you're going to do," Adrian murmured, "I suggest you do it soon."

The crowd parted all at once, giving way to a new Tranquil. He was an elven man, with long white hair and an air of dignity. It took Adrian a moment to realize this was the same elf they'd seen in the laboratory, but untwisted by demonic possession. The only thing the same was his blue eyes, radiating gentleness as they took in the group.

"Ah, Wynne, you have come." He smiled.

Her grim expression did not soften. An aura of white power radiated from her staff. Adrian could feel the mana being summoned within the old woman, even though she made no move to attack. It might be prudent to begin preparing her own spells, just in case. The tension in the chamber was palpable.

"You are not Pharamond," Wynne said.

"Am I not? We are one, now and forever more."

"I will cast you out."

He chuckled lightly, and gestured to the Tranquil around him. *"Look around you, Wynne. Why do you struggle so? This is the future that awaits you. I know it, Pharamond knows it, and so do you."*

"That is *not* our future," she insisted.

"And what have you done to prevent it? All those extra years given you, and what have you accomplished but to have your efforts slip through your fingers like so much sand?"

Adrian watched in amazement as his words hit home. Wynne's expression crumpled into doubt. "I . . . am doing what I can," she mumbled.

He laughed at her. *"And what is that, exactly? Tell me, great heroine of the dreaded Blight. I see a woman whose soul has shriveled, caring for nothing other than a purpose that now escapes her."* The handsome elf walked close and cupped her chin in his hand. She did not resist. *"You would be happier as Tranquil, dear Wynne. Your life has been a mistake, and a waste of all you were given."*

Sweat beaded on her brow. The light emanating from her staff began to dim, and her knees buckled. There was an invisible contest of wills going on between Wynne and the demon . . . and she was losing.

Shale realized it the same instant Adrian did. With a furious cry the golem charged. It bashed the elf aside with a stone fist, sending him flying away from Wynne with barely a sound. The old woman collapsed to the floor, dropping her staff.

All at once the Tranquil burst into action. They surged toward Shale and Adrian, their faces still placid and completely silent as they clutched at them with strong hands. Adrian tried to back away, horrified, and felt her hair being pulled. She was surrounded by bodies, and someone was trying to tear her staff from her grip.

"Enough!" she cried. The mana rushed out of her in a corona of flame, burning everyone around her. They screamed in agony and recoiled. She gritted her teeth, reminding herself they weren't really people—they were figments of a dream. The demon was the real target here.

She concentrated, digging even deeper into the well of her power. The flames intensified, and she pushed them toward where she saw the demon just getting back to his feet. A ball of white fire soared toward him, everything she had poured into it, and when it struck him it exploded into an inferno.

He was engulfed, as were the Tranquil nearest to him. They shrieked as they lit up, trying in futility to run away. The entire room was filled with smoke and the smell of burning flesh. Adrian fell to her knees, drained. She barely saw Shale through the fiery haze, thrashing about with its fists, sending bodies sailing left and right.

And then the demon . . . walked out of the flames. He was untouched, and smirked in amusement. *"You think to challenge me in the heart of my demesne? You were fools even to come."* He held up a hand as if beckoning, and the entire tower began to shake. Adrian's heart quailed.

And then Wynne rose.

Something had changed within her. Gone was the old woman; instead a force radiated from within. She stood tall and defiant. *"You are mistaken, creature of Pride."* Her voice rang out with unearthly power that pushed back the darkness. Adrian felt it pass through her soul like a cleansing wind. *"You read my mind, but there is a place you could not and cannot reach . . . and that is what you fear."*

The demon's cool demeanor vanished. He hunched down low, baring his teeth in a furious hiss. Adrian saw his features change, subtly shifting from the handsome elf he presented to something ugly and evil, as if what lay beneath the skin were now bubbling up to the surface. *"You do not belong here, spirit!"* he screamed. *"He is mine and you cannot take him from me!"*

Wynne walked toward him . . . no, not walked. Glided. Her robes had transformed into diaphanous silver, flowing in the air as her aura of power became even brighter.

"You have already lost him," she said. Her hand snatched the demon by the neck and lifted him up off the ground. He struggled, clawing uselessly at her arms, and then began to scream. Cracks formed along his skin, white light bursting out of them. He burned, until the light eclipsed him . . .

Adrian heard the music.

It was everywhere. She welcomed it and feared it at the same time, and in a single moment it swept her away. Up into the sky she was borne, away from the tower, from the fire, and the agonized screams of the Tranquil . . . the exquisite glory of it sharpened until she wanted to cry out for it to stop.

And then she awoke.

13

The world came into clarity only slowly, and it took Rhys several minutes before he realized he was on the floor of the laboratory. The others scattered around him, some standing, but all of them looking befuddled. It was as if a fog lifted from his mind, but at the same time it felt as if this were the dream and the world he'd just left behind was the reality.

Magic trilled through the air like electricity. The Fade was torn—as if an invisible window had been left open, and a foul wind was now blowing in. He shivered in reaction, desperately wanting to scratch everywhere the magic touched.

He looked around. Everything about the laboratory was unchanged: the air just as still, the darkness just as oppressive. The only thing different was the demon. Gone was the twisted abomination, replaced by an older elven man with long white hair. His face was ashen, his tattered robes soaked through with sweat, and he gripped the arms of the chair so tightly his knuckles were bone white.

"Is . . . is this real?" he asked through ragged breaths.

All eyes turned toward him, as if the sound of a voice had shattered the unnatural calm. Wynne got to her knees and crawled closer, but remained just outside the binding circle. "Pharamond?" she whispered, her voice laden with concern. "Are you . . . ?"

The elf stared at her in disbelief. Tears welled in his crystal blue eyes, and he began to tremble . . . and then suddenly burst out into jarring laughter. He leapt to his feet, looking about at every corner of the room with a goofy grin even as the tears rolled down his cheeks. "I'm me!" he shouted. "I'm actually me!"

Pharamond let out a joyous whoop and ran over to the startled Wynne, dragging her to her feet. He held her hands tightly, opening his mouth several times as if unable to formulate the words he needed. Then he crushed her in a tight hug. "Thank you, Wynne," he sobbed. "Thank you, oh, I can't even begin to tell you . . ."

Rhys winced as he stood, his bones aching. There was no way to tell how long they'd lain there. Time in the Fade was not the same as in the real world. It could have been a day, a few hours, or even a few minutes. It felt like forever. They were probably lucky they'd slain the rest of the demons before the ritual was performed. Had they not, they'd likely all be dead. Trapped in the Fade forever, unaware of why they couldn't leave the land of dreams until finally they forgot they even needed to.

He saw the golem standing nearby, its stony brow furrowed in consternation. Adrian was next to it, rubbing her shoulders. She seemed uncharacteristically quiet, watching Wynne with a distrustful glare. What was going on in her head, he couldn't even imagine—had something happened with Wynne after they'd parted ways? Evangeline, meanwhile, was just getting to her feet. He realized her intention even before she drew her sword.

"Stand away from him," Evangeline ordered Wynne. The blade was pointed not at her, but at Pharamond.

The elf stared at her, his expression turning instantly from joy to stark terror. "What are you doing?" he spluttered. He retreated, almost stumbling in his haste, but Evangeline kept pace. Her sword did not waver.

"I think it's clear what I'm doing."

Wynne interposed herself between the two of them. She ignored the fact that the tip of the sword was little more than inches from her breast. "I will not allow you to slay him, templar," she said firmly. Shale stood beside her, looming dangerously in a scene reminiscent of what had just happened in the Fade.

"Is that so?" Evangeline ignored the golem, her eyes remaining fixed on Pharamond. "Can you even be certain he is no longer possessed? His appearance has changed, but you know that means nothing. It could be a trick."

"It is not a trick." Wynne gestured to the binding circle, the blood runes now scuffed. Her meaning was obvious: Pharamond had crossed the threshold of his own accord.

Evangeline stared at the runes, the truth sinking in, and reluctantly she lowered her sword. She did not sheathe it, however. "Very well," she said. She hesitated before addressing Pharamond again. "You, however, have much to answer for."

"Answer for?" He seemed genuinely perplexed.

"Your actions have led to the death of every innocent in this keep."

The words seemed to strike him like a thunderclap. The elf recoiled, staring at Evangeline with wide eyes . . . and when Wynne tried to approach him out of concern he backed away from her as well. "You can't mean . . ." he began, his voice trailing off as realization dawned. Suddenly he darted toward the laboratory door.

"Hold!" Evangeline cried. She paused long enough to glare accusingly at Wynne before racing after him. The others followed quickly on her heels.

Pharamond hadn't gone far, however. They found him in the outside chamber, sunk to his knees in horror. The entire room was still littered with burnt corpses, the smoky haze carrying the stench of charred and rotting meat. It was almost too dark to see, and for that Rhys's churning stomach was grateful.

"I never . . ." Pharamond was overcome, shaking his head in denial. He took a deep breath. "I thought I had protected them from . . ."

"You sealed the doors," Evangeline pointed out.

"A precaution!" he objected. "The Lord Mayor's suggestion!"

"They knew about this?"

He nodded slowly. "They . . . supported me. They believed in me. At the time I thought it was logical, but I never . . ." Staring around at the dead bodies, the elf began to shake. A mournful groan escaped his lips as he began to sob. "I killed them, didn't I? I'm responsible."

Rhys watched uncomfortably as the elf broke down in tears. This was no ordinary grief, but more like a wretched pain forcibly extracted from the man. His whole body convulsed with sobs, and he covered his face as he rocked back and forth on the floor.

Wynne hesitated only a moment before she ran to kneel at his side, a pained look on her face as she reassuringly held his shoulders. "Pharamond," she murmured, "I know this distresses you greatly, but we cannot stay. You must pull yourself together."

He looked up from his hands, his eyes bleary and red with tears. "I can't!" he cried. "I . . . can feel everything now, and I can't stop! Oh, Maker help me!"

Pharamond collapsed onto the floor, writhing in grief. He called out like a child might, pawing at the ashes on the floor. Wynne tried to help him, but he could not be moved. She looked to the others in alarm—and to Rhys specifically.

Surely this was worse than being Tranquil—to feel nothing at all for so long, and then to feel everything at once? The man was at the mercy of his emotions, in such pain it was like watching a trapped animal. Part of Rhys cried out that he should try to help, but still he stood frozen in place.

Finally, Evangeline strode forward. Wynne raised a hand in objection, but the templar ignored her. She pulled Pharamond up by his shoulder . . . and then roundly slapped him across the face. It was a hard blow, made all the worse by her metal gauntlets, and the elf crumpled with barely a whimper.

"I could have done that," the golem sniffed.

Wynne rose, her face twisted in fury, but stopped before a word was said. Pharamond was already picking himself off the floor. It seemed the blow had proven effective: his weeping had ceased. Now he rubbed his cheek, a red welt already forming, and stared warily up at Evangeline.

"Tell me what you did," she demanded.

Pharamond paused, glancing at Wynne as if for permission. The old woman nodded, a gesture Evangeline did not miss. "I've been studying the nature of the Rite of Tranquility for many years—how it severs one from the Fade so they no longer dream, why that prevents them from demonic possession, and whether an alternative was even possible. It has been . . . my life's work."

"The Tranquil do nothing they're not asked to."

"That's not true! We have free will. We just . . . desire nothing, we strive for nothing." He paused, staring off into the distance. "But it doesn't matter. I *was* asked to do this. I was commissioned to perform my research by the Chantry."

"The Chantry?" Evangeline frowned. "They knew about this?" She looked accusingly at Wynne, but the old woman merely shook her head. Evidently she didn't know about this either.

"Of course they knew about it," Pharamond said, almost affronted. "How else could I have been here? Why else would I even have come?"

"But did they know what you were doing?" Evangeline gestured at the carnage around them. "Did they know you intended to summon a demon?"

"I didn't summon it!" He paused, considering his words. "I realized early on that Tranquility wasn't repairable on this side of the Fade. It needed to be done from the other side. A spirit had to bridge that gap—and it could only do that if it knew exactly where to look. The Rite renders the Tranquil invisible to spirits."

"They're not just invisible, they're immune . . ."

"Not immune!" The elf became excited, in the manner of a

scholar speaking on his favorite subject. "Undesirable! A demon looks to possess a man because it wishes to experience life. To them a Tranquil is no better than an inanimate object. Worse, since a Tranquil will resist. If it is going to cross that bridge to possess a Tranquil, it needs to be *lured* . . ."

Wynne furrowed her brows in confusion. "So you sought to become possessed on purpose? Pharamond, whatever did you hope to gain?"

He sighed. "I didn't mean to be possessed. I only needed the bridge to be crossed, to see if it could be done. I came to a place where the Veil was thin, where a spirit could be found and communicated with."

Pharamond knelt down by one of the charred bodies, his expression full of grief. He held out a hand as if to touch it, but could not. He pulled his hand back quickly, clamping his eyes shut to fight against renewed tears. "These people were so welcoming. Like a family. They believed I was scarred, and wanted me to be healed. They were willing to accept the risk, and logically I believed . . ." He choked up.

Evangeline shook her head angrily. "You killed them all for nothing. Whatever knowledge you've gained is useless."

He shook his head. "It's not, actually."

Now Adrian stepped forward, her expression curious. "What do you mean it's not?"

"I believed a demon needed to *try* to possess me, that the act of trying would itself restore my connection to the Fade." He opened his eyes and stared intently at Adrian. "But that wasn't it at all. I only needed the demon to reach across that gap and touch my mind, nothing more. The instant it happened, I was cured. The possession came . . . later."

"But any spirit could do that," Rhys pointed out. When Evangeline looked at him incredulously, he repeated it: "Any spirit could do it, provided they were strong enough. It doesn't have to be a demon."

Pharamond nodded. "It would take a spirit medium to coax one."

"*I'm* a spirit medium."

The room was quiet as that sank in. Adrian nodded in approval, but Evangeline refused to be budged. "You must be mad," she scoffed. "None of you can honestly think this should be attempted again. Look around you!"

"And instead they should have died for nothing?" Adrian demanded. "This man is no longer Tranquil. If his work can be used without repeating what happened here, it's worth pursuing!"

"Reversing Tranquility is not in anyone's best interest." Before Adrian could retort, Evangeline gestured to Pharamond. "Look at him! Is his condition so much better? What if he never improves?"

"What if he does?"

"And what if the entire reason he was made Tranquil in the first place is still valid? We do not use the Rite without cause. This man could now be a danger, to himself as well as others—such as the people of this very keep."

Pharamond nodded glumly. "It's true."

"Don't listen to her!" Adrian ordered him. When she saw Evangeline raising her sword, she leapt between the templar and Pharamond. "I won't let you do this! Tranquility isn't an answer— Pharamond already knows more about it than anyone's cared to find out. He should be allowed to find another solution!"

Evangeline's expression was grim. "There is blood on this knowledge, as there would be on anything that comes of it. You would give false hope to those who deserve better." She made to move around Adrian, her blade held ready, but Adrian intercepted her.

"No!" she cried. She looked helplessly at Rhys. "This is what the Libertarians have always talked about! The templars have no right to do this! Don't you see? This is our chance to undo what the Circle has done to us for centuries!"

Of course that's what it would be about, to her. Rhys wasn't so certain himself. Even if he could repeat Pharamond's ritual safely, should he? Evangeline wasn't wrong. "Adrian, I . . ."

She abandoned him and spun around to face Wynne. "This is your friend, the one you were determined to save! You can't possibly let him be condemned for this!"

Wynne said nothing at first, merely looking at Adrian inscrutably. Rhys couldn't believe Wynne was being so calm about this. "I'll admit," she finally said, "it brings me no pleasure to see Pharamond tormented, and I dislike the notion he might be punished out of hand. But he *did* invite the demon in. This was no accident."

"And what difference does it make?" Adrian demanded. "You *of all people* should know that!"

Wynne stood up, the grip on her staff tight as she glared at Adrian. "Yes, I believe I *of all people* know exactly the difference."

"Hypocrite!"

Rhys was confused. There was a tension between the two that went beyond Adrian's usual hostility. He would have intervened had Evangeline not interrupted.

"We are done speaking of this," she said curtly. She faced Pharamond, holding up her sword. "You have employed forbidden magic and exacted a terrible price from innocents. This crime cannot be overlooked. In the name of the Order of Templars I hereby—"

Adrian screamed in outrage, firing a magical blast from her staff. It struck Evangeline directly in the breastplate, sending her flying back. The templar fell to the floor amid several bodies, letting out a grunt of surprise. The sword did not leave her hand.

"Adrian!" Rhys cried. "What are you doing?"

"What we should have done when we arrived!"

He turned to Wynne in alarm, but she remained where she was, frowning as she watched the scene unfold. She made no indication she would intervene. Shale moved closer to protect her.

Evangeline got back up, wiping at the scorch mark left on her armor. Her expression was fearsome to behold; she was clearly done with playing nice. "That was a mistake," she growled. As she assumed a combat stance, white power coursed through her blade— the power of a templar ready to battle a mage. Adrian summoned mana, a ball of red flame already coalescing about her hand.

"Wait!"

Rhys realized the shout was his. Once again, his mouth had acted with a mind of its own. *Stupid mouth,* he chided himself. *Why must you always do the talking?*

Evangeline hesitated, and even Adrian looked in his direction. The tension in the room was thick, and it seemed like all it would take was a spark and there would be no turning back. Rhys licked his lips, suddenly aware just how dry they were. His heart was beating rapidly.

"There is another option," he said slowly. When nobody responded, he moved to stand between the two of them. Both eyed him carefully. Adrian in particular seemed filled with mute fury. Her eyes said *You should be helping me,* but he knew he couldn't do that, no matter how much she might want him to.

"What other option?" Evangeline asked, her tone skeptical.

"The Chantry asked Pharamond to do his research. Perhaps they didn't know what he intended to do, but isn't it possible they might consider his findings important, even so?" He paused, but Evangeline didn't respond. Her eyes remained fixed on Adrian, their standoff unabated. "Why not bring him to the Chantry and let them decide? Why must you pass sentence here?"

"I have my orders," she stated.

Wynne stepped beside him, her interest suddenly kindled. "Your orders come from the Lord Seeker, but where do his come from? My mission was approved by the Divine herself. If anyone would have an interest in this, it would be she."

Adrian bristled at the talk, the magical fire curling its way up her arms. She wanted to fight, Rhys could see that. Evangeline, however, appeared to consider the idea. Her sword still crackled with energy, but instead of staring at Adrian, she was looking thoughtfully at Pharamond.

"Do you really want to be the one who decides this?" Rhys asked.

Slowly she lowered her blade, and its power vanished. "No," she said. "I have a duty to the Templar Order . . . but I have one to the Chantry, as well. In the end their decision may be the same, but I cannot deny them the opportunity to make it."

Adrian almost seemed disappointed. She released the magical flame and backed off. A single glance at Rhys told him just what she thought of his interference.

"Then it's solved," Wynne said. "We return to Val Royeaux, and I'll send word ahead for the Divine to expect our arrival. Let her solve this business."

"And what's to become of Pharamond, then?" Adrian demanded. "What if the Chantry doesn't like what it hears?"

"We shall see."

"That was your answer before."

"And it remains true."

Evangeline nodded and sheathed her blade, although the room seemed no less tense for her agreement. She and Adrian exchanged a dire look that said there would eventually be a reckoning between the two. Rhys didn't understand why Adrian kept pushing it—if Evangeline had wished to be unreasonable, she could have been. Instead she chose to relinquish her decision to a higher authority. Surely that had to count for something?

Wynne helped Pharamond to his feet. The elf seemed confused, uncertain if the matter was now truly decided. Would he be leaving? Was he being spared? Rhys could understand his hesitance. Like himself, Pharamond's fate was likely only delayed. In the meantime, however, bloodshed was averted.

Pharamond gazed sadly at the corpses surrounding him, his eyes hollow. Once they were gone from this place, it would be as dead as the land surrounding it. Would anyone ever come to take the place of those who had lived here, knowing what had happened to them? It seemed unlikely; the keep would become a tomb.

A fitting monument, perhaps, to the search for forbidden knowledge.

Cole hid within the shadows of the upper keep's entry chamber. It was nighttime outside. He could see the moon in the clear sky through the few windows. That meant the place was blessedly dark, which was just as well. He didn't want to look at it. He didn't want to be reminded of what had happened here. Far worse was the stillness that had now settled over everything, a quiet so total it was overwhelming.

Not long ago, it hadn't been nearly as quiet. He'd awoken to the sound of angry shouting. Slowly he'd made his way through the pitch black halls until he found the source: Rhys and the others arguing in a chamber full of death and smoke, the light from their staves offering a hint of the battle which had occurred there—bodies twisted and burned, scattered among the ashes in a way not unlike the soldiers he remembered from the city square.

They weren't arguing about the bodies, however. This had something to do with a strange elven man in the tattered robes, someone Cole had never seen before. Knight-Captain wanted to kill him. Red Hair refused to let her. Nobody seemed to care what the elven man wanted. Even from a distance, Cole could see the despair in his eyes. He wanted death. Had it come for him, he would have embraced it gladly and let it wash him away into that dark and peaceful oblivion.

But he wasn't killed. Cole hovered on the edge of the room, keeping one hand on his dagger in case Rhys needed him, and watched the tension build . . . and then eventually come to an end. Nobody seemed happy with the result, even though Cole wasn't certain what that was. Least happy of all was the elven man.

Cole felt sorry for him, kneeling there so hopeless and alone.

Now he didn't know what he should do next. The memories of the dream world plagued him. Many of the details were already slipping away, like dreams sometimes did, but the essence remained. Memories had bubbled up like some rotten buried thing, and its stink lingered in his nostrils.

There was a vague recollection of sitting on top of his father's chest. Blood gurgled out of the man's mouth. Cole held the dagger up in front of his eyes, let him look at it. He wanted the man to know that it was Cole who was ending his life, stopping him from hurting anyone else. He remembered his father trying to speak, and imagined the man would have pleaded for his life, but nothing came out but more blood.

The satisfaction of sinking the dagger into his father's heart was imprinted on his soul. His mother's dagger. The only piece of the wilder folk she'd kept, and when his father tried to sell it she'd buried it in the field. Cole had watched, and he now remembered digging the dagger up, clawing at the earth with bare fingers as tears stung his eyes.

He remembered his sister, too. All too well. The thought of her made him wince, and he wanted to wipe the thoughts from his mind. Go back to forgetting. But the memories refused to leave, and every time he closed his eyes he saw unbidden images there, waiting.

"Are you all right?"

The voice was startling, primarily because Cole thought he had been listening. Instead he'd been so wrapped up in his own thoughts he hadn't noticed Rhys enter the room. The silvery-blue light from his staff drove back the shadows a little, at least for the moment, and he felt grateful.

"You didn't need me," Cole admitted glumly. "I came all this way because I thought they would hurt you, but they didn't. I should have gone back when you told me to."

Rhys didn't say anything. He had the look he always had when he came to see Cole in the tower, one of pity and concern. It was hard for Cole to look at him when he did that. He looked at the floor instead, and tried not to flinch when Rhys sat on the stair next to him.

For several minutes they said nothing, the only sound the faint hum emitted by Rhys's staff. Finally Rhys broke the silence. "That house in the Fade," he began hesitantly, "that was your home? That's where you come from?"

"I don't know. Yes."

"And that man was your father?"

"Yes."

Another pause, and then Rhys nodded slowly. "I'm sorry that happened to you, Cole. I was born in the Circle, so I don't know what it's like for mages who aren't . . . but you hear things. Most don't want to talk about it."

Cole didn't know how to respond. He'd never spoken to any other mages. It was true that he'd never overheard any talking about their old lives. He'd thought it was because they didn't want to think about what they couldn't have. But perhaps they wanted to forget, too?

Rhys looked at him. After a moment, Cole lifted his eyes and met his gaze. He felt oddly uncomfortable, like Rhys had been exposed to something private, something Cole couldn't take back. That was odd only because Cole hadn't known it even existed before they'd gone into that dream realm . . . but there it was now, this awkward thing lying between them.

"You're not responsible for what happened to her, Cole."

And there it was. Cole looked away, feeling the flush rising in his cheeks. He wanted to cry, or scream, or . . . something. A dark lump deep down inside of him clenched, something that had been there all along, but he'd become accustomed to it. Silently gnawing away at him.

"I don't even remember her," he muttered.

"That's not true."

He shifted uncomfortably on the stairs. "I didn't mean to do it."

"I know."

"I was just trying to keep her quiet, so Papa wouldn't hear us. I thought she was being so good, too, so quiet . . ." He choked up, unable to continue.

"I know." Rhys put his hand on Cole's shoulder. Such a simple gesture, yet it was reassuring.

He also found himself incredibly glad that Rhys wasn't angry at him any longer. Ever since the fight in the crypt, he'd been worried that Rhys would never want to see him again. And he'd have deserved it, too, after the way he'd pushed Rhys away. The relief was so unbearable he felt the tears come. They pushed their way up like a wellspring, and before he knew it he was weeping.

Rhys put an arm around him and hugged him tight, and he buried his face in the man's shoulder. He couldn't remember the last time he'd cried. It felt like he never had, like he was so dry inside these tears were a foreign and unwelcome thing. But it felt good as much as it felt wretched.

And then Cole froze as he realized someone else was in the room.

Rhys realized it, too, and paused to look over at the entrance to the chamber. Knight-Captain stood there, staring at them. There was an ugly scorch mark across her breastplate, right where that sunburst crest was. It looked like someone had crossed it out.

"I'm sorry I doubted you, Rhys," she said.

He cleared his throat. "I didn't realize you'd followed me."

"The others are helping Pharamond collect his things. I noticed you'd wandered off . . . again. It wasn't difficult to imagine who you'd gone looking for."

"You can . . . see me?" Cole asked.

"I can." She stepped forward, but paused when he sat up in alarm. "Could it be your curse is broken?"

"I don't know."

"It's possible seeing him in the Fade changed something," Rhys said. "But we have no idea whether that will last. You could easily forget him again."

It was true. The thought troubled Cole, but at the same time he was being seen by someone with whom he hadn't gone out of his way to interact. And she *remembered* him. In the dream world that didn't seem so real, but here? Here it was everything.

The way she looked at him was strange, however. It was like she couldn't quite believe he was there, or expected him to transform into something else. An insect, maybe. Or a demon. "Are you going to kill me?" he finally asked.

Rhys looked at Knight-Captain in alarm. Then she shook her head, a troubled expression on her face. "No. I think I've made enough threats today."

She walked toward him again, more slowly this time, and knelt at the foot of the stairs not far away. She scrutinized Cole with her pretty eyes. "I was there," she said. "I saw what happened to you. I *felt* it. I can't say you won't be judged for your crimes, but it won't be by me."

He didn't know what to say.

"Return to the Circle with us," she continued. "If Rhys is going to be cleared of the Lord Seeker's suspicions, he'll need evidence. If your curse isn't broken, we'll make him see you just as I've seen. What happens after that . . . I will speak on your behalf. That's all I can offer."

Rhys smiled at her gratefully, but she didn't look his way.

Knight-Captain's eyes remained intently on Cole. There was honesty there. Cole believed her. "Why would you defend me?"

"Because the first duty of the templars is to protect mages. Rhys told me we failed you, and he's right. If there's any chance the Circle can help you, I believe we should try."

"They'll probably make him Tranquil," Rhys said. "You know that."

Her expression filled with compassion. "Would that be so terrible?"

A life without dreams, and without memory. Without the terror of being swallowed up by the darkness and fading away forever. "No," Cole murmured. "That wouldn't be so bad."

Knight-Captain held out her hand to him . . . and he took it.

14

Rhys tried not to think about what awaited him at the White Spire as the group journeyed back to Val Royeaux. It wasn't easy. Tension simmered just beneath the surface in the group, ready to spill over into hostility if anyone so much as spoke the wrong word, and thus everyone kept to themselves. That gave him far too much time to think.

He tried to keep a close eye on Cole. It was easy to tell the young man was having difficulty spending so much time in the company of those who could see him, and each morning when they awoke he was surprised all over again to discover he was not only still visible, but remembered.

By everyone but Pharamond, that is. As heartbreaking as it was to watch Cole's realization that his curse still affected him, it was also interesting to watch it in operation. As long as Rhys had known the young man, he'd never had the opportunity to see what happened when he was in someone's company for an extended period. Pharamond never saw Cole at all unless attention was brought to him, and each time that happened the elf was surprised anew to find a "stranger" suddenly among them. He barely recollected the introductions made previously, and within minutes Cole would slip out of his notice once again.

What kind of magic could do this? Prior to entering the Fade, Rhys had told the others about Cole and they never forgot his name afterward. Why did Pharamond? Was it only because Cole was present? If meeting him in the Fade was what allowed the others to see and remember him, was that the solution to ending the curse for good? It was a puzzle, and very likely one Rhys would never get a chance to unravel.

Adrian was not making things any easier. She seemed to be angry at everyone. Evangeline, she said, was going to betray them, and made no bones about voicing her suspicions. She seethed in Wynne's presence, making acidic comments about how the woman should have supported her—comments no doubt intended for Rhys, as well—and argued with her over the importance of Pharamond's research. She believed a confrontation awaited them the moment they stepped back into the White Spire, and Wynne's dismissal only made her more furious. Cole she avoided like the plague, glaring accusingly at him if he got too near.

To Rhys she said nothing at all. The icy silence was unnerving, all the more because she sat behind him now that Pharamond rode with Wynne. He could feel her eyes boring into the back of his neck, and she gripped his chest so stiffly it felt awkward. Part of him wondered if he would ever have his friend back. The other part felt a little angry that, once again, everyone had to see things her way.

Evangeline concentrated on keeping them moving. She'd said little since they left the keep. He assumed it had something to do with the templars outside. She'd taken them aside, and at one point appeared to be arguing heatedly with their leader. Adrian's whispered warnings that they should prepare for a fight didn't seem so far-fetched.

But then it was over. The templar leader waved for his men to surrender a horse to Evangeline, along with feed and supplies. They complied, albeit sullenly, and once they were done, the leader turned back to Evangeline. Rhys couldn't make out what the man said, but the expression of disgust on his face said plenty. The templars rode off without another word.

Had they expected to attack? Had Evangeline dissuaded them? She wouldn't say when she returned, and tersely ordered the group to get underway—as soon as possible. They hastened to do just that.

As they passed through the badlands, Shale became cantankerous. *More* cantankerous, rather. The golem complained constantly at the slow speed of the horses through the sand and the blowing wind. The first night when they finally stopped to rest, it moaned for over an hour . . . a long litany of offenses by "soft" humans, exhaustion not being the least of them.

The group endured the golem's complaints, though Rhys caught Evangeline rolling her eyes from time to time. Pharamond appeared delighted to encounter an actual golem, however, and plied Shale with all manner of questions. Shale's answers were, for the most part, sarcastic. When asked what kind of rock it consisted of, Shale answered "petrified nug droppings." When asked how it was created, Shale responded with a long explanation of mother golems and father golems which Pharamond believed for five whole minutes. When asked how it could see through those points of lights in its eye sockets, Shale commented that it actually preferred tearing the eyeballs out of flesh creatures and using them instead—elven ones in particular.

That, at least, gave Pharamond pause.

Shale began the next morning by commenting on the noises everyone made as they slept. Then more observations on how slowly they got underway through what was the worst windstorm since they arrived in the badlands. Many of the golem's amused barbs were aimed at Wynne, with words like "decrepit" and "rusting" popping up.

Finally Wynne turned her horse about. With a beaming smile she asked if Shale wouldn't be so kind as to lead the way instead. It was a challenge the golem was only too happy to undertake, and it actually worked out quite well. The path it trudged through the sand was much easier to follow. The golem only vanished into a sinkhole once, requiring an hour's worth of effort for the horses to haul it back out.

Shortly after they left the badlands and green grass appeared on the hills, Wynne made the suggestion that Shale deliver a message to the Circle of Magi at Montsimmard. It was the nearest, and the mages there could use the sending stone to contact the White Spire. Sendings were not done lightly, she said, but considering the interest of the Chantry it might be a good idea to let them know of their expected arrival—and the urgent need for an audience with the Divine. Montsimmard, however, was well out of their way.

Evangeline seemed almost relieved to agree. Shale sighed at being reduced to the level of messenger—did Wynne expect it to fetch a chair, next? Perhaps she'd prefer to place a saddle on its back and ride it instead of her horse? A withering look from the old woman was enough to silence the golem. It accepted her letter and was off.

Rhys had a moment of amusement imagining the golem showing up at the gates of the Montsimmard Circle. He supposed it might, in fact, make Wynne's letter all the more convincing. How many golem messengers could there be, after all, especially ones with such an endearing attitude?

After Shale was gone, things were quiet again. Evangeline led them along the same back roads they took getting there, hurrying them as much as she dared. They didn't meet a single soul until late on the third day of travel, when a dwarven merchant on a small wagon met them going in the opposite direction.

The man almost didn't stop, and eyed even the Chantry insignia on Evangeline's armor with suspicion. When questioned, he said he was planning on taking the long route to Montsimmard on account of all the unrest since the battles began. Their raised eyebrows made him chuckle with amusement. Hadn't they heard?

There was war in the east. Who was fighting whom was the subject of rampant rumor, but the flood of citizens fleeing into the Heartlands had turned the countryside upside down. They would be lucky to reach the capital, he said.

They stood there, stunned, as the dwarf urged his horses onward. A civil war, then? But there had been no mustering of the chevaliers, no call to arms under the Imperial banner? What had happened while they were in the badlands?

It was ill news of the worst sort. A civil war, then? Had the chevaliers been musters, or a call of arms made to the Imperial banner? What had happened while they were in the badlands? Rhys watched Evangeline staring pensively off into the distance, as if she could somehow discern what awaited them at the capital. The wind howled through the hills as the group waited for her to lead them, but she did nothing.

"Ser Evangeline?" Wynne asked hesitantly.

The templar remained quiet.

"Ser Evangeline, we've still an hour of light left."

"If we travel into the night we could reach Velun," Rhys suggested. "Maybe we could ask for news there?"

That seemed to get her attention. "No," she said firmly. "We stay away from any settlements. If there is anarchy, we're at risk now more than ever." She turned in her saddle and scanned the rest of them, frowning as her eyes fell on Pharamond.

Rhys could almost read the thoughts running through her head. Bring the elf into a populated area and the chance he might run away became even greater. Would he do so? Rhys couldn't say for certain—but short of Evangeline spending every waking moment watching Pharamond, not to mention Cole, there was no way to ensure he didn't have the chance.

"Let's make camp now," she said.

It was raining. Rhys didn't think he would miss the rain, but after that trek through the badlands it felt almost glorious to stand out in the open and let the sand wash off. He turned his face up to the night sky, closing his eyes and enjoying the icy raindrops pelting his skin. The sound of thunder off in the distance seemed welcoming rather than ominous.

Everyone had finally succumbed to nervous exhaustion at the camp, leaving only Evangeline to stand guard. He couldn't join the others in sleep, and so sat in silence by the smoldering remains of the campfire. He'd offered to let Evangeline get some sleep, but she'd barely responded except to shake her head. Perhaps she thought he would try to run, as well. He certainly had every reason to.

Cole was curled up next to him, as close as he could get to the fire without burning. He didn't even stir as the rain fell on him, although Rhys saw fluttering behind his eyelids. Bad dreams. Considering all the young man had been through, he couldn't blame him for wanting to forget. He might not understand why Cole felt the impulse to kill, and couldn't let himself forget what Cole was, but he wasn't without sympathy.

He wiped a wet lock of blond hair out of Cole's eyes, and prayed silently that the Maker might deliver him a few days of peaceful rest before they got to the tower. The Maker owed him that much, at least.

"They may not listen to us," Evangeline suddenly said.

Rhys looked up, startled. The templar stood next to the campfire, watching him with a pensive expression. Her silvery armor glistened from the rain, her scarlet cloak dark and soaked through. Even with her black hair wet and plastered against her face, she was beautiful. He didn't want to admit it to himself, but there it was. "The templars?" he prompted.

She nodded. "I do not know Lord Seeker Lambert well. I believe he's a fair man, if harsh, but if there's war in the land . . ."

"You think he might not be inclined to listen."

"I think he might see our duty to keep order as being more important than finding the truth. Convincing him that Cole is not a demon will be . . . difficult enough." She paused, considering. "And the templars I spoke to . . . they will return to the Lord Seeker with their own tale. I have no control over that, and indeed any defense I offer might be considered biased. I wish I could say otherwise."

He thought about it, and then let out a slow sigh. "What other option do we have?"

"You could run." He was startled, and stared at Evangeline as she knelt down by the fire. She picked up a stick and stirred the coals, sending up sparks and thick smoke into the rain. "I have to bring Pharamond to the tower. You, on the other hand, were not the object of this mission. You could take Cole and flee. To Ferelden, if you dared to cross the Dales with these rumors of war, or north to Tevinter."

He gulped. Was this a test? "I would just be hunted," he said.

She reached into her cloak and pulled out a small glass vial. It glowed a deep and sinister red, something within it making the hairs on the back of his neck prickle. Magic, but something more as well. "This is your phylactery," she explained. "I would use it to track you if you escaped. If you overpowered me and broke it, however . . ."

"Why would you do this?"

The question made her pause. She stared at the coals, a grim frown etched onto her face. "I don't like being forced to choose between my duty and what's right. Knight-Commander Eron used to say that a templar's duty should always be questioned, and that the moment we stopped doing so was when we stopped being templars."

"He . . . sounds like a good man."

"He is. Wherever they've sent him, I hope he's treated fairly."

She looked back at Rhys, her eyes intense. "You saved my life, Rhys. You could have left me to die when Adrian cast that spell in the keep, but you didn't."

"Oh, I doubt you would have *died*."

"I don't."

He grinned, embarrassed. "I didn't think about it. I just knew I had to warn you . . . though by rights we probably both should have burned."

Evangeline watched him carefully. Perhaps she was trying to determine if he was just being modest; he couldn't tell. After a moment she nodded, as if coming to a decision. "I was wrong about you. You're a good man, and if there were anyone able to resist a demon it would be you. Letting you go would be endangering no one."

"And what about Cole?"

"Teach him. Keep him safe. He deserves a second chance."

"Even after what he's done?"

"I won't judge Cole, not after what I've seen. I'll leave that to the Maker."

They were both quiet for a long time, only the slow hissing of the coals and the occasional peal of thunder overhead to keep them company. "You could come with us," he said quietly.

"I have to bring Pharamond to the tower."

"Pharamond be damned! Let Wynne take him back. It was her mission all along, not yours. If you go back with him still alive and me vanished . . ."

Evangeline smiled at him, faintly. She replaced the vial in her cloak, and then took out a small bundle of purple silk. Without speaking, she placed it on the ground and unwrapped it. There were five tiny vials within. Four seemed empty, but one of them had a small amount of shimmering blue liquid inside. He didn't need to hear the music in his mind to know what it was.

"Lyrium," he breathed.

She nodded. "We're not mages, Rhys. Our training would not be enough to deal with magic unless we used lyrium, I'm sure you know this."

"But what does . . ."

"There's only one vial left." Carefully she wrapped the vials back up in the silk and put the bundle away. "Once that is gone, I'll have perhaps a week before I start to feel the effects. Within a month, perhaps two, I'll go insane."

"You're addicted."

"And there's nothing to be done about it. The Chantry controls the supply of lyrium, and thus they control the templars. There is no turning back from the order once you're within." She shrugged. "My course is set. Yours need not be."

He thought about it. After a while, he stood up. There was just no way he could sit there with her staring at him and think this through rationally. He turned to leave the camp, hoping she would let him be alone. She'd just suggested he run, after all, so arguing he shouldn't leave camp didn't seem likely.

She didn't. Rhys walked off into the distance, far enough away that the faint light from what remained of the campfire was gone. The moon was obscured by the rain clouds, and thus the darkness seemed almost complete. He walked up the nearest hill, marveling at the slush of the wet grass and the fresh, crisp smell of the air.

When he got to the top, he stared out over the horizon. He couldn't see far—more hills were in the distance, with only a lingering mist glowing faintly silver under the moonlight. The patter of the rain was almost hypnotic. Soothing. He took a deep breath and let the chill air steady him.

Fleeing. That would make him an apostate, of course. Even without a phylactery, the templars would still look for him. He would be on the run, with Cole to look after . . . assuming Cole would even be willing to join him. And where would they go? Anywhere might be safer than the tower, but it still seemed hopeless.

Then again, he'd promised to help Cole. Now that he'd seen it was possible for people to remember the man, he might actually be able to do something. He could continue his research into spirits, something he hadn't been able to do for the last year. Perhaps he could find some remote location, some place where the locals weren't so inquisitive, set up a workshop . . .

. . . and end up exactly like Pharamond.

That wasn't a cheerful thought. As much as he disliked the constant supervision of the templars, their vigilance meant he couldn't harm anyone. Without them, all it would take was one mistake, one encounter with the wrong demon, and he would doom far more people than just himself.

"Don't go," someone said behind him.

He spun around. Adrian stood there, wet and bedraggled and hugging herself as the rain poured down. As miserable as she looked, however, her expression was determined. Her jaw was set, and he knew what *that* meant.

"You were eavesdropping," he sighed.

"You were talking right next to me."

Rhys turned away, staring out over the valley and trying to recapture the serenity he'd felt only a moment before. It had vanished with the wind, evidently. "I don't want to argue, Adrian. And why would you not want me to go, anyhow? You've made it perfectly clear how much you hate me."

She threw her hands up. "I don't *hate* you," she sighed irritably. "I hate that you're not doing anything to stop the templars before they kill you. I hate that you're letting one pretty templar turn you into a fool."

"So this is about Evangeline."

Adrian scowled. She walked to the top of the hill and stood beside Rhys, looking out over the dark valley below as he was. "Fine, I'm jealous," she admitted. "Is that what you want to hear?"

"Evangeline is a good person. You heard her offer."

"I heard her telling you to spend the rest of your life on the run, to give the templar order one more reason to believe mages are exactly who they think we are." She shook her head in dismay. "You need to face them, Rhys. For you, and for all of us."

"And what would you have me do, exactly?"

Adrian grabbed his arm, turning him to face her. Her gaze was intense. "Return to the tower. Let them refuse to see the truth. Let them try to make an example of you. Show them for what they are."

"Maker's breath, Adrian! You want me to become a martyr?"

"The mages know you, Rhys. They'll rise to defend you."

He pulled away, trying not to look as angry as he felt. It was easy to send others to fight her battles, wasn't it? Let them die for the cause, while she stands on the sidelines rabble-rousing? But perhaps that wasn't fair. He knew how much Adrian cared—too much, perhaps. As long as he'd known her, she'd always kept her eyes on the goal. It was what he had always admired about her.

"And what about Cole?" he asked.

"Haven't you done enough for him?"

"No, I don't think anyone has."

Adrian frowned. He could tell she was struggling to find the words, ones that wouldn't upset him. It was an effort she usually didn't make. "If you really wanted to help Cole," she said carefully, "you wouldn't bring him to the tower. You know the templars aren't going to try and help him." She cut him off before he could interject. "And, yes, I know Ser Evangeline said she would help. But she can't, and she knows it. That's why she suggested you run."

"And so maybe I should."

She gave him a knowing look. "Cole's managed to live right under the noses of the templars for years. I imagine he's in no danger of being hunted. You, on the other hand, would be. It isn't a better choice."

"You think I don't know that?"

"You're not acting like you do." She put a hand on his shoulder, looking at him earnestly. "If news of what Pharamond learned gets out, it will remind everyone how desperate the templars are to keep power over us. When they try to punish you, it will be just like in Kirkwall. This is our chance, Rhys. This is what the Libertarians have been waiting for."

"And I'm the sacrificial lamb; that's great." He sighed, rubbing a hand over his wet hair. The rain was beginning to slacken, although somehow it seemed like it should be coming down stronger than ever. He expected thunderstorms, lightning, the sky opening up above him. Instead, all he got was drenched. "Not everyone lives in a world of black and white like you do, Adrian," he said. "It doesn't have to end in a rebellion. There are other options."

"Such as?"

"My mother, for one. I refuse to think she'll—"

Adrian's face hardened, and she pulled back. "I know Wynne is your mother," she said, "and I know how much that means to you. But you can't put your hopes in her. You can't trust her."

"You don't trust anyone."

"It's not that." She considered carefully, glancing at Rhys in a way that suggested he wasn't going to like what she had to say. "I couldn't say anything earlier, not in front of Ser Evangeline."

"Now you're making me nervous."

Adrian steeled herself. "When we reached the demon, Wynne defeated it—by herself, without any help from me. I don't think she even really wanted me there."

"And that's bad?"

"It's *how* she did it. Rhys, there's a spirit inside of her, a powerful one. I saw it emerge. It wasn't a spell, and she didn't summon it. I think it was there all along."

He stared at her, stunned. "Are you saying . . . ?"

"I think Wynne is an abomination."

—————

The next morning, just as the sun began to creep over the horizon, the camp stirred. Rhys had spent the rest of the night jittery and sleepless, and finally convinced Evangeline to get some sleep. How she managed to stand guard every evening and not succumb to exhaustion, he had no idea. An effect of the lyrium, or a sense of vigilance?

It had been strange, sitting there in the quiet camp and watching the sleeping faces of the others. Wynne, in particular. Even in sleep, she looked tired and pale. An old woman who chose to travel across half the Empire and sleep out in the rain. She certainly didn't look possessed—abominations were twisted, hideous things like what Pharamond had become. Even when a demon didn't twist its host's body, there should still be some evidence of its presence. He should be able to sense it.

Could Adrian be wrong?

Everyone got to their feet sluggishly, wiping off their clothes and rubbing themselves vigorously to get rid of the chill. The dawn sky was clear, bursting with red and orange, and Rhys might have thought it pretty had he not been so preoccupied.

As Evangeline collected the mounts from where they were grazing, Rhys called out to her. "Leave one of them here," he said. "I'd like to speak to Wynne. Alone."

Wynne stopped brushing her hair and looked up in surprise. The others were similarly curious, but no one said anything. Evangeline merely nodded. "We'll go slowly. Catch up as soon as you can." He could only imagine what she thought he was planning. She hadn't asked him anything since he and Adrian had returned to the camp.

Everyone quietly mounted and rode off, leaving Rhys and Wynne behind. Cole was the only one to look back. He seemed worried. Perhaps he thought Rhys was planning to leave him? Reluctantly, the young man turned back to the road ahead . . . and within moments they were gone.

Wynne kept brushing as if nothing were amiss. She took several pins from her robe and put her hair up into a bun, all the while not looking in Rhys's direction. He was stumped as to where he should begin. He'd spent the night waiting for this moment, but all the things he'd rehearsed evaporated from his mind. How did you accuse someone of being an abomination?

"She told you," Wynne said.

He stared at her, his mouth agape. It hadn't been a question, simply an observation. Wynne sat with hands folded in her lap and looked at him with a wary expression. "I . . . guess she did, yes," he muttered.

"Close your mouth, dear. It's unbecoming."

His mouth snapped shut with an audible click.

"I suppose this was inevitable," she sighed.

He almost didn't want to ask. "Is it true?"

"Is it true I've been possessed by a spirit? Yes, that is true." Before he could ask another question, however, she held up a finger and smiled patiently. "No, it is not what you believe has changed me. The spirit was with me when we first met."

"But that was . . ."

"Many years ago, yes." She frowned thoughtfully, staring into the ashes of the campfire. "I died, you see. It happened at the beginning of the Blight. The Tower of Magi in Ferelden had been taken over by abominations, and I was killed in the battle. As I lingered on the precipice between life and death, a spirit came to me. Not a demon, not anything horrid or selfish, and it offered me a second chance."

He waited, as it seemed there was more to the story, but Wynne said nothing. She continued to stare, and he wondered what she was thinking. This felt like a confession. "A second chance to do what?" he asked.

Wynne shrugged. "I wish I knew. Years ago I thought my time short, that I had been given only a temporary reprieve. I was alive for some greater purpose, and once that was done I would die as I was meant to." She shook her head sadly. "I fought to keep the Circle from collapsing, to prevent a war that would have cost untold lives . . . and nothing. I live still."

Whatever Rhys had expected to come of this conversation, this wasn't it. He walked a few steps away, rubbing his forehead like that would get his brain functioning, and then turned back. Wynne still sat there, looking at him expectantly. He sat down on the grass, a little too suddenly.

"Are you sure it's not a demon?" he asked. "I mean . . . I've never heard of a benevolent spirit possessing anyone. They can be curious about our world, but they don't go out of their way to enter it like demons do."

"Demons and spirits are not so different from one another. They are two sides of the same coin. As for why this spirit chose to come to me . . ." Her voice trailed off, and she became contemplative. "I don't know. It happened so quickly. I think it had always been with me before, and simply chose that moment to act."

"But you don't know why?"

"We did not speak. I . . . felt it come, like a warm glow spreading throughout my body. It provided the spark of life that was fading from me, and I think that's where it remains. A part of me, of my soul."

"Is that why I can't sense it?"

"I believe so. The spirit and I are not separate."

"But Adrian said she saw it appear."

Wynne allowed herself a private smile. "It may have seemed that way. In the Fade I have power in the same way the spirit does. If I didn't show it earlier, it's because I didn't wish to tip my hand to the demon."

Rhys chewed his lip and considered, while Wynne busied

herself packing. There were so many questions he should be asking, yet what he faced was simply too large to think of anything else. He remembered her anger when the subject of saving Pharamond arose, back when he'd told her and Adrian about Cole. Now it made sense.

I'd like you to meet my mother, the abomination.

Oh, how charming! She doesn't look at all twisted like most of them do.

No, she looks quite good for a dead woman, doesn't she?

He let out a slow breath. "So what now?"

Wynne paused, closing her pack. "That's an excellent question. In a way, this is very convenient. I'd hoped to speak with you away from Ser Evangeline, but there was never a convenient excuse."

"What do you mean?"

She looked at him intently. "I want you to learn Pharamond's ritual."

"You . . . want me to do what?"

"The Divine is trying to change the Circle, Rhys. What Pharamond has learned will be the first step toward that. His knowledge can't die with him, and if what Ser Evangeline tried to do at the keep is any evidence, that may very well come to pass."

He jumped to his feet, his anger resurfacing as several realizations combined at once. Learning she was possessed or dead . . . truth be told, those he couldn't wrap his head around, but *this* was something he understood. "You knew all along what he was doing!"

"I knew his goal."

"And . . . you were just going to let Evangeline kill him? After all that?"

She waved her hand dismissively. "I wouldn't have let it come to that. Shale would have intervened. As it happened, Adrian's outburst made that unnecessary. I still think it was foolish for Pharamond to go so far . . . only a Tranquil could rationalize an attempt at possession . . . but the Divine's purpose is very clear, as is my own."

"So all this, helping a friend in dire need, that was all just a ruse."

"For the templars' benefit, yes. I've been visiting Pharamond off and on for several years, in the hope his research would bear fruit. And it has."

"You could have told me."

She chuckled ruefully. "Like you were so quick to tell me of Cole? Or Evangeline's true mission? I must guard my purpose, as well as the Divine's involvement." When he stormed angrily toward the horse, she leapt to her feet and chased after him. Catching his arm, she pulled him about. "Listen to me, Rhys: Libertarians like Adrian believe that the Circle must be destroyed. I believe it can be made better. The templars must be shown the truth."

"And why doesn't the Divine simply order the templars to do as she asks?"

"Because it isn't that simple. The Divine must contend with centuries of tradition, and there are those in the Chantry who resist. Or do you *truly* believe a single mage managed to sneak out of the White Spire and infiltrate the ball at the Imperial Palace, all on his own?"

That gave him pause. "You don't mean . . ."

"Of course I do. The templars are unruly beasts. They must be led to the water; they cannot be forced to drink. Until they do, we must protect ourselves." Wynne hesitated. She cupped Rhys's cheek in a moment of unexpected tenderness. "And you must be protected. Learning the ritual would make you the only person other than Pharamond who knows and can use it. That will have value the Divine cannot overlook . . . and neither can the Lord Seeker."

Rhys scowled, reaching up and removing her hand. "You knew a spirit medium could learn it. That's why you brought me."

"I knew this could save you."

He turned back to the horse. Taking the reins, he pulled himself up into the saddle. Wynne remained where she was, watching him without comment. He thought he'd had her figured out, but clearly he hadn't even been close. "You're a piece of work." He shook his head. "You're no better than Adrian. Neither of you can see beyond your cause, to whom it affects."

She sighed patiently. "Rhys, I'm trying—"

"Trying to justify why a spirit chose to bring you back to life. Because it couldn't be a random act, something without meaning. You need to be a crusader. I get it."

His words were sharper than he'd intended, but they silenced her nevertheless. Perhaps she meant well. Adrian meant well, too. Somehow taking Cole and running didn't seem like such a bad idea.

"Get on the horse," he muttered bitterly. "I'll keep your secret. And I'll learn the ritual."

She nodded slowly. "May I ask why?"

"Because running won't help anyone. It's time I made a stand."

15

They were a day away from the capital city. That's what Knight-Captain told them, and Cole greeted the news with a mixture of eagerness and apprehension. He felt strangely naked out under the open sky, in places he didn't belong. It would be good to be back in the tower, to walk down dark hallways he didn't need to see in order to know where they led. It was only the thought of being brought before the templars that frightened him. They would judge him, and find him wanting.

Just not a cell, he prayed silently. *Anything but a lonely dungeon cell.*

It was even worse being with people who could see him. He'd wished for it for so long, and yet now he felt their eyes upon him even when they weren't looking his way. It made his skin crawl, and he couldn't help it. Each time he spoke and they responded, he jumped. So he tried to speak as little as possible.

They would have been at the city sooner, except that Knight-Captain—*Evangeline,* he mentally corrected himself—had taken them off the main road the day before last. She said it would be better to stay out of sight, travel through rural areas, and approach the city from the west rather than the south. Everyone looked worried when she said that, but nobody objected. Not even Red Hair, who objected to almost everything.

He imagined it had something to do with the army they'd encountered. Well . . . not an army, really. There'd been maybe a dozen men on the road, but Evangeline said later there were probably more nearby. Hundreds more. An older man wearing a fancy purple cloak had ridden down to speak to them. His helmet had a plume of white feathers sprouting from it—Cole had never seen anything so silly. The man would have looked wealthy if it hadn't been for all the mud stains and rust.

He'd spoken with Evangeline and Old Woman. Boring, friendly talk to which Cole hadn't listened. Instead he'd dismounted and wandered to where the other soldiers were grouped, just down the way. Rhys made a strangled noise when he did that. He probably would have tried to stop Cole if that didn't mean calling attention to them both.

But he didn't. In a way it was strangely comforting to walk among those men and not have them even glance in his direction. Their horses noticed, however. He saw their big black eyes swivel, and they made nickering noises when he got too close. He'd never been near a horse prior to all this, that he could remember. They'd be more impressive if they didn't all smell like dusty manure.

It was the soldiers who interested him more, regardless. They were big, brutish-looking men who wore their armor like it didn't belong to them. Cole disliked the way they looked down the road, or how they nervously fingered their weapons. It wasn't fear that agitated them, however. It was anticipation. He could almost smell the bloodlust.

One of them said, "How long til the others get here?"

"Soon," another replied. "Let's hope he stalls them long enough."

That was all he needed to hear. Cole ran back to Rhys and quickly told him, and then Rhys rode forward and whispered it in Evangeline's ear. When she made her farewells to Purple Cloak, everything changed. His smile became strained. Cole couldn't hear the words, but he understood what was happening well enough when Purple Cloak signaled to the soldiers and they rode toward them at full speed, their weapons drawn.

And then they stopped, on account of the shimmering curtain

of magic that blocked their way. That was Rhys's doing; Cole could see his staff raised, glowing as brightly as the sun. He also heard what Rhys said next very clearly: "We're exactly what we appear to be, Baron. I suggest you take your men and go—unless you *want* to be toads; I won't judge."

Purple Cloak's face went white as a sheet, and he made haste to retreat with his men, all of them shouting curses as they rode off. Evangeline brought them off the road immediately, saying the men would be back with more. Cole felt vaguely disappointed. Could Rhys really turn them into toads? He wanted to see that.

They fled swiftly across a grassy dale, hopping a farmer's fence and then passing through a small forest. Eventually they stopped, the horses sweating and needing to be fed. Evangeline seemed convinced that any chase had been eluded. When Cole asked why Purple Cloak had wanted to attack them, it was Old Woman who answered: "For ransom," she said. "He thought we were traveling in disguise, pretending to be templars and mages so nobody would meddle with us."

"He wanted coin?" Cole asked, perplexed.

"If he could get it, from whatever families we belonged to. And if he couldn't get it, I imagine a few of us would have ended up on the slave market."

"The Empire is falling apart." Rhys shook his head, amazed.

Evangeline agreed. "Bandits first, then roving mobs of starving peasants if things get worse. We might expect to see press gangs as well, if the nobility are gathering armies. Val Royeaux could be in chaos when we arrive."

The others seemed to digest that news as if it tasted unpleasant. The elven man fretted and worried, to the point where Old Woman needed to talk to him in kind words until he calmed.

Cole didn't know what to make of it. Press gangs? What would they press? He would have asked, but he'd likely exceeded his allowance for stupid questions. So instead he remained quiet as

Evangeline got back on the horse, and he held on for dear life as they tried to make up for lost time.

That was two days ago. Now they were camping inside an old hay barn, half falling apart with the field overgrown with lavender. There was purple everywhere he looked, flowers gently swaying in the evening's breeze along with a scent that was both pleasant and somehow too sweet. Cole saw no livestock, and Evangeline said she suspected the run-down farmhouse off in the distance might be abandoned, but didn't want to risk checking.

Cole didn't mind. The farmhouse looked lonely. He watched from the edge of the field, wondering who might have once lived there. The dark windows over the door stared back at him like a pair of malevolent eyes. *There are secrets in this house,* they said, *secrets in the floors and the walls that will remain until they are dust and gone.*

He shivered and turned away. Camping among the flowers was preferable. Besides, the sky was clear. The day had been warm, and the evening was no less so. If there was anything to enjoy about being out in the open it was this.

He might not have a choice soon enough.

Old Woman—Wynne, as she kept reminding him—was in the stable, mending a tear in her robe. She listened patiently as Red Hair berated her about the same topic she always talked about: freedom. Cole didn't really understand what kind of freedom she meant, but he had the suspicion she didn't either. Whatever she thought it was, she was determined to have it.

That argument went on for what seemed like hours, until finally Red Hair stalked off and spent her time brushing the horses. She liked the horses. She talked to them in a soothing voice and gave them names. When the tiny mage was with the horses, she became pretty, all the anger and hard lines on her face dissolving away. Cole would suggest she do more of that if he didn't think she would yell at him for it.

Evangeline had left hours ago. There was a small village nearby, she said, where she intended to buy food. That left Rhys and the elven man, Pharamond, sitting and talking off among the flowers. What they talked about, he hadn't a clue. People stopped speaking when they could see you standing there. It had never really occurred to him someone might not want to be overheard.

Even among a group of people who could see him, Cole still felt like an outsider. Maybe it was supposed to be that way. Maybe that was part of his curse.

Rhys said that there might be a way to end it, that people remembering Cole after seeing him in that dreamland could be the key. Cole hadn't mentioned to Rhys that he'd already started to notice changes. He'd seen the perplexed look on Evangeline's face when she looked at him in the morning, like she couldn't quite place who he was. Red Hair kept complaining Cole was sneaking up on her when he'd been standing beside her the entire time.

All of them were starting to forget, and they weren't even aware of it. Cole was aware. It was like the ground was slowly turning to quicksand under his feet, while everyone else kept walking on, oblivious to his sinking. He was fading away, that familiar feeling creeping like a chill over his bones.

"Is something wrong, Cole?"

It was Evangeline. She was strolling toward him from afar, a sack hefted over one shoulder. Her scarlet cloak streamed in the wind behind her. The moon was coming up just over the horizon, and it cast her in a silvery light that made his heart clench. The way the templar looked at him, as if she knew things about him even he didn't know, made him nervous. But it wasn't in a bad way, somehow.

"I . . . thought you were going to the village?" he stuttered.

"I was," she said. When she got to the rotted remains of the pasture fence he stood by she let the sack drop to the ground with a relieved grunt. "Thankfully I encountered a farmer coming back from the market with a full cart. No business, he said. Whatever's happening, it hasn't touched this part of the Heartlands yet."

"That's a good thing."

"For us it is." She glanced over at where Rhys and Pharamond sat, and then regarded Cole curiously. "Why don't you go over and talk to them? I could see you looking forlornly at them from across the field. I'm certain they wouldn't mind."

The elven man was laughing at something Rhys said, so boisterously he was rolling around on the ground. That's how the elf laughed at anything, it seemed. The slightest amusing remark and he would roar with amusement, and keep it up until everyone else stared at each other uncomfortably. The man was awash in a sea of feeling, carried away by whatever current took him.

"I . . . can't." Cole shook his head, feeling an embarrassed blush rise up his cheeks. He imagined he must seem like some kind of shy, awkward child to Evangeline. A child who didn't know anything.

She leaned against the fence and scrutinized him while he deliberately avoided her gaze. "Let me ask you a question," she finally said. "How did you know about my mission?"

"I heard the man in black armor tell you."

"The Lord Seeker? There was a moment in my quarters when he sensed . . . something. That was you?"

"Yes."

"Were you there before then?"

"Yes," he answered hesitantly.

"When I was undressing."

It wasn't a question. He remembered watching Evangeline remove her armor, and he averted his eyes, feeling his blush burn even hotter. All the times he'd watched people in the tower, and never once did he consider they might object . . . until now.

"Do you do that often?" she asked.

He shook his head vigorously. "You were taking Rhys away. I

had to know why! All I wanted was . . ." Looking into Evangeline's eyes, he couldn't continue. The way she studied him so intently, her brow knitted, it was clear she was upset. Considering how kind she had been to him, he desperately wanted nothing more than to take it back. "I'm sorry," he said lamely.

They stood by the fence for a time, an awkward silence between them. Evangeline stared down at the sack, nudging it with her foot. It seemed like she was trying to decide something.

"What was the book?" he finally asked.

She looked up, startled by the question. "What book?"

"In your room. You took out a book . . . you seemed to like it a lot."

Evangeline's expression changed. It became softer, almost sad, just as he remembered her looking when she held the book. "It . . . was my father's," she said, her voice suddenly thick. She glanced away. "The Chant of Light. We used to read the verses together. Do you . . . know anything about the Chant?"

"No."

She nodded, as if his answer was expected. Then she favored him with an embarrassed smile. "You would have liked my father. He was a good man." With that, she sighed ruefully and shook her head as if dispelling dark thoughts. Then she leaned in and kissed Cole on the forehead.

"Go," she said gently. "Talk to Rhys. He doesn't blame you for anything."

With that, she picked up the sack and walked toward the hay barn. He watched her go, rubbing his forehead in confusion. It tingled where she'd kissed him, and he felt it all the way down to his toes.

It also made him sad. Evangeline was going to forget him. A week from now, or a month, he'd be the only one who remembered this.

Cole walked over to where Rhys and Pharamond sat. Rhys's

staff was sitting on the ground, glowing so as to provide them light. A book lay open between them, one of several the elven man brought with him, and both were studying it.

He lingered several feet from the pair, watching glumly and secretly hoping they wouldn't notice him at all.

No such luck. "Oh, hello!" the elven man exclaimed with surprise, spotting Cole. "Where did you come from?"

Rhys grinned. "This is Cole," he explained—for the tenth time since they'd left the keep. "I've mentioned him before, remember?"

Pharamond knitted his brow, clearly confused. "The fellow who people forget? I didn't realize I'd meet him so soon. I rather thought nobody knew we were out here." Then he brightened, and burst out with amused laughter. "Unless it's me, isn't it? He's been here all along and I'm the one who's forgotten! Oh, how wonderful!"

The man continued to laugh until he wiped tears from his eyes. Cole scowled, and Rhys gave him a wry look that said *Be patient.* So Cole tried. "What's so wonderful about it?" he asked.

Pharamond's chuckling faded in fits and starts, and then completely disappeared. Just as quickly, the elven man turned contemplative. He gazed sadly down at the book before him, running a finger along its pages. "It would not be so bad," he said, "to have your deeds forgotten. Better yet to forget them yourself."

"Nobody remembers anything I do."

He scratched his chin, and looked at Rhys. "What about writing it down? If there was a written account of the young man, might that jog the memory?"

Rhys shrugged. "I don't know. I couldn't find any records related to Cole, and I looked. For all I know, the words on the page might disappear."

"Remarkable!" The elf stared at Cole with those strange blue eyes, like he was some kind of puzzle to figure out. The scrutiny made him squirm. "Tell me, young man, are you able to do magic?"

"I don't think so."

"Hmm. Arcanist derangement, perhaps?"

Rhys exchanged a confused look with Cole. "What . . . kind of derangement?"

"A term coined by the Magister Allineas at the height of the Towers Age. He posited that magical talent is like a flowing river. Properly channeled, it finds its way to the ocean—mages such as yourself, possessing the ability to cast spells." He gestured at Cole. "Left to its own devices, however, it might flow in a different and unexpected direction. But that talent *will* express itself somehow."

Rhys frowned. "You're saying he's a hedge mage."

"A derogatory term, one created by the Chantry. Prior to the Circle, magical talent expressed itself in many ways, often guided by ancient tradition. Some of these 'hedge mages,' as you call them, possessed powers no Circle spell could replicate. Their unpredictability was considered a threat."

"You make it sound like a good thing."

The elf spread his hands in surrender. "I only go by the old texts. I will say the term 'derangement' was no accident, however. These wild talents were more than unpredictable; they were chaotic. Allineas mentions these people communing with spirits, being lured into darker paths . . . many of them went insane. Few lived long lives."

Cole hung his head. That was it, then. Just as he thought, there was no cure for what he was despite what Rhys hoped. He turned and walked away, and heard Rhys hiss something angry. The elven man leapt up and chased after Cole, catching him by the arm. "Dear me!" he exclaimed. "I spoke without thinking! Please don't listen to me!"

"But it's true."

"Words on a page!" His eyes fretted, and he spoke with raw emotion. "If there's anything that what I've done proves," he said, "it's that theories and assumptions can be wrong. Don't ever forget that, young man."

Cole wondered if he didn't have more in common with this white-haired elf than he'd thought. Pharamond had sunk into that oblivion, and even after he'd crawled out of it he still wasn't real. A paper-thin version of himself ready to blow away at the slightest wind. Cole could feel the shadow spreading over the man's heart as surely as over his own.

"What's it like to be Tranquil?" he suddenly asked.

Pharamond turned away as if stricken. He clamped his eyes shut, fighting back a wave of tears. Rhys stood up, a concerned look on his face. "Cole, I don't think this is something—"

"No," the elf said, his voice thick. He shook from the effort of controlling himself. "You said a young man was returning to the tower to absolve you of those murders. This is he, is it not? He may very well face Tranquility . . . as may you." Rhys nodded glumly. "As may I," Pharamond finished. He shuddered as if the thought were too horrible to contemplate.

Cole thought he might not continue, but then Pharamond nodded, steeling himself. "I find it ironic the Rite of Tranquility cuts one off from the land of dreams, because a dream is exactly what it feels like. Everything in a dream is as it should be, nothing is out of place . . . yet part of you knows something is not right. This isn't your home, this isn't your life . . . it isn't you.

"Yet one cannot act other than the dream allows. It follows its course, and you follow it believing nothing is real. You will turn the corner and awaken, safe and sound. Yet you never do. Instead you are slowly smothered in a crystal-clear silence that has no meaning."

The three of them stood there, a wind slowly weaving through the field of purple flowers, and no one said a thing. For the first time since they left the keep, Cole began to feel truly frightened.

"That's a grim sight."

Evangeline had to agree with Rhys. They were approaching Val Royeaux from the western hills, and now they could see with their own eyes what they'd been hearing about. For much of the day they'd encountered swarms of people on the road heading in the opposite direction, all of whom said the same thing: the capital was in chaos.

News of war in the eastern provinces had struck the city like lightning, leading to a panicked exodus by the nobility. Then a rumor had circulated that the Empress was dead, the first of dozens of wild tales that set the city on fire with speculation—and when the Imperial Chancellor issued the decree calling for conscription of the peasantry, the riots began.

It seemed impossible that so much had happened in two weeks, and each story they'd heard on the road had been wilder and less credible than the last . . . but here, at least, was proof they weren't all wrong.

An army was gathered outside the city gates, a veritable sea of tents. Easily ten thousand men camped down there, she figured. The smoke from all the campfires was compounded by the fact that half the city was aflame, or had been recently. The sky was a blanket of soot, the stench of it filling the nostrils and made only worse by the smell of humanity from the camps.

The palace on its hill couldn't be seen through the smoky haze. Even the far-off Grand Cathedral was lost amidst the sprawl of buildings that made up the Empire's largest city. The one thing still plainly visible was the White Spire. It rose above the other buildings like a shining beacon of normality.

"The city gates are closed," Adrian pointed out.

And she was right. The Sun Gates were a marvel of construction, made of steel and covered with a golden façade that depicted the rise of Emperor Drakon. In full sunlight, it was said, they shone so brilliantly they would blind an attacking army. A foolish superstition to be sure, but the Orlesians held the gates with a certain reverence. *Sooner or later everyone in Orlais passes through the Sun Gates,* as the old saying went. But that wasn't true today. The last time Val Royeaux had been sealed, it had been attacked by dragons—a terrible event from which it had taken the city years to recover. Hopefully this wasn't nearly as bad as that.

"Is the army here to lay siege?" Rhys asked.

Wynne shook her head, and pointed at the mass of tents. "See the red banner with the stag's head? That belongs to the Marquis de Chevin, one of Celene's closest allies. I also see Ghyslain, Morrac, the Countess d'Argent . . . the Marquis has gathered the northern host."

"Then why close the gates?"

"I imagine they don't want people fleeing into the farmlands to avoid conscription. Either that or it's a plague—I believe that was one story, was it not?"

Evangeline waved her hand dismissively. "In two weeks? Most of those people never even got inside the city. We'll have to see for ourselves . . . if they let us in."

She led the way, riding down the steep path that led directly into the heart of the army camp. They could avoid it by traveling all the way around to the smaller Night Gate, but that would require crossing the river. Theoretically there shouldn't be a problem. They were expected.

Though that also worried her.

They moved through the army camp slowly. There were a lot of worried faces, men and women dressed in the meanest of armor if they wore any at all, hungrily lapping up gruel as they sat by their campfires. They contrasted sharply with the chevaliers: knights in full battle dress, each adorned with a colorful family crest. They rode down the lines, shouted orders, and darted from tent to tent like buzzing bees. Not a single one appeared to be standing still, and from Evangeline's perspective they looked more nervous than the rank and file.

The air was thick with expectation. It made her wonder if there was an army marching on Val Royeaux. Were these men preparing to march? It also made her curious if the Templar Order was planning to take a side. They had in the past, at the Chantry's behest. If so, she might find herself marching with these men.

There also seemed to be a great number of people who weren't part of the army at all. She saw children scurrying about, and women who were either camp followers or fully intended to become such. There were cooks, elves running errands, merchants trying to hawk protective "charms" to the men, even shifty-looking rogues slipping between the shadows.

A group of city guardsmen stood in front of the city gates—a large group, in fact. At least twenty of them kept an eye on several hundred supplicants, travelers who evidently intended to wait until the gates finally opened. It was a makeshift shantytown full of dispirited people who sat about with nothing better to do than stare at the guardsmen as if they could open the gates by force of will alone.

Evangeline and the others were clearly unusual enough to elicit notice. As they rode up, a number of the campers jumped to their feet, perhaps sensing an opportunity. So, too, did one of the guardsmen step forward, holding out his pike in warning. "Ho there! The gates of Val Royeaux have been sealed by order of the Lord Chancellor!"

"And is no one to get in?" she asked. "We have business at the White Spire."

"Wait!" a voice called from behind the man. A more seasoned-looking guard stepped forward, a grizzled fellow wearing an Imperial tunic over his armor. Clearly a commander, or at least someone of ranking. "I suppose you have a name, templar?" he demanded, eyeing her warily.

"You suppose correctly. My name is Ser Evangeline de Brassard."

He scowled and spat on the ground. "Figures you would show up on my rotation. I was almost ready to retire to the tavern, too."

"Does that mean you'll open the gate?"

"Yes, but you're not going inside until the Lord Seeker arrives. I'm to inform him you're here—personally—and you're not to move from this spot. The man was very specific." The commander irritably waved away the confused-looking guard with the pike and marched back to the gatehouse, disappearing into the sally port.

"So what do you suppose that means?" Rhys asked once he was gone.

"It means the Lord Seeker is angry."

"Oh dear!" Pharamond exclaimed. He anxiously pulled at the collar of his robe, flinching as a group of travelers pushed by them to get closer to the gates. They were anxious, and clearly aware that something was happening. "I'd forgotten how much I used to dislike crowds!"

Adrian seemed similarly displeased. "Perhaps we shouldn't stay here."

"Do you have somewhere else you need to be?" Evangeline asked.

"Ask me that once your templars have thrown us in prison."

Eventually the crowd was driven back, but not until a pair of loud Tevinter merchants were beaten severely. A rough-looking thug whom Evangeline presumed to be a hireling of the merchants drew his sword, and was quickly run through by a guardsman's pike. That appeared to sap the crowd of its interest, and they recoiled from the gates so quickly they almost trampled each other in their haste.

Evangeline and the others were safe on their horses, though the mounts grew nervous at all the tension. They became even more so when thunder roiled in the clouds overhead. It might be a good thing if it rained—perhaps some of the soot and stench could be washed out of the air. While the clouds threatened a downpour, however, nothing came. Instead they hovered on the edge of expectation.

Over an hour passed. It had been well into the evening when they arrived, and waiting proved difficult.

Evangeline felt tense. Who knew what Ser Arnaud might have told the Lord Seeker? He'd been less than pleased to see the group emerge from Adamant alive, and more than a little furious when Evangeline commanded him to surrender supplies and then left. She imagined his report would be less than kind. Not that the Lord Seeker would need more ammunition against her than he already had. Trying to explain to him where she thought her true duty lay would no doubt be like arguing with a wall. There would be a consequence for the decision she made, and it was coming to greet her now.

When the clang of the gears sounded, Evangeline jumped. The effect on the sullen travelers was electrifying. Many immediately leapt up at the sudden noise, raising a hue and cry to their fellows, and began to run toward the gates. Evangeline saw many snatching up their packs, clearly presuming their chance to enter the city had finally come.

The commander walked out of the sally port at the same time, his scowl deepening as he took in the activity. "Keep them back, for the love of Andraste!" he barked to the guards. "Cut down any one of them that tries to get past you!"

When the great doors finally parted with an ominous booming

sound, they did so rapidly. For a moment, there was blinding light. Evangeline shielded her eyes and blinked, and then watched as a full regiment of templars rode out. Thirty knights, all carrying torches. At their head was Lord Seeker Lambert, impressive in his black armor and riding the same massive charger she'd seem him arrive at the tower with so many weeks before.

The surge of travelers stopped dead in their tracks. They shrank back in fear, not a one engaging the threatening guardsmen, and before long Evangeline's group was the only one near the gate. Everything became still and quiet.

The Lord Seeker's face was rigid with fury. She could see it in the tightness of his jaw, in the flash of his grey eyes, almost hear the way he crushed the leather reins in a viselike grip. That did not bode well.

"Lord Seeker Lambert." She greeted him with as warm a nod as she could muster. "It's good to see you again."

"I suppose I should be thankful you made it at all," he said, every word crisp. "No untoward events on the road? You were not waylaid by bandits? They've become very common in recent days."

"None we could not evade, my lord."

"I see." He urged his horse forward, riding up beside Wynne and Pharamond. Wynne regarded him with a pleasant smile, but the elf quaked in obvious terror. "And this was the object of your rescue?"

"He is," Wynne answered. "Pharamond's research has—"

"I'm already well acquainted with his research," the man interrupted. He turned an icy glare on Wynne. "*Someone* sent word through the sending stones. The White Spire is simply buzzing with speculation." He turned to the waiting templars, waving them closer. "Escort them to the Grand Cathedral. Do not delay, and do not permit any of them to leave your sight."

Wynne looked puzzled. "Are we not to return to the White Spire?"

"Most Holy has commanded an immediate audience." Every word he spoke was laced with contempt. "Evidently she has a sending stone in her possession as well, though I'm certain you knew that. I am here to facilitate the meeting."

Within moments, Evangeline's group was surrounded. The templars didn't draw their weapons, and whatever expressions they held were hidden behind their helmets. Still, there was no arguing with them. The group slowly rode with them toward the gates.

"Not you, Ser Evangeline," the Lord Seeker called. "You are with me."

She halted her mount, trying not to let her dismay show. The others continued ahead. Rhys looked back, catching her eyes and silently expressing his sympathy. Behind him, Cole was doing his best to hide. Whether or not the Lord Seeker would have taken notice of the young man even if he could see him didn't seem to matter—Cole would clearly have been much happier if he could have crawled inside Rhys's robe and disappeared.

Within moments they were gone. "Ride with me" was all the Lord Seeker said as he turned his mount about and followed after them. Evangeline kept pace, and as soon as they were through the gates the gears began turning once again. A minute later the great doors slammed shut, the thunderous sound filled with such finality it chilled her bones.

They rode quietly through the Avenue of the Sun. During the day this would be a bustling place, the wide street lined with merchants of every kind as well as "greeters" who coaxed travelers to follow them to a special shop, a whorehouse, an inn . . . everyone would be bombarded with shouts the moment they entered Val Royeaux. At night it was quieter, and the greeters far seedier in their purpose.

This night it was deserted. The glowlamps, installed at great expense along the avenue and maintained by the Tranquil, cast a sapphire shroud over the area that was almost eerie. So much smoke hung in the air she knew it must be worse in the poor quarters. There were enough city guardsmen patrolling the streets to make her believe a strict curfew had been laid down.

"Perhaps I was unclear in my instruction," the Lord Seeker finally said.

"I do not believe so."

"Then can you tell me why these people are here? I sent a group of experienced templars to assist you should the inevitable occur. You dismissed them. Yet here I am confronted with the specter of the very chaos you were to prevent."

"My lord, I—"

"Not only do you allow them to leave the badlands with the Tranquil in tow, you let them go to the Circle of Magi to send word!" He glared at her scornfully. "A sending is seen by the mages before anyone else, leaving me no ability to stop word from spreading, and even if I had wished to keep this news from the Divine it did not matter! She received her own sending!"

He paused in his rant, clearly expecting her to speak now. "My Lord Seeker," she said stiffly, "there were circumstances that—"

"*Circumstances.*"

"Yes, my lord. Most Holy has a personal interest in the results of Enchanter Wynne's mission. I decided it was best to permit her the opportunity to decide what should be done regarding the matter."

"You decided." He repeated the word with disgust and shook his head. They rode in silence, and he stared at the street ahead. Perhaps he pondered what to do with her? She doubted that—far more likely he'd decided what to do with her before she even neared the capital. "I gave you an order, Knight-Captain. Does that mean nothing?"

"I took vows to serve the Chantry," she insisted. Inwardly she despaired at the hole she was digging for herself, but a part of her was beginning to grow angry. "We have a responsibility to the

Divine, as well as to the mages we protect—not only to keep order. With all due respect, my lord."

"I see no respect here. I see a woman who has left me no opportunity to deal with this matter in a way that will not lead to
more upheaval. Is this what you intended?"

"I did what I judged to be best, and if you'll permit me the
chance to explain myself fully, I'm hoping you'll agree."

"And yet there is no time for explanations, is there? We ride to
the Grand Cathedral, our course set." The Lord Seeker clenched
his jaw, refusing to look at her. "When we return to the White
Spire, you will report to Ser Arnaud. He will be relieving you as
Knight-Captain."

"Yes, my lord." Evangeline stifled her outrage. It was true she'd
left him few options, having allowed the matter to go over his
head, but she was increasingly certain that was for the best. She
wasn't about to let fear of losing her position prevent her from doing what was right.

The streets led them briefly through the market district. Here
she could see evidence of the turmoil the capital had suffered.
Whole buildings burnt to the ground, some recently enough to
still be smoldering, and enough refuse littered the cobblestones to
make her think a battle had occurred. Even in the dim evening
light the dark splatters of blood were unmistakable.

Lord Seeker Lambert was clearly finished with their conversation, but she couldn't leave it at that. "There is one other matter,"
she said reluctantly. "I have new information on the murders."

"Indeed?" His tone was acidic. "Strange how there have not been
any more murders since Enchanter Rhys left us."

"Be that as it may, he is not responsible."

"Then who is?"

"That . . . will require some explanation."

He turned in his saddle to level an incredulous glare at her. She
tried not to look away. She knew that Cole would be difficult to

explain, even under the best circumstances, but that didn't mean she shouldn't try. "You will be debriefed at the White Spire," he stated. "You can make your explanations then, Ser Evangeline. Until that time, we have an audience to contend with."

The Lord Seeker appeared annoyed by the prospect, but it gave Evangeline hope. The Divine she remembered from the failed assassination in the palace struck her as a fair and just person. All Evangeline could do was silently pray to the Maker that His holy servant was granted the wisdom to see them through this.

It was a small hope, but she clung to it with all her might.

16

Rhys had been to the Grand Cathedral only once before. Shortly after his elevation to senior enchanter, he'd been brought in with Adrian and several others who had been elevated along with him to meet Divine Beatrix III. A courtesy, really, and Rhys remembered standing there in the stifling heat for several hours before Most Holy made her appearance.

It had been less than a year before her death, and at the time he wouldn't have been surprised if she'd expired on the spot. He remembered a shriveled old woman helped into the chamber by no less than four attendants, all but collapsing under the weight of her scarlet robes. The thick, golden medallion hanging around her neck seemed to pull her head down toward the ground, and her great headdress hung askew.

When she reached the Sunburst Throne, the Divine had blinked her eyes and looked around in confusion. "Where are we?" she'd asked, Rhys noting that not more than three teeth remained in her mouth. "Is it time to break my fast already? I told them I wasn't hungry. No more porridge, I said!"

One of the attendants had leaned in close. "The mages, Most Holy."

The woman's beady eyes went wide in shock. "Mages?!" She searched the room, almost falling over in her agitation. "Andraste's grace, are we under attack?!"

It had taken the attendants, as well as a pair of nearby templars, to finally calm the Divine down and assure her that, no, the evil mages were not here to attack anyone. They got her settled, a pile of rags seated on a throne that dwarfed her in both size and majesty, and then she immediately proceeded to fall asleep. Rhys and the others had been "introduced" one after the other, everyone pretending not to notice the old woman's thunderous snoring.

He had never considered himself the most faithful of Andrastians. Perhaps it was being raised by the Chantry, or simply being a mage and thus less impressed by events some might call miraculous. Still, he remembered being disappointed. All that preparation, and the vast humility he'd felt stepping into that chamber, only to discover the most exalted person in all of Thedas was simply . . . human.

Now here he was, seven years later, and the Grand Cathedral looked just the same. The structure stood in a walled compound on the far end of Val Royeaux, once having existed outside the capital until the city literally grew around it. It was an imposing fortress of grey stone and arches that seemed to reach high up to the sky. Despite the beauty on display, golden statues and colorful stained glass that reached from one end of the structure to the other, the place possessed a somberness that told of its bloody past.

The Chantry, after all, was a religion born from a war that had shaken all of Thedas. Places like the Grand Cathedral and the White Spire had once been fortresses that had endured countless battles, and all were built upon the bones of countless dead.

It made him wonder if more would be added to that count today.

Once again he stood in the audience chamber, staring at the empty throne. This late at night the stained glass windows were dark, and only the Eternal Brazier cast any light, the flames in its marble basin making every shadow dance. The forty-foot-tall statue of Andraste, depicted as a robed woman with the sword of justice held aloft, seemed particularly ominous now. It was as if she stared down, knowing what lay ahead and pitying him for it.

Lord Seeker Lambert stood near the throne with the templars lined up on either side of the chamber, all of them standing at attention. Evangeline stood with them, her face an unreadable mask. Cole was . . . somewhere nearby, in the shadows. Watching. Only the mages stood out on the open floor. Rhys found the wait almost excruciating.

Then a gong rang. A line of priests filed into the chamber, each of them holding their hands in prayer and chanting. Their voices filled the room with echoes, sending a shiver down his spine.

Immediately following them was the Divine. This was no wizened crone, but a much younger woman who walked straight and proud. She needed no assistance save for the single attendant that carried the train of her voluminous red robes. Everyone in the room fell to one knee as she passed. For a long moment there was nothing but the hushed sound of the Divine's footsteps as she ascended to the Sunburst Throne.

"All hail the Most Holy Justinia, Fifth of Her Name, Exalted Servant of the Maker!" a templar shouted, his voice booming across the chamber.

"Grant us wisdom," a chorus of voices answered.

There was a pause, and then the Divine spoke: "Rise, all of you."

Everyone stood. The woman sat upon the throne, and unlike its previous occupant she appeared to fill it. She sat up straight, utterly in command, and took in her audience with a warm and welcoming gaze.

The attendants hung to the rear of the chamber. Only one of them actually stood on the dais next to the throne: a pretty woman with short red hair, wearing a priest's robes but standing with such ease and grace that Rhys couldn't help but get the impression she was a bodyguard. Rumor said the Divine was employing bards in her personal service. He'd assumed the tales were exaggerated, as so many of them were, but perhaps that wasn't so?

"Such a late hour for an audience," the Divine commented. Her voice carried easily in the room's acoustics; it was almost as if she spoke directly in Rhys's ear. "But it is good you all are here. I have awaited this for some time."

"Your Perfection, if I may." The Lord Seeker strode toward the dais. He made a perfunctory bow, and did not wait for permission to continue. "There is no need for this. With the state of the Empire, I'm positive you have more important concerns than an internal matter of the Circle of Magi."

"Your advice is appreciated, Lambert," she said. Rhys thought he detected a hint of sarcasm in her tone, and certainly the lack of an honorific did not go unnoticed by the man. He glared indignantly, but said nothing. "The Empire faces war, and while we pray for the souls of the many innocents trapped in its wake, the Chantry cannot forsake its responsibility for the sake of politics."

"I am dealing with the matter, Your Perfection . . ."

"Indeed?" Her eyebrows shot up. "And yet a mage made an attempt on my life scant weeks ago. The templars have had an increasingly difficult time of managing the Circle ever since that unfortunate business in Kirkwall. Perhaps some assistance is in order, wouldn't you say?"

His nod of assent was grudging, at best. "If you believe it so, Your Perfection."

"I do." The Divine cast her gaze around the room, clearly looking for someone, until she spotted her amid the line of templars. "Speaking of the attempt on my life, I never did have the opportunity to thank the one personally responsible for my rescue. Ser Evangeline, be so kind as to step forward."

Rhys saw Evangeline's eyes go wide in shock. She hestitated, until the Divine finally beckoned her over. Reluctantly she left the templar line, and when she reached the bottom of the dais she instantly dropped to one knee.

"The report I received on the events at Adamant fortress were quite thorough," the Divine said. "I understand you're responsible for ensuring the mission's completion and safe return to Val Royeaux."

Evangeline didn't look up. "I . . . did my best, Most Holy."

"Indeed you did. Here I find myself thanking you for not one service rendered to the Chantry, but two." The Divine looked over at the Lord Seeker. "You have a most promising templar in your ranks, Lambert. I trust you'll see her adequately rewarded?"

The Lord Seeker said nothing. For a long moment there was tense silence as he and the Divine locked stares, until finally he relented. "As you wish, Your Perfection."

"Good. Someone will need to look after the White Spire when you return to your regular duties, after all."

"Most Holy!" Evangeline spluttered. "I . . . cannot ask you to . . ."

"You did not ask. Rather, it is I who am asking you to continue serving the Maker." She waved for Evangeline to come closer. "Stand at my side while I deal with the matter at hand."

Evangeline exchanged a look with the Lord Seeker. Standing behind both of them, Rhys couldn't see the details . . . but from the man's rigid posture, it was easy to tell he wasn't pleased. Someone was being overruled. Rhys would be a liar if he claimed that didn't make him at least a little happy.

He watched Evangeline walk up the steps toward the throne, where she was met by the red-haired woman. She looked proud, if a little flustered. *Good for her,* Rhys thought to himself. *At least someone's going to benefit from all this.*

"Now then," the Divine began. "Let us continue. Enchanter Wynne?"

Wynne stepped forward, leading Pharamond by the hand. The

elf was shaking so badly from terror, he looked ready to vomit. As soon as he reached the dais, he prostrated himself before the Divine. "Please, Your Perfection!" he begged in a quavering voice. "I did only as you asked of me, I swear it!"

Wynne knelt down and tried to console him, but the elf was having none of it. He trembled and sobbed, snot running out of his nose in a pathetic display almost painful to watch. Finally the Divine raised her hand. "Stand," she commanded him. "For the moment, I wish only to speak."

Slowly Pharamond allowed Wynne to help him up. He attempted to collect himself, though not very well. "I . . . did only as you asked, Most Holy," he repeated.

The Lord Seeker strode forward, wheeling on the Divine with an expression of outrage. "What does he mean by that, *exactly*?"

"I believe you are forgetting yourself, Lambert."

"And I believe the templars have a right to know what transpires in our own domain!" he snapped. "We have a difficult enough time dealing with the mages, we most certainly do not need interference!"

She frowned, and Rhys wondered if things were about to come to a head. These were two of the most powerful people in Thedas butting heads, right there in front of everyone. The unease in the chamber was conspicuous, and he couldn't help but notice the templars were not only armed but also handily outnumbered everyone else. But . . . they served the Chantry. The templars would never openly oppose the Chantry, would they? That was unthinkable.

"Allow me to explain, then," the Divine said in a crisp tone. "Five years ago I asked someone to undertake an investigation into the nature of the Rite of Tranquility. It is a process we use even though we do not fully understand it. I wished to know if the Rite could deny a mage their power without also neutering their mind. I also wished to know if the process could be reversed."

She gestured to Pharamond. "As you can see, that much appears to be true."

"But why?" the Lord Seeker demanded. "The Rite of Tranquility has served the Circle for centuries. It is our last defense against mages who cannot master their own powers. We must keep order, Most Holy! We must protect the innocent from the mages, and the mages from themselves!"

She nodded. "A convenient tale, so we may sleep better at night. The Maker says that magic is to serve mankind . . . but we possess a responsibility to those who serve us, Lord Seeker. We cannot hail them when their magic is useful and then lock them in a cage when it is inconvenient. They are the Maker's children, not to be tolerated, but to be cherished."

Rhys was stunned. He'd never thought to hear such words from anyone in the Chantry before, never mind the Divine. From the murmurs that traveled around the room, he suspected many others felt the same way. Looking to his right, he caught a glimpse of Adrian standing not far from him and watching the throne.

She was crying.

The Lord Seeker furrowed his brow, staring at the Divine in consternation. "And what price would you have us pay for such idealism, Most Holy?"

"Idealism is our stock-in-trade, Lambert. A religion without ideals is tyranny. As for the price"—she turned back to Pharamond—"that is what I intend to discover."

Wynne bowed low. "Your Perfection, with your permission, perhaps I could answer your questions. Since Pharamond's . . . restoration . . . he has had difficulty controlling his emotions. I fear this may be overwhelming for him."

The elf smiled gratefully at her, but the Lord Seeker was not nearly as impressed. "And this is a man we should now trust to resist possession?" he growled.

The Divine silenced him. "Your report was very detailed,

Enchanter Wynne. For that I thank you. There are, however, questions remaining. If you would be so kind as to answer them, it would be appreciated."

"Of course, Your Perfection."

The Divine sat back in the throne. She steepled her hands together and rested her chin on them, narrowing her eyes in thought. "First I wish to know what happened to the people of Adamant."

Wynne appeared reluctant to speak, and Rhys could well imagine why. He remembered the room full of charred corpses, the blood smearing the walls, and shuddered. "They are dead," she whispered.

"Speak up!" the Lord Seeker snapped.

"They are dead," Wynne said, more loudly.

The Divine closed her eyes, moving her mouth in a prayer. All was quiet for a long minute until she opened her eyes again. Rhys could see they were moist—she was clearly moved, and it made him feel guilty. As horrified as he'd been by the carnage, other concerns had seemed far more pressing than that of lost lives.

"How?" she asked, her voice hoarse with emotion.

Wynne hesitated. "The Veil was already thin at Adamant. Pharamond's experiment allowed demons to pass into our world. They possessed the keep's people . . ."

"And tore each other apart," the Lord Seeker finished for her. She nodded.

"And then possessed the corpses."

She nodded again.

The Lord Seeker didn't look at the Divine. He didn't have to.

"And this experiment," the Divine continued, "is there promise in it? Is it an accident the Rite of Tranquility has been reversed in this man, or can it happen again?"

Wynne made to answer, but now Pharamond spoke up. "I did not intend to be possessed, I swear it," he said. He cleared his throat uncomfortably. "In fact, I believe the process can be replicated far more safely . . . if, that is, you wish it to be. . . ." His voice trailed off into silence.

"But have you learned more of the Rite's nature?"

"Yes, I believe I have."

"And do you believe a way can be discovered to allow the Rite to restrict a mage without rendering them Tranquil?"

Rhys noticed the nervous sweat pouring down Pharamond's brow. He glanced helplessly at Wynne, but she merely nodded for him to answer. He faced the Divine again, stuttering several times before he managed a response: "No," he said quietly. "I don't believe that's possible."

His answer hung in the air.

"Then there's nothing further to discuss," the Lord Seeker declared. "If the only result of this man's research is to discover the Rite may be reversed, then I deem it a failure . . . and a dangerous one, Most Holy. Even now there are those in the White Spire who believe we are about to turn every Tranquil back into a mage!"

The Divine pondered his words and did not respond. She did not have to, however, as Adrian suddenly stepped forward. Rhys groaned inwardly, seeing the outrage written clearly on her face right next to the tears. "And so you should!" she shouted. "They should never have been mutilated in the first place!"

The man glared at her in fury, but it was the Divine who responded. "And what would you have us do, my dear? Execute them?"

"Yes!" Adrian looked around at the shocked glances she received, and they only seemed to fuel her outrage. "Yes! You think it's *kinder* to turn them into automatons, into servants? If you really fear us so much, then kill us! Don't pretend that killing everything that makes us human isn't the same thing!"

The Lord Seeker angrily waved at several of the templars off to the side, but the Divine shook her head. He stared at her in disbelief, but she ignored him. "I understand your frustration," she said to Adrian, "but we are placed in a difficult position."

"One that is about to be made even more difficult, Most Holy," the Lord Seeker said. He got down on one knee before the throne, a show of earnest supplication Rhys found surprising. So did Ser Evangeline and the red-haired woman on either side of the throne. Both stared at the man in surprise. "We cannot indulge this research any further," he said. "By the elf's own words, it leads nowhere. We must put our efforts toward keeping order before word of this spreads."

More surprising still, the Divine appeared to consider his words. She frowned thoughtfully, staring off into the distance as she weighed the options. Rhys almost expected Adrian to object, but then he saw her shaking her head in dejection. She was giving up.

"No!" he cried out. The words were almost ripped from him before he realized what he was saying. They sounded too loud in the massive audience chamber, reverberating until all eyes were turned toward him.

There you go again, he scolded himself. *When will you learn, exactly?*

Steeling his nerves, Rhys approached the dais, kneeling down in the same manner the Lord Seeker had before him. "Forgive me, Most Holy, but I have to speak."

The corner of the Divine's mouth twitched in amusement. "Why not? It seems as if none of us are standing on ceremony today. Who might you be?"

"Enchanter Rhys, Most Holy."

She smiled. "Ah! The son, is it? I can see the resemblance."

He was taken aback by that, a combination of Wynne clearly having told the Divine about their relationship and the woman even remembering. Plus, he didn't look like Wynne . . . did he? In the space of his hesitation, however, the Lord Seeker interrupted. "Do not listen to this man. He is under suspicion of murder, and anything he says will undoubtedly be an effort to save his own skin."

The Divine chuckled, lowering her hands and easing back in the throne. "We all have our biases, Lambert. Seeing as you allowed this man to accompany the mission, I'm willing to listen to what he has to say." She nodded to Rhys. "Please continue."

"I believe setting aside this man's research would be a mistake," he said. "So much of what we know of the Rite of Tranquility, indeed of magic itself, is based on tradition and hearsay. What he has learned may not be an alternate solution to the Rite, but that does not mean one *cannot* be found."

"And how do you know this?" the Lord Seeker demanded.

"I have been speaking with Pharamond since we left Adamant. Considering my own research deals with spirits, I've found what he has to say quite illuminating."

The Lord Seeker stared, stunned. He spared a withering glance at Evangeline, who kept her own expression stony and did not look away, and then turned to face the Divine. "Do you see? Already it spreads. Next he'll be trying to convince us that demons are required to further this agenda!"

"Not demons," Rhys insisted. "Spirits!" At the incredulous look from both the Lord Seeker and the Divine, he spoke more emphatically. "Not everything about spirits is evil. We use spirits to heal, and the Chantry accepts this because it's useful. This is no different."

"Of course it's different!" the Lord Seeker boomed. "We have an entire keep of innocents horribly slaughtered to show us how different it is!"

"And would you make their deaths meaningless?"

"Not I!" he said. "Their deaths were made meaningless by the selfish act of a man who used them to reverse something that should never have been reversed! It is blasphemy!"

Rhys laughed bitterly. "Blasphemy? This door is opened. You

can try to slam it shut, or you can see what's on the other side! It might just be a way to avoid the rebellion even you must know is coming!"

The Lord Seeker drew his sword. The metallic sound it made as it left its scabbard rang throughout the room, and the reaction was instantaneous. At least half of the templars drew their blades, and Rhys didn't get the impression they intended to stop him; rather the opposite. Rhys fell back, alarmed, and immediately channeled mana. Adrian rushed to his side, summoning a wreath of fire to her hands.

"Enough!" the Divine cried. "There will be no bloodshed!"

Evangeline ran toward the Lord Seeker, weapon already in hand, but the red-haired priest got there first. She grabbed his sword hand, and when he wheeled about to force her off she glared at him with steely eyes. "Don't be a fool," she warned, her voice low and deadly.

He scowled, though he did lower his blade. Pulling his hand from hers, he turned to face Rhys. "I see no rebellion coming," he seethed. "I see mages who take every inch they're allowed and demand ten more, forgetting the very reasons the Circle exists. And what I hear are threats, coming from a Libertarian who would be the very first corrupted if power were ever placed in his hands."

Rhys allowed his power to fade, but it was difficult. The Lord Seeker was so full of contempt and self-righteousness it was sickening, and Rhys wanted nothing more than to wipe that sneer off his face . . . even though it would surely mean his own death.

"I'm not making threats," he said. "I'm telling you there are alternatives, but you're too blind to see them. If you keep trying to strangle the mages, you'll lose us. That I promise you."

The Lord Seeker ignored him, instead turning to the Divine. "Do you see what we contend with? Resistance at every turn. End this, here and now, before it spreads beyond these walls."

"It's too late," a voice cried out. It was Wynne. She reassuringly patted the anxious Pharamond's hand and then left him to approach the dais. "I'm sorry, Most Holy, but the Circle of Magi already knows about Pharamond."

"What do you mean?" the Lord Seeker demanded.

She smiled sweetly at him. "The sending that went to the White Spire and the Grand Cathedral was also sent to every other Circle in Thedas. The first enchanters are already on their way to Val Royeaux as we speak."

Adrian gasped, and Rhys was similarly stunned. Had that been Wynne's plan all along, then? Had the golem been so incredibly caustic just so Evangeline would be happy to see it leave? He couldn't help but feel a little chagrined at the realization.

The Lord Seeker wheeled on the Divine. "Execute them," he growled. "Execute them all. This flies in the face of everything the Chantry stands for, a direct challenge to our authority!"

The Divine frowned and regarded Wynne with a speculative look, tapping her fingers on the arm of the Sunburst Throne. Wynne bowed, and spoke in a carefully guarded tone. "This is a chance for you to work with the Circle, to greet Pharamond's findings as an opportunity rather than as a threat."

"You put us in a difficult position," the Divine said. Rhys could tell she was displeased, perhaps even backed into a corner. She exchanged a dire look with the Lord Seeker, one that made Rhys nervous. Might she refuse, after all this? Had Wynne alienated a woman who had seemingly been their ally?

"None more difficult than we mages are in, Your Perfection," Wynne answered.

The Divine's fingers thrummed on the throne for several more moments before she nodded curtly. "So be it." Before the Lord Seeker could object, she held up a hand. "Expedite the arrangements, Lambert. They will hold conclave here at the White Spire, rather than in Cumberland. Set it to happen in one month's time. Let the mages debate a policy that both of us can live with."

The Lord Seeker ground his teeth, but it was easy to see he was just as caught as she. "Very well," he said curtly. "I believe it a fool's errand, but it appears we are left with no choice. The templars will allow this, but I have three conditions."

"Name them."

"One, that we restrict the size of the conclave. I do not wish to see the tower packed with every senior enchanter from here to Ferelden. Too much power in one place may give these mages foolish ideas."

The Divine nodded. "I believe those in this chamber will be required at the conclave. Beyond that, I agree. First enchanters only."

"Two, I wish these mages imprisoned. I do not want them stirring up trouble, not in the White Spire or anywhere else."

"Confine them to quarters." She looked at Wynne. "I believe we can make an exception for you, Enchanter, in recognition of your past service. You will remain in the White Spire until the conclave. Should Lord Seeker Lambert believe you are abusing this privilege, you will join the others."

Wynne nodded. "I understand, Most Holy."

"Lastly"—the Lord Seeker gestured at Pharamond—"I wish this man to undergo the Rite of Tranquility once again."

There was silence as his words sank in, and then Pharamond let out a heart-wrenching wail of despair. The elf sank to his knees, staring at the Lord Seeker in utter horror. Tears welled in his eyes. "Please," he gasped. "Please do not do this, I beg you . . ."

Wynne ran to the man's side, keeping him upright. She pleaded to the Divine, "For the love of the Maker, have mercy!"

The Lord Seeker scowled. "The reasons he underwent the Rite are true today as they once were. Moreover, look at him. The man can barely control himself. How will he fare against a demon? Whatever knowledge he possesses will remain."

Pharamond collapsed to the ground. The desperate keening sound he made was like an animal caught in a trap, and it tugged at Rhys's heart. "You can't do this!" he shouted. "After all he's been through, it's inhumane!"

"Perhaps you'd like to join him," the Lord Seeker said icily.

The Divine shook her head. "Enough, Lambert. The elf shall become Tranquil once again. It is done." With that, she rose from the throne. Every templar in the chamber immediately stood at attention. Before she left the dais, however, she paused and regarded Wynne with a warning look. "Let us hope you are correct, Enchanter, and this conclave allows the Circle and the Chantry to build a new accord. If not, may the Maker have mercy on you all."

The red-haired attendant took the Divine by the hand and led her away. All was silent as the two of them left the dais, save for the sound of Pharamond's pitiful sobbing. It echoed throughout the holy chamber, and Rhys found himself standing there, stunned.

What had just happened? There was to be a conclave . . . and he was to attend? It seemed he had another reprieve, though the way the Lord Seeker glared at him he imagined it wouldn't last much beyond that.

He was far luckier than poor Pharamond. Rhys walked toward the man, Adrian beside him, but neither could offer any more comfort than Wynne could. The old woman cradled him like a child beneath the Eternal Brazier as he howled in grief.

Whatever he had done in the keep, whatever mistakes he had made, he was paying for it now. If there was anything worse than being stripped of all your emotion and made to live as a hollow shadow of what you once were . . . it was knowing exactly what it was like, and having it about to happen to you again.

17

Three weeks.

Evangeline was Knight-Captain in name only, now. Despite pronouncements from the Divine, that did not make the Lord Seeker appreciate her presence any more. In fact, it made things worse. She had been relegated to tasks no Knight-Captain before her ever had the pleasure of doing: guard duty in the dungeons, for one. Alone.

Arnaud showed up on occasion to gloat. The man carried around his insufferable smile like a victory flag, taunting her with the knowledge that as soon as the first enchanters' conclave was done, so was her position within the White Spire. The Divine's favor only went so far. He was probably right. That didn't make her want to wipe that smile off his face any less. It might even be worth it, despite the consequences.

Not all the other templars felt as Arnaud did, of course. Some of them came to the dungeons late at night, offering their sympathies and advice. Apologize, they said. Throw yourself at the Lord Seeker's mercy, lest you lose whatever standing you've earned in the order forever. This was ignoring the fact that Lord Seeker Lambert didn't *have* any mercy. That, and she no longer cared.

Well . . . that was a lie. She did care. She cared so much the helpless rage smoldered inside her like a burning coal. This wasn't the Templar Order she joined. That order was filled with protectors, people doing their best with an awful situation. People who believed the mages needed help just as much as the innocents outside the tower, and had a Maker-given duty to be compassionate with the power they wielded.

Knight-Commander Eron had believed that. Her father had believed that. She saw none of it in the Lord Seeker, however—just a cold certainty that froze out any hope of compromise. What made it worse was that many of the other templars feared the Lord Seeker, and saw him clamping down on them just as much as the mages, yet none of them were willing to raise a voice of opposition. Seeing their Knight-Captain serve as the perfect example of what happened to someone who did made that willingness fade all the more rapidly.

So there she was, stuck for days on end down in the darkness. She'd tried several times to request an audience with the Lord Seeker, all to no avail. He didn't want to speak with her, or even acknowledge she existed. Evangeline knew he was watching her like a hawk, however, just waiting for the slightest opportunity to accuse her of insubordination.

Which meant she couldn't seek out Rhys, or any of the others. Even Wynne she'd spoken to only in passing, and the old woman had been understanding when Evangeline suggested they'd best not meet for both their sakes. Rhys was confined to his chambers, and it nagged at her that she couldn't go and speak with him about . . . someone.

Evangeline stood there, brow knitted in confusion, and then suddenly dug into her tunic. From there she pulled out a small piece of parchment. Quickly she walked over to the sapphire light of the glowlamp and read it:

> *His name is Cole.*
>
> *He's not that old, perhaps twenty years. No more. He has blond hair that hangs in front of his eyes and wears dirty leathers—perhaps the only clothes he owns. He was*

*there when you found Rhys in the templar crypt, but you
couldn't see him. Nobody can, and those who do forget him.
Just like you are doing right now.*

Remember the dream.

She lowered the parchment, closing her eyes and trying to cling
to the memory. The dream in the Fade. That awful farmhouse,
and finding a boy hidden away in a kitchen cupboard. She remembered everything about it, but Cole himself slipped past her
mind's eye. She couldn't see his face, or hear his voice. But she
wanted to. It was her duty to remember.

What had happened to him? He had come to her, in the days
after the audience with the Divine. Her recollection was like that
of the dream—an impression of an event rather than something
solid. He'd asked her about Rhys, and asked her if he was going
to be given over to the templars.

I'm sorry, Cole, she'd said. *I really don't know.*

She'd felt helpless, and it had been terrible to watch him sag in
defeat. He'd been so terrified on the ride back to the White Spire,
she remembered that much. All his hopes and fears wrapped up
in anticipation of a moment that never arrived. They'd gone to the
Grand Cathedral, and then everything afterward had been a blur
of activity. The Lord Seeker had shut her out completely, and
Cole had undoubtedly retreated back into the depths of the tower.

In fact, he might even be watching her right now.

"Light reading, Ser Evangeline?" a voice asked.

She jumped. Lord Seeker Lambert was standing in the dungeon entrance, regarding her with an arched eyebrow. He was in
full armor, the lamp's blue light glinting off its polished black
surface. When she didn't respond, he walked over to the small
table and idly moved around the playing cards she'd laid out for
herself. "I see you're keeping busy. Guard duty can be tedious, but
it's an important task nevertheless."

"Is there something you wished, Lord Seeker?"

He looked at her and frowned. "I appreciate a subordinate who challenges me—to a point. Considering where you stand, I would suggest modifying your tone."

Evangeline took a deep breath. He was right, of course. There was no point in antagonizing him further. "I've been requesting an audience with you all week," she said. "I'm simply surprised to see you come to the Pit. I would have gone to your office."

"Indeed." He paced about the room, hands clasped behind his back, and for several moments did not speak. Evangeline wasn't certain what to make of it. "I wished to meet you in private, away from prying eyes. It has to do with your report."

"You read it."

"I did, yes. Very thorough. I have a question, however. You claim that Enchanter Rhys is not, in fact, responsible for the murders—there is another, a young mage by the name of Cole."

"That's correct."

"Moreover, you claim he is invisible, and forgotten by anyone who meets him. This does not, however, include yourself?"

"I . . . am starting to forget, my lord."

The Lord Seeker stopped pacing, peering at her curiously. "I see" was all he said. "And yet you claim you can provide evidence of this Cole's existence? That he will manifest at your command?"

"He said he would show himself, to help Rhys."

"Then do so. I would like to meet this man."

She squirmed uncomfortably. "I'm afraid I don't know where he is."

He nodded, as if this was the answer he was expecting. "So he's . . . somewhere in the tower? Let's assume this man does exist—"

"He exists, my lord."

"Let's *assume* that is so. Did it occur to you his abilities are the hallmarks of blood magic? Strange, never-before-seen powers, fueled by the letting of blood from his victims?"

"I don't believe that's true."

"You don't *believe*." His frown deepened, and he shook his head as if disappointed. "So you wouldn't agree if I suggested that perhaps this Cole is influencing your mind? Perhaps he is influencing Enchanter Rhys as well? Can you be *absolutely certain* this is not the case?"

She sighed. On one hand, it was true—she couldn't be certain. She'd met Cole in the Fade, and everything about his presence seemed convenient. For all she knew, he might be the demon she first suspected him to be. Or he might be a maleficar, a user of forbidden magic who was bending her thoughts and memories into thinking him harmless. Perhaps he was manipulating them all.

On the other hand, she didn't think of him as harmless. She remembered him as dangerous, what she could remember at all. He was also troubled, little more than a child left to fend for himself in a world he didn't fully understand. She had to believe her gut, and her gut told her he was what he appeared to be. That he needed help.

"No, I can't be absolutely certain," she admitted. "But I still believe it. Somehow Cole's talents became . . . twisted . . . after he was brought to the tower. Through fear or I don't know what. He needs to become Tranquil before he loses his mind completely and hurts someone else."

The Lord Seeker nodded, pleased. "It's good to see you still believe in the Rite of Tranquility. I'd almost suspected you'd thrown in with those Libertarians."

"The Rite has its place. I do agree with Enchanter Rhys that we need an alternative, however. He is not wrong, and he is no murderer. We have a responsibility to rise above our differences and see the truth."

"Bold words." The man paced again, rubbing his chin and clearly pondering. He was cold, she decided. Everything to him was a problem that must be neatly solved and put away on a shelf to be forgotten. Anything that couldn't be was a threat. "Let me make you a proposition," he said. "I will agree to see this Cole, once you find him. He won't be harmed. Provided there's truth to what you say, Enchanter Rhys will be free to go."

"And in return?"

"You will stand before the first enchanters' conclave and denounce the research of this Pharamond."

So that was it, the entire reason for his coming to the dungeon to speak with her. He didn't want to be seen as lenient, and he most certainly didn't want to be seen making an arrangement regarding her testimony. "You can't ask me to do that," she said.

"I certainly can. It's your actions that have put me in this position, and thus I believe it's your responsibility to see it rectified." He raised a finger before she could speak. "I've read your report. It's obvious you're sympathetic to the mages, and that's commendable. I'll even go as far as to say we may look into this matter in the future, under closely monitored conditions. Perhaps you will be the one in charge of that. But we cannot do this now, not while the mages are casting about for reasons to rebel."

"And you would rather give them one?"

The Lord Seeker snorted derisively. "We are not playing games. There was a day when magic ruled this land and all lands, and it took the Maker to send us His chosen bride in order to tear them down. *We* are the bulwark preventing that from happening again. No one else."

"And can that not be done with compassion?"

"Let me tell you where compassion gets us." He wandered over to the doorway that led into the dungeon cells, staring down the length of the hall as if seeing ghosts in its shadows. "I come from the Tevinter Imperium. For ten years I served with the Imperial Chantry, did you know that?"

"No."

"I'm not surprised. I left because the Circle of Magi had been corrupted beyond hope of redemption. The magisters slowly took back power within the Circle . . . inch by inch. After all, what harm could there be in allowing the mages to govern themselves? Who better to know what mages need, and how to teach them to resist the lures of demons?"

"Those are excellent questions," she said.

"I agree. At the time, I believed the answer was yes, that the mages were best served when trained by their own." He noticed Evangeline's incredulous look, and almost smiled. "I did not begin my service convinced they could not be trusted. How many of us do?"

"Considering what the Chantry teaches us . . ."

He shrugged. "I entered the order because I believed I could make things better. I found allies among the magisters, and I was convinced they could serve as examples for the others. One I even considered a friend. Together we were going to change the world."

"And he betrayed you."

The Lord Seeker shook his head. "He became the Black Divine. The perfect position to make our dreams a reality, yet once there it became more about keeping his power than using it. Those who sought to replace him turned to forbidden arts, and he did the same to compete. I had no idea."

Evangeline was hesitant to speak. "You can't be blamed."

"I can. My investigations turned up less and less. The templars became stonewalled, unable to look into even the simplest matter, and I refused to accept it was because those mages—men and women I had helped rise—did not wish their own corruption revealed."

"But you found out eventually."

His laugh was a short and bitter bark. "Yes. I confronted my friend, and he told me I was naïve. He said I knew nothing of power. But I learned a great deal that day."

Evangeline shifted uncomfortably. She didn't like this insight into the Lord Seeker's past, and she had to wonder if it was simply because she preferred to think of him as unreasonable. The sad truth, she supposed, was that every templar had their reasons, and they were all good. At the same time, they all sounded like excuses. "That need not be what happens here," she said.

He turned from the doorway to stare at her intently. "We give them leeway now, and they will demand more and more until that is *exactly* what will happen."

She shook her head. "We're not always right, my lord. If we push them too far, they'll turn into exactly what you make them out to be. There has to be another way."

The Lord Seeker sighed heavily, walking back to the dungeon entrance. "There is no other way," he said, "but I see it is pointless to speak more of it. Say what you will at the conclave, then . . . but once it is done you will not be serving in this tower any longer, no matter what the Divine says."

"And what about Cole?"

"If he exists, we will hunt him down." He made to leave, but hesitated. "It seems my first impression of you was incorrect. Knight-Commander Eron evidently chose subordinates with as poor judgment as his own. How unfortunate." With that, he walked out.

I am happy to disappoint you, she thought.

Three weeks.

Rhys had never considered his quarters in the tower small before. Certainly if one had to spend three weeks confined somewhere, it was better than a dungeon cell. Far better, in fact. That didn't stop time from dragging incredibly slowly. All he had to do in his chambers was either stew in his frustration or read— and there was only so much he could read of Brother Genitivi's dry dissertations on the New Exalted Marches before he went mad.

Not that he wanted to read. What he wanted to do was march out of his quarters and tell the entire tower exactly what had happened in Adamant, what Pharamond had done, and what the templars were going to brush under a rug if they could get away with it. He wanted to shout it from the rooftops, no matter how much trouble it got him into. He was already up to his eyeballs in trouble, and had been ever since this whole thing started.

Or perhaps that was just the frustration talking.

Mostly he worried. He was certain Evangeline was in trouble for trying to help, and she knew that was a possibility even when she made her offer. That she did so anyhow made her worthy of respect. If only there were more templars like her, the Circle wouldn't be in the mess it was.

That was wishful thinking, however. There weren't many templars like her. Most were so wrapped up in their authority they couldn't see past it. They were jailors, and the mages were prisoners to be either reviled or pitied. The Divine might be sympathetic to mages, but that didn't stop centuries of Chantry doctrine teaching people to blame magic for events that happened a thousand years ago.

Rhys was also worried about Cole. He hadn't come to visit the entire week. Not that Cole had ever ventured up to his quarters before, but if there were anyone who could sneak past the guards it would be him. Did something happen to him? Was he frightened by the audience with the Divine, or did he feel betrayed? Rhys had desperately looked for Cole when they were being led out of the Grand Cathedral, but seen nothing.

And now there was only silence. There was only one person

who visited Rhys on a regular basis, and that in and of itself was a mixed blessing.

As if on cue, a quiet knock sounded on his door.

"I'm here, Wynne."

The door opened, and the old woman peeked inside. She wore a new robe, this one black just as the first enchanters wore. The fact she technically hadn't earned such a robe was irrelevant, considering the unique place Wynne held in the Circle. She mentioned to Rhys that she'd had the old robes burned; after traveling in the rain and sleeping in the mud for weeks, she didn't want to see them ever again.

Wynne spotted him and smiled. "I didn't think you'd be anywhere else. I simply didn't want to wake you." She came in carrying a tray of food: biscuits and cheese, plus a bowl of steaming soup. The aroma immediately awakened his appetite. The Lord Seeker wasn't trying to starve him, exactly, but it seemed like the templars brought meals only when they remembered to—which wasn't very often. If it weren't for Wynne's frequent visits, he'd likely be eating his fingers by now.

"Thank you." He took the tray and immediately began shoving the biscuits into his mouth. Perhaps a little greedily, but Wynne didn't appear to notice. She sat on the edge of his cot and watched him, folding her hands in her lap.

"You'll be happy to know the army has finally marched," she said. "It appears the Marquis is going to support the Empress after all."

"I didn't realize that was in question," he said between mouthfuls.

She shrugged. "There's apparently been talk of deposing the Empress, especially with all the rumors coming from the east. Some say she's dead, others say she's been captured. Still others say she's holed up with her army at Jader, and that Gaspard has cut off the western highway. I think that's more likely."

"Is the Circle going to be called on to fight?" He chuckled lightly. "I mean, I can just *imagine* how that would go over . . ."

"The Divine wishes to wait until after the conclave, which is a prudent move on her part. Leliana seems to think it'll be unlikely even then, not unless Gaspard marches on Val Royeaux."

"Leliana?"

"You saw her in the Grand Cathedral, next to the Divine. An old friend."

Ah, another "old friend" of Wynne's. Rhys was beginning to wonder just how many of those she had. "I suppose the first enchanters have started to arrive?" he asked.

"You suppose correctly. Many are already here. Briaus arrived from Hossberg last night, and Irving from Fereldem this morning. I understand the Grand Enchanter is in Val Royeaux as well, but if so she hasn't shown up at the tower yet." The last she said with a frown.

"I guess you'd rather she'd stayed in Cumberland?"

"Fiona was once a Grey Warden. Considering one does not normally *leave* the Wardens, this makes her something of a . . . an anomaly." She considered, frowning. "Of course, so am I, so I suppose it makes little difference. Still, it was her election to the position that caused the conclave to be disbanded in the first place."

"You make it sound like her fault."

"Who else's? Mine?" She shrugged. "Fiona campaigned diligently for independence from the Circle. Grand Enchanter Briaus had never allowed such a vote, correctly believing it would only antagonize the Chantry. With her election, everything changed."

Rhys stopped eating, and studied Wynne carefully. She was torn, even he could see that. With the conclave less than a week away, she had to be considering what she was going to say. He wondered that himself. "So," he began carefully, "all these visits and we haven't yet talked about what we're going to do at the conclave."

"Are we going to do something?"

"I thought we might." In the face of her amused expression, he scowled. "I mean, considering how you alienated the Divine, I figured you'd abandoned her whole 'fix the Circle' plan." When she laughed out loud, his scowl deepened. "Or not."

"Oh my dear boy." Her laughter subsided, and she looked at him apologetically. "Do forgive me. Of course you don't know— who do you think asked me to send those messages? The Divine had no more idea than I did what we would find in Adamant, but her instructions were clear: if I discovered Pharamond's research had born fruit, I was to contact the first enchanters immediately."

"So it's a game, then?"

"She came into power within a Chantry accustomed to a Divine too senile to rule. There are those who resent her fiercely, and will look for the slightest opportunity to circumvent her wishes. If she pursues a policy of reform, she must do so very carefully."

"Reform? You think the templars will allow that?"

Her smile was mysterious. "I believe it's our duty to try."

Hadn't she already tried? Everyone had tried, for centuries now. If the rebellion at Kirkwall proved anything, it was that the middle path allowed everyone to pretend an amicable solution was possible. Still, there was no point in arguing with Wynne about it. Her path was clearly set.

He cut off a large wedge of cheese and offered some to her. She shook her head politely. "Last time you were here," he said as he ate, "you said you were going to speak to Pharamond."

That saddened her. She idly pulled at the hem of her robe for several moments before responding. "He's . . . not doing well. Lord Seeker Lambert has scheduled the Rite of Tranquility for the night before the conclave, and the wait is killing him."

"What? Why are they waiting?"

"Why do you think? Everyone in the tower already knows

what happened to him. Lambert wishes to leave it until the last minute so no one has a chance to react."

"Ah."

They were quiet then. Rhys finished his meal and Wynne watched him. Other than the wind howling outside of his tiny window, there wasn't a single sound. Not more than a week ago he'd been arguing with his mother, accusing her of using him to further her ends . . . and now there was this odd familiarity with her visiting and bringing him food. He didn't know what to make of it.

Rhys put aside his tray, finishing the last biscuit, and stared at her. She stared back at him, the moment intensely awkward. "You don't need to keep coming here," he finally said. "I already told you I would keep your secret."

She nodded, looking off into the distance. She seemed pained, he thought. And tired. So very tired. "I said that when I first came to see you," she began. "I wanted to see what my son had become without any guidance from me. That is true, but . . . I thought I was dying. The war in Ferelden was over, and I believed the spirit could not keep me alive for long. I had to see you, at least once."

"Then why didn't you come back?"

She looked at him, her eyes moist. Reaching out, she cupped his cheek; it was a gentle, affectionate gesture. "Because you were fine. You were lovely. What could I do except cause you damage?"

"Damage? But . . ."

"What use would you have for an old woman, Rhys? You lived your entire life without me, and here I was an abomination and a crusader to save the Circle? You joined the Libertarians, and I was content to let you find your own path."

"So that's it?" He shook his head, moving her hand away from his face. "You thought you were dying, and when you didn't the only reason you came back was because you thought you could use me?"

Wynne shook her head, horrified. "No, you don't understand. Rhys, I . . ."

There was a knock at the door.

Who could it be? One of the guards? Both of them sat there, at a loss. "Go away!" he called.

From behind the door, he heard an angry whisper: "Rhys, it's me!" It was Adrian. She quickly darted through the door and closed it behind her, skidding to a startled halt when she realized Wynne was also present.

"For the love of Andraste," Rhys breathed, "what are you *doing*? Shouldn't you be locked in your room?"

Wynne stood up. "I'll leave the two of you to your business."

Adrian blocked her path. "Actually, I wanted to talk to you as well."

"I think you and I have spoken enough. If anyone asks, I never saw you." She walked around Adrian and slipped out the door. Rhys watched her go, and had a sinking feeling she wasn't going to come back. Suddenly he regretted saying what he did. That wasn't a good way to leave things.

He frowned as Adrian plopped herself down on the cot. "Rhys, she's here!" she gushed, positively vibrating with excitement. "The Grand Enchanter is here!"

"So I've heard."

"No, I mean *here*. In the tower!"

"How do you know that? And how did you even get here?"

She waved the question away dismissively. "Says the man who snuck out of his own room not too long ago. I've been busy all week, staying in contact with the Libertarians. What have *you* been doing?"

"Keeping low."

"Well, stop it. We need you. The Grand Enchanter is going to call for a new vote at the conclave."

He sat back, stunned. "That's insane. We're supposed to be

debating Pharamond's research, not talking about independence. The Lord Seeker will be watching us like hawks. There's no way he'll let that happen."

Adrian was thrilled. He could see the determination in her eyes. What she was waiting for her entire life seemed close at hand, but what was that? War? Would they all be slaughtered? How far did they want to push it?

"That doesn't matter," she said. "It's a gesture, and one that needs to happen. If the templars do anything, the entire Circle of Magi will know about it." She grabbed Rhys by the shoulders, almost shaking him in her intensity. "Just think! We'll be there, right at the center of everything when it happens. History in the making!"

"A lot of bad things happen in history, Adrian."

She pulled away, instantly switching to a hurt expression. For a moment she was silent, and then she frowned. "It's that templar, isn't it?" she asked suspiciously. "Are you worried she'll get hurt? If the Lord Seeker makes a move, you think she'll be forced to stand with him?"

He sighed. "No, that's not it."

"Then what?" Adrian stood up, agitatedly pacing around the tiny room before wheeling on him and holding her hands out in desperate appeal. "Tell me what's changed! We joined the Libertarian fraternity together. We used to sit up at night and talk about what a Circle run by mages would be like, how we would help run it. Don't you still want that?"

Rhys ran a hand through his hair, trying to control his frustration. She was looking at him in helpless confusion, and he gestured toward the bed. "Sit down, Adrian." When she hesitated, he repeated it more forcefully: "Sit. Down."

She sat.

He took her hands in his, to make certain she listened. "I *do* still want that," he stated. "I just don't want anyone to get hurt. Not Evangeline, not you, not Cole, not anyone."

Her brow furrowed. "Who's Cole?"

"Never mind that. We have to be careful, that's all I'm saying. If we do this the wrong way, if we act too rashly—especially when the Lord Seeker will be expecting us to—we could ruin it, for everyone."

Adrian sighed, shaking her head sadly. She looked at him almost like he were naïve, and she didn't quite know how to tell him. "It may come to violence, Rhys. We have to be prepared for that. And if it does, we have to be prepared to work together."

He scowled, but he had to admit she had a point. He had just been thinking, after all, about how there seemed to be no middle way. "What do you need me to do?" he asked.

"Talk to Wynne."

"I've *been* talking to Wynne. She's come almost every day this week."

"There are a lot of Aequitarians wavering. Astebadi of Antiva and Gwenael of Nevarra are both going to be here, and the Grand Enchanter said it wouldn't take much to convince them to act." Adrian paused dramatically. "Rhys, this is our chance. The winds are changing. If Wynne stands up in front of the conclave and says she believes the Circle should separate, the entire Aequitarian fraternity will fall behind her. Even the Loyalists might agree."

"She won't do it."

"Then you have to *convince* her."

"Wynne has a plan, and she has the Divine's help. I think she should at least be given the opportunity to see if she can pull it off."

"No, no." She shook her head, refusing to even consider the idea. "They're giving us a conclave to placate us. No matter what we say in there about the Tranquil, you think that will change anything?

This is the only opportunity we're going to get to actually make a stand."

"Then we have to do it without Wynne."

"No!" she said, frustrated. She made as if to stand up from the cot, but he held her hands fast. With a growl of anger she pulled them away. "You have to make her listen, Rhys! She's your mother. If anyone could convince her, it's you."

She might be right. He could even picture in his head what he might say: *If I mean anything to you, Wynne, you'll help us. I've never asked you for anything, but I'm asking now. Please . . . do this. For me.*

Even so, it felt wrong. Wynne had used him, so now he was supposed to use her back? Exploit whatever connection was between them, no matter how slight, to get what he wanted?

"Adrian, I . . . can't."

She gave up. She sat there, defeated, and for a moment Rhys thought she might actually cry. She had so much of herself wrapped up in this cause, it made him wonder: What would happen to her if she ever got what she wanted? When there was no one left to fight? They used to talk about what they would do if the Circle were ever free, yes, but was there anything of that girl still left? He'd watched that part of her get swallowed up over the years, while he remained the same. Left behind.

Rhys started to formulate an apology when Adrian leaned in and kissed him. He was taken completely by surprise, and grabbed her by the shoulders to push her back—perhaps more forcefully than he intended. "What . . . what are you doing?"

"I don't want to lose you." She *was* crying. Now that the tears were coming, they came forcefully, her entire face twisted in grief. "All those years I told myself it was better to be your friend. I assumed we would always be together, and that together we could do anything. But . . . I *feel* you drifting away from me."

"Adrian." He tried to console her, but she turned away from

him, embarrassed by her tears. "Adrian, this isn't the way to keep us together."

"Isn't it?" She looked at him, her eyes red and pleading. "Don't you love me?"

He couldn't answer that, just like he couldn't answer it the last time she'd asked him so long ago. The question had hung between them ever since, and it had taken Adrian forever to get over those feelings of rejection . . . and here she was digging them up again.

The truth was that the woman he loved had been gone for a very long time.

Adrian didn't need him to say anything. She could see it on his face. Quickly she stood up and collected herself, wiping away her tears. "It doesn't matter," she said, her voice controlled. "We'll find a way . . . with or without you."

"I said I'll help, Adrian."

She regarded him with a withering look. "Rhys, you can't even help yourself." With that she turned and walked out the door, and he was left there in his chambers . . . alone.

18

Something big was happening. It had been building up for weeks, like the charge in the air right before a storm. Everyone in the tower was on edge. They didn't want the storm to begin, but couldn't stand waiting for it to happen.

Cole understood only a little. There was going to be a meeting, and it involved important mages who had been slowly arriving from faraway places. Everyone called them "First Enchanter," though he had no idea how so many people could be first at something. Didn't there have to be a second, and a third?

As important as they might be, however, they were afraid of the templars. When they argued, they did so quietly because there were templars nearby . . . watching, always watching. They folded their arms and scowled at the mages, the same way the kitchen cooks scowled when they spotted a rat. These mages could wear all the fancy black robes they wanted, it didn't mean they weren't prisoners.

Big Nose showed up sometimes. Cole didn't know where he got his new suit of armor, but it was polished to a shine. He had a scarlet cloak now, as well, just like the one Evangeline wore. Big Nose liked to loom over the mages. He circled them, feigning interest in their discussions until they slowly quieted. They didn't like Big Nose much, and Cole didn't blame them. Cole didn't like him, either.

It was strange. Once Cole would have said there was nothing

he was more afraid of than templars . . . but now? Now he walked up to them. He stood inches away, looking into their eyes, and knew they saw nothing. They stared right through him. *I can see you,* he wanted to say. *I can see what you are, now.*

Rhys couldn't help him. They'd locked Rhys into his room, and while Cole had considered going to visit, what would he say? Cole had caused him enough grief. It was better to stay away—maybe that would make things easier for Rhys.

Evangeline couldn't help Cole, either. She was so pretty and gentle it made Cole's heart ache. When she'd promised to take him before the templars, he'd been afraid . . . but it gave him hope as well. She seemed strong, and who would know the templars better than she? But now she was down in the Pit, forced to do things a Knight-Captain wasn't supposed to do. That's what the other templars said. They gossiped about her, saying mean things that made Cole angry.

Old Woman couldn't help Cole either. He'd seen her coming and going, sometimes heading up to Rhys's room. She was watched closely at all times, and she knew it. Maybe she even knew Cole watched her, and pretended not to notice. He suspected she'd always been able to see him, right from the very beginning. It just didn't matter, because he didn't fit into her plans.

Red Hair—Rhys called her Adrian—she wouldn't help Cole even if she could. The templars had locked her inside her room, just like Rhys, but that didn't change anything. There were others who snuck up to her door to deliver messages, and she even managed to get out once or twice. The lengths she and her friends went to in order to distract the guards was fascinating for him. Adrian had just as many plans as Old Woman, and while Cole could probably have listened in and discovered what her plans were, he didn't want to know. Whatever she planned, it wasn't going to help him.

None of them could help him.

But he might be able to help them. When they'd ridden back to the city, he'd been listening. The things the others said about the templars made sense. They were the problem. When he looked into their eyes he didn't see the danger he used to. He saw fear. A terrible fear that was going to burn up everything in its path.

For so long the templars had been the demons haunting his world, and all he'd done was hide in the shadows . . . but maybe it was time to stop hiding. He wasn't locked in a room, after all, or banished to the Pit. Nobody was watching him. He was free to act.

Cole moved through the dark hall carefully, acutely aware of everything around him. The tower was asleep, or trying to be. The meeting everyone had been waiting for was tomorrow morning, and the tension had reached such a fever pitch it screamed at his senses. One false move and he would turn a corner and bump into a guard, and everything would be over.

A fat templar was waiting outside the doorway Cole sought, half-asleep. His head kept drooping and then snapping up again. If he'd just nod off, this would be easier, but there was no such luck. Fear kept him awake. Fear of the man in the black armor.

Cole shuddered at the memory. That man was made of steel, honed to a fine edge. When Cole had been in Evangeline's chambers, that man had *sensed* him. He had something in him, something different from the other templars, but Cole couldn't put his finger on it. He didn't want to find out what it was.

Slowly he walked over to the guard, heart pounding in his chest. Pharamond said that everyone forgetting him wasn't just something that happened. It was something Cole did. A power. If so, maybe he could use it.

You don't see me. You won't notice anything I do. He stared into the guard's eyes, concentrating, summoning up . . . something. He could feel it. Way down inside of him, in the dark place he never dared to look, something was there. He tried not to let it frighten him. Instead, he told it to come.

Reaching out, ever so carefully, Cole plucked the keys from the templar's belt. He maintained eye contact the entire time. The keys jingled, and he froze. Nothing. The man didn't blink, didn't react at all.

I can do it. I can make *them not see me.*

It was an exhilarating feeling. He carefully backed away from the guard, clutching the keys to his chest. When he moved to the doorway, he watched for any signs of a response. Nothing.

Cole closed his eyes and took a deep breath. Now that he'd summoned the dark place, it was spilling up inside of him. He tried to will it away, tried to push it back down, but it wouldn't go. It seeped into every part of him, trying to take him away. It was trying to make him fade.

No, I won't let you.

He clenched his teeth. He breathed, each moment slow and excruciating, until finally it wasn't so bad. It almost felt like the shadows in the hall lengthened, like they stretched out toward him, but he tried to ignore them. He was real. He was standing right there, and he was going to act.

Cole unlocked the door. The slightest click as he turned the key, and then the faintest noise as he pulled the handle. Even though the guard stood not two feet away, he didn't look. Quickly Cole slipped inside.

The bedroom was tiny and dark. The barred window showed only night sky, and a hint of snow—the first of the season. A single candle burned on the table, reduced almost to a puddle of melted wax. It did nothing but make the shadows seem all the more mournful. This room was a tomb, or was waiting to become one.

"Who . . . who's there?" A quavering voice from the darkness. Cole could barely make out the figure of a man lying on the small cot. Not that he needed to. He knew exactly who it was.

"It's Cole," he said.

Pharamond jumped up, staring at Cole in bewilderment. He had the look of a man who hadn't slept in days, perhaps in weeks. Worn and pale, dark circles under his eyes, haggard and stretched to the very limits of his endurance. Once someone might have said this elf was handsome with his silky white hair and his blue eyes . . . but not tonight. Tonight he just looked old.

"I can see you," Pharamond breathed in amazement. "And I remember who you are. Why is that? Has something changed?"

"You've changed." Cole walked over to the elf and sat down on the edge of his cot. Pharamond glanced down at the dagger in Cole's hands, his eyes widening in fear. "You can see me and re- member me because you want to die."

The elf gulped once, loudly. He didn't look away. He didn't question how Cole could know such a thing. He also didn't say Cole was wrong. "Tomorrow morning they're going to make me Tranquil again," he whispered, the words a croak torn from the depths of his throat. "I want to die more than anything."

Cole nodded sadly, but didn't respond. He stared at the flicker- ing candle instead, and for a long time the two of them sat in si- lence. Being Tranquil didn't sound so bad to him. He'd been terrified of being swallowed up by the darkness for so long it seemed like it would be a relief to get it over with. You were only scared of becoming nothing until you were nothing.

Just like dying.

"I can get you out of here," he said. "That's why I came."

"Get me . . . out? How?"

"The same way I got in." Cole considered the idea carefully. "I think . . . I think I could make them not notice you either, if you were with me. We could walk out the doors together, and they won't ever be able to harm you."

"What if that didn't work?"

"Then you would die."

Pharamond looked shocked, like the possibility of escape had never entered his mind. He stood up, pacing back and forth on the floor with growing agitation . . . and then he paused, staring grimly out the window at the blowing snow. "And where would you take me?" he asked.

"Where do you want to go?"

"I don't know there's anyplace I *can* go."

Cole didn't have any suggestions. He didn't know anything of the world outside the tower. What little he'd seen during the voyage to the keep made it seem frightening and cold, full of people who paid less attention to each other than they did even to him. "Wouldn't anywhere be better than here?"

Pharamond walked up to the window, running his fingers lightly along the bars. They were already covered in a faint layer of frost. "Winters in Adamant are horrible," he said. "The badlands become cold as ice, and that sand . . . the winds blow so hard the sand feels like it's going to strip the flesh from your bones. The people at the keep spend months preparing, yet every year a few still die. Hunters caught out in a storm, visiting merchants who don't know any better, a foolish child . . ."

Cole didn't know why the elf told him this, but he listened even so. It was all very strange. Every time before when he'd sought out some lost and hopeless soul, it had been because a burning need had driven him there. He needed them just as much as they needed him. There was no time for talking because he needed that recognition in their eyes, that moment when they made him real.

What did he feel now? Even with the darkness unleashed, crawling up inside of him like a horde of hungry insects, there was still no burning need. He ran his thumb along the edge of the dagger. Sharp. Giving Pharamond that way out would be easy. If he didn't *need* to do it, did that make it mercy instead of murder?

"The first snowfall," Pharamond continued, "there is always a celebration. I thought it so strange. The winter is dangerous, not something to celebrate. But the badlanders still put up their wreaths and hold a great feast, with dancing. I am always included and asked to dance, even though they know I won't. I just watch them, puzzled by it all." He stopped, his voice catching, and looked at Cole. He was crying. "There won't be any celebration in Adamant tonight."

"Are you saying you don't want to escape?"

"I don't want to escape. I want you to kill me."

The last conclave Rhys attended had been a spectacle.

The College of the Magi in Cumberland was a palace—once the home of a Neverran Duchess and given to the Chantry, it was rumored, because her daughter had been discovered to have magical talent. The Duchess wished her daughter to live in the opulence to which she was accustomed, and not in a dark tower a hundred miles away.

Rhys believed it. If the White Spire was impressive for its oppressive grandeur, the College was impressive for the sheer wealth on display: marble pillars, brightly painted frescoes, vases, and gilded vines that crawled up the walls. The entry hall had been especially interesting, with sandstone busts of every grand enchanter who had held the office in the last six hundred years. Everything glittered. It didn't seem like the sort of place mages would be allowed to gather, but it had been exactly that.

The "red auditorium," so named because of its domed mahogany ceiling, easily held the two hundred people in attendance: first enchanters, the heads of every fraternity, senior mages, and even intrigued apprentices. They argued, postured, split into cliques, and made speeches. Some were there simply to watch, the eldest with no small amusement at the "excitable" newcomers. Rhys had spent his time wandering amidst the cacophony, confused as to the schedule of events until he realized there wasn't one. Any attempt to enforce order was swept aside in favor of conversation.

Very little had been accomplished and, according to those who attended, that wasn't unusual. Still, nobody seemed to mind. It made the mages feel like they were a part of something bigger than just their own tower, and that when they chose they could speak as a unified voice.

This conclave, if it could really be called such, was nothing like that.

The White Spire's great hall dwarfed those present: fifteen first enchanters, short four who couldn't make it in time, plus the Grand Enchanter. Other than that there was simply himself, Adrian, and Wynne. The templars watching balefully from the walls more than doubled their number. It was intimidating, and everyone felt distinctly uneasy.

Rhys stood off to one side, not really feeling welcome in their inner circle . . . unlike Adrian, who hadn't left the Grand Enchanter's side since they'd arrived. No one was talking. They waited for Pharamond to be brought in, and that alone was cause for tension: Wynne had already explained what was being done, and none of the first enchanters were pleased. When the elf finally entered, Tranquil once again, Rhys wasn't sure what the reaction would be. Nothing good.

Grand Enchanter Fiona was an elven woman, black hair greying at the temples, and almost as short as Adrian. It might have been comical to watch the two of them standing next to the taller mages had they both not possessed an intensity which made them larger than life. Fiona glared daggers at the templars, and it was apparently a sentiment shared by the others.

As he stood there watching, Evangeline walked over to him. Her armor had been newly polished, but he noticed she'd left the red cloak behind. It made her seem . . . less imposing, somehow.

Not that he ever thought her imposing, per se, but he had always pictured her as an authority figure. If she was trying to downplay that now, she was the only templar present making the attempt.

"You're not standing with the others," she observed.

He grinned at her. "That's because I'm special."

"Are you, now?"

"Oh yes, didn't you know? I'm the mage who might be a murderer. The ladies found my dangerous allure too much to bear and started fainting, so they asked me to wait over here."

She laughed, and then gave him a scandalous look for making her do so—though he noticed she still couldn't quite hide her amusement. "I'm certain they don't really think that."

He shrugged. "Maybe. Either way, I'm no first enchanter."

"Neither is Adrian, but that doesn't seem to be stopping her."

"Adrian is currently attached to the Grand Enchanter's hip. That makes her more of an accessory, I suppose, like a nice belt or an extra pair of shoes."

She smirked and followed his gaze to where Adrian stood on the floor. Adrian noticed the attention, and when her eyes caught Evangeline's the smirk faded instantly. "They don't seem to be in a hurry to get this conclave underway," she noted.

"They're waiting for Pharamond."

"Ah."

"Do you know when he's to arrive? How long does the Rite of Tranquility usually take?"

Evangeline stared off at the row of watching templars, and her eyes flashed with anger. "It should be done by now. I've asked, but the most I've been told is that Pharamond is 'on his way.'" She grinned wryly when Rhys's eyebrows shot up at that. "I'm not exactly in favor with the order right now."

"I've caused you all sorts of trouble, haven't I? I'm so sorry."

His apology clearly took her by surprise. "You're not to blame, Rhys," she said. "I said I would try to help . . . Cole. I told you that was my duty as a templar, and I meant it. If the order is un-willing to bend, it's no fault of yours."

She remembered Cole. There had been a moment of hesitation, but he could see her struggling to hold on to his name. He found the effort touching, though he couldn't say exactly why. For a long moment the two of them stood there, comfortable in their silence as they scanned the group of mages milling about on the center floor.

"I have to tell you something," he finally said. "I admire you, Evangeline. Of all the things I've ever thought templars were like, you've managed to prove me wrong about every single one. If more of them were like you . . ."

She was actually blushing, though she hid it well under a ca-sual air. "The order is a place where ideals are set aside for the sake of necessity. There simply isn't room for compassion or mercy, and those who feel there should be . . ." She hesitated, and then shrugged. "They find themselves on the outside, as an example to the others."

"Just like the rest of us?"

"Seems that way."

He grinned. "Somehow that makes you more attractive than ever."

Evangeline looked at him incredulously, perhaps wondering if he was serious. He was tempted to laugh it off, pretend it was a bit of teasing and nothing more . . . but he just couldn't. He held her gaze, and something passed between them. Something neither was willing to acknowledge, but it was there nevertheless.

"I've had enough of this!" someone cried from the great hall's floor.

It was enough to break the moment. Evangeline averted her eyes, her cheeks flushed, and Rhys felt a moment of loss. He should have said something else, something better.

The commotion on the floor was centered around the Grand

Enchanter, who was now stamping her staff on the marble floor
to get the others' attention. The staff flared brightly, making her
white robes stand in stark contrast to the dark ones around her.
The watching templars whispered angrily in response, and several
headed toward the doors.

"We're not waiting," Fiona declared. "We're here now, and we're
well aware of what we're to discuss. We don't need another Tranquil to underline the kind of contempt in which the templars
hold us."

"Will you keep it down!" one of the first enchanters hissed fear-
fully, an Antivan man with a braided black beard.

"No, I will not." Her staff flashed as she turned her glare on
the other mages before her. "This is the first time we've been allowed together in a year, and I'm not going to waste it." She took
a dramatic breath. "I am putting forward a motion to separate the
Circle of Magi from the Chantry."

Everyone in the room took a shocked breath. More templars
moved toward the doors, these ones propelled as if chased. Rhys
sensed that something bad was about to happen—the air bristled
with anger, ready to explode. He followed Evangeline, running
onto the floor.

"We are to discuss Pharamond's research," Wynne insisted.
"Nothing more. If you derail this conclave, Fiona, we'll never get
another."

Fiona snorted derisively. "This isn't a conclave. This is a joke!
We could discuss what to do about the Rite of Tranquility until
we were blue in the face; do you believe the templars would even
think about following our advice?"

"The Divine is willing to—"

"Fuck the Divine." She sighed when the others stared at her,
stunned by her blasphemy, and rubbed her forehead in agitation.
"I'm certain the Divine is a perfectly nice person," she continued
in a more conciliatory tone. "So was Grand Cleric Elthina in

Kirkwall. She did her best to keep everyone happy, and what happened? Nothing was resolved, until finally her inaction killed her."

Wynne frowned. "She was killed by the act of one madman."

"I'm not going to condone what Anders did," Fiona said, "but I understand why he did it. I'm only suggesting that we act, not blow up the White Spire."

"Aren't you? How do you think the templars will respond to this?"

"We are not responsible for their actions. We're only responsible for our own." Fiona turned her gaze to each of the first enchanters in turn. "You all know who I am. I came to the Circle from the Grey Wardens because I saw something had to be done. In the Wardens, we learn to watch for our moment and seize it—and that moment is now."

"And what would you have us do? Battle the templars when they attempt to take us captive?" Wynne stepped in front of the Grand Enchanter, holding her hands out imploringly to the others. "What Pharamond discovered has given us an opportunity. In the face of evidence that the Rite of Tranquility is faulty, the Divine has the excuse she needs to ask for reform. That will be a beginning, I promise you."

"You promised as much at our last conclave," Fiona said. Her words weren't harsh, however . . . Rhys thought she sounded weary more than anything. "And look where we are. We know how you feel, Wynne, but the Chantry can't wait to decide when it's safe to do what's right."

"And the Libertarians are going to decide for us?" one of the first enchanters asked, a heavyset bald man with an Ander accent.

The mage with the braided beard frowned. "I'd like to know if this Pharamond actually found something significant, or if this is all just so much smoke."

"He managed to heal himself," Adrian interjected, "and now

the templars have made him Tranquil again. What does that tell you? They don't care what we learn, or what the Rite does or doesn't do. All they care about is keeping us controlled."

The first enchanters appeared to accept her words, nodding uneasily. Wynne looked upset, perhaps because she sensed the same thing Rhys did—the mood was swinging in the Grand Enchanter's favor. Even the ones whom Rhys assumed would speak up in Wynne's defense remained silent. First Enchanter Edmonde was an Aequitarian like her, for instance, but he simply scowled and rubbed his long beard.

Rhys saw Evangeline watching nervously as more templars left the great hall. Only a dozen remained clustered near the door, eyeing the proceedings with a dangerous air. The sounds of many booted feet could be heard from the halls. "I know my opinion isn't welcome here," Evangeline told the mages, "but whatever you're going to do, I suggest you do it quickly."

Edmonde seemed surprised. "You're not going to stop us?"

"The conclave has always existed to allow the mages to decide their own path," she said, her tone carefully neutral. "So decide."

Nobody spoke. Wynne looked pensive, but Rhys imagined she'd already said all she could—likewise for the Grand Enchanter. Everyone already knew what everyone else thought, and knew the issue at hand. They merely appeared reluctant to step off the precipice.

"If I may speak?" he quietly asked. Surprisingly, they all turned and paid attention. Even the Grand Enchanter. "I know I'm not one of you . . ."

"We know who you are, Rhys," the bald-headed first enchanter said. "Wynne has spoken of you frequently. For a Libertarian, your views have always proven moderate. Speak, and we will listen."

Rhys licked his lips nervously. "The Grand Enchanter isn't wrong," he said. "This is the only chance you've had to gather, and it's the only one you'll get. The Lord Seeker will consider this vote treason no matter how it goes. So there's only one question left." His gaze met Adrian's, and he could almost read her thoughts: *Do it. Say it. Convince them.* "What do you want to tell the rest of the Circle? Will you try not to make things worse, and trust the Divine, or will you make a stand?"

There was a crash outside. The templars were coming—all of them, by the sound of it. He could see in the eyes of the mages that they knew exactly what Rhys meant: the die was cast. There was no turning back now.

"I put forward the motion," the Grand Enchanter said urgently. "Who says aye?"

But it was too late. All heads turned as Lord Seeker Lambert marched through the great hall's doors, a crowd of templars at his back. All had swords drawn. Three men who wore the same black armor as the Lord Seeker walked at his side—more seekers, Rhys realized. The thunderous noise of their entrance was like death approaching.

The templars and seekers spread out, surrounding the mages in a heartbeat, as the Lord Seeker strode toward them. The cold fury in his expression left no mistake as to his intent. "This conclave is at an end," he declared. "Like children, you cannot even be trusted to do as you are commanded. I will not have treason under this roof."

Grand Enchanter Fiona stepped ahead of the others, almost protectively. Considering how short the elven woman was compared to the Lord Seeker, it might have seemed laughable were her incredible power not obvious. Her staff flared brightly, mirroring the outrage in her eyes. "This is no treason. The Divine gave us leave to hold conclave, and you've no right to tell us what we may or may not do with it."

"The Divine is a fool," he snarled at her. "As are all of you, both for thinking this might even be permitted . . . as well as for listening to the words of a murderer." It took Rhys a moment to realize the man was referring to him. "The Tranquil, Pharamond, was found dead this morning. Stabbed to death. I took the liberty of having Enchanter Rhys's chambers searched, and found this."

He tossed something on the floor between them: a knife with a black hilt, the smear of blood on its blade clearly visible. It wasn't Rhys's, nor did it look anything like Cole's dagger. Rhys had never seen it before. "But . . . that's not mine," he objected.

"Of course you would say that."

"It's true!"

Evangeline stepped forward. "I told you who was responsible for the murders, my lord. If you'd listen to me—"

"I did listen. Now I have evidence that proves you were mistaken."

"There must be another explanation!" she insisted. "Someone placed that in his room, they're trying to—"

"Be silent!" the Lord Seeker shouted. "Do not make this any worse for yourself, stupid girl! We are dealing with a blood mage. If you are not under his influence then you have allowed your infatuation with these mages to cloud your mind." He gestured to the templars. "Take Enchanter Rhys into custody."

"No!" Wynne pulled Rhys back by the arm. "This is beyond reason! The Divine shall hear of this, I swear it!"

Rhys felt bewildered. He knew the Lord Seeker had it in for him, but to go to such lengths? As he stood there, the templars closed in with their blades at the ready. The mages responded by brandishing their staves, the room crackling with mana. They spread out, facing off against the templars—a battle was imminent.

The Lord Seeker seemed unimpressed. "I am done listening to the Divine," he announced. "She will lead this land into chaos it can ill afford. All of you have a choice: stand down and return to your towers, unharmed, or be treated as the rebels you clearly are."

"No, it is *you* who have a choice," Grand Enchanter Fiona

warned. "Leave us to our lawful conclave. Allow us to investigate this claim against Enchanter Rhys in a rational manner. Or face the consequences."

His eyebrows shot up. "Threats?" He looked at Evangeline. "And what of you? Do you stand with these traitors, or will you salvage some shred of sanity?"

Evangeline clenched her jaw. She drew her sword. "The only insanity I see here is that of a man who refuses to see what he does is wrong."

"So be it."

With a wave of his hand, the templars attacked. Even prepared as the mages were, they weren't ready for the wave of disruption unleashed—the powers of a templar are uniquely designed to counter a mage's spells, and here that counted for everything. Blades came down against magical shields, shattering them and sending blinding sparks flying about the hall.

It did not stop the mages. The Grand Enchanter shouted in rage, unleashing a ball of blinding energy at the nearest group of templars. Several raised their own shields in time, but that didn't stop them from being scattered as the ball exploded. The concussive wave shook the entire chamber.

Templars charged toward Rhys. A nearby first enchanter raised her hands. "I surrender!" she cried in a panic. Whether the templars didn't hear her over the cacophony or thought she readied an attack, he couldn't tell. Either way, the first templar that reached her ran her through.

The surprised look on the young man's face said he hadn't expected that. He watched in horror as the mage stared down, confused by the sword now piercing her chest. As she opened her mouth to speak, blood spurted out. Quietly she slid off his blade and slumped to the floor, a dark stain spreading on her robes.

The reaction was electrifying. A cry went out as more mages saw what had happened, and suddenly they were no longer merely defending themselves. Rhys heard Adrian scream in fury, and deadly fire rained down on the templars—men burned, screaming horribly. The entire chamber exploded in chaos, a cyclone of lightning and smoke summoned in their very midst. The templars attacked indiscriminately now, hacking down any mage they could reach.

The confusion was too much to follow. Rhys ducked his head as a large chunk of masonry fell from the ceiling, just missing him. Another templar charged out of the smoke, uttering a war cry with his sword raised high. Rhys held out his staff and unleashed a bolt of force, knocking the man back into the fray.

He turned and saw Wynne cradling the fallen woman in her arms. She desperately summoned healing spirits to mend the woman's injuries, but the magic she poured into the body was pointless. The woman was dead and gone. Wynne shook her head in horror, tears running down her face. "No! No, this is all wrong! That can't be happening!"

Rhys tried to pull her away, but she resisted. So he grabbed Wynne by the shoulders and dragged her up, forcing her to look at him. She did so, staring with wide eyes, perhaps not comprehending what he was doing. "We have to get out of here!" he shouted.

Evangeline appeared out of nowhere. He noticed blood on her sword, and from her grim expression it was clear she hated all of this. She saw the two of them and ran over. "The front gates!" she cried, wincing as another explosion rocked the great hall. "They're sealed, but you can blow them open!"

Evangeline grabbed his hand and pulled him along, and he pulled Wynne. Together the three of them stumbled through the battle. Spirits swirled about, their ethereal forms attacking templars without any defense against them. The Veil had been torn asunder by the magic ripping through the hall, and it made Rhys uneasy. How long before one of the mages gave in to rage and despair and allowed a demon to possess them? Then the battle would become something much, much worse.

"And where do you think you're going?"

Fear clutched his heart as Rhys saw the Lord Seeker standing before them, a glittering obsidian blade held casually before him. He appeared undisturbed by the chaos, grey eyes focused on them and only them.

"Get out of our way, Lambert," Evangeline warned.

"No one is leaving this room," he said, his tone cold as ice. "Not a single one." A dozen templars appeared behind him, and Rhys saw more coming. Mages were scattering now, some trying desperately to flee even as they were cut down. Others were being overwhelmed, their mana disrupted until they couldn't cast a single spell. The mages were losing.

Wynne pushed herself away from Rhys, wiping the tears from her face. "You won't get away with this!" she cried, her voice hoarse.

"Get away with bringing a murderer to justice? With stopping a new rebellion in its tracks? The Maker's work is being done today, nothing else." He strode forward, summoning power into his sword as the other templars surrounded them.

Evangeline raised her blade with a look of determination. Wynne, too, gripped her staff and prepared for battle. Rhys couldn't let it happen. He dug deep down into the reserves of mana within him, deeper than he ever had before. With a cry of rage, he held up his staff and unleashed a torrent of magic.

The wave of force that expanded from him sent every templar flying back, as if they weighed nothing. The entire building shook, and for a single moment Rhys felt exhilarated. The power . . . it was like nothing he had ever tapped into before. It flowed through his veins, filling him up.

It would have been so easy to do more. The Veil was fragile, and he could sense the demons, lurking just beyond and eager to enter this world. A single call would give him all the power he needed. He could take many of these templars with him, one last hurrah they would never forget.

Forbidden power at his fingertips, beckoning.

With a shout of exquisite agony, Rhys pulled back from the brink. He turned to Wynne and Evangeline, his eyes flashing with power. "Go!" he shouted. They stared at him in shock, but neither budged. "GO!" he roared.

Without waiting, he spun around to face the templars. A sparkling wall of pure force rose up between them, the men slamming against it uselessly. Holding up his staff, Rhys summoned a storm of energy, adding it to the maelstrom. He would tear the entire hall down, if he had to, stone by stone.

The Lord Seeker reached the wall of force. He channeled his own power, shattering it with a single blow of his black sword. Hot pain flashed through Rhys. He fired one magical bolt after another at the Lord Seeker. The man blocked each one, but it was enough to give him pause. His brows knitted in effort as he fought to get closer.

And then something hit Rhys from behind. A blow to the back of his head, making his vision swim. He lashed out with a spell, flinging the unseen attacker up into the ceiling with enough force to shatter his bones. Then something else slashed at Rhys's side. He unleashed a spell in that direction as well, not even bothering to look.

Then the Lord Seeker was there. The man's eyes were filled with hate. "Andraste guide my blade," he uttered, and swung his sword with all his might.

The shock of the disruption sent Rhys stumbling back. The world spun around him, and he fell to the ground. Several templars leapt on him instantly, beating him with metal gauntlets and sword hilts. The pain was blinding until he surrendered to it.

As the world began to fade, he looked around. The Lord Seeker was standing over him, watching the beating Rhys received with his cold, cold eyes. But Wynne and Evangeline were nowhere in sight. They were gone.

Good. At least I did something right.

And then the blackness reached up and claimed him.

19

Evangeline and Wynne trudged through the sewers, knee-deep in water so foul Evangeline didn't even want to think about it. The tunnels had originally been built as a refuge against siege—a means to transport supplies behind enemy lines, and at times even a way to house the city's population. The years since those days had not been kind, and now this was a decrepit and forgotten place filled with nothing but waste.

That included the human kind, as well. There was evidence of habitation: tattered shelters, cold firepits, bits of clothing, and even weapons. The poorest of the poor lived in these depths, called the *sous des gens* by the city folk, but none of them seemed to be here. No doubt the press gangs had scoured the sewers weeks ago, looking for anyone they could drag into the army no matter how sickly. For a square meal, some of these people might even have jumped at the chance. She supposed she should be grateful for the lack of eyes to witness their passing.

The sewers were freezing. Frost gathered around each of the grates that led up to the surface, sometimes in piles several feet thick. The murky water chilled Evangeline's legs even through her armor. Wynne was far worse off in her robes, now stained up to the waist.

The woman was in no mood to complain, however. Ever since they'd eluded their pursuit and fled beneath the streets, Wynne had said nothing. She walked fast, her expression one of cold fury, and it wasn't even clear she knew or cared Evangeline was behind her. Save for the echoing sounds of sloshing water, it was completely quiet. Evangeline had no idea where they were going.

She'd started off leading Wynne, forcibly pulling the old woman along despite her screams that they needed to save Rhys. He'd been right, however. Either someone kept the other templars at bay or they would all have been caught. That hadn't made it any easier to do, and it hadn't made Wynne any more forgiving.

Evangeline understood completely. Even now, she wanted to turn around and march right back to the White Spire. What if Rhys was still alive? What were the rest of the tower's mages going to do? They must have heard the explosions. She imagined the Lord Seeker had dealt with them before coming to the conclave—separated them into the dormitories and kept them under close watch. That way they could be left frightened and guessing. For all they knew, every mage who wasn't in the room with them was being made Tranquil, and they could easily be next.

The Lord Seeker had clearly planned it all, possibly since the audience in the Grand Cathedral. The templars would call it another rebellion, an excuse for even harsher restrictions. It filled her with disgust. They wouldn't be satisfied until they made the mages bleed, and would feel completely justified doing it.

They proceeded through the old tunnels for some time, Wynne leading the way with her glowing staff the only source of light. Occasionally they passed a sewer grate, the lack of visible sunlight telling Evangeline it was now evening. An entire day spent running, then. What would the morning bring? Would they have to leave Val Royeaux?

"Wait," she said. "Where are we going?"

Wynne didn't slow down. "Leliana always told me to be prepared, and thankfully this time I listened to her." As she turned another corner, her staff showed what appeared to be a metal casement embedded into the sewer wall. Its locking mechanism looked incredibly complex. "Ah, here it is. I thought I'd forgotten the way."

Evangeline watched dubiously as the old woman began fiddling with the lock's dial. "This is yours? Here in the middle of the sewers?"

"I rented this from an upstanding young man from the local thieves' guild when I first arrived in the city . . . just in case." The casement opened with a loud clang, revealing two things: a staff made of a burnished red metal, and a sack. She took the staff out first, running her hand along its length lovingly.

"Don't you already have a staff?" Evangeline asked.

"This one is different." She placed her white staff in the casement, and handed the sack to Evangeline. It felt heavy, clinking as if it were full of coin. It probably was. "Something from my time in the Blight, given to me by the Hero of Ferelden. It's not something I dare use casually."

"Couldn't you have used that at Adamant?"

"Not unless I also wanted the templars to know I possessed it." She turned to Evangeline, regarding her with a serious look. "Tell me: What will the templars be doing now? Still hunting for us, no doubt."

Evangeline considered. "They'll scour the streets, searching anywhere they think we might hide. Presumably the Lord Seeker will claim a fugitive apostate is on the run—that will get the co-operation of the citizens rather quickly. Then they'll close off the city gates, and as soon as they realize we haven't left they'll come down here."

"So we still have time."

"Some. Are we going to the Grand Cathedral?"

"We're not." The red staff began to glow. This wasn't the comforting light of her old staff, however. It was dim and menacing, making every shadow in the sewers writhe as if alive. Evangeline's skin crawled. She wanted to get away from it, run back up to the surface and keep running until she stopped shuddering.

"I intend to go back," Wynne stated, the determination in her eyes leaving no room for denial. "I will tear down the White Spire brick by brick if I have to, but I intend to either find my son alive or make the man who murdered him pay."

Evangeline felt uneasy. It was obvious why the old woman had kept the staff a secret—the templars held to the belief that any mage, no matter how noble, would resort to forbidden magic when backed into a corner. That Wynne had access to such an artifact would only serve as proof that she considered using it an option, and she would be censured accordingly.

Even so, Evangeline found it difficult to credit the templar position when it was they who backed the mages into that corner. She didn't remember any of the desperate first enchanters in the great hall turning into abominations—but if they had, could she truly blame them? Out of fear, the templars were driving the mages to do the very things of which they were accused. It was a vicious cycle that needed to be stopped.

She said nothing. Instead, she met Wynne's gaze and nodded. It was an intense moment, and the old woman appeared satisfied by the answer. Wynne spun on her heel and marched through the tunnels once more, quicker this time. "You realize if you do this, your future with the templars is done?" she asked.

"My future with the order is already done."

"And what of lyrium?"

"There's more than one way to get lyrium." One of her duties over the years had been, in fact, hunting down the various dwarven smuggling rings that brought lyrium into the district. Before today, she'd never have believed that knowledge might come in handy, though convincing men she'd once hunted to trust that she now only wanted a transaction would be . . . difficult. "I have at least a week before I'm useless to you."

"Let's not waste time, then."

As they walked into another tunnel, however, Evangeline became aware of something ahead in the shadows. It was no rat. Someone was down there with them, moving quietly enough so as not to disturb the sewage—but enough to alert her. She swiftly drew her sword. "Wait," she told Wynne.

The figure approached, crouched low and cautious. It wasn't a templar, but a young man in rough leathers with shaggy blond hair hanging over his eyes. If he was one of the *sous des gens,* then he was also dangerous, for he held a wicked-looking dagger at the ready. Still, she hesitated. There was something about him that seemed oddly familiar, like he was someone she should know. Someone important.

"Cole," Wynne said, scowling.

The young man seemed relieved. "You remember me."

Remember the dream. It all came back to Evangeline in a rush. She sheathed her sword and walked toward Cole, who stared at her in confusion. When she got near, she hugged him close. "I'm glad you're safe," she breathed. Initially he squirmed in her embrace, clearly unaccustomed to it, but then he relaxed and hugged her back. For a moment they were two lost souls, embracing in the darkness.

"Step away from him," Wynne warned. The menacing glow of her staff deepened, casting the old woman in sinister shadow.

Evangeline let Cole go and turned to face her, but instead of leaving his side she placed herself protectively in front of him. "Why? What do you think he's done?"

"Isn't it obvious? Pharamond was murdered in his chambers. I can believe Lord Seeker Lambert capable of many things, but not this."

Evangeline hesitated. The knife the Lord Seeker threw down hadn't been Cole's . . . but could he have been mistaken? She didn't want to believe the young man had killed someone yet again, but what if he had? How big a fool would she be, sympathizing with someone who endangered his friends? Rhys might be dead because of him.

She looked at Cole questioningly, her suspicions slowly giving way to dread at his guilty expression. "I didn't kill him," he said . . . but the way his eyes stared at the floor said otherwise.

Wynne's gaze intensified. "Stand aside, Evangeline."

"Wynne, I . . ."

"I said stand aside!" The old woman stamped the staff on the ground, and suddenly black flame leapt from it. It twisted and curled around her, ribbons of some dark power that fed on her rage and drew strength from it. She was a force of vengeance now, eyes red as blood, and Evangeline was terrified.

Cole ran. He darted down the tunnel, splashing through the brackish water even as Wynne unleashed a bolt of flame at him. Cole leapt to one side, the bolt narrowly missing, and as it struck the sewage it burst into a curtain of cold fire. The *whoomp* of expanding air struck Evangeline like a fist, and she staggered back. Wynne remained unmoved, searching for Cole through the smoke.

"Stop!" Evangeline cried. She lunged toward Wynne, grabbing the red staff. It was so cold it burned, blistering her hands . . . but she refused to let go. As they struggled for control, gouts of black flame spurted from its tip. One blast just missed Evangeline's face, the lick of it caressing her cheek.

"Leave me be!" the old woman growled at her like an animal.

With great effort, Evangeline shoved forward and drove Wynne against the tunnel wall. The impact forced her to release her grip, and Evangeline tore the staff away. Spinning around, she smashed it against the ground with all her might . . . and it shattered.

Wynne screamed, a primal cry of loss and fury. Evangeline didn't have time to react as a blast of force struck her. She was lifted off her feet, tumbling end over end down the tunnel. With a grunt she landed in the sewage, inhaling evil-tasting water, and for a moment all was blackness. She flailed about in confusion, her shout a muffled roar in her ears.

Then she broke to the surface. A single gasp of air filled her lungs with agony, and she floundered to reach the embankment. Blinking, she looked up and saw Wynne standing over her. The old woman's eyes were narrowed in outrage.

"That was a foolish thing to do, Ser Evangeline."

She raised a hand and summoned mana, a sphere of power coalescing in her hand. Evangeline tried to speak, to somehow reason with the woman . . . but all that came out were hoarse coughs.

And then the spell simply vanished. Wynne froze in place . . . and Evangeline realized it was because Cole stood behind the old woman, dagger at her throat.

"I won't let you hurt her," he said.

For a moment, Evangeline thought he might cut Wynne's throat. He didn't. He carefully forced her to back away with him. Evangeline crawled onto the embankment, retching and spitting that foulness up from her lungs. Once the world stopped spinning, she gave one last cough and wiped her mouth.

"You defend him," Wynne seethed.

"That staff was evil," Evangeline said. Slowly she got to her feet. "Whatever happened, whatever you plan, it should never have been an option and you know it."

The old woman scowled. Evangeline could see the regret in her eyes, however. Finally she relented, the rage draining out of her all at once. She would likely have fallen to her knees had Cole not still held the blade to her neck.

"It's all right, Cole," Evangeline said. "You can let her go."

He did, quickly hopping away. His expression was morose. "I didn't kill Pharamond," he said. "He begged me to. He wanted to die. But I . . . I couldn't. I knew Rhys would be unhappy, and I didn't want to cause him any more trouble . . ."

Cole wasn't guilty because he was lying . . . he was guilty because he *didn't* kill Pharamond? Even though he thought he should have? It made a strange sort of sense. Evangeline remembered the elf's pleas, the stricken look on his face as the templars dragged him away. Had she the chance, and he'd asked her to show him mercy . . .

"Then who did kill him?" Wynne asked, confused. "Surely not the Lord Seeker."

"Why not?" Evangeline said. "Pharamond was a threat to his authority. As is Rhys. He'd already ordered me to kill all of you once, remember?"

Wynne slowly nodded . . . and turned away, unable to look at either of them. "I'm so sorry," she whispered. "I feel like such a fool. I just can't stop thinking . . . what if Rhys is dead? After all this, all I've been through, to have him die before me . . ."

"He isn't dead," Cole said.

Wynne stared at him in astonishment. "What . . . did you say?"

"Rhys is hurt. They put him in the dungeon, but I can't get him out. There's too many templars there, now." He paused, looking at both of them uncertainly. "That's why I came looking for you. I can't help him alone."

"Why would you do anything at all?"

He squirmed. "Rhys always wanted to help me. I don't know why he did, but he did. Everything that's happened to him is my fault. I have to do *something*."

Wynne stared at him. Then she shook her head, ashamed. "I am an old fool. I acted without thinking, doing all the things I've cautioned other mages against. I . . . hope you can forgive me, young man. What I did was . . . inexcusable."

"You're Rhys's mother," he said simply. "My mother tried to protect me, too."

"And did she succeed?"

"No. She died." Cole's face twisted with grief. He backed away from them, stumbling once as he hit the tunnel wall. There he crouched down, placing his head between his knees and his hands over his head. Like he was shutting down.

Evangeline knelt beside him. She put a hand on his shoulder, whispering soothing things. Her father had done that. Just the once, the day her mother died. Even wrapped up in his own grief, he couldn't stand to watch his daughter in pain. She imagined he'd felt as helpless as she did right now.

"I . . . attacked you as well, Ser Evangeline," the old woman said. "I can't even—"

"Templars guard the mages, remember?" Evangeline interrupted. "Even if it's from themselves. I may not believe in the order, but that doesn't mean I stopped believing in what we stood for."

Wynne looked at her strangely, as if seeing her for the first time. "I think I know what Rhys sees in you, Ser Evangeline."

"Just save him." Evangeline stood up, and Cole stood with her. He suddenly seemed calm, as if he'd never broken down at all. That wall Cole put up around himself was there again. It made her sad, but there was nothing she could do. "If we're going to do this, we need a sensible plan," she said. "Running around half-cocked and full of rage isn't going to help anyone. We have to find a way into the dungeon that won't have the entire White Spire blocking our way out."

"I know a way in," Cole said.

Both women stared at him.

"There are old places in the Pit," he continued, "places nobody even knows about. Some of the walls are crumbled, and you can get into the sewers. That's how I got here."

Evangeline smiled, her thoughts already racing ahead of her. There would still be the matter of dealing with whatever guards the Lord Seeker had placed at the dungeons, not to mention the deadly traps protecting it, but if they could get *inside* without assaulting the front entrance . . .

"I know what we're going to do," she said.

Rhys coughed, and his whole body shook with agony. More blood gurgled into his mouth, the revolting coppery taste making him gag. He spit, and the blood dribbled out onto the cell's stone floor. He spit again, the effort making his stomach clench painfully—so he closed his eyes and waited for the spasm to pass.

Someone had stabbed him. He remembered that much, a hazy moment shortly before he'd finally succumbed to unconsciousness. One of the templars had loomed over him, a fellow with a large nose—the same one that had been waiting at Adamant. *"Now you'll get what you deserve, all of you,"* he'd said . . . and then stabbed Rhys. He could still feel the cold blade sliding into his stomach as if it were yesterday.

Seemed petty, really.

Why didn't they kill him? They had every justification. He could easily be branded a rebel . . . and it wasn't like his death would make the mages *more* angry. After that pitched battle in the great hall, the White Spire would either be in open rebellion or in complete lockdown. He could only guess what would happen once the other Circles heard the news. The templars would have their hands full.

One chop to the neck and everything he knew about Pharamond's work would be gone forever . . . unless that was the point. Perhaps the templars wanted information they thought only he had? If so, they were bound to be disappointed. The elf had explained his theories on making the Tranquility cure work—but little else. There'd been no time.

The thought of Pharamond made him sad. The elf had

experienced a brief moment of release from the awful oblivion that was Tranquility, only to be murdered in his chambers while waiting for his sentence to be carried out.

It couldn't have been Cole. The dagger that the Lord Seeker had thrown down hadn't been Cole's, and why would Cole use another? That meant the templars had executed Pharamond and purposefully framed Rhys for it. Whenever they came to speak to him, he'd find out why.

Cole. . . . Sometime recently he'd awoken in the cell and seen Cole crouching over him. At the time he'd thought it another fever dream, brought on by his injuries. Indeed, he'd imagined Evangeline there, and Wynne. Even Adrian. An entire array of people parading through his cell to either pity or accuse him in turn. Of them all, however, Cole had seemed the most plausible.

"I'll get you out of here, I promise."

Had that been what Cole said to him? Rhys could hardly be confident. He hoped it wasn't true. He didn't want Cole risking himself any more than he wanted Wynne or Evangeline doing so. They should leave, get as far away from Val Royeaux as they could before whatever came next swallowed them whole.

Because something *was* coming. The rebellion in Kirkwall would be nothing compared to this. He'd seen several first enchanters slain, and the rest of them . . . ? It didn't even matter now, did it?

There was a noise at the cell door. A key turning in the lock. Rhys tried to push himself up, and managed to do so only with an accompanying jab of agony. He waited in the darkness, staring at where the light would momentarily be blinding him.

It didn't disappoint. With a great clang, the metal door swung open and a great flood of light filled the room. Rhys closed his eyes, waiting to let the glare stop being so painful, and instead listened as several pairs of heavy, booted feet tromped in.

So this was it. An execution, then? Or something else?

"Leave us," a voice said.

The boots left without comment, slamming the door shut behind them. Rhys opened his eyes again, blinking away the swirl of afterimages and focusing on the figure standing before him. It was a man in armor, holding a glowlamp . . . and its gentle blue light revealed him to be the Lord Seeker.

The man looked down at Rhys with contempt.

"You're awake. Good." The Lord Seeker hung the glowlamp on the wall and sat down in a chair—brought in, Rhys assumed, as he didn't remember noticing it before. Of course, in the utter darkness of his cell the chair could have been right by his head and he wouldn't have noticed it then, either.

"What? No cookies? I'm disappointed."

The Lord Seeker ignored him. "We're going to talk, you and I. It seems past time that we did."

Rhys burst into laughter, but it was interrupted by a bloody coughing fit. "Talk?" he finally managed. "I'd rather the execution. It'd be less painful, and frankly, why should I be more special than everyone else?"

The Lord Seeker's smile was patient, but it didn't touch his eyes. "There have been no executions. All who didn't perish in the great hall have joined you in imprisonment . . . as have many others. I daresay the White Spire's dungeons haven't been this full in ages."

"You're going to keep us all here?"

He leaned back in the chair, folding his arms and staring at Rhys sternly. "What happens to the others depends entirely on you."

"What do you want?"

"A confession."

"Very well. I confess: I'm a mage."

"Don't be a fool."

Rhys snorted. "I didn't kill Pharamond. You must know that."

"Must I?" The Lord Seeker raised a disapproving brow. "I imagine you'll tell me it was the 'invisible man,' yes? Cole, is it? He murdered this Pharamond as he murdered the other mages?"

Rhys felt a chill run down his spine. At some level he'd hoped the templars would forget about Cole, just like everyone else. Learning about him from Evangeline might mean that wasn't going to happen now. "Cole didn't kill Pharamond," he said. "At least, he didn't do it with that dagger."

"Are you certain?" The Lord Seeker leaned close, making Rhys recoil. Those grey eyes seemed to bore into him with their intensity, and was it . . . concern? There was concern there as well, though whether it was for Rhys or something else he really couldn't imagine. The idea that this man might feel sympathy for anything seemed laughable. "What do you believe Cole is, exactly?"

"A mage who was brought to the tower, and then lost."

"With abilities never before recorded, outside of blood magic?"

"He's not a blood mage."

"Perhaps he's not. Where did you see him first?" When Rhys didn't answer, the Lord Seeker stood up from the chair. Pacing around the small cell, he continued. "Here in the tower, I suspect. Perhaps glimpses of a stranger that nobody else could see? It took you seeking him out to actually speak with him, however."

"I'm not the only one who's seen him. Evangeline, for instance."

"She saw him in the Fade first, however."

"Yes, but he followed us . . ."

"Did he? Followed you halfway across the Empire? Somehow keeping pace with you the entire way without you once spotting him? And let me guess: the first time you did see him, you were seeking him out." He stopped pacing, giving Rhys an incredulous look. "Come now, Enchanter. You're a clever man. I figured you to have better reasoning than this."

"Cole isn't a demon," Rhys objected, but suddenly he wasn't so certain. He'd rejected the idea plenty of times. When he spoke with Cole, his gut said the young man was real, a lost soul who needed help. As human as he. But still a doubt lingered . . .

No! He's trying to trick you! This was just one more attempt to twist him about. He only wanted a confession—whatever good that did him.

"Allow me to refresh your memory." The Lord Seeker reached behind the chair and picked up a tome from the floor. Rhys recognized it: one of the volumes he'd written during his years researching spirits, no doubt rescued from some corner of the archives where it languished. Rhys had barely thought of his research since he discontinued it a year ago, and thus it was surprising to see now . . . and even more surprising that the Lord Seeker had bothered to dig it up.

The man walked over to the glowlamp and flipped through several pages until he found the one he wanted. *"Demons often become confused when they pass through the Veil,"* he read. *"They find themselves in a world they have no control over, and no connection to. They seek out such connections, possessing whatever they can see and touch, and seek to make it conform to the world they left behind—a world embodied by concepts and emotion rather than immutable reality. They subsume themselves in the world of the living, and this is what drives them mad."*

He snapped the book shut and looked inquisitively at Rhys, but said nothing. Rhys felt uneasy. "You're saying Cole is a confused spirit, but that doesn't—"

"Tell me," the Lord Seeker interrupted, "when did the murders begin? Before or after you first met Cole?"

Rhys hesitated. "After."

"Why not before? How long did Cole claim he'd lived in the tower?"

"I . . . don't know. Years, I think."

"So for years he lived in the tower, out of sight and forgotten, and never felt the need to murder anyone until he met you." The

Lord Seeker shrugged, replacing the book behind the chair. "That's certainly possible. Did he say *why* he killed these people?"

"Because he felt like he was fading away, but—"

"Fading away. As if he lacked a connection to our world, and the killings somehow strengthened it." He rubbed his chin thoughtfully, and Rhys felt even more uneasy than before. He would have expected threats, condemnation . . . anything but this. "Blood magic is the manipulation of life energy," he continued, "the strongest source of mana and the only one forbidden to mages. Such life energy could provide a spirit the connection it needed, no matter how temporarily?"

Rhys nodded slowly.

"But only a mage can perform blood magic. So either this Cole has possessed the body of some unfortunate soul and is an abomination, and thus able to use that body's magic, or he is a disembodied spirit trying desperately to maintain a connection to our world, his only power the ability to influence the minds of others." The Lord Seeker spread his hands. "The question is: Which one are we dealing with?"

"What if he's neither of those things?" Rhys asked. He sat up again, wincing as a jab of pain lanced through his chest. "And even if he is, what would this have to do with my confession? If Cole is a spirit and you know it, then why accuse me of murder?"

The Lord Seeker nodded, as if this were an excellent question. "You're a compassionate man, Enchanter. Always willing to help those in need. It's made you quite popular." His eyes narrowed as he looked pointedly at Rhys. "It must have been quite distressing to encounter a young man so desperate and alone."

"But I would never—"

"Only you could help him. You couldn't tell anyone else, for fear of what they might assume, and no one else could see the lad. Why you could, who knows? Coincidence, perhaps. Some aspect of your own talents you were unaware of."

It sounded eerily familiar. Rhys said nothing.

"What would you do to help this poor young man, I wonder? Blood magic could help him, and only you can do that. Seek out some imprisoned mage, so eager to die you could even call it mercy, draw the life force from them—"

"But I didn't do that!" Rhys shouted.

The Lord Seeker stared at him knowingly. "The spirit chose you. You encountered many during your research. They would know who you are, and could follow you back to the tower. That's why you see him."

"No!"

"I've searched the records high and low. They contain the details of every apostate found, the orders given to bring them to the Circle, testimony from the templars sent . . . there is nothing for a boy named Cole, or anyone by his description. You can choose to believe this young man's abilities extend to erasing records, or you can accept that Cole never existed in the first place."

Rhys twisted to look away. He couldn't stand it. His heart pounded, and all he wanted to do was scream *No! You're wrong!* But now Rhys was besieged by doubt. If Cole could make people forget him, what if he could make them forget other things? What if Rhys *had* agreed to help? What if he'd let Cole in, opened his mind up just enough for a single evening? And then forgotten. Could it be?

The Lord Seeker leapt forward and grabbed Rhys by the throat. The steel gauntlets pressed painfully into his skin as the man forced Rhys to look at him. Those grey eyes burned now, his patience at an end. "Confess," he demanded. "You will tell the first enchanters you have been under the influence of a demon. You killed the elf, killed all of them, and unwittingly empowered this demon to manipulate the mages of this tower."

"And if I don't?" Rhys said between gritted teeth.

"Then you will die." He released his grip, stepping back once again. Rhys collapsed to the ground, coughing and choking, the agony in his chest almost too much to bear. "The first enchanters will be executed, as will Enchanter Adrian and any other mages we've imprisoned. We cannot abide rebellion, and I will either find a solution or deal with it however I must."

Rhys laughed. It was a wheezing, weak laughter coupled with painful gasps, but he couldn't help himself. More blood filled his mouth, and he spit it out, but still he couldn't stop laughing. The Lord Seeker stared at him in disbelief, his expression slowly changing to fury. "Is something amusing?" he demanded.

"You almost had me convinced," Rhys chuckled. He rolled over, sweating profusely from the exertion, and shakily pushed himself up. The Lord Seeker did not appear impressed by his efforts.

Slowly Rhys's mirth subsided. He wiped his mouth and looked at the Lord Seeker seriously. "Even if Cole is what you believe," he said, "I doubt he knows it. He most certainly isn't manipulating the entire tower. If you're looking for someone to take the blame, look somewhere else."

"But you did murder those people."

"Or you framed me, precisely so we could have this conversation." Rhys smiled sweetly. "I guess we'll never know."

The Lord Seeker paused. He looked at Rhys speculatively, and Rhys wondered if he shouldn't take it back. What if he *was* a murderer, and Cole a demon? He was dead either way; at least confessing would spare the lives of everyone else.

But spare them for what? Tranquility? Feed them a lie, so they could go on swallowing everything else the templars chose to heap upon them? Deep down, Rhys didn't believe it. He couldn't. Cole was what he appeared to be, and so was the Lord Seeker: a man grasping at straws to keep the Circle of Magi from crumbling around his ears.

"As you wish," the Lord Seeker said. He turned and left, taking the glowlamp with him. The moment the cell door slammed shut, Rhys was left once again in darkness.

Maker help me, he prayed. *Don't let them try to save me. Tell them to run and save themselves.* And then he closed his eyes, suddenly shaking from pure exhaustion. *And help Cole. Wherever he is, whatever he is, I believe he means well.*

I believe it.

20

"I preferred the tower in Ferelden," Shale muttered.

Wynne snorted. "How can you say that?" she whispered. "The one and only time you were in Ferelden's tower, it was half-filled with abominations and corruption of every kind."

"It was an improvement."

"Quiet, you two!" Evangeline hissed. Trying to remain quiet with the golem accompanying them was challenging enough without the two of them chattering. How Wynne had managed to find Shale, Evangeline couldn't imagine. After reaching Mont-simmard, the golem had followed them to the capital—where it had spent its time terrorizing the local pigeons, evidently. Stealthy or not, she imagined it would prove quite useful with what lay ahead.

Things had gone smoothly so far. They'd entered the tower through an ancient section of the sewer system—that the tunnels had ever connected to the White Spire was clearly long forgotten. Evangeline had certainly never known about it, and the decrepit ruins in the deepest part of the Pit hadn't seen human traffic in centuries. It wasn't an easy way to enter, either, requiring near submersion in brackish waters and scaling half a mortar wall she was certain would crumble.

But it didn't. It even held the weight of the golem, and before long they were inside. Cole knew the Pit like the back of his hand, and had led them unerringly through the darkness. There were so many twists and turns, so many collapsed passages and remnants of fortifications blocking the way, they would never have found their way without him.

When they finally reached the area near the dungeons, they discovered it exactly as reported: teeming with templars. At least twenty were in the guard station, with more just outside. Half the mages must be locked up, if not all—the Lord Seeker would have needed to reopen the cells on the lower levels, which could easily hold twice the tower's population if required.

They could have assaulted the dungeons right then. Evangeline didn't relish the idea of fighting her former comrades again, but she'd be foolish to believe what she did now wouldn't end in blood spilled. Regardless, it wasn't the templars that worried them. All it would take was one of those templars pulling the wrong lever and the defenses at the dungeon entrance would be activated. No one would be getting in or out.

That presented a problem.

"I'm simply worried about Rhys," Wynne whispered, chewing her lip nervously. "I wish we'd stayed with Cole and Leliana. Rhys is hurt. Who will heal him?"

"He'll be fine," Evangeline assured her. "We're doing our part."

They crept up the long flight of stairs toward the main floor of the tower. Wynne kept her staff dark, so they needed to move carefully. Even at this time of night, it was still possible for a templar to come or go. All it would take was one, and all their efforts would be for naught.

They were lucky. No one appeared, and when they entered the tower proper it was deathly quiet. What guards were awake would be stationed at the great hall entrance or in the mage commons— that would be standard procedure, though tonight she'd half expected it to be an armed camp with guards at every doorway and stairwell. She was glad to see she was wrong.

"Shoddy security," the golem sniffed.

"They're not as worried about attacks from within, it seems."

"Why not? That's exactly what they should be worried about."

"The mages are kept confined. The tower is too large for templars to be everywhere at once. If we wait around long enough, however, we're bound to encounter a patrol." She waved them forward, and slowly they ascended the central staircase.

They passed several levels without incident. Then, as they neared those occupied by the mages, they began to hear muffled voices. Evangeline peeked over the edge of the banister and saw her suspicions confirmed: an entire group of templars occupying the commons. They were not on alert—several of them sat around, playing cards by the light of a single glowlamp. The others conversed in whispers or nodded off in a corner. Not a single mage was in sight.

The Lord Seeker would have their heads to see them so relaxed, but that wasn't what was important. They wouldn't be able to pass by on the stairs without the risk of being spotted.

"Wynne, could you . . . ?"

"Yes."

The old woman held out a hand and concentrated. A faint glow coalesced over it, growing stronger and brighter until Evangeline became alarmed. Then Wynne opened her eyes. "Hush," she told the shimmering orb floating before her . . . and it dimmed in response. "Do you understand what I ask of you?"

The orb bounced in a way that could have been acknowledgment, and then it flew up into the air. There it split into a dozen tinier orbs, and these were so faint they could barely be spotted in the darkness. All at once they scattered, floating toward the templars.

"What are they going to do?" Evangeline whispered nervously.

"Just watch."

The orbs sailed over the templars' heads, with not one of them bothering to look up. Fortunate, to say the least, though why would they? Then the orbs split up, each heading toward a different door . . . and passed through the crack at the bottom.

They waited in the staircase anxiously, each moment making it more likely that someone else would come along and complicate matters immensely. They didn't want to get into a pitched battle. Not here, not yet.

Then, just as one of the men threw down his cards with a triumphant shout, loud popping noises began to sound behind the doors. They sounded like small explosions. The reaction from the templars was immediate. They leapt to their feet, stumbling about in shock as they drew their swords. Several of them ran to the doors, throwing them open even as the fearful shouts from the mages beyond rang out.

It was enough. The cacophony of noise and confusion provided the cover they needed to slip past. Now all they had to do was hope the commotion drew others only from below, and not above.

"I hope that doesn't end with anyone being harmed," Evangeline whispered as they drew far enough away from the commons. "There are mostly apprentices in those dormitories, and with tensions being as they are . . ."

"I hope so, too," Wynne said.

There was nothing more to discuss. They entered the upper levels of the tower, normally reserved for the officers. Evangeline's own quarters were here—or would be, if the Lord Seeker hadn't reassigned them. Perhaps Arnaud had triumphantly moved in? A part of her wanted to check. There was only one thing she wanted: her father's book. But she reminded herself it was too risky. A keepsake of a life that was behind her now.

It was quiet as the grave, with barely a single glowlamp to light their way. Every footstep seemed like a thunderclap. She felt certain someone was going to hear them.

And then they turned a corner on the staircase . . . and someone blocked their way.

Wynne gasped in surprise, and the golem lurched forward with stony fists raised to attack—only to be stopped by Evangeline. The person before them was an elven woman, her grey robes and the sunburst mark on her forehead marking her as Tranquil. She stood on the dark landing, frozen . . . but not in fear. Merely the calm curiosity of one who had encountered something unexpected.

A beat passed in silent confrontation, with nobody making a move. "Do you know who I am?" Evangeline asked.

"I do, Knight-Captain," the Tranquil answered. "You have been declared an enemy of the Circle by Lord Seeker Lambert."

"Are you going to warn the tower we're here?"

She hesitated. "Do you intend to harm anyone?"

"Only if they harm us first."

The elf nodded slowly, as if this answer was acceptable. "The Lord Seeker was delivered an urgent summons to the Grand Cathedral, and left with many templars. He declared he would not be gone long. Whatever it is you plan, I suggest you be quick."

Evangeline exchanged a glance with Wynne. It appeared Leliana had been successful in convincing the Divine to aid them after all. That explained the emptiness of the tower. "Why are you telling us this?" she asked. "I've never known the Tranquil to do anything but what they're told."

The woman tilted her head curiously, as if the answer should be obvious. "Obedience is prudent. To interpret it as a lack of free will would be an error." She turned to leave, and then paused. "Good luck, Knight-Captain." And with that she walked away, vanishing into the shadows.

"That's it?" Shale asked incredulously. "We just let it go?"

Wynne nodded, her expression almost sad. "Yes," she said.

Evangeline had to agree. There was no reason to harm the woman, after all. Still, the encounter made her wonder. Was this tantamount to tacit approval, a sign that even the Tranquil found the actions of the order objectionable? She'd always wondered what the Tranquil might do if they ever found a reason, somewhere in those logical minds of theirs, to rebel. What would that look like?

Whatever the case, they had no time to waste. Evangeline led Wynne and Shale up the final flight of stairs, more urgently now. This was a walk she remembered well—it wasn't so long ago she'd ascended these steps with First Enchanter Edmonde at her side, seeking the very same thing.

They reached the very top of the tower . . . the foyer containing the massive vault door that led to the phylactery chamber. It was as she remembered, and by the vault stood a single templar just as before. This time, however, the man had his sword drawn. He held it nervously, sweat pouring down his brow as he found himself confronting not only another templar but an archmage, her staff ablaze with power, and a looming golem of stone and crystal.

"Stop! Who goes there?" he cried, his voice quivering. Evangeline recognized him. The name escaped her, but this was a young man—barely recruited a year ago and still full of dreams and ideals. Terrified as he was, still he stood his ground and was prepared to defend his post.

"You know who I am," Evangeline said, drawing her own sword. He shifted uneasily as she stepped into the foyer, his eyes flickering between Shale and Wynne behind her. He didn't lower his blade an inch, though its shakiness proved he was no swordsman. She could easily disarm him. In fact, she could easily skewer him, if she wanted.

"You shouldn't be here, Knight-Captain."

"Yet here I am."

That answer didn't please him. The young templar backed away farther, until he bumped into the vault. That made him jump, and for a moment Evangeline thought that might propel him into attacking—but he controlled himself, just enough.

"Listen to me carefully," she said. Her blade remained steady, and followed him wherever he moved. "You're not going to die here. You're going to leave your post, run down those stairs, and tell the templars where we are. Do it as quickly and as loudly as you can."

He licked his lips nervously. "But . . ."

"It's your duty to raise the alarm. Not to fight against impossible odds."

He took an exploratory step toward her, sword shaking even more than before. Evangeline backed away, to allow him past. That appeared to encourage him, and he took two more steps toward Wynne and Shale. He swung his sword around to point it at them, on the verge of panic.

Wynne stared at him calmly. The magic swirling around her white staff ebbed, and she too stood aside. The golem appeared far more reluctant. It glowered at the young templar before grudgingly making way. The path to the stairs was now clear.

He moved slowly, in fits and starts and clearly becoming more certain this was all some trick. Nothing happened. When he got to the doorway he suddenly bolted, rushing down the stairs and shouting so loudly his cries echoed. Evangeline listened, and sighed.

That was it, then. Soon it would begin.

"Let's get this over with," Wynne said. She briskly walked over to the plate on the far side of the vault, placing her hand upon it. Evangeline did the same on the other side. The key to entering the phylactery chamber: one templar and one mage, working in tandem. Evangeline only hoped the Lord Seeker hadn't somehow managed to change it.

He hadn't. Both of them channeled power into their plates, the reddish glow changing into blue . . . and then the vault began to shake. Its mechanisms turned loudly, each metal layer of the door shifting until they aligned. Far below, down the stairs, shouts could be heard.

"It should have killed him," Shale muttered.

Evangeline didn't respond. When the vault's handle revealed itself, she ran over and pulled. The massive door swung open with a shuddering groan. Beyond lay the phylactery chamber, just as she'd seen it last: great glittering pillars reaching up to the very roof of the tower, each holding hundreds of red vials—the blood of every mage in the White Spire, and many more besides. The chamber pulsed with its dark energy, sending a shiver of dread down Evangeline's spine.

The three of them walked in, forgetting for the moment about the growing commotion down the stairs. Wynne stared up at the pillars, eyes wide. Perhaps she had never seen a phylactery chamber before? She was either amazed or repulsed, it was difficult to tell.

Evangeline approached the large central pillar. "I think I remember where Rhys's vial is located. Hopefully the Tranquil put it back where it—"

"Wait." Wynne studied the nearest pillar. She reached out with a hand, running her fingers along the glass vials . . . and slowly her expression hardened. There was rage there, a towering anger that grew stronger by the minute.

"We can't wait, Wynne."

"Even if we find Rhys's phylactery, the First Enchanters have theirs here as well. Freeing them will do nothing if they can be tracked down again."

Evangeline felt uneasy. "What do you propose?"

Wynne looked over at Shale. "Tear it down," she said. "Tear it all down."

The golem might have smiled. Eagerly it approached the central pillar. For a moment, Evangeline wondered if she should try to stop it. Destroy the phylacteries? It was . . . unthinkable. Or was it? She had always felt leery of the templars using blood magic simply because it was convenient. And what would be the purpose of backing down now?

She'd made her choice. They all had.

Evangeline watched as Shale reached the pillar. It stared up briefly, and then it clutched its hands together . . . like a great hammer it struck the pillar with tremendous force. The sound of shattering glass was earsplitting. The entire column shook, whole shelves of vials emptying their contents and raining down upon the floor.

Shale swung again, and this time the pillar moved. Evangeline could feel the force of the blow in her bones. The twisting metal staircase that circled the pillar suddenly detached itself, first bending almost in two before finally crashing down. It just missed the golem, sending up a cloud of debris. The other pillars began to shake now, as well, each of them shedding vials by the dozens.

With a great cry, the golem smashed the pillar once more. This time it gave way. It teetered slowly, the last of its phylacteries showering the golem in red glass, and then it toppled. With a thunderous groan, it struck one of the surrounding pillars, and that one collapsed as well. It fell against the one next to it, and that one fell against another . . . a chain reaction had begun that had the entire chamber collapsing. Portions of the roof were even caving in.

Both Wynne and Evangeline backed out into the foyer, covering their faces as a cloud of dust billowed out of the chamber. It almost felt as if the entire tower was going to fall down around their ears. Evangeline felt dumbstruck; the magnitude of the destruction was awe-inspiring.

As the clamor began to dim, they stared into what remained beyond the vault door. Very little could be seen except darkness and dust. It seemed impossible that anything remained intact therein, or that the golem could have survived. Yet even as they watched, a hulking silhouette approached, each step crunching in shattered glass.

Shale appeared, a stone monstrosity completely covered in sparkling motes of glass . . . and grinning widely. "That was strangely satisfying," it said.

Now the sounds of booted feet could be heard, rushing up the stairs and accompanied by the shouts of men. Many men.

Evangeline prepared herself. Now there would be blood.

Cole's legs were getting cramped. He waited in the shadows, not far from the entrance to the dungeons, and watched.

He wouldn't have needed to stay hidden at all if it wasn't for the fact he was with a stranger: a woman with short, red hair that Old Woman had called Sister Leliana. He supposed that meant she was a priest? If so, she didn't look like one. She was dressed in coppery chain mail, with black leather boots that reached almost to her thighs and a longbow around her shoulders more ornate than anything he'd ever seen. She looked like someone who fought as easily as she breathed. Were there priests like that? He had no idea.

Since Evangeline and the others left, the Sister and Cole hadn't spoken a word. She crouched next to him, her gaze intent on the templars. He wanted to ask her questions. How did she know Old Woman? Did she know Rhys? He vaguely remembered her standing by the woman with the tall hat on, in the holy place that stunk of perfume, but she'd looked different then.

But it didn't really matter, did it? He wasn't here to ask questions—he was here to save Rhys. When Cole saw him in his cell, he'd been pale and barely coherent. The wound in his stomach had looked bad. Cole didn't know anything about medicine, or healing spells, or he'd have tried to help. If Rhys had died while he was gone . . .

Finally, after what seemed like hours, it began.

First there was a sound like thunder, high overhead and so distant Cole wasn't certain he heard it at all. Then it got louder, and a tremor shook the ceiling—just enough to dislodge clumps of dust and alarm the templars. They jumped up all at once, drawing their swords and shouting at each other. Before they could do anything, another templar came running down the stairs, so quickly he almost tripped.

"We're under attack!" he screamed.

"What? By whom?" said one of the others. "Where's the Lord Seeker?"

"I don't know!"

There was a moment of confusion, followed by another sound from far above: an explosion this time. That jolted them into action. One of the templars took command, ordering three men to remain behind as he gathered up the others and ran off. The sound of their boots on the stairs was growing faint when the Sister finally shifted.

She unslung the longbow and notched an arrow, but didn't draw it. She seemed displeased. "That's not good," she whispered. "They left three. I'd hoped for less."

"Is three too much?"

"It's not that. It will only take one to activate the defenses, and killing all three quickly enough may be . . . tricky." She gave the slightest smile as she raised her bow, aiming carefully as she drew back the arrow.

Cole put his hand on her shoulder. "I can do it," he said.

The Sister looked at him curiously, but didn't object. So he stood up. He'd never hurt a templar before. He wasn't going to let them keep him from saving Rhys, however, and Evangeline had said they wouldn't have much time.

Clutching his dagger tightly, Cole crept down the hallway toward the guard station. He reached the first templar, an older man who stood near the entrance. He had tanned, weathered skin and a bushy black mustache flecked with grey. The man looked right through Cole, staring nervously in the direction of the stairs. At every faint sound of battle he twitched.

"Another rebellion," he growled.

One of the other two, a square-jawed woman who wore a helmet that covered most of her face, shook her head in disgust. "Foolish," she sighed. "The Lord Seeker will have their heads this time. You'd think they'd learn."

The old templar merely grunted. Cole stared into his eyes, so close he could smell the man's sour breath. Concentrating, Cole reached down into the well of darkness inside him. He steeled himself against the fear that came with it.

I won't let myself be washed away, he thought. *Rhys is the only friend I have in the entire world, and I would do anything to help him. Anything.*

Cole raised the dagger. Gently he placed the serrated edge against the templar's neck. It pressed against his skin, drawing the slightest bit of blood . . . but the man didn't react. He continued to stare, as if nothing was happening.

You won't see me. Cole cut deep, the man's neck gushing bright blood down the front of his armor. His eyes went wide and he gasped, clutching at his throat in panic. The blood flowed more quickly now, staining his tunic and dripping onto the floor. He raised his gauntlet to stare at it, confused. Then he let out a single gurgle and dropped to one knee.

You can't see what I do. Cole left the old templar behind and moved to the woman. He could feel it, feel the shroud he'd lain over her eyes. She struggled against it, not even aware she was doing so. His temples throbbed painfully.

You can't stop me. He placed the point of the dagger against the base of her throat and pushed, pressing his weight against it. The blade plunged deep. The woman grunted, the slightest bit of blood spurting from her mouth. Still she seemed transfixed, unable to surface from the sea of oblivion in which she swam.

None of you can stop me. He pulled the blade out, watching as she reeled back and fell against the wall. Her sword dropped to the floor with a clatter. She tried in vain to staunch the flow of blood with her hands. She turned to the last templar, reaching out with a shaking hand to try to warn him, but all that came out was a strangulated cry.

If he's dead, I'll hunt every last one of you. Every last one, I swear it. The last templar was a younger man. His blond hair was long and messy, and in some ways he reminded Cole of himself. The young man's brow furrowed, as if he detected something amiss but couldn't quite put his finger on it. Cole struggled to maintain his concentration, but felt it slipping through his fingers. His heart thudded so loudly in his ears it was all he could hear.

The woman finally slumped to the ground, and the sound she made suddenly alerted the young templar. He spun around, shouting in surprise, and at the same moment spotted Cole. "No!" he shouted, raising his sword to strike.

It was too late. Cole lunged, slashing the dagger across his neck. The templar staggered back, his clumsy swing easy for Cole to evade. He tried to lift his blade again, but the blood was gushing freely now. He was too weak. The sword wavered, and then dropped. He fell to his knees, staring at Cole in utter astonishment. Then, ever so slowly, he collapsed.

Cole let out an explosive breath. He reeled away from the body, leaning against the wall and struggling against the urge to vomit. That dark power was in every inch of him now, like a sickly oil that filled every fiber of his being. He shook, sweat pouring down his brow, and closed his eyes. *Push it down, back down . . .* it took every ounce of willpower he possessed to regain control.

When he shakily got back to his feet, the Sister was already entering the guard station, bow still in hand. She noticed the fallen templars, but her attention remained fixed on Cole. There was wariness in her eyes. Fear, even. Of him.

"That . . . is an interesting thing you do," she said carefully.

"It's okay. You won't remember it."

She didn't appear to believe him. He didn't mind. He wiped the dagger on the cloak of one of the templars. The sounds of shouting up the stairs was louder now. Closer.

The Sister grabbed the glowlamp from the wall, as well as the key ring from the older templar's belt, and together they ran into the hallway with all the cells. Cole could hear muffled shouts behind some of the doors—lots of them, in fact. There were more people here than he'd ever seen before, including some on the lower levels, and they all seemed to be calling for help.

"I need to find Rhys," he said nervously.

"We will!" The Sister ran to the nearest cell and unlocked it. When the door opened, it revealed a short woman with an ugly bruise covering one of her cheeks. She glared at them angrily, crouching in the corner like a cornered cat ready to leap. Cole realized he recognized her: it was Red Hair. Adrian. The one who argued all the time.

"What do you want with me?" she demanded.

The Sister chuckled. "That's a fine way to greet your rescuers."

Red Hair's eyes narrowed suspiciously. "Rescuers?"

"Unless you'd prefer to stay."

It only took a moment for Red Hair to realize the truth. She stood, holding out her manacled hands. "Get me out of these, then," she said. "We have to find the Grand Enchanter. If anyone escapes, it has to be her."

The Sister nodded and turned to Cole. She tore one of the keys off the ring and passed it to him. "Let the others out. Quickly."

"I need to find Rhys," he repeated.

"We need to let them *all* out." She immediately ran over to Adrian and unlocked her cuffs. Cole ran out into the hall. The noises were louder now. The cries of those in the cells were a rising swell of fear, and he let it wash over him.

Cole closed his eyes, reaching out with his thoughts. Rhys was alive. He could feel him close by, weak and slipping away, but still holding on. Cole wasn't too late. The Sister could help the others—he wasn't here for them.

Don't die, he called out. *I've come for you, just as I said I would. I won't let you die.*

21

Rhys felt himself being roughly dragged from the haze of pain in which he lingered. Someone was shaking him by the shoulders. He wanted to cry out, tell them to stop. *For the love of the Maker, you're hurting me!* All he could do, however, was weakly groan.

"Rhys! You have to get up!"

The voice was Cole's. It felt so far away . . . like he was looking down at himself lying there in the darkness, but none of this had any relation to *him*. It wasn't real. Just some dream he couldn't quite wake up from.

"Rhys!"

He reluctantly opened his eyes. The reality that greeted him was sharp and unrelenting, a knot of agony that burned in his stomach and spread its tendrils into the rest of his body. He wanted to retreat from it, back into the darkness, but the insistent shaking wouldn't let him. "Cole," he mumbled, "stop, I'm awake . . ."

Cole looked relieved. He began unlocking Rhys's manacles, and as Rhys slowly came to his senses he realized something was wrong. There was shouting outside his cell. Doors slamming and people running. Voices filled with urgency. Off in the distance, an explosion sounded.

That made him sit up. Was the tower under attack? "Wait, what's going on?" he asked. "What have you done? I hope you didn't . . ."

The cuffs fell from his wrists and landed on the floor with a dull thud. Rhys hadn't realized how heavy they were, but now that they were off it was a blessed relief. "We came to rescue you," Cole said, as if it were the simplest matter in the world. He looked Rhys straight in the eyes. "Can you stand? I'll carry you if you can't."

Rhys doubted Cole was strong enough, but he didn't doubt the young man would try. Still, that wasn't what made him hesitate. He watched Cole now, the way he moved, the worry in his expression, and wondered if there was something there he hadn't seen before. The words of the Lord Seeker came rushing back.

What if it was true? What if it was *all* true? "Cole, I . . . need to tell you something." He spoke the words before he had time to think them through.

Cole didn't question him, or suggest that now wasn't the best time. He merely nodded and sat back, waiting for Rhys to continue.

What could he say? He had no more evidence than the Lord Seeker did, a man who had every reason to manipulate the truth in his favor. The Lord Seeker never met Cole, never looked him in the eyes. He hadn't been in the Fade and witnessed the kind of pain that made the young man what he was today. Cole was real. Rhys knew it in his bones.

Why, then, did he feel so guilty? Slowly he lowered his gaze. "Never mind."

Cole helped him to his feet, and together they walked out into the hallway. It wasn't easy; each step was agony, a jolt that made his guts feel like they would fall out. He tried holding his stomach tightly, but it was no use. Sweat poured down his brow, and he shook uncontrollably.

"I . . . I can't," he grunted.

"It's just a little farther," Cole urged him.

Rhys tried to summon mana to heal himself. He closed his eyes and concentrated, but the pain was simply too great. It was a white blaze he just couldn't fight his way past, and trying only made it worse. He doubled over, the light-headedness threatening to make him swoon.

Someone else ran up to them, carrying a glowlamp. It was Adrian. Rhys had never been so happy to see someone in his life. He thought for certain she'd been killed in the great hall—if anyone was the sort to go down fighting, after all, it was her. From the bruise on her face, it seemed it wasn't for lack of trying.

Adrian skidded to a halt. "What's the matter with him?" she asked Cole. "Why won't he heal himself?"

"He's too hurt."

Adrian scowled. "A thousand potions in this tower, and nobody thought to bring one?" She lifted his chin up and studied his face. He gritted his teeth, feeling like he would burn up and yet freeze at the same time. "I'm sorry, Rhys," she said, her irritation dissolving into obvious worry. He must look worse than he felt. "You know I don't have healing spells, and I can't spare the time to find someone who does."

"Are . . . *you* okay?" he asked her weakly.

The question took her by surprise. She seemed disconcerted, almost suspicious. It was odd, though he couldn't quite place his finger on why. He'd known Adrian for so long, but now he was reminded of the last time they'd spoken in his chambers. Perhaps the friend he'd known was gone forever, now. That made him sad.

"I'm fine," she said. "Try to get out safely, Rhys."

And with that she ran off. Rhys watched her go, and then nodded gratefully as Cole helped him forward. It took effort, and his steps were both stumbling and uncertain, but he was able to walk. Barely.

There were people rushing past them. Rhys recognized a couple: some were first enchanters from the great hall. Others were mages he knew from the tower. All of them were terrified, and unwilling to slow down. There was a red-haired woman with a glowlamp ahead at the entrance to the hall, waving everyone onward. She looked vaguely familiar, but Rhys couldn't place her. He had other things to worry about.

Like walking. He tried his best to keep pace, Cole and he falling into a strange gait: step-shuffle-hop, step-shuffle-hop . . . it was agonizingly slow, but Rhys gritted his teeth and kept going. He felt so useless it was maddening, but Cole didn't appear to mind. He patiently urged Rhys on.

Before long they fell behind the others. The red-haired woman yelled for everyone to keep up. He saw the Grand Enchanter beside her, as well as Adrian. And then they were gone. Rhys and Cole were alone in the darkness, with only the sounds of distant battle and the shouts of the mages far ahead to give them a sense of direction. Not that Cole needed it. He knew these passages well.

Step-shuffle-hop, step-shuffle-hop.

Time passed slowly. The sounds drew farther and farther away, and the darkness became complete. Rhys was left blind. He knew they were descending deeper and deeper into the Pit, but he had no idea where they were. He relied on Cole to guide him, the only sounds their footsteps on the cold stone and the thudding of his heart in his ears.

Where was Evangeline? Was Wynne here, as well? Were they part of the fighting? Where were they going, and what if the templars came hunting them? He wanted to ask Cole these questions, but it was all he could do just to control the pain and keep moving.

After what seemed like an hour of torture, Rhys heard water splashing beneath his feet. He could smell something sour and putrid, like sewage, layered thick amid all the dust. "Where are we?" he asked through gasped breaths.

"Close now," Cole said. The man might as well be invisible, but for the voice in the darkness and the arm supporting Rhys's waist. "There's a wall ahead. You'll need to climb down."

"Fall down, you mean," Rhys chuckled grimly.

"We'll find a way."

Suddenly Rhys heard something behind them: the sound of many booted feet, running. Men shouting orders. Templars. He froze, instinctively trying to summon mana to his defense, but the surge of pain was too much. He staggered back, tripping over a rock, and Cole quickly caught him before he fell.

Rhys's heart beat wildly. He crouched down, wincing as the gash in his stomach protested, and waited. Maybe the templars wouldn't come this way? Maybe they . . . but his hopes sank as he spotted the telltale light of a glowlamp off in the distance. Several, in fact. The light grew brighter as the templars rushed in their direction.

"Cole, we have to run!"

"Wait," Cole urged. "It's okay."

How could it be okay? Not that Rhys's limping gait would have gotten them far, but to sit still and hope for the best?

He felt a rush of panic as the first templar came into sight. There were five of them, big and burly men in heavy armor splattered with streaks of blood. Their grim faces said they were ready to kill whatever lay in their path.

The lead man held his glowlamp high as he peered off into the passage. Rhys was confused. The templar wasn't five feet away. His light should have revealed them, plain as day. How could he not see?

"I could have sworn I heard splashing," he muttered.

"It's us," another said. "Those are just echoes."

"Maybe. Are we sure any came this way? What's down here?"

A templar with a bushy black beard walked forward, swinging his sword irritably against the wall. "Maker's breath, who knows? We should go back. The last thing we should be doing is wandering down here, chasing ghosts."

"The Lord Seeker said we're to find whoever escaped the dungeon. He'll be following as soon as he can."

"And what if he doesn't? Are we supposed to fight a dozen first enchanters ourselves? Have sense, man!"

The lead man gave the other a sour look. "Tell the Lord Seeker that, if you're willing. Maybe you want to join Ser Evangeline? She's fighting alongside those mages, both you and I saw it. It's insanity."

The rest said nothing, avoiding each other's gazes so as not to betray their private thoughts. The lead templar spat in disgust, and then marched off down the passage. The others quickly followed. Each splashed by Cole and Rhys, not a one noticing them.

Then Rhys felt it: a power so faint he barely noticed it was there. It was a hush that surrounded him like a blanket, thick and smothering. And it came from Cole. In the last vestiges of the light from the templar lamps, he could see Cole's eyes clamped shut. The man was concentrating hard, a trail of blood seeping out of his nose.

"Cole," he whispered. "They're gone."

Cole's eyes snapped open. He looked at Rhys in surprise . . . and then winced in pain. He curled up on the ground, placing his head between his legs and whimpering. Rhys didn't know what was wrong. He helplessly patted the young man's shoulder, and when the templars were fully gone they sat in complete darkness once again.

Eventually Cole's breathing slowed. "I . . . I think I'm okay now."

"How did you do that?"

Cole didn't answer. Instead he pulled Rhys to his feet and led him onward once again. This new ability of Cole's disturbed him. It hadn't felt like any kind of magic Rhys had encountered before. It was . . . something else completely. That wasn't a comforting thought.

The templars had also mentioned Evangeline. Did that mean

she was still alive? He hoped so. If the Maker truly looked after the faithful and the good, He would let her escape.

They reached the wall Cole mentioned. It wasn't easy to descend in the dark. It took forever, Rhys clutching at stones he couldn't see, breathing in short gasps and praying he wouldn't fall. And then he *did* fall. Luckily, Cole was there to catch him. The pain was unimaginable. Rhys lay there in the cold and clammy sewer water until the spasms subsided, and all Cole could do was pat his head and urge him to keep moving.

Eventually they entered the sewers. It had to be the sewers, from the foul smell. Clearly the rest of the mages had come this way. Faint voices echoed in the passages, and Cole quickly led him in the opposite direction.

It didn't take long for more templars to come. Many templars, in fact. They shouted orders at each other and splashed through the water, the sounds seemingly coming from every direction. It was confusing, but Cole seemed to know where he was going. Rhys trusted him.

They turned down one passage, and then another. It went on forever, time blending into a haze of pain, and Rhys might have blacked out more than once—if he did, when he came to he found himself still walking. Finally Rhys tugged at Cole's sleeve. "I . . . have to stop," he panted. His legs wobbled so badly they felt about to collapse from under him.

Cole didn't say anything, but took Rhys by the shoulder and guided him to an embankment. There they sat, Rhys trying to bring his breathing under control. His guts burned. It felt like they were bleeding again, his life oozing out of him uncontrollably. His head spun from exhaustion.

A faint light drifted down from a grate in the ceiling. The light of Val Royeaux at night, he assumed. It was enough to hint at the edges of the passage walls, and show the rats scurrying about in the corners. Rhys wondered if they shouldn't try to reach it, maybe escape into the city. Then he quickly discarded the idea. Even if there was a ladder, he couldn't imagine climbing right now . . . and what if the grate was sealed? Without magic, he was useless.

Rhys froze. Someone was coming toward them. They weren't running, however . . . they were walking. Cole grabbed his hand, and Rhys shuddered as he felt that dark shroud settle over them once again. They were hidden.

Then their pursuer came into view: it was the Lord Seeker.

The man waded slowly through the water, a glowing red vial held before him. Rhys's heart sank—it had to be his phylactery. The Lord Seeker was tracking him with it. He moved casually, gracefully . . . a hunter on the prowl.

Would Cole's ability hide them? Rhys held his breath, watching as the Lord Seeker paused. The man slowly moved the vial around, studying how the crimson lights within responded. Then he frowned.

"Come out," he said. "I know you're here. All that effort to destroy your phylactery, and here I've kept it with me all along."

Neither of them moved.

"Ah yes," the Lord Seeker chuckled. "Invisibility is an interesting trick, I'll give you that. Of course, every trick is worthless once the truth is revealed." He put away the vial . . . and took out a small book. It was an odd thing, the size of his palm and bound in shiny gold. The man opened it and began reading aloud. The words were old, Ancient Tevinter . . . almost a chant, really. What he thought he was doing, Rhys couldn't imagine.

Then something changed. The tingle of magic, prickling along his neck. It swept through the passage like a wind, and with it went the shroud that hid them. Cole gasped in shock.

The Lord Seeker's head instantly spun around at the sound. Those grey eyes narrowed as he spotted them, and he smiled coldly. "And there we are," he said. "Cole, I assume?" Tossing the book aside, he raised his sword and charged.

Cole leapt to his feet, dagger in hand. He ran to meet the seeker without a sound. Rhys tried to grab at him, alarmed. "No! Don't be a fool! You need to run!"

Cole didn't stop, however, and Rhys only managed to tumble off the edge of the embankment. He fell into the water, blood rushing to his head and making him dizzy. He tried to summon mana, reached desperately down for power—anything at all—but his head only reeled in agony. He screamed.

Cole dodged the first swing of the Lord Seeker's sword, ducking low and stabbing at him with the dagger. It glanced uselessly off the man's black armor. The seeker instantly spun around, faster than Rhys would have thought possible, and kicked at Cole. The metal boot connected, sending the young man flying back into the sewer water with a grunt of pain.

Cole didn't stay down long. He jumped up in one smooth motion, crouching low in a fighting posture. The two circled each other now, the Lord Seeker appraising his opponent carefully.

"I won't let you hurt Rhys," Cole growled. He darted toward the Lord Seeker, striking fast like a snake. As the seeker swung his blade down, Cole jumped aside at the last second and let it strike the water. Then he leapt up and slashed at the man's neck. The dagger connected, and had the Lord Seeker not twisted aside he would have received much more than just a gash.

As it was, he seemed infuriated. He held a gauntlet up to his neck, and then studied the blood on it. "You're fast," he said. "I'll give you that." He pointed his sword at Cole, the tip tracking the young man as he moved from side to side . . . and then he charged. The Lord Seeker's swings were fast, each coming one after the other, Cole barely able to dodge in time. The young man was forced back, and when he stumbled against the bank, the Lord Seeker moved in for the kill.

"Cole!" Rhys shouted.

Cole tried to parry the swing, but only succeeded in having the dagger ripped from his grasp. It fell to the ground, and the Lord Seeker kicked it off into the water. When Cole jumped after it, the seeker nimbly swung the hilt of his sword against Cole's head. The young man flew back, slamming against the passage wall.

Not letting up, the Lord Seeker stabbed his blade into Cole's shoulder. It sank deep, and Cole screamed in agony.

When the seeker removed the sword, Cole made a growling sound like a rabid animal and leapt on him. The Lord Seeker was taken by surprise. Cole was all over him, clawing and biting at his face. It was enough to stagger the man, and he dropped his sword, but his confusion lasted only a moment. Reaching up, he grabbed Cole by the hair and threw him aside like a rag doll.

Cole landed in the water with a great splash, and instantly jumped back up. The Lord Seeker expected that, however, and kicked him in the stomach. It was a solid blow, sending Cole flying several feet to splash in the water again. He tried to rise, but the Lord Seeker kicked him again. Blood flew from his mouth as he sailed back.

"No!" Rhys cried. "Cole! Run!" He crawled through the murky water toward where the Lord Seeker had kicked the dagger. It must be there somewhere! He felt around in the slime, his hands shaking.

The Lord Seeker marched over to Cole, yanking him up by the hair. This time Cole was too weak to do more than struggle. The seeker curled his fist and punched Cole in the face. He went down, but still tried to get back up. The Lord Seeker picked him up by the hair and repeated the punishment. Twice. Three times. With the last blow, Cole's nose exploded in a shower of blood. He stayed down, slowly crawling through the water toward the embankment.

Rhys found the dagger. His hand closed around the hilt, and

he shakily got to his feet. The entire world swam around him. He tried to charge, but only succeeded in stumbling toward the Lord Seeker. "Leave . . . him . . . alone!" he shouted.

The Lord Seeker turned and grabbed his wrist, crushing it until he dropped the dagger. Then he contemptuously backhanded Rhys across the face. The blow sent him careening back, slamming against the wall, where he crumpled in a heap. His stomach blazed with piercing agony, and he writhed along the floor, his scream a mere ragged gasp.

Sighing irritably, the Lord Seeker walked over to his sword and picked it up. He paused then, watching as Cole pulled himself back up. The young man stood there, his face a mess of blood with one eye swollen shut, and swaying on his feet . . . but ready to fight. The seeker seemed impressed. "So desperate to have your prey, demon? It would be wiser for you to flee into the Fade, and never return."

Cole spat out dark blood. "I'm . . . *not* . . ."

"Not a demon? Of course you are." The Lord Seeker looked around, and spotted where he'd tossed the small book. He picked it up and showed it to Cole. "The Litany of Adralla. Do you know what that is?"

Cole glared at him and said nothing.

"Of course not," the man continued. "It was created by a magister of Tevinter to dispel demonic influence over the mind. It works on nothing else."

Rhys's heart sank. He watched as the anger drained out of Cole. He stared at the seeker in confusion.

"Poor, stupid spirit," the Lord Seeker said. He put the book away and walked toward Cole. The young man tried to retreat, but he couldn't stop staring, his mouth agape. "Did you try so hard to pretend you were one of us, pretend you were real, that you forgot what you really were?"

He snatched out with a hand, grabbing Cole around the neck

and hoisting him off the ground. Cole choked and flailed weakly, but there was nothing he could do. "You're *not* real," the Lord Seeker said, his tone biting. "You're just another parasite that's wormed its way into our world, feeding off all the things you can't have."

"Let him go!" Rhys called out. "He's nothing to you!"

The Lord Seeker turned and looked at Rhys in honest consternation. "This creature preys upon those I am sworn to protect, no matter how undeserving. It has fooled you, turned you into a murderer, and would have made you its host before long. Why defend it?"

"You're wrong about him." Rhys steeled himself, and slowly stood. "Not all spirits are the same, just as not all mages are the same. Not everyone possessed is an abomination. Not all magic is equal." He reached deep down inside and summoned mana. The pain was incredible, almost blinding, but he fought through it with sheer will alone. White fire curled around his fists, the air crackling with magic.

That got the Lord Seeker's attention. Rhys could see the calculation in the man's eyes: *Is he bluffing? How much power does he truly have?* He released Cole's neck, letting the young man slump to the ground, and pointed his sword at Rhys in warning. "Don't be a fool."

Rhys did not waver. "A fool is a man who reaches beyond his grasp. A fool is a man that refuses to accept there are limits to his knowledge. *I* am no fool."

Cole scrambled away from the Lord Seeker, and then stopped. He looked over at Rhys, their eyes meeting . . . and Rhys saw he was crying. There was no denial there, no refusal or anger. There was a realization. Cole's world had crashed down around him, the one thing he'd always feared finally come true: he wasn't real.

And just like that, Cole faded away.

In that moment, Rhys knew the truth. A part of him, deep down, had always known.

It was if a gaping hole opened underneath him, and into it fell all his strength to fight. His mana fled, the white fire dissipating, and he sank to his knees. *Let him kill me,* he thought. *Let's end it, here and now.*

"I'm disappointed." The Lord Seeker strode toward Rhys, mouth pressed into a thin frown. "It seemed like you had more fight in you, Enchanter. I've awaited this rebellion for some time, and quite frankly I was expecting it to be difficult."

Rhys barely looked up. "You can strike me down," he said, "but that won't stop the others."

"Their turn will come. Order will be restored, one mage at a time if need be."

"I fear it's too late for that, my Lord Seeker," a new voice said from the shadows. It was Evangeline. She walked into the dim light, and it was plain to see she'd been in battle: her armor was covered in streaks of blood, and her eyes held the grim intensity of a woman forced to kill those who'd once been her comrades. The way she walked with her sword held at the ready, however, said she would not be denied.

"Ser Evangeline." The Lord Seeker seemed surprised. He turned to face her, warily raising his own blade and ignoring Rhys. "You should have fled while you had the chance. You are a disgrace to the order, to your family, and to the Maker."

They slowly circled each other in the water, eyes locked. "Of all those things," she said, "you're wrong about my family. My father would be proud of what I've done. He always said tyranny was the last resort of those who have lost the right to lead."

"He taught you poorly."

"Evangeline," Rhys croaked. He felt utterly drained, barely able to keep himself upright. Even speaking was difficult. "Cole, he . . ."

She didn't take her eyes from the Lord Seeker. "I heard. It changes nothing." With that she lunged. The two of them clashed, sword meeting sword. They danced around each other, skilled combatants giving no quarter. Rhys could only watch. He tried to summon his magic, but the effort almost made him black out.

There were others coming. He could hear the echo of their distant voices, the splashes as they ran. Mages, or more templars? *Hold on, Evangeline.*

She fought valiantly. Several times Rhys thought Evangeline might actually get the better of the Lord Seeker, coming in for a fast attack as soon as she spotted an opening. Each time, however, the man deflected her swing or spun out of the way at the last moment.

Slowly he pressed his advantage. Evangeline was forced onto the defensive, doing all she could just to parry his strikes as she backed up. The Lord Seeker knew he was winning. He began hammering her sword, each blow ringing loudly and making her fight all the harder just to hold on to it.

Finally, more people came into view. It was the mages after all. Wynne was at the lead, staff shining brilliantly, with at least a dozen others right behind her. They ran through the water, intent on stopping the Lord Seeker.

But it was too late.

All it took was that single distraction for the Lord Seeker to go in for the kill. One solid blow to Evangeline's sword caused it to fly out of her hand. It spun wildly, landing with a resounding splash not a foot away from Rhys. The man lunged before she could react, thrusting his blade through her breastplate.

"Evangeline!" Rhys cried. He stretched out a hand toward her, cursing his weakness . . . and for a moment in time, everything was still. Rhys saw nothing else save Evangeline's eyes turning to meet his. There was pain there, the loss of what might have been, and he felt it as keenly as she. Evangeline mouthed the words *I'm sorry*, blood spurting from her lips. Then she slumped from the Lord Seeker's sword, falling silently into the water as Rhys watched in disbelief.

The charge of the mages ground to a halt. Wynne walked ahead of them, looking first at Evangeline's body and then at Rhys . . . and then at the Lord Seeker, her expression unforgiving. "Your templars have been defeated," she told him. "You have lost."

He said nothing at first. He stood tensely poised, calculating his chances. Against a single, wounded mage with barely a spell to defend himself? Against a young man armed with only a dagger? He would win without question. Even against a single, skilled templar he was more than a match. Against a dozen angry mages, however . . . that was another matter entirely. "And you have gained nothing," he finally stated. "Whatever you do here, you will not be permitted to run free. We will track you down and put you back in your cages, I swear it."

Wynne's eyes narrowed. "Not today."

The Lord Seeker backed off. He held his sword up, warning any of the mages he would strike if they dared approach him, and then turned and fled into the shadows. The mages immediately gave chase, their staves flashing with fire. Within moments they were all gone, the sound of their spells fading into the tunnels . . . all except for Wynne. The old woman remained behind, shaking her head sadly.

Rhys hardly cared. He crawled through the water, fighting against the pain and the weakness to reach Evangeline. He was barely aware of his tears—inside he was screaming. This wasn't fair. It wasn't right. Evangeline should have let the Lord Seeker kill him, not intervened and suffered for it.

He reached her body and pulled it up out of the water. It took all his strength. There he cradled her in his arms, wiping the wet locks of hair from her bloody face. She seemed almost peaceful, her eyes staring off into some distant place. "No . . . no, no, no," he repeated, the grief spilling out of him freely now.

He didn't want to let her go. He wanted her back. Rhys reached into himself, pulled up what little mana he possessed . . . he shook from the pain of it, and what came was pitifully little, but he poured whatever he had into Evangeline's body. He knitted flesh with healing magic, closed her wounds with healing magic. But it did nothing. She remained pale and lifeless.

A hand gently touched his shoulder. "Rhys." Wynne's voice ached with pity. "It's too late. You can't . . ."

He shook his head, almost incoherent in his grief. "She's the best of them. She doesn't deserve this. The Maker *can't* take her from me now. . . ." He laid his head on Evangeline's breast, sobbing and praying silently for death to come for him, too. He'd lost Cole, lost Evangeline, lost *everything*. All he'd wanted to do was help, but instead he'd destroyed it all.

Wynne brushed his hair with her hand. It was an affectionate gesture . . . and when he looked up he saw there were compassionate tears in her eyes. He was reminded of the woman he'd met so long ago—that hero of the Blight who had walked into the White Spire with a warm smile and an open heart, the one he'd felt so proud to call his mother.

"Let me," she whispered.

"But you can't. She's . . ."

"Shhhh." Wynne put her hand over his lips to quiet him. Then she cupped his cheek lovingly, yet there was sadness and regret in her eyes. "I never knew why the spirit kept me alive, when I should have died all those years ago. Now I do."

Wynne turned her attention to Evangeline. She placed both her hands on the body and closed her eyes. There was a rush of power. Rhys didn't know quite how to describe it. It expanded out of Wynne, filling the sewer tunnel with its warm light, and he watched in amazement as *something* flowed out of her and into Evangeline. It wasn't dark or terrible. It was life. It was a spark.

At first it seemed like nothing would happen. But then he saw it—the color returned to Evangeline's cheeks. All at once she took a great, gasping breath. Her eyes opened and she surged up in a panic. Rhys had to catch her to keep her from splashing about in the water.

Their eyes met. It was her. She was alive.

Then Rhys realized what that meant. He looked at Wynne . . . and saw his mother smile. It was a smile that said good-bye. And then she fell back and was gone forever.

22

Rhys surveyed the ruin from its highest remaining tower, the chill wind rustling his hair. The dark clouds had been threatening snow all afternoon, the air heavy with anticipation of a winter storm, but nothing had materialized. It seemed the weather was as restless as his mood.

Andoral's Reach lay at the very fringes of Orlais, long ago a mighty fortress of the Tevinter Imperium, which had been sacked when Andraste rose up with her barbarian armies to end the rule of mages. How fitting that it should be here the mages gathered for their first conclave since the White Spire.

They had been coming in dribs and drabs since the first enchanters arrived a month ago. A dozen per day for a while, then slowing in the weeks that followed, until now the ruin was near bursting with over a hundred mages—apostates all. Rhys wasn't certain how they heard of the ruin, or why they came, but they did. Where else did they have to go?

They came hungry, with empty hands and fear in their eyes as well as tales of what was now happening in the other Circles. The templars had cracked down. In some places they received news of the White Spire even before the mages there did, and had struck preemptively. It made no difference. In each tower, the mages reacted the same way: They fought. Many died. The rest fled.

Rhys supposed he should worry. The destruction of so many phylacteries had protected them so far, but if the mages at other towers could hear of Andoral's Reach, then so could the templars. They wouldn't need phylacteries. If the templars were going to come, however, they would need to come with an army. The ruin was decrepit, its walls crumbling and covered in ivy, but its fortifications still offered protection. With hundreds of mages to man the battlements, they could hold off an army ten times their size—if not more.

Let them come, he thought grimly.

He scanned the horizon for the hundredth time, but saw only snowy hills and black skies. Not a templar in sight. The civil war in Orlais was rumored to be growing worse. There'd been a terrible battle in the Heartlands. Val Royeaux was said to be burning. If any of it was true, the templars might very well have their hands full and thus be unable to deal with apostates hiding at the edge of the Empire.

Rhys heard Adrian's footsteps on the tower's stairs long before she arrived at the top. She looked none the worse for their ordeal, which wasn't surprising. Adrian was tough. She wore the black robes of a first enchanter now—the elderly Edmonde had perished in the flight from the White Spire, and Adrian had been elected his replacement by the survivors a week ago. What that made her the first enchanter of, he couldn't rightly say. She had no Circle. None of them did.

It didn't stop her from being enthusiastic regarding her appointment, as brief a time as she intended to keep it. She nodded to him as she approached, holding the red curls from her face as a sudden gust of wind made them flutter. "They're calling for you, Rhys," she said. "It's going to start soon."

"I know."

She could have left, but instead remained at his side. She stared out at the barren hills with him, the silence between them strained. "Ser Evangeline tells me you've left the Libertarian fraternity." She said it lightly, as if it were a matter of no consequence. Rhys wasn't fooled. He could always tell when Adrian was mortally offended. "She says you plan on joining the Aequitarians."

And this was why she'd sought him out, of course. "I already have," he answered. "First Enchanter Irving asked me this morning to take my mother's place and represent them at the conclave. I accepted."

"*You're* their representative?"

"Apparently they trust my judgment."

She frowned thoughtfully. "And how are you going to vote?"

"I haven't decided yet."

She eyed him carefully, no doubt trying to discern the reason for his ambivalence. Perhaps the Grand Enchanter had sent her assuming their friendship would make Rhys confide in Adrian before the conclave commenced? If so, it was a mistake. If Rhys had felt estranged from Adrian before, it was complete now. Their friendship had evaporated, replaced by an awkwardness he couldn't account for. It went beyond his rejection of her that night in his chambers. There was something in the way she refused to meet his eyes . . . and he'd been thinking on it carefully.

Adrian turned to go, abandoning her efforts, but he caught her shoulder. "Wait," he said. "I have something to ask you."

She tensed. When she turned back, however, she assumed an air of nonchalance. "Go on."

"How did Pharamond die?"

That startled her. "The templars killed him, and framed you."

"The Lord Seeker denied it." He waved away her retort. "I know you'll say he was lying—but why? He told the truth about everything else, why lie about that? Why go through all that effort to frame me? It doesn't make sense."

She shrugged. "Then whoever murdered the others must have murdered Pharamond as well."

"His name is Cole. You met him, but you don't remember it." Rhys met Adrian's gaze, forcing her to look at him. He frowned when she broke the contact again and looked away. "The thing is, Cole told Evangeline he hadn't. He'd never lied about the other murders, why lie about that one?"

"I don't know. Why does anyone lie about murder?"

Rhys stepped toward Adrian, glaring at her angrily. She retreated, startled, until she hit the parapet and could back up no farther. She glanced behind her at the long drop to the ruin's courtyard, and then back at him. "I think there's another answer," he growled.

They faced off in tense silence. She stubbornly refused to budge, or answer him. Then, slowly, she lowered her eyes. "Fine," she said. Her voice was so quiet and laced with guilt he knew the answer even before she said it: "I killed Pharamond, and I placed the knife under your bed."

"Tell me why."

"Why do you think?" Adrian said angrily. "It was the only way Wynne was going to change her mind. She went to that conference to talk everyone out of voting for independence *again,* and she would have succeeded." She looked up at him, her eyes challenging. "She wouldn't ever have stood up to the templars, not unless she had a reason to. Not unless someone she loved was threatened by them."

Rhys felt his rage boiling over. He grabbed Adrian by the front of her robe, and was sorely tempted to throw her over the side. It would have been easy. There was no magic that would save her from the fall, and she wasn't even fighting him. In fact, she almost appeared to be daring him to do it. That made it worse. "You killed her," he seethed. "You killed Evangeline, and all those other people. Their blood is on your hands."

"I accept responsibility for my actions," she said, "but not for the templars'. I never thought it would go that far. Even so, I would do it again. Pharamond wanted to die. He begged me."

"You're proud of what you did."

"It had to be done. For us all."

For us all. Rhys roughly let her go and turned away. He couldn't stand to look at her . . . but, in a way, she was right. What was one more body amongst foundations? He couldn't claim innocence, after all. He played his own role in what happened. There was just as much blood on his hands.

He couldn't help but be reminded of the Kirkwall rebellion, however. A mage named Anders had slain the Grand Cleric and set off a series of events that led to the slaughter of nearly every member of the city's Circle . . . and he'd done it for the good of them all, because he saw no alternative other than to force a confrontation with the templars. No matter who got caught in the middle.

Was that all there was left for them? Was each side to spill blood, kill the other in the name of righteousness until only one was left standing? It wasn't so long ago he'd been convinced the Circle needed to end, that Wynne was wrong. She'd changed her mind, thanks to Adrian, but had he? All he felt now was disgust.

"We're through, you and I," he said coldly. "We were friends once, but no longer. I want you to know that."

She seemed sad, but unsurprised. "I understand."

"You don't understand anything."

He left her behind and marched down the tower stairs. It began to snow.

This conclave was far different from the last. Instead of a vast hall filled with marble and stained glass, the mages gathered in a ruined chamber that might have once been the barracks but now wasn't much of anything. Half the walls were little more than piles of crumbling stone, and much of the ceiling had long since collapsed. Weeds thrust up through the floor, and moss clung to every surface it could. They might as well have stood in a field for all the shelter it offered.

There were far more than a dozen-odd first enchanters, as well. Hundreds of mages packed into the chamber, so many they couldn't all hope to stand under what little ceiling remained. Snow fell upon them, slowly collecting in piles on the floor. They stood practically shoulder to shoulder, leaving only space for a collapsed column in the center—what would pass for a stage, he supposed.

And there was but one templar. Evangeline smiled with relief when she saw Rhys enter. He smiled in return, putting what happened with Adrian out of his mind. As Evangeline approached him, more eyes turned his way. The conversation in the chamber ebbed and then vanished completely. Everyone knew the conclave was ready to begin.

Grand Enchanter Fiona approached the collapsed column. The elf climbed carefully up, and when she turned to face the solemn crowd there was no doubting her position. She seemed indomitable. Defiant. It was easy to believe she'd been a Grey Warden. Whether she was now about to lead them to freedom or back into the arms of the Chantry remained to be seen.

"We have two choices," she announced, her words carrying easily. No one so much as whispered. "I believe it is clear to everyone here what they are: we submit, or we fight."

Her eyes scanned everyone present, daring them to object. None did. "If we submit," she continued, "then we do so as a group. Even the Libertarians. We return to the Chantry and throw ourselves at their mercy. Many of you do not know this, but the Divine aided us in our flight from the White Spire. She is a friend. Perhaps she could even spare some from Tranquility or execution . . . but surely not all."

No one spoke. "If we fight, we fight as one. We declare the Circle dead, and with it any attempt by the templars or the Chantry to govern us. This will mean war. The Divine will not be able to restrain the templars, if indeed she would even try. Many of us will perish in the battles that follow . . . but surely not all."

Still no one spoke. The snow fell harder through the gaps in the ceiling, but no one noticed. A shiver ran down Rhys's spine. "The time for debate is done," the Grand Enchanter said. "Now we must act, before the templars come and all choice is taken from us. As Grand Enchanter of the Circle of Magi, I hereby call for a vote on our independence."

A susurrus of whispers fluttered through the chamber, but quickly died down. "Not all first enchanters are present. I have received word that the Right of Annulment has been invoked upon the Circle of Dairsmuid. All within have been slain, as has First Enchanter Rivella." She paused again, waiting for the gasps of shock to pass. "Others are unaccounted for. The mages here today have elected to instead be represented by their fraternities. I ask those leaders to stand now, and make your votes heard."

The first to do so was a bent old man, a newly appointed first enchanter who claimed to represent the Loyalists. He delivered a short speech in a quavering voice, calling on the mages to submit. There was no hope in fighting the templars, he said. The people of Thedas would never accept free mages, and as in Andraste's time they would rise up as one and cast them down. The Circle was their only hope.

It was no less than anyone expected from the Loyalists, but perhaps less expected were those who followed. The smaller fraternities stood in turn, and each elected to follow the Loyalist lead: submission over resistance. Few as their followers were, their words still cast a gloom over the chamber. The life almost seemed to drain out of the Grand Enchanter's eyes.

Then Adrian strode through the doorway, not far from Rhys. "The Libertarians vote to fight!" she cried out. The crowd rustled as all eyes turned to her. "Are you all such cattle you would lie down and accept the inevitable? If you think anything will change if we submit, you're right! It'll be worse! Every Circle will become a prison. Every mage who came within a mile of this place will be made Tranquil. They know *no other way*, and never will unless we teach it to them!"

Louder mumbling greeted her words, but little of it was angry. Few could deny what she said. From the heads that lowered and the tears that some shed it seemed to Rhys to only be a question of which result brought more pain than the other. There was no easy choice to be made here.

As the din settled, the Grand Enchanter turned her eyes toward Rhys. The Aequitarians were the largest fraternity, and now as always before they held the balance of power. If they sided with the Libertarians, together they would outnumber the others. If they sided with the Loyalists, the question would be settled irrevocably. Some might have wondered at the Aequitarian choice for spokesman: a man who wasn't a first enchanter, and who hadn't even been part of their fraternity until this morning. Rhys wondered himself. He felt like a poor substitute for his mother. Even so, nobody presumed what his answer would be.

He felt Evangeline's hand wrap around his own and give it a squeeze.

"You all know who my mother was," he said to the crowd, "and she taught me something before she died. It was that the time has come for us to put aside our assumptions of the past—the assumptions of others as well as our assumptions about ourselves. We know nothing of Tranquility, or of demons, or even our own limitations. Whatever comes next, we will only survive if we learn to look upon it with new eyes. If we don't, we will simply make those old mistakes over again . . . and whatever our fate, we will deserve it."

Some nodded at his words, but no one spoke. Grand Enchanter Fiona waited, and then looked at him with a perplexed expression. "Forgive me, Enchanter Rhys," she said, "but I do not believe you made your vote clear."

Rhys took a deep breath, and then cast the final die.

"I vote that we fight."

The snow fell hard that night, but Rhys paid it no heed.

He sat in a dark corner of the ruin's courtyard, alone with his thoughts at last. He had expected an uproar after his vote, but instead there had been only silence. The realization that the Circle of Magi was irrevocably finished had left a question in its wake: What now? It wasn't something he could face yet, and so he'd left. Other mages had done the same, each needing to come to terms with the inevitable.

Evangeline appeared, crossing through the snow and wind. Anyone else he might have considered an intrusion on his solace, but not her.

"It's done," she said as she reached him, her expression grim.

"It is."

Evangeline held out a hand to help him to his feet, and he took it. "What are you thinking of?" she asked.

"My mother."

She nodded sadly, needing no explanation. "I stood on the other side of that blackness and Wynne sent a golden light to bring me back. It was . . . beautiful."

Evangeline hadn't spoken of that night since it happened. Rhys was still amazed to see her alive. Magic had never breached the wall between life and death before. It wasn't supposed to be possible, and yet here Evangeline was: not a spirit, not some facsimile of the woman he knew. A miracle.

"Is . . . it inside of you?" he asked uneasily.

"The spirit? I don't know. I don't feel any different."

"Do you remember what happened before?"

Evangeline said nothing at first. "I remember Cole. I remember the look in your eyes when you . . . realized what he was." Rhys nodded, feeling the shame burn his cheeks, but she laid a reassuring hand on his shoulder. "You shouldn't torment yourself."

"Shouldn't I? He fooled me. I, of anyone, should have known better."

"I was there in the Fade. That wasn't a lie, Rhys."

He shook his head. "But that can't be. There was never any boy named Cole. That never happened. It must have all just been some . . ."

"And who just told the assembled mages that it was time to put aside our assumptions?" Evangeline chuckled ruefully as he clamped his mouth shut. "I don't know what Cole was. All I know was that he was a lost soul, and you tried to do right by him. That's all that matters."

"I think I killed those people."

"I know. It doesn't change anything about you."

They were quiet for a time. "Do you think we'll ever see Cole again?" he finally asked.

"I don't know. I don't think so."

Rhys nodded in agreement. "So . . . what will you do?" he asked quietly. "The Circle's done. The templars will come for us and it will be war, just as Fiona said. Are you going to fight against them?"

She looked at him then and didn't smile, her expression utterly serious. "If it means I fight at your side, I'll gladly die again and regret nothing."

"Then we'll face the future together." Evangeline nodded and hugged him tight, and he accepted the embrace gladly. Rhys realized the question of what lie ahead no longer seemed as daunting. With her . . . the thought was lost as he looked into her eyes. He'd nearly lost her forever. There in the ruined courtyard, the snow quietly falling around them, they kissed. It felt natural and right.

She smiled and took his hand as they parted. "Come with me."

They walked together to a place not far from Andoral's Reach. There a massive oak tree stood alone in a field, a gnarled and grey thing so old it seemed impossible it should still be standing . . . yet also so majestic it took one's breath away to behold. That tree had watched the ages pass. It had seen Blights fill the land with darkspawn and yet suffered no corruption. Perhaps it had even watched Andraste's armies tear down the mighty fortress, stood witness to battles that had slain thousands upon thousands of men, yet it had not fallen.

It was at the foot of that tree that Wynne's ashes were now buried. It had been Leliana's suggestion. Wynne would have wanted no monument, she said, no marble crypt or fanfare. Just a place to finally rest, someplace where those who knew her could come and remember her as she was: a woman who had fought for what she believed in, who had stood against darkspawn and chaos alike. A woman who'd used the years she'd been given to leave the world a better place than she found it.

Leliana was there now, as was Shale. First Enchanter Irving, too. There were others as well, all hanging their heads in sad memory, marking the passing of their friend. Even the golem had no sarcastic quips to offer, the light in its eyes now dim and grey.

Rhys and Evangeline watched quietly from a distance. He tried to remember his mother, and that last smile she had given him. His heart ached, wondering at the life he might have had if she'd never been forced to give him away, the different life *she* might have had. Maybe they could have been good for each other.

Leliana began to sing. The words were elven, but Rhys understood them even so: they spoke of joy and loss, and how all things must come to an end.

It was at once the most haunting and beautiful melody he'd ever heard.

made it through the entire letter without expiring on the spot. Well, it didn't matter, so long as it was written and delivered tonight. He unstrapped his armor as he dictated:

> Most Holy,
>
> The Seekers are well aware of the part you played in the rebellion. You call me to the Grand Cathedral in the middle of the night on "urgent" business only to speak of trivial matters? And then, when I return to the White Spire, I discover chaos . . . and one of your agents in the midst of the apostates.
>
> Did you think I would not notice? Did you believe yourself above repercussions for such acts? It was a dark day when the Chantry placed such an incapable woman upon the Sunburst Throne. I will not stand idle and watch you destroy what ages of tradition and righteousness have built.
>
> In the twentieth year of the Divine Age, the Nevarran Accord was signed. The Seekers of Truth lowered our banner and agreed to serve as the Chantry's right hand, and together we created the Circle of Magi. With the Circle no more, I hereby declare the Accord null and void. Neither the Seekers of Truth nor the Templar Order recognize Chantry authority, and instead we will perform the Maker's work as it was meant to be done, as we see fit.
>
> Signed this day on the fortieth year of the Dragon Age,
> Lord Seeker Lambert van Reeves

He walked over to the desk and snatched the letter up just as the page finished. Scanning it over, he nodded approvingly. "Fix it with my seal and place it in Ser Arnaud's hands. Tell him he is to personally bring it to the Grand Cathedral. *Personally*. Is that understood?"

"Yes, my lord." The page rushed out of the chamber so quickly he almost tripped. Lambert slammed the door shut and allowed himself a smile. He imagined the Divine reading that. Without the templars, the Chantry was toothless—nothing more than a bunch of old women armed only with words. What would she do? Try to convince the people, after ages of teaching them mages were to be feared and contained, that now everything was different?

In three days the templar host would march on Andoral's Reach. With any luck, by the time he returned victorious the Chantry would have come to its senses and chosen a new Divine . . . one that would be eager to reach a new Accord with the seekers, placing the power much more firmly where it belonged.

The Lord Seeker removed the rest of his armor, dimmed the glowlamp, and crawled into his bed. He would sleep well tonight. Soon he would be a hero, the mages would be put back in their place, and all would be right with the world. It was a good day, indeed.

As sleep slowly came, he became aware that something was wrong. A sound in the darkness—the faintest creak, like his door opening. Immediately he reached for his sword by the bed, but before he could reach it something was upon him. A man pushed him back down and placed a dagger against his throat. He froze.

In the dim moonlight that filtered in through the window, he caught a glimpse of the intruder's shaggy blond hair and immediately recognized him. "Demon," he growled, and hissed in pain as the blade pressed against his flesh.

The young man leaned close, his expression one of deadly intent. "There *was* a Cole," he whispered. "You forgot him in that cell, and I heard his cries when no one else would. I went to him, and held his hand in the darkness until it was over. When the templars found him, they erased everything to hide their shame . . . and I was helpless to act." Sorrow, and perhaps even regret, crossed

the young man's face, but only for a moment. "I'm not helpless any longer." The words sent a chill through Lambert's heart.

"What do you want from me?"

The young man smiled coldly.

"I want you to look into my eyes."

For more fantastic fiction from Titan Books check out our website:

of all our exciting titles, including:

EPILOGUE

Lord Seeker Lambert strode into his chambers, his face flush with satisfaction. Swiftly he removed his black cloak and tossed it to an elven page that trailed behind him. Fifteen Knight-Commanders in one room, and not a single one had raised a voice in protest. They all knew what needed to be done. Those few that held private reservations would either remain silent or be replaced.

An army would be assembled and the pathetic mages gathered at Andoral's Reach would be crushed . . . or starved out, it didn't matter which. Their deaths would serve as an example to all who came after. The Circle of Magi was gone, and soon it would be replaced by a new order that would finally have the power to establish a real peace. Where even the Chantry had failed, the Seekers of Truth would stand triumphant in the eyes of the Maker.

"Take a letter, boy," he snapped.

The page nearly yelped in fear, dropping the cloak as well as the papers he carried. The Lord Seeker waited impatiently as the boy scrambled to recover it all. He hung up the cloak and then sat at the tiny desk, dipping a writing pen into the inkwell with a shaky hand.

"Maker's breath, boy. If that letter ends up illegible, I'll have your hide."

The page gulped. "Yes, my lord." His hand slowed, even if his panicked breaths did not. Lambert would be fortunate if the boy